EVERYMAN,

I WILL GO WITH THEE,

AND BE THY GUIDE,

IN THY MOST NEED

TO GO BY THY SIDE

EVERYMAN'S POCKET CLASSICS

CHRISTMAS
STORIES

EDITED BY DIANA SECKER TESDELL

EVERYMAN'S POCKET CLASSICS

Alfred A. Knopf New York London Toronto

THIS IS A BORZOI BOOK
PUBLISHED BY ALFRED A. KNOPF

This selection by Diana Secker Tesdell first published in
Everyman's Library, 2007
Copyright © 2007 by Everyman's Library
A list of acknowledgments to copyright owners appears at the back
of this volume.

US website: www.randomhouse.com/everymans

ISBN: 978-0-307-26717-7 (US)
1-84159-600-0 & 978-1-84159-600-6 (UK)

A CIP catalogue reference for this book is available from the
British Library

Library of Congress Cataloging-in-Publication Data
Christmas stories / edited by Diana Secker Tesdell.
p.   cm.—(Everyman's pocket classics)
ISBN 978-0-307-26717-7 (alk. paper)
1. Christmas stories, American.   2. Christmas stories, English.
I. Tesdell, Diana Secker.
PS648.C45C4579   2007   2007028109
808.83'108334–dc22

Typography by Peter B. Willberg
Typeset in the UK by AccComputing, North Barrow, Somerset
Printed and bound in Germany by GGP Media GmbH, Pössneck

CHRISTMAS
STORIES

Contents

CHARLES DICKENS

THE STORY
OF THE GOBLINS
WHO STOLE
A SEXTON

(from *The Pickwick Papers*)

'IN AN OLD Abbey town, down in this part of the country, a long, long while ago – so long, that the story must be a true one, because our great grandfathers implicitly believed it – there officiated as sexton and grave-digger in the churchyard, one Gabriel Grub. It by no means follows that because a man is a sexton, and constantly surrounded by emblems of mortality, therefore he should be a morose and melancholy man; your undertakers are the merriest fellows in the world, and I once had the honour of being on intimate terms with a mute, who in private life, and off duty, was as comical and jocose a little fellow as ever chirped out a devil-may-care song, without a hitch in his memory, or drained off a good stiff glass of grog without stopping for breath. But notwithstanding these precedents to the contrary, Gabriel Grub was an ill-conditioned, cross-grained, surly fellow – a morose and lonely man, who consorted with nobody but himself, and an old wicker bottle which fitted into his large deep waistcoat pocket; and who eyed each merry face as it passed him by, with such a deep scowl of malice and ill-humour, as it was difficult to meet without feeling something the worse for.

'A little before twilight one Christmas eve, Gabriel shouldered his spade, lighted his lantern, and betook himself towards the old churchyard, for he had got a grave to finish by next morning, and feeling very low he thought it might raise his spirits perhaps, if he went on with his work at once.

As he wended his way up the ancient street, he saw the cheerful light of the blazing fires gleam through the old casements, and heard the loud laugh and the cheerful shouts of those who were assembled around them; he marked the bustling preparations for next day's good cheer, and smelt the numerous savoury odours consequent thereupon, as they steamed up from the kitchen windows in clouds. All this was gall and wormwood to the heart of Gabriel Grub; and as groups of children bounded out of the houses, tripped across the road, and were met, before they could knock at the opposite door, by half a dozen curly-headed little rascals who crowded round them as they flocked up-stairs to spend the evening in their Christmas games, Gabriel smiled grimly, and clutched the handle of his spade with a firmer grasp, as he thought of measles, scarlet-fever, thrush, whooping-cough, and a good many other sources of con-solation beside.

'In this happy frame of mind, Gabriel strode along, returning a short sullen growl to the good-humoured greet-ings of such of his neighbours as now and then passed him, until he turned into the dark lane which led to the churchyard. Now Gabriel had been looking forward to reaching the dark lane, because it was, generally speaking, a nice gloomy mournful place, into which the towns-people did not much care to go, except in broad day-light, and when the sun was shining; consequently he was not a little indignant to hear a young urchin roaring out some jolly song about a merry Christmas, in this very sanctuary, which had been called Coffin Lane ever since the days of the old abbey, and the time of the shaven-headed monks. As Gabriel walked on, and the voice drew nearer, he found it proceeded from a small boy, who was hurrying along, to join one of the little parties in the old street, and who, partly to keep himself company, and partly to prepare himself for the occasion, was shouting out the song at the highest pitch of his lungs. So Gabriel waited till the boy came up, and then dodged him into a corner, and rapped him over the head with his lantern five or six times, just to teach him to modulate his voice. And as the boy hurried away with his hand to his head, singing quite a different sort of tune, Gabriel Grub chuckled very heartily to himself, and entered the churchyard, locking the gate behind him.

'He took off his coat, set down his lantern, and getting into the unfinished grave, worked at it for an hour or so, with right good will. But the earth was hardened with the frost, and it was no easy matter to break it up, and shovel it out; and although there was a moon, it was a very young one, and shed little light upon the grave, which was in the shadow of the church. At any other time, these obstacles would have made Gabriel Grub very moody and miserable, but he was so well pleased with having stopped the small boy's singing, that he took little heed of the scanty progress he had made, and looked down into the grave when he had finished work for the night with grim satisfaction, murmuring as he gathered up his things –

"Brave lodgings for one, brave lodgings for one,
A few feet of cold earth, when life is done;
A stone at the head, a stone at the feet,
A rich, juicy meal for the worms to eat;
Rank grass over head, and damp clay around,
Brave lodgings for one, these, in holy ground!

' "Ho! ho!" laughed Gabriel Grub, as he sat himself down on a flat tombstone which was a favourite resting place of his; and drew forth his wicker bottle. "A coffin at Christmas – a Christmas Box. Ho! ho! ho!"

' "Ho! ho! ho!" repeated a voice which sounded close behind him.

'Gabriel paused in some alarm, in the act of raising the wicker bottle to his lips, and looked round. The bottom of the oldest grave about him, was not more still and quiet, than the churchyard in the pale moonlight. The cold hoar-frost glistened on the tombstones, and sparkled like rows of gems among the stone carvings of the old church. The snow lay hard and crisp upon the ground, and spread over the thickly-strewn mounds of earth so white and smooth a cover that it seemed as if corpses lay there, hidden only by their winding sheets. Not the faintest rustle broke the profound tranquillity of the solemn scene. Sound itself appeared to be frozen up, all was so cold and still.

' "It was the echoes," said Gabriel Grub, raising the bottle to his lips again.

' "It was *not*," said a deep voice.

'Gabriel started up, and stood rooted to the spot with astonishment and terror; for his eyes rested on a form which made his blood run cold.

'Seated on an upright tombstone, close to him, was a strange unearthly figure, whom Gabriel felt at once, was no being of this world. His long fantastic legs, which might have reached the ground, were cocked up, and crossed after a quaint, fantastic fashion; his sinewy arms were bare, and his hands rested on his knees. On his short round body he wore a close covering, ornamented with small slashes; and a short cloak dangled at his back; the collar was cut into curious peaks, which served the goblin in lieu of ruff or neckerchief; and his shoes curled up at the toes into long points. On his head he wore a broad-brimmed sugar-loaf hat, garnished with a single feather. The hat was covered with the white frost, and the goblin looked as if he had sat on the same tombstone very comfortably, for two or three hundred years. He was sitting perfectly still; his tongue was put out, as if in derision; and he was grinning at Gabriel Grub with such a grin as only a goblin could call up.

' "It was *not* the echoes," said the goblin.

'Gabriel Grub was paralysed, and could make no reply.

' "What do you here on Christmas eve?" said the goblin sternly.

' "I came to dig a grave, Sir," stammered Gabriel Grub.

' "What man wanders among graves and churchyards on such a night as this?" said the goblin.

' "Gabriel Grub! Gabriel Grub!" screamed a wild chorus of voices that seemed to fill the churchyard. Gabriel looked fearfully round – nothing was to be seen.

' "What have you got in that bottle?" said the goblin.

' "Hollands, Sir," replied the sexton, trembling more than ever; for he had bought it off the smugglers, and he thought that perhaps his questioner might be in the excise department of the goblins.

' "Who drinks Hollands alone, and in a churchyard, on such a night as this?" said the goblin.

' "Gabriel Grub! Gabriel Grub!" exclaimed the wild voices again.

'The goblin leered maliciously at the terrified sexton, and then raising his voice, exclaimed –

' "And who, then, is our fair and lawful prize?"

'To this inquiry the invisible chorus replied, in a strain that sounded like the voices of many choristers singing to the mighty swell of the old church organ – a strain that seemed borne to the sexton's ears upon a gentle wind, and to die away as its soft breath passed onward – but the burden of the reply was still the same, "Gabriel Grub! Gabriel Grub!"

'The goblin grinned a broader grin than before, as he said, "Well, Gabriel what do you say to this?"

'The sexton gasped for breath.

' "What do you think of this, Gabriel?" said the goblin, kicking up his feet in the air on either side of the tombstone, and looking at the turned-up points with as much complacency as if he had been contemplating the most fashionable pair of Wellingtons in all Bond Street.

' "It's – it's – very curious, Sir," replied the sexton, half dead with fright, "very curious, and very pretty, but I think I'll go back and finish my work, Sir, if you please."

' "Work!" said the goblin, "what work?"

' "The grave, Sir, making the grave," stammered the sexton.

' "Oh, the grave, eh?" said the goblin. "Who makes graves at a time when all other men are merry, and takes a pleasure in it?"

'Again the mysterious voices replied, "Gabriel Grub! Gabriel Grub!"

' "I'm afraid my friends want you, Gabriel," said the goblin, thrusting his tongue further into his cheek than ever – and a most astonishing tongue it was – "I'm afraid my friends want you, Gabriel," said the goblin.

' "Under favour, Sir," replied the horror-struck sexton, "I don't think they can, Sir; they don't know me, Sir; I don't think the gentlemen have ever seen me, Sir."

' "Oh yes they have," replied the goblin; "we know the man with the sulky face and the grim scowl, that came down the street to-night, throwing his evil looks at the children, and grasping his burying spade the tighter. We know the man that struck the boy in the envious malice of his heart, because the boy could be merry, and he could not. We know him, we know him."

'Here the goblin gave a loud shrill laugh, that the echoes returned twenty fold, and throwing his legs up in the air, stood upon his head, or rather upon the very point of his sugar-loaf hat, on the narrow edge of the tombstone, from whence he threw a summerset with extraordinary agility, right to the sexton's feet, at which he planted himself in the attitude in which tailors generally sit upon the shop-board.

' "I – I – am afraid I must leave you, Sir," said the sexton, making an effort to move.

' "Leave us!" said the goblin, "Gabriel Grub going to leave us. Ho! ho! ho!"

'As the goblin laughed, the sexton observed for one instant a brilliant illumination within the windows of the church, as if the whole building were lighted up; it disappeared, the organ pealed forth a lively air, and whole troops of goblins, the very counterpart of the first one, poured into the churchyard, and began playing at leap-frog with the tombstones, never stopping for an instant to take breath, but overing the highest among them, one after the other, with the most marvellous dexterity. The first goblin was a most astonishing leaper, and none of the others could come near him; even in the extremity of his terror the sexton could not help observing, that while his friends were content to leap over the common-sized gravestones, the first one took the family vaults, iron railings and all, with as much ease as if they had been so many street posts.

'At last the game reached to a most exciting pitch; the organ played quicker and quicker, and the goblins leaped faster and faster, coiling themselves up, rolling head over heels upon the ground, and bounding over the tombstones like foot-balls. The sexton's brain whirled round with the rapidity of the motion he beheld, and his legs reeled beneath him, as the spirits flew before his eyes, when the goblin king, suddenly darting towards him, laid his hand upon his collar, and sank with him through the earth.

'When Gabriel Grub had had time to fetch his breath, which the rapidity of his descent had for the moment taken away, he found himself in what appeared to be a large cavern, surrounded on all sides by crowds of goblins, ugly and grim; in the centre of the room, on an elevated seat, was stationed his friend of the churchyard; and close beside him stood Gabriel Grub himself, without the power of motion.

' "Cold to-night," said the king of the goblins, "very cold. A glass of something warm, here."

'At this command, half a dozen officious goblins, with a perpetual smile upon their faces, whom Gabriel Grub imagined to be courtiers, on that account, hastily disappeared and presently returned with a goblet of liquid fire, which they presented to the king.

' "Ah!" said the goblin, whose cheeks and throat were quite transparent, as he tossed down the flame, "this warms one, indeed: bring a bumper of the same, for Mr Grub."

'It was in vain for the unfortunate sexton to protest that he was not in the habit of taking anything warm at night; for one of the goblins held him while another poured the blazing liquid down his throat, and the whole assembly screeched with laughter as he coughed and choked, and wiped away the tears which gushed plentifully from his eyes, after swallowing the burning draught.

' "And now," said the king, fantastically poking the taper corner of his sugar-loaf hat into the sexton's eye, and thereby occasioning him the most exquisite pain – "And now, show the man of misery and gloom a few of the pictures from our own great storehouse."

'As the goblin said this, a thick cloud which obscured

the further end of the cavern, rolled gradually away, and disclosed, apparently at a great distance, a small and scantily furnished, but neat and clean apartment. A crowd of little children were gathered round a bright fire, clinging to their mother's gown, and gambolling round her chair. The mother occasionally rose, and drew aside the window-curtain as if to look for some expected object; a frugal meal was ready spread upon the table, and an elbow chair was placed near the fire. A knock was heard at the door: the mother opened it, and the children crowded round her, and clapped their hands for joy, as their father entered. He was wet and weary, and shook the snow from his garments, as the children crowded round him, and seizing his cloak, hat, stick, and gloves, with busy zeal, ran with them from the room. Then as he sat down to his meal before the fire, the children climbed about his knee, and the mother sat by his side, and all seemed happiness and comfort.

'But a change came upon the view, almost imperceptibly. The scene was altered to a small bed-room, where the fairest and youngest child lay dying; the roses had fled from his cheek, and the light from his eye; and even as the sexton looked upon him with an interest he had never felt or known before, he died. His young brothers and sisters crowded round his little bed, and seized his tiny hand, so cold and heavy; but they shrunk back from its touch and looked with awe on his infant face; for calm and tranquil as it was, and sleeping in rest and peace as the beautiful child seemed to be, they saw that he was dead, and they knew that he was an angel looking down upon, and blessing them, from a bright and happy Heaven.

'Again the light cloud passed across the picture, and again the subject changed. The father and mother were old and helpless now, and the number of those about them was diminished more than half; but content and cheerfulness sat on every face, and beamed in every eye, as they crowded round the fireside, and told and listened to old stories of earlier and bygone days. Slowly and peacefully the father sank into the grave, and, soon after, the sharer of all his cares and troubles followed him to a place of rest and peace. The few, who yet survived them, knelt by their tomb, and watered the green turf which covered it with their tears; then rose and turned away, sadly and mournfully, but not with bitter cries, or despairing lamentations, for they knew that they should one day meet again; and once more they mixed with the busy world, and their content and cheerfulness were restored. The cloud settled upon the picture, and concealed it from the sexton's view.

' "What do you think of *that?*" said the goblin, turning his large face towards Gabriel Grub.

'Gabriel murmured out something about its being very pretty, and looked somewhat ashamed, as the goblin bent his fiery eyes upon him.

' "*You* a miserable man!" said the goblin, in a tone of excessive contempt. "You!" He appeared disposed to add more, but indignation choked his utterance, so he lifted up one of his very pliable legs, and flourishing it above his head a little, to insure his aim, administered a good sound kick to Gabriel Grub; immediately after which, all the goblins in waiting crowded round the wretched sexton, and kicked him without mercy, according to the established and invariable custom of courtiers upon earth, who kick whom royalty kicks, and hug whom royalty hugs.

' "Show him some more," said the king of the goblins.

'At these words the cloud was again dispelled, and a rich and beautiful landscape was disclosed to view – there is just such another to this day, within half a mile of the old abbey town. The sun shone from out the clear blue sky, the water sparkled beneath his rays, and the trees looked greener, and the flowers more gay, beneath his cheering influence. The water rippled on, with a pleasant sound, the trees rustled in the light wind that murmured among their leaves, the birds sang upon the boughs, and the lark carolled on high her welcome to the morning. Yes, it was morning, the bright, balmy morning of summer; the minutest leaf, the smallest blade of grass, was instinct with life. The ant crept forth to her daily toil, the butterfly fluttered and basked in the warm rays of the sun; myriads of insects spread their transparent wings, and revelled in their brief but happy existence. Man walked forth, elated with the scene; and all was brightness and splendour.

' "*You* a miserable man!" said the king of the goblins, in a more contemptuous tone than before. And again the king of the goblins gave his leg a flourish; again it descended on the shoulders of the sexton; and again the attendant goblins imitated the example of their chief.

'Many a time the cloud went and came, and many a lesson it taught to Gabriel Grub, who although his shoulders smarted with pain from the frequent applications of the goblin's feet thereunto, looked on with an interest which nothing could diminish. He saw that men who worked hard, and earned their scanty bread with lives of labour, were cheerful and happy; and that to the most ignorant, the sweet face of nature was a never-failing source of cheerfulness and joy. He saw those who had been delicately nurtured, and tenderly brought up, cheerful under privations, and superior to suffering that would have crushed many of a rougher grain, because they bore within their own bosoms the materials of happiness, contentment, and peace. He saw that women, the tenderest and most fragile of all God's creatures, were the oftenest superior to sorrow, adversity, and distress; and he saw that it was because they bore in their own hearts an inexhaustible well-spring of affection and devotedness. Above all, he saw that men like himself, who snarled at the mirth and cheerfulness of others, were the foulest weeds on the fair surface of the earth; and setting all the good of the world against the evil, he came to the conclusion that it was a very decent and respectable world after all. No sooner had he formed it, than the cloud which had closed over the last picture, seemed to settle on his senses, and lull him to repose. One by one, the goblins faded from his sight, and as the last one disappeared, he sunk to sleep.

'The day had broken when Gabriel Grub awoke, and found himself lying at full length on the flat gravestone in the churchyard, with the wicker bottle lying empty by his side, and his coat, spade, and lantern, all well whitened by the last night's frost, scattered on the ground. The stone on which he had first seen the goblin seated, stood bolt upright before him, and the grave at which he had worked, the night before, was not far off. At first he began to doubt the reality of his adventures, but the acute pain in his shoulders when he attempted to rise, assured him that the kicking of the goblins was certainly not ideal. He was staggered again, by observing no traces of footsteps in the snow on which the goblins had played leap-frog with the gravestones, but he speedily accounted for this circumstance when he remembered that, being spirits, they would leave no visible impression behind them. So Gabriel Grub got on his feet as well as he could, for the pain in his back; and brushing the frost off his coat, put it on, and turned his face towards the town.

'But he was an altered man, and he could not bear the thought of returning to a place where his repentance would be scoffed at, and his reformation disbelieved. He hesitated for a few moments; and then turned away to wander where he might, and seek his bread elsewhere.

'The lantern, the spade, and the wicker bottle, were found that day in the churchyard. There were a great many speculations about the sexton's fate at first, but it was speedily determined that he had been carried away by the goblins; and there were not wanting some very credible witnesses who had distinctly seen him whisked through the air on the back of a chestnut horse blind of one eye, with the hind quarters of a lion, and the tail of a bear. At length all this was devoutly believed; and the new sexton used to exhibit to the curious, for a trifling emolument, a good-sized piece of the church weathercock which had been accidentally kicked off by the aforesaid horse in his aerial flight, and picked up by himself in the churchyard, a year or two afterwards.

'Unfortunately these stories were somewhat disturbed by the unlooked-for re-appearance of Gabriel Grub himself, some ten years afterwards, a ragged, contented, rheumatic old man. He told his story to the clergyman, and also to the mayor; and in course of time it began to be received as a matter of history, in which form it has continued down to this very day. The believers in the weathercock tale, having misplaced their confidence once, were not easily prevailed upon to part with it again, so they looked as wise as they could, shrugged their shoulders, touched their foreheads, and murmured something about Gabriel Grub's having drunk all the Hollands, and then fallen asleep on the flat tombstone; and they affected to explain what he supposed he had witnessed in the goblin's cavern, by saying that he had seen the world, and grown wiser. But this opinion, which was by no means a popular one at any time, gradually died off; and be the matter how it may, as Gabriel Grub was afflicted with rheumatism to the end of his days, this story has at least one moral, if it teach no better one – and that is, that if a man turns sulky and drinks by himself at Christmas time, he may make up his mind to be not a bit the better for it, let the spirits be ever so good, or let them be even as many degrees beyond proof, as those which Gabriel Grub saw in the goblin's cavern.'

NIKOLAI GOGOL

THE NIGHT
BEFORE
CHRISTMAS

Translated by Richard Pevear
and Larissa Volokhonsky

THE LAST DAY before Christmas had passed. A wintry, clear night came. The stars peeped out. The crescent moon rose majestically in the sky to give light to good people and all the world, so that everyone could merrily go caroling and glorify Christ.* The frost had increased since morning; but it was so still that the frosty creaking under your boots could be heard for half a mile. Not one group of young lads had shown up under the windows of the houses yet; only the moon peeked stealthily into them, as if inviting the girls sprucing themselves up to hurry and run out to the creaking snow. Here smoke curled from the chimney of one cottage and went in a cloud across the sky, and along with the smoke rose a witch riding on a broom.

If the Sorochintsy assessor had been passing by just then, driving a troika of hired horses, in a hat with a lamb's wool

*Among us, to go caroling [koliadovat] means to sing songs called koliadki under the windows on Christmas Eve. The master or mistress of the house, or anyone staying at home, always drops into the carolers' sack some sausage or bread or a copper coin, whatever bounty they have. They say there used to be an idol named Koliada who was thought to be a god, and that is where the koliadki came from. Who knows? It's not for us simple people to discuss it. Last year Father Osip forbade going caroling around the farmsteads, saying folk were pleasing Satan by it. However, to tell the truth, there's not a word in the koliadki about Koliada. They often sing of the nativity of Christ; and in the end they wish health to the master, the mistress, the children, and the whole household. (The Beekeeper's note.)

band after the uhlan fashion, in a dark blue coat lined with astrakhan, with the devilishly woven whip he used to urge his coachman on, he would surely have noticed her, for no witch in the world could elude the Sorochintsy assessor. He could count off how many piglets each woman's sow had farrowed, and how much linen lay in every chest, and precisely which of his clothes and chattels a good man had pawned in the tavern of a Sunday. But the Sorochintsy assessor was not passing by, and what business did he have with other people, since he had his own territory. And the witch, meanwhile, rose so high that she was only a black spot flitting overhead. But wherever the spot appeared, the stars disappeared from the sky one after another. Soon the witch had a sleeve full of them. Three or four still shone. Suddenly, from the opposite direction, another little spot appeared, grew bigger, began to spread, and was no longer a little spot. A near-sighted man, even if he put the wheels of the commissar's britzka on his nose for spectacles, still wouldn't have been able to make out what it was. From the front, a perfect German:* the narrow little muzzle, constantly twitching and sniffing at whatever came along, ended in a round snout, as with our pigs; the legs were so thin that if the headman of Yareskov had had such legs, he'd have broken them in the first Cossack dance. To make up for that, from behind he was a real provincial attorney in uniform, because he had a tail hanging there, sharp and long as uniform coattails nowadays; and only by the goat's beard under his muzzle, the little horns sticking up on his head, and the fact that he was no whiter than a chimney sweep, could you tell that he was not a German or a provincial attorney, but simply a devil who

*Among us, anyone from a foreign land is called a German, whether he's a Frenchman, a Swiss, or a Swede – they're all Germans. (The Beekeeper's note.)

had one last night to wander about the wide world and teach good people to sin. Tomorrow, as the first bells rang for matins, he would run for his den, tail between his legs, without looking back.

Meanwhile the devil was quietly sneaking toward the moon and had already reached out his hand to snatch it, but suddenly pulled it back as if burnt, sucked his fingers, shook his leg, and ran around to the other side, but again jumped away and pulled his hand back. However, despite all his failures, the sly devil did not give up his pranks. Running up to it, he suddenly seized the moon with both hands, wincing and blowing, tossing it from one hand to the other, like a muzhik who takes a coal for his pipe in his bare hands; at last he hastily hid it in his pocket and ran on as if nothing had happened.

In Dikanka nobody realized that the devil had stolen the moon. True, the local scrivener, leaving the tavern on all fours, saw the moon dancing about in the sky for no reason and swore to it by God before the whole village; but people shook their heads and even made fun of him. But what led the devil to decide on such a lawless business? Here's what: he knew that the wealthy Cossack Choub had been invited for kutya by the deacon, and that there would also be the headman, a relative of the deacon's in a blue frock coat who sang in the bishop's choir and could hit the lowest bass notes, the Cossack Sverbyguz, and others; that besides kutya there would be spiced vodka, saffron vodka, and lots of other things to eat. And meanwhile his daughter, the beauty of the village, would stay at home, and this daughter would certainly be visited by the blacksmith, a stalwart and fine fellow, whom the devil found more disgusting than Father Kondrat's sermons. The blacksmith devoted his leisure time to painting and was reputed to be the best artist in the whole neighborhood. The then still-living chief L—ko himself had summoned him specially to Poltava to paint the wooden fence around his house. All the bowls from which the Dikanka Cossacks supped their borscht had been decorated by the blacksmith. The blacksmith was a God-fearing man and often painted icons of the saints: even now you can find his evangelist Luke in the T— church. But the triumph of his art was one picture painted on the church wall in the right-hand vestibule, in which he portrayed Saint Peter on the day of the Last Judgment, with the keys in his hand, driving the evil spirit out of hell; the frightened devil is rushing in all directions, sensing his doom, and the formerly confined sinners are beating him and driving him about with whips, sticks, and whatever else they can find. All the while the artist was working on this picture, painting it on a big wooden board, the devil tried as hard as he could to hinder him: shoved his arm invisibly, raised up ashes from the forge in the smithy and poured them over the picture; but the work got done despite all, the board was brought to church and set into the wall in the vestibule, and ever since then the devil had sworn vengeance on the blacksmith.

One night only was left him to wander about the wide world, but on this night, too, he sought some way to vent his anger on the blacksmith. And for that he decided to steal the moon, in hopes that old Choub was lazy and not easy to budge, and the deacon's place was not all that close to his: the road went beyond the village, past the mills, past the cemetery, and around the gully. If it had been a moonlit night, the spiced vodka and saffron vodka might have tempted Choub, but in such darkness you would hardly succeed in dragging him down from the stove and getting him out of the cottage. And the blacksmith, who had long been on bad terms with him, would never dare visit his daughter with him there, for all his strength.

So it was that, as soon as the devil hid the moon in his pocket, it suddenly became so dark all over the world that no one could find the way to the tavern, to say nothing of the deacon's. The witch, seeing herself suddenly in the dark, cried out. Here the devil, sidling up to her, took her under the arm and started whispering in her ear what is usually whispered to the whole of womankind. Wondrous is the working of the world! All who live in it try to mimic and mock one another. Before, it used to be that in Mirgorod only the judge and the mayor went about during the winter in cloth-covered sheepskin coats, and all of petty clerkdom wore plain uncovered ones; but now both the assessor and the surveyor have got themselves up in new coats of Reshe-tilovo astrakhan covered with broadcloth. Two years ago the clerk and the local scrivener bought themselves some blue Chinese cotton for sixty kopecks a yard. The sacristan had baggy summer trousers of nankeen and a waistcoat of striped worsted made for himself. In short, everything tries to get ahead! When will these people cease their vanity! I'll bet many would be surprised to see the devil getting up to it as well. What's most vexing is that he must fancy he's a hand-some fellow, whereas – it's shameful to look him in the face. A mug, as Foma Grigorievich says, that's the vilest of the vile, and yet he, too, goes philandering! But it got so dark in the sky, and under the sky, that it was no longer possible to see what went on further between them.

'So, chum, you haven't been to the deacon's new house yet?' the Cossack Choub was saying as he came out the door of his cottage to a tall, lean muzhik in a short sheepskin jacket with a stubbly chin that showed it hadn't been touched in

31

over two weeks by the broken piece of scythe a muzhik usually shaves with for lack of a razor. 'There'll be good drinking there tonight!' Choub continued, with a grin on his face. 'We'd better not be late.'

With that, Choub straightened the belt that tightly girded his coat, pulled his hat down hard, clutched his knout – a terror and threat to bothersome dogs – but, looking up, he stopped . . .

'What the devil! Look, look, Panas! . . .'

'What?' said his chum, and also threw his head back.

'How, what? There's no moon!'

'What the deuce! It's a fact, there's no moon.'

'None at all,' said Choub, somewhat vexed at the chum's unfailing indifference. 'Not that you care, I suppose.'

'But what can I do?'

'It had to happen,' Choub went on, wiping his mustache on his sleeve, 'some devil – may the dog have no glass of vodka in the morning – had to interfere! . . . Really, as if for a joke . . . I looked out the window on purpose as I sat inside: a wonder of a night! Clear, snow shining in the moonlight. Everything bright as day. The moment I step out the door – it's pitch-dark!'

Choub spent a long time grumbling and swearing, all the while pondering what to decide. He was dying to chatter about all sorts of nonsense at the deacon's, where, without any doubt, the headman was already sitting, and the visiting bass, and the tar dealer Mikita, who went off to the Poltava market every two weeks and cracked such jokes that good people held their sides from laughter. Choub could already picture mentally the spiced vodka standing on the table. All this was tempting, it's true; but the darkness of the night reminded him of the laziness so dear to all Cossacks. How good it would be to lie on the stove now, with his knees bent, calmly smoking his pipe and listening, through an entrancing drowsiness, to the carols and songs of the merry lads and girls coming in crowds to the windows. He would, without any doubt, have decided on the latter if he had been alone, but now for the two of them it would not be so boring or scary to walk through the dark night, and he did not really want to appear lazy or cowardly before the others. Having finished swearing, he again turned to the chum:

'So there's no moon, chum?'

'No.'

'It's odd, really! Give me a pinch. Fine snuff you've got there, chum! Where do you get it?'

'The devil it's fine,' replied the chum, closing the birch-bark pouch all covered with pinpricked designs. 'It wouldn't make an old hen sneeze!'

'I remember,' Choub went on in the same way, 'the late tavern keeper Zozulia once brought me some snuff from Nezhin. Ah, what snuff that was! such good snuff! So, then, chum, what are we going to do? It's dark out.'

'Let's stay home, then, if you like,' said the chum, grasping the door handle.

If the chum hadn't said it, Choub would certainly have decided to stay home, but now something seemed to tug at him to do the contrary.

'No, chum, let's go! It's impossible, we have to go!'

Having said that, he was already annoyed with himself for it. He very much disliked dragging himself anywhere on such a night; but it was a comfort to him that he himself had purposely wanted it and was not doing as he had been advised.

The chum, showing not the least vexation on his face, like a man to whom it was decidedly all the same whether he stayed home or dragged himself out, looked around,

scratched his shoulders with the butt of his whip, and the
two chums set out on their way.

Now let's have a look at what the beautiful daughter was
doing, left alone. Oksana had not yet turned seventeen, but
already in almost all the world, on this side of Dikanka and
on the other, the talk was of nothing but her. The young
lads, one and all, declared that there had never been, nor
ever would be, a better girl in the village. Oksana knew and
heard all that was said about her, and was capricious, as
beauties will be. If she had gone about not in a checkered
wraparound and a woolen apron, but in some sort of capote,
she would have sent all her maids scurrying. The lads chased
after her in droves, but, losing patience, gradually dropped
out and turned to others less spoiled. The blacksmith alone
persisted and would not leave off his wooing, though he
was treated no better than the rest.

After her father left, she spent a long time dressing up
and putting on airs before a small tin-framed mirror, and
couldn't have enough of admiring herself. 'Why is it that
people decided to praise my prettiness?' she said as if distractedly, so as to chat with herself about something. 'People
lie, I'm not pretty at all.' But in the mirror flashed her fresh
face, alive in its child's youngness, with shining dark eyes
and an inexpressibly lovely smile which burned the soul
through, and all at once proved the opposite. 'Are my dark
eyebrows and eyes,' the beauty went on, not letting go of
the mirror, 'so pretty that they have no equal in the world?
What's so pretty about this upturned nose? and these cheeks?
and lips? As if my dark braids are pretty! Ugh! they could
be frightening in the evening: they twist and twine around
my head like long snakes. I see now that I'm not pretty at all!'
and then, holding the mirror further away from her face, she

exclaimed: 'No, I am pretty! Ah, how pretty! A wonder! What joy I'll bring to the one whose wife I become! How my husband will admire me! He won't know who he is. He'll kiss me to death.'

'A wonderful girl!' the blacksmith, who had quietly come in, whispered, 'and so little boasting! She's been standing for an hour looking in the mirror and hasn't had enough, and she even praises herself aloud!'

'Yes, lads, am I a match for you? Just look at me,' the pretty little coquette went on, 'how smooth my step is; my shirt is embroidered with red silk. And what ribbons in my hair! You won't see richer galloons ever! All this my father bought so that the finest fellow in the world would marry me!' And, smiling, she turned around and saw the blacksmith . . .

She gave a cry and stopped sternly in front of him.

The blacksmith dropped his arms.

It's hard to say what the wonderful girl's dusky face expressed: sternness could be seen in it, and through the sternness a certain mockery of the abashed blacksmith; and a barely noticeable tinge of vexation also spread thinly over her face; all this was so mingled and so indescribably pretty that to kiss her a million times would have been the best thing to do at that moment.

'Why have you come here?' So Oksana began speaking. 'Do you want to be driven out the door with a shovel? You're all masters at sidling up to us. You instantly get wind of it when our fathers aren't home. Oh, I know you! What, is my chest ready?'

'It will be ready, my dear heart, it will be ready after the holiday. If you knew how I've worked on it: for two nights I didn't leave the smithy. Not a single priest's daughter will have such a chest. I trimmed it with such iron as I didn't

35

even put on the chief's gig when I went to work in Poltava. And how it will be painted! Go all around the neighborhood with your little white feet and you won't find the like of it! There will be red and blue flowers all over. It will glow like fire. Don't be angry with me! Allow me at least to talk, at least to look at you!'

'Who's forbidding you – talk and look at me!'

Here she sat down on the bench and again looked in the mirror and began straightening the braids on her head. She looked at her neck, at her new silk-embroidered shirt, and a subtle feeling of self-content showed on her lips and her fresh cheeks, and was mirrored in her eyes.

'Allow me to sit down beside you!' said the blacksmith.

'Sit,' said Oksana, keeping the same feeling on her lips and in her pleased eyes.

'Wonderful, darling Oksana, allow me to kiss you!' the encouraged blacksmith said and pressed her to him with the intention of snatching a kiss; but Oksana withdrew her cheeks, which were a very short distance from the blacksmith's lips, and pushed him away.

'What more do you want? He's got honey and asks for a spoon! Go away, your hands are harder than iron. And you smell of smoke. I suppose you've made me all sooty.'

Here she took the mirror and again began to preen herself.

'She doesn't love me,' the blacksmith thought to himself, hanging his head. 'It's all a game for her. And I stand before her like a fool, not taking my eyes off her. And I could just go on standing before her and never take my eyes off her! A wonderful girl! I'd give anything to find out what's in her heart, whom she loves! But, no, she doesn't care about anybody. She admires her own self, she torments poor me; and I'm blind to the world from sorrow; I love her as no one in the world has ever loved or ever will love.'

'Is it true your mother's a witch?' said Oksana, and she laughed; and the blacksmith felt everything inside him laugh. It was as if this laughter echoed all at once in his heart and in his quietly aroused nerves, and at the same time vexation came over his soul that it was not in his power to cover this so nicely laughing face with kisses.

'What do I care about my mother? You are my mother, and my father, and all that's dear in the world. If the tsar summoned me and said: "Blacksmith Vakula, ask me for whatever is best in my kingdom, and I will give it all to you. I'll order a golden smithy made for you, and you'll forge with silver hammers." I'd say to the tsar: "I don't want precious stones, or a golden smithy, or all your kingdom: better give me my Oksana!" '

'See how you are! Only my father is nobody's fool. You'll see if he doesn't marry your mother,' Oksana said with a sly smile. 'Anyhow the girls are not here . . . what could that mean? It's long since time for caroling. I'm beginning to get bored.'

'Forget them, my beauty.'

'Ah, no! they'll certainly come with the lads. We'll have a grand party. I can imagine what funny stories they'll have to tell!'

'So you have fun with them?'

'More fun than with you. Ah! somebody's knocking; it must be the lads and girls.'

'Why should I wait anymore?' the blacksmith said to himself. 'She taunts me. I'm as dear to her as a rusty horse-shoe. But if so, at least no other man is going to have the laugh on me. Just let me see for certain that she likes some-body else more than me – I'll teach him . . .'

The knocking at the door and the cry of 'Open!' sounding sharply in the frost interrupted his reflections.

'Wait, I'll open it myself,' said the blacksmith, and he stepped into the front hall, intending in his vexation to give a drubbing to the first comer.

It was freezing, and up aloft it got so cold that the devil kept shifting from one hoof to the other and blowing into his palms, trying to warm his cold hands at least a little. It's no wonder, however, that somebody would get cold who had knocked about all day in hell, where, as we know, it is not so cold as it is here in winter, and where, a chef's hat on his head and standing before the hearth like a real cook, he had been roasting sinners with as much pleasure as any woman roasts sausages at Christmas.

The witch herself felt the cold, though she was warmly dressed; and so, arms up and leg to one side, in the posture of someone racing along on skates, without moving a joint, she descended through the air, as if down an icy slope, and straight into the chimney.

The devil followed after her in the same fashion. But since this beast is nimbler than any fop in stockings, it was no wonder that at the very mouth of the chimney he came riding down on his lover's neck, and the two ended up inside the big oven among the pots.

The traveler quietly slid the damper aside to see whether her son, Vakula, had invited guests into the house, but seeing no one there except for some sacks lying in the middle of the room, she got out of the oven, threw off her warm sheepskin coat, straightened her clothes, and no one would have been able to tell that a minute before she had been riding on a broom.

The mother of the blacksmith Vakula was no more than forty years old. She was neither pretty nor ugly. It's hard to be pretty at such an age. Nevertheless, she knew so well how to charm the gravest of Cossacks over to herself (it won't hurt to observe in passing that they couldn't care less about beauty) that she was visited by the headman, and the deacon Osip Nikiforovich (when his wife wasn't home, of course), and the Cossack Korniy Choub, and the Cossack Kasian Sverbyguz. And, to do her credit, she knew how to handle them very skillfully. It never occurred to any one of them that he had a rival. If on Sunday a pious muzhik or squire, as the Cossacks call themselves, wearing a cloak with a hood, went to church – or, in case of bad weather, to the tavern – how could he not stop by at Solokha's, to eat fatty dumplings with sour cream and chat in a warm cottage with a talkative and gregarious hostess? And for that purpose the squire would make a big detour before reaching the tavern, and called it 'stopping on the way'. And when Solokha would go to church on a feast day, putting on a bright gingham shift with a gold-embroidered blue skirt and a nankeen apron over it, and if she were to stand just by the right-hand choir, the deacon was sure to cough and inadvertently squint in that direction; the headman would stroke his mustache, twirl his topknot around his ear, and say to the man standing next to him, 'A fine woman! A devil of a woman!'

Solokha nodded to everyone, and everyone thought she was nodding to him alone. But anyone who liked meddling into other people's affairs would have noticed at once that Solokha was most amiable with the Cossack Choub. Choub was a widower. Eight stacks of wheat always stood in front of his house. Two yoke of sturdy oxen always stuck their heads from the wattle shed outside and mooed whenever they saw a chummy cow or their fat bull uncle coming. A bearded goat climbed on the roof and from there bleated in a sharp voice, like a mayor, teasing the turkey hens who strutted about the yard and turning his back whenever he caught sight of his enemies, the boys who made fun of his beard. In Choub's chests there were quantities of linen, fur coats, old-style jackets with gold braid – his late wife had liked dressing up. In his kitchen garden, besides poppies, cabbages, and sunflowers, two plots of tobacco were planted every year. All this Solokha thought it not superfluous to join to her own property, reflecting beforehand on the order that would be introduced into it once it passed into her hands, and she redoubled her benevolence toward old Choub. And to keep Vakula from getting round his daughter and laying hands on it all for himself, thus certainly preventing any mixing in on her part, she resorted to the usual way of all forty-year-old hens: making Choub and the blacksmith quarrel as often as possible. Maybe this keenness and cunning were responsible for the rumors started here and there by the old women, especially when they'd had a drop too much at some merry gathering, that Solokha was in fact a witch; that the Kizyakolupenko lad had seen she had a tail behind no longer than a spindle; that just two weeks ago Thursday she had crossed the road as a black cat; that the priest's wife once had a sow run in, crow like a rooster, put Father Kondrat's hat on her head, and run back out.

It so happened that as the old women were discussing it, some cowherd by the name of Tymish Korostyavy came along. He didn't fail to tell how in the summer, just before the Peter and Paul fast, as he lay down to sleep in the shed, putting some straw under his head, he saw with his own eyes a witch with her hair down, in nothing but a shirt, start milking the cows, and he was so spell-bound he couldn't move; after milking the cows, she came up to him and smeared something so vile on his lips that he spent the whole next day spitting. But all this was pretty doubtful, because no one but the Sorochintsy assessor could see a witch. And so all the notable Cossacks waved their hands on hearing this talk. 'The bitches are lying!' was their usual response.

Having climbed out of the oven and straightened her clothes, Solokha, like a good housekeeper, began tidying up and putting things in order, but she didn't touch the sacks: 'Vakula brought them in, let him take them out!' Meanwhile the devil, as he was flying into the chimney, had looked around somehow inadvertently and seen Choub arm in arm with his chum, already far from his cottage. He instantly flew out of the oven, crossed their path, and began scooping up drifts of frozen snow on all sides. A blizzard arose. The air turned white. A snowy net swirled back and forth, threatening to stop up the walkers' eyes, mouths, and ears. Then the devil flew back down the chimney firmly convinced that Choub and his chum would turn back, find the blacksmith, and give him such a hiding that it would be long before he was able to take his brush and paint any offensive caricatures.

In fact, as soon as the blizzard arose and the wind began cutting right into their eyes, Choub showed repentance and, pulling his ear-flapped hat further down on his head, treated himself, the devil, and the chum to abuse. However, this vexation was a pretense. Choub was very glad of the blizzard. The distance to the deacon's was eight times longer than they had already gone. The travelers turned back. The wind was blowing from behind them; but they could see nothing through the sweeping snow.

'Wait, chum! I don't think this is the right way,' Choub said after a short while. 'I don't see any houses. Ah, what a blizzard! Go to that side a little, chum, maybe you'll find the road, and meanwhile I'll search over here. It was the evil one prompted us to drag around in such a storm! Don't forget to holler if you find the road. Eh, what a heap of snow the devil's thrown in my face!'

The road, however, could not be seen. The chum went to one side and, wandering back and forth in his high boots, finally wandered right into the tavern. This find made him so happy that he forgot everything and, shaking off the snow, went into the front hall, not the least concerned about his chum who was left outside. Choub, meanwhile, thought he had found the road; he stopped and began shouting at the top of his lungs, but seeing that his chum didn't appear, he decided to go on by himself. He walked a little and saw his own house. Drifts of snow lay around it and on the roof. Clapping his hands, frozen in the cold, he began knocking at the door and shouting commandingly for his daughter to open.

'What do you want here?' the blacksmith cried sternly, coming out.

Choub, recognizing the blacksmith's voice, stepped back a little. 'Ah, no, it's not my house,' he said to himself, 'the blacksmith wouldn't come to my house. Again, on closer inspection, it's not the blacksmith's either. Whose house could it be? There now! I didn't recognize it! It's lame Lev-chenko's, who recently married a young wife. He's the only one who has a house like mine. That's why it seemed a bit odd to me that I got home so soon. However, Levchenko is now sitting at the deacon's, that I know. Why, then, the blacksmith? . . . Oh-ho-ho! he comes calling on the young wife. That's it! Very well! . . . now I understand everything.'

'Who are you and why are you hanging around the door?' the blacksmith, coming closer, said more sternly than before.

'No, I won't tell him who I am,' thought Choub. 'He

may give me a thrashing for all I know, the cursed bastard!' and, altering his voice, he replied:

'It's me, good man! I've come to your windows to sing some carols for your amusement.'

'Go to the devil with your carols!' Vakula cried angrily. 'Why are you standing there? Clear out right now, do you hear?'

Choub himself was already of that sensible intention; but he found it vexing to have to obey the blacksmith's orders. It seemed some evil spirit nudged his arm, forcing him to say something contrary.

'Really, why are you shouting so?' he said in the same voice. 'I want to sing carols, that's all!'

'Oh-ho! there's no stopping you with words! . . .' Following these words, Choub felt a most painful blow to his shoulder.

'So, I see you're already starting to fight!' he said, retreating a little.

'Away, away!' the blacksmith cried, awarding Choub another shove.

'What's with you!' said Choub, in a voice that expressed pain, vexation, and timorousness. 'I see you fight seriously, and painfully too!'

'Away, away with you!' the blacksmith shouted and slammed the door.

'What a brave one!' Choub said, left alone outside. 'Try going near him! Just look at the big jackanapes! You think I can't get justice against you? No, my dear, I'll go, and go straight to the commissar. You'll learn about me! I don't care that you're a blacksmith and a painter. If I could see my back and shoulders, I suppose they'd be black and blue. He must have beaten me badly, the devil's son! A pity it's cold and I don't want to take my coat off! You wait, fiendish blacksmith, may the devil smash up you and your smithy,

I'll set you dancing! So there, you cursed gallowsbird! He's not at home now, though. I suppose Solokha is sitting there alone. Hm ... it's not so far from here – why not go! No one else would come in such weather. Maybe it'll be possible ... Ohh, what a painful beating that cursed blacksmith gave me!'

Here Choub rubbed his back and set out in the other direction. The pleasantness waiting ahead in the meeting with Solokha lessened the pain somewhat and made him insensible to the frost itself, which crackled in all the streets, not muffled by the blizzard's whistling. At times his face, on which the snowstorm soaped the beard and mustache more deftly than any barber tyrannically seizing his victim by the nose, acquired a half sweet look. And yet, had it not been for the snow that criss-crossed everything before the eyes, you could long have seen Choub stopping, rubbing his back, saying, 'A painful beating that cursed blacksmith gave me!' and moving on again.

While the nimble fop with the tail and the goat's beard was flying out of the chimney and back into it, the little pouch that hung on a strap at his side, in which he had put the stolen moon, somehow accidentally caught on something in the oven and came open, and the moon seized the opportunity and, flying out of the chimney of Solokha's house, rose smoothly into the sky. Everything lit up. It was as if there had been no blizzard. The snow gleamed in wide, silvery fields and was all sprinkled with crystal stars. The frost seemed to grow warmer. Crowds of lads and girls appeared with sacks. Songs rang out, and it was a rare house that had no carolers crowding before it.

Wondrously the moon shines! It's hard to describe how good it is to jostle about on such a night with a bunch of laughing and singing girls and lads ready for every joke and prank that a merrily laughing night can inspire. It's warm under your thick sheepskin; your cheeks burn still brighter with the frost; and the evil one himself pushes you into mischief from behind.

A crowd of girls with sacks barged into Choub's house and surrounded Oksana. Shouts, laughter, stories deafened the blacksmith. Interrupting each other, they all hastened to tell the beauty some new thing, unloaded their sacks and boasted about the loaves, sausages, and dumplings, of which they had already collected plenty for their caroling. Oksana seemed perfectly pleased and happy; she chatted, now with this girl, now with that, and laughed all the while. With some vexation and envy the blacksmith looked on at their merriment, and this time he cursed caroling, though he used to lose his mind over it.

'Ah, Odarka!' the merry beauty said, turning to one of the girls, 'you have new booties! Oh, what pretty ones! and with gold! You're lucky, Odarka, you have a man who buys everything for you; and I don't have anyone to get me such nice booties.'

'Don't grieve, my darling Oksana!' the blacksmith picked up. 'It's a rare young lady who wears such booties as I'll get for you.'

'You?' Oksana said, giving him a quick and haughty glance. 'I'd like to see where you're going to get booties such as I could wear on my feet. Unless you bring me the ones the tsaritsa wears.'

'See what she wants!' the crowd of girls shouted, laughing.

'Yes,' the beauty proudly continued, 'you'll all be witnesses: if the blacksmith Vakula brings me the very booties the tsaritsa wears, I give my word that I'll marry him at once.'

The girls took the capricious beauty with them.

'Laugh, laugh!' said the blacksmith, following them out. 'I'm laughing at my own self! I think, and can't decide what's become of my reason. She doesn't love me – so, God be with her! As if Oksana's the only one in the world. Thank God, there are lots of nice girls in the village besides her. And what is this Oksana? She'd never make a good house-wife; she's only good at dressing herself up. No, enough, it's time to stop playing the fool.'

But just as the blacksmith was preparing to be resolute, some evil spirit carried before him the laughing image of Oksana, saying mockingly: 'Get the tsaritsa's booties for me, blacksmith, and I'll marry you!' Everything in him was stirred, and he could think of nothing but Oksana.

Crowds of carolers, the lads separately and the girls sepa-rately, hastened from one street to another. But the black-smith walked along without seeing anything or taking part in the merriment that he used to love more than anyone else.

The devil meanwhile was indulging himself in earnest at Solokha's: kissed her hand, mugging like an assessor at a priest's daughter, pressed his hand to his heart, sighed, and said straight out that if she did not agree to satisfy his passions and reward him in the customary way he was ready for anything: he'd throw himself in the water and send his soul straight to hellfire. Solokha was not so cruel, and besides, the devil, as is known, acted in cahoots with her. She did like seeing a crowd dangling after her, and she was rarely without company; however, she had thought she would spend that evening alone, because all the notable inhabitants of the village had been invited for kutya at the deacon's. But everything turned out otherwise: the devil had just presented his demand when suddenly the voice of the stalwart headman was heard. Solokha ran to open the door, and the nimble devil got into one of the sacks lying there.

The headman, after shaking the snow off the earflaps of his hat and drinking the glass of vodka that Solokha handed him, said that he had not gone to the deacon's on account of the blizzard, and seeing a light in her house, had stopped by, intending to spend the evening with her.

Before the headman finished speaking, there came a knocking at the door and the voice of the deacon.

'Hide me somewhere,' the headman whispered. 'I don't want to meet the deacon right now.'

Solokha thought for a long time where to hide such a stout guest; she finally chose the biggest sack of coal; she dumped the coal into a barrel, and the stalwart headman got into it, mustache, head, earflaps, and all.

The deacon came in, grunting and rubbing his hands, and said that none of his guests had come, and that he was heartily glad of this opportunity to *sport* a little at her place and the blizzard did not frighten him. Here he came closer to her, coughed, smiled, touched her bare, plump arm with his long fingers, and uttered with an air that showed both slyness and self-satisfaction:

'And what have you got here, magnificent Solokha?' And having said it, he jumped back slightly.

'How – what? An arm, Osip Nikiforovich!' replied Solokha.

'Hm! an arm! heh, heh, heh!' said the deacon, heartily pleased with his beginning, and he made a tour of the room.

'And what have you got here, dearest Solokha?' he uttered with the same air, having accosted her again and taken her lightly by the neck, and jumping back in the same way.

'As if you can't see, Osip Nikiforovich!' replied Solokha. 'A neck, and on that neck a necklace.'

'Hm! a necklace on the neck! heh, heh, heh!' And the deacon made another tour of the room, rubbing his hands.

'And what have you got here, incomparable Solokha? . . .' Who knows what the deacon would have touched this time with his long fingers, but suddenly there came a knocking at the door and the voice of the Cossack Choub.

'Ah, my God, an extraneous person!' the frightened deacon cried. 'What now, if someone of my station is found here? . . . It'll get back to Father Kondrat! . . .'

But the deacon's real apprehensions were of another sort: he feared still more that his better half might find out, who even without that had turned his thick braid into a very thin one with her terrible hand.

'For God's sake, virtuous Solokha,' he said, trembling all over. 'Your kindness, as it says in the Gospel of Luke, chapter thir–th– Knocking! By God, there's knocking! Oh, hide me somewhere!'

Solokha poured the coal from another sack into the barrel, and the none-too-voluminous deacon got in and sat down at the bottom, so that another half sack of coal could have been poured on top of him.

'Good evening, Solokha!' said Choub, coming in. 'Maybe you weren't expecting me, eh? it's true you weren't? maybe I'm interfering with you? . . .' Choub went on, putting a cheerful and significant look on his face, which let it be known beforehand that his clumsy head was toiling in preparation for cracking some sharp and ingenious joke. 'Maybe you've been having fun here with somebody? . . . Maybe you've already hidden somebody away, eh?' And, delighted with this last remark, Choub laughed, inwardly triumphant that he alone enjoyed Solokha's favors. 'Well, Solokha, now give me some vodka. I think my throat got frozen in this cursed cold. What a night before Christmas

God has sent us! When it struck, Solokha, do you hear, when it struck – eh, my hands are quite numb, I can't unbutton my coat! – when the blizzard struck . . .'

'Open up!' a voice came from outside, accompanied by a shove at the door.

'Somebody's knocking,' Choub said, breaking off.

'Open up!' the cry came, louder than before.

'It's the blacksmith!' said Choub, clutching his earflaps. 'Listen, Solokha, put me wherever you like; not for anything in the world do I want to show myself to that cursed bastard, may the devil's son get himself blisters as big as haystacks under each eye!'

Solokha, frightened, rushed about in panic and, forgetting herself, gestured for Choub to get into the same sack where the deacon was already sitting. The poor deacon didn't even dare to show his pain by coughing or grunting when the heavy fellow sat almost on his head and stuck his frozen boots on both sides of his temples.

The blacksmith came in without saying a word or taking off his hat and all but collapsed on the bench. He was noticeably in very low spirits.

Just as Solokha was closing the door after him, someone knocked again. This was the Cossack Sverbyguz. This one could not be hidden in a sack, because it would have been impossible to find such a sack. He was more corpulent than the headman and taller than Choub's chum. And so Solokha led him out to the kitchen garden to hear all that he had to tell her.

The blacksmith looked distractedly around the corners of the room, catching from time to time the far-resounding songs of the carolers. He finally rested his eyes on the sacks: 'Why are these sacks lying here? They should have been taken out long ago. I've grown all befuddled on account

49

of this stupid love. Tomorrow's a feast day and there's all this trash lying around the house. I must take them to the smithy.'

Here the blacksmith crouched down by the huge sacks, tied them tightly, and was about to haul them onto his shoulders. But it was obvious that his thoughts were wandering God knows where, otherwise he would have heard Choub hiss when his hair got caught by the rope that tied the sack and the stalwart headman begin to hiccup quite audibly.

'Can it be that this worthless Oksana will never get out of my head?' the blacksmith said. 'I don't want to think about her, yet I do, and, as if on purpose, about nothing but her. What makes the thought come into my head against my will? Why the devil do these sacks seem heavier than before! There must be something in them besides coal. Fool that I am! I forgot that everything seems heavier to me now. Before, I used to be able to bend and unbend a copper coin or a horseshoe with one hand, and now I can't lift a sack of coal. Soon the wind will knock me down. No,' he cried, cheering up after a pause, 'what a woman I am! I won't let anybody laugh at me! Let it even be ten sacks, I'll lift them all.' And he briskly hauled sacks onto his shoulders that two strong men would have been unable to carry. 'This one, too,' he went on, picking up the small one, at the bottom of which the devil lay curled up. 'I think I put my tools in it.' Having said which, he left the house whistling the song:

No bothering with a wife for me.

Noisier and noisier sounded the songs and shouts in the streets. The crowds of jostling folk were increased by those coming from neighboring villages. The lads frolicked and horsed around freely. Often amidst the carols one could hear some merry song made up on the spot by some young

Cossack. Then suddenly one of the crowd, instead of a carol, would roar a New Year's song at the top of his lungs:

> *Humpling, mumpling!*
> *Give me a dumpling,*
> *A big ring of sausage,*
> *A bowl full of porridge!*

Loud laughter would reward the funny man. A little window would be raised, and the lean arm of an old woman – they were the only ones to stay inside now with the grave fathers – would reach out with a sausage or a piece of pie. Lads and girls held up their sacks, trying to be the first to catch the booty. In one spot the lads came from all sides and surrounded a group of girls: noise, shouts, one threw a snowball, another grabbed a sack with all sorts of things in it. Elsewhere the girls caught a lad, tripped him and sent him flying headlong to the ground together with his sack. It seemed they were ready to make merry all night long. And the night, as if on purpose, glowed so luxuriantly! And the glistening snow made the moonlight seem whiter still.

The blacksmith stopped with his sacks. He imagined he heard Oksana's voice and thin laughter in the crowd of girls. Every fiber of him twitched: flinging the sacks to the ground so that the deacon on the bottom groaned with pain and the headman hiccuped with his whole gullet, he trudged on, the small sack on his shoulder, with the crowd of lads that was following the crowd of girls in which he thought he had heard Oksana's voice.

'Yes, it's she! standing like a tsaritsa, her black eyes shining! A handsome lad is telling her something; it must be funny because she's laughing. But she's always laughing.' As if inadvertently, himself not knowing how, the blacksmith pushed through the crowd and stood next to her.

'Ah, Vakula, you're here! Good evening!' said the beauty with the very smile that all but drove Vakula out of his mind. 'Well, did you get a lot for your caroling? Eh, such a little sack! And the booties that the tsaritsa wears, did you get them? Get me the booties and I'll marry you!' She laughed and ran off with the crowd.

The blacksmith stood as if rooted to the spot. 'No, I can't; it's more than I can bear...' he said at last. 'But, my God, why is she so devilishly pretty? Her eyes, and her speech, and everything – it just burns me, burns me... No, I can't stand it anymore! It's time to put an end to it all: perish my soul, I'll go and drown myself in a hole in the ice and pass out of the picture!'

Here, with a resolute step, he went on, caught up with the crowd, came abreast of Oksana, and said in a firm voice:

'Farewell, Oksana! Seek whatever suitor you like, fool whomever you like; but you won't see any more of me in this world.'

The beauty looked surprised, wanted to say something, but the blacksmith waved his hand and ran away.

'Where to, Vakula?' called the lads, seeing the blacksmith running.

'Farewell, brothers!' the blacksmith called out in reply. 'God willing, we'll see each other in the next world; but we're not to carouse together anymore in this one. Farewell, don't remember any evil of me! Tell Father Kondrat to serve a panikhida for my sinful soul. I didn't paint the candles for the icons of Saint Nicholas and the Mother of God, it's my fault, I got busy with worldly things. Whatever goods you find in my chest, they all go to the church! Farewell!'

After saying which, the blacksmith went off at a run with the sack on his back.

'He's cracked in the head!' said the lads.

'A lost soul!' an old woman passing by mumbled piously. 'I'll go and tell them the blacksmith has hanged himself!'

Meanwhile Vakula, having run through several streets, stopped to catch his breath. 'Where am I running, in fact?' he thought, 'as if all is lost. I'll try one more way: I'll go to Paunchy Patsiuk, the Zaporozhets. They say he knows all the devils and can do whatever he likes. I'll go, my soul will perish anyway!'

At that the devil, who had lain for a long time without moving, leaped for joy inside the sack; but the blacksmith, supposing he'd caused this movement by somehow catching the sack with his arm, punched it with his hefty fist, gave it a toss on his shoulder, and went off to Paunchy Patsiuk.

This Paunchy Patsiuk had indeed been a Zaporozhets once; but whether he had been driven out of the Zaporozhye or had run away on his own, no one knew. He had been living in Dikanka for a long time – ten years, maybe fifteen. At first he had lived like a real Zaporozhets: didn't work, slept three-quarters of the day, ate like six mowers, and drank nearly a whole bucket at one gulp; there was room enough for it all, however, because Patsiuk, though short, was of quite stout girth. Besides, the balloon trousers he wore were so wide that, however long a stride he took, his legs were completely invisible, and it looked as though a wine barrel was moving down the street. Maybe that was why they nicknamed him 'Paunchy'. A few days after his arrival in the village, everybody already knew he was a wizard. If anyone was sick with something, he at once called in Patsiuk; and Patsiuk had only to whisper a few words and it was as if the illness was taken away. If it happened that a hungry squire got a fish bone caught in his throat, Patsiuk could hit him in the back with his fist so skillfully that the bone would go where it belonged without causing any harm to the squire's throat. Of late he had rarely been seen anywhere. The reason for that was laziness, perhaps, or else the fact that it was becoming more difficult each year for him to get through the door. So people had to go to him themselves if they had need of him.

The blacksmith opened the door, not without timidity, and saw Patsiuk sitting on the floor Turkish fashion before a small barrel with a bowl of noodles standing on it. This bowl was placed, as if on purpose, at the level of his mouth. Without lifting a finger, he bent his head slightly to the bowl and sipped up the liquid, occasionally catching noodles in his teeth.

'No,' Vakula thought to himself, 'this one's lazier than Choub: he at least eats with a spoon, but this one won't even lift his arm!'

Patsiuk must have been greatly occupied with his noodles, because he seemed not to notice at all the coming of the blacksmith, who, as he stepped across the threshold, gave him a very low bow.

'I've come for your kindness, Patsiuk,' Vakula said, bowing again.

Fat Patsiuk raised his head and again began slurping up noodles.

'They say, meaning no offense...' the blacksmith said, plucking up his courage, 'I mention it not so as to insult you in any way – that you have some kinship with the devil.'

Having uttered these words, Vakula became frightened, thinking he had expressed himself too directly and hadn't softened his strong words enough, and, expecting Patsiuk to seize the barrel with the bowl and send it straight at his head, he stepped aside a little and shielded himself with his sleeve, so that the hot liquid from the noodles wouldn't splash in his face.

But Patsiuk shot him a glance and again began slurping up noodles. The heartened blacksmith ventured to continue.

'I've come to you, Patsiuk, may God grant you all good things in abundance, and bread proportionately!' The blacksmith knew how to put in a fashionable word now and then; he had acquired the knack in Poltava, while he was painting the chief's wooden fence. 'My sinful self is bound to perish! nothing in the world helps! Come what may, I must ask for help from the devil himself. Well, Patsiuk?' said the blacksmith, seeing his invariable silence, 'what am I to do?'

'If it's the devil you need, then go to the devil!' replied Patsiuk, without raising his eyes and continuing to pack away the noodles.

'That's why I came to you,' replied the blacksmith, giving him a low bow. 'Apart from you, I don't think anybody in the world knows the way to him.'

Not a word from Patsiuk, who was finishing the last of the noodles.

'Do me a kindness, good man, don't refuse!' the blacksmith insisted. 'Some pork, or sausage, or buckwheat flour – well, or linen, millet, whatever there may be, if needed . . . as is customary among good people . . . we won't be stingy. Tell me at least, let's say, how to find the way to him?'

'He needn't go far who has the devil on his back,' Patsiuk pronounced indifferently, without changing his position.

Vakula fixed his eyes on him as if he had the explanation of these words written on his forehead. 'What is he saying?' his face inquired wordlessly; and his half-open mouth was ready to swallow the first word like a noodle. But Patsiuk kept silent.

Here Vakula noticed there were no longer either noodles

or barrel before the man; instead, two wooden bowls stood on the floor, one filled with dumplings, the other with sour cream. His thoughts and eyes involuntarily turned to these dishes. 'Let's see how Patsiuk is going to eat those dumplings,' he said to himself. 'He surely won't want to lean over and slurp them up like noodles, and it's not the right way – a dumpling has to be dipped in sour cream first.'

No sooner had he thought it than Patsiuk opened his mouth wide, looked at the dumplings, and opened his mouth still wider. Just then a dumpling flipped out of the bowl, plopped into the sour cream, turned over on the other side, jumped up, and went straight into Patsiuk's mouth. Patsiuk ate it and again opened his mouth, and in went another dumpling in the same way. He was left only with the work of chewing and swallowing.

'See what a marvel!' thought the blacksmith, opening his mouth in surprise, and noticing straightaway that a dumpling was going into his mouth as well and had already smeared his lips with sour cream. Pushing the dumpling away and wiping his lips, the blacksmith began to reflect on what wonders happen in the world and what clever things a man could attain to by means of the unclean powers, observing at the same time that Patsiuk alone could help him. 'I'll bow to him again, and let him explain it to me . . . Though, what the devil! today is a *hungry* kutya, and he eats dumplings, non-lenten dumplings! What a fool I am, really, standing here and heaping up sins! Retreat! . . .' And the pious blacksmith rushed headlong from the cottage.

However, the devil, who had been sitting in the sack and rejoicing in anticipation, couldn't stand to see such a fine prize slip through his fingers. As soon as the blacksmith put the sack down, he jumped out and sat astride his neck.

A chill crept over the blacksmith; frightened and pale,

he did not know what to do; he was just about to cross himself... But the devil, leaning his doggy muzzle to his right ear, said:

'It's me, your friend – I'll do anything for a friend and comrade! I'll give you as much money as you like,' he squealed into his left ear. 'Oksana will be ours today,' he whispered, poking his muzzle toward his right ear again.

The blacksmith stood pondering.

'Very well,' he said finally, 'for that price I'm ready to be yours!'

The devil clasped his hands and began bouncing for joy on the blacksmith's neck. 'Now I've got you, blacksmith!' he thought to himself. 'Now I'll take revenge on you, my sweet fellow, for all your paintings and tall tales against devils! What will my comrades say now, when they find out that the most pious man in the whole village is in my hands?' Here the devil laughed with joy, thinking how he was going to mock all the tailed race in hell, and how furious the lame devil would be, reputed the foremost contriver among them.

'Well, Vakula!' the devil squealed, still sitting on his neck, as if fearing he might run away, 'you know, nothing is done without a contract.'

'I'm ready!' said the blacksmith. 'With you, I've heard, one has to sign in blood; wait, I'll get a nail from my pocket!' Here he put his arm behind him and seized the devil by the tail.

'See what a joker!' the devil cried out, laughing. 'Well, enough now, enough of these pranks!'

'Wait, my sweet fellow!' cried the blacksmith, 'and how will you like this?' With these words he made the sign of the cross and the devil became as meek as a lamb. 'Just wait,' he said, dragging him down by the tail, 'I'll teach you to set

57

good people and honest Christians to sinning!' Here the blacksmith, without letting go of the tail, jumped astride him and raised his hand to make the sign of the cross.

'Have mercy, Vakula!' the devil moaned pitifully. 'I'll do anything you want, anything, only leave my soul in peace – don't put the terrible cross on me!'

'Ah, so that's the tune you sing now, you cursed German! Now I know what to do. Take me on your back this minute, do you hear? Carry me like a bird!'

'Where to?' said the rueful devil.

'To Petersburg, straight to the tsaritsa!'

And the blacksmith went numb with fear, feeling himself rising into the air.

For a long time Oksana stood pondering the blacksmith's strange words. Something inside her was already telling her she had treated him too cruelly. What if he had indeed decided on something terrible? 'Who knows, maybe in his sorrow he'll make up his mind to fall in love with another girl and out of vexation call her the first beauty of the village? But, no, he loves me. I'm so pretty! He wouldn't trade me for anyone; he's joking, pretending. Before ten minutes go by he'll surely come to look at me. I really am too stern. I must let him kiss me, as if reluctantly. It will make him so happy!' And the frivolous beauty was already joking with her girlfriends.

'Wait,' said one of them, 'the blacksmith forgot his sacks. Look, what frightful sacks! He doesn't go caroling as we do: I think he's got whole quarters of lamb thrown in there; and sausages and loaves of bread probably beyond count. Magnificent! We can eat as much as we want all through the feast days.'

'Are those the blacksmith's sacks?' Oksana picked up.

'Let's quickly take them to my house and have a better look at what he's stuffed into them.'

Everyone laughingly accepted this suggestion.

'But we can't lift them!' the whole crowd suddenly cried, straining to move the sacks.

'Wait,' said Oksana, 'let's run and fetch a sled, we can take them on a sled.'

And the crowd ran to fetch a sled.

The prisoners were very weary of sitting in the sacks, though the deacon had made himself a big hole with his finger. If it hadn't been for the people, he might have found a way to get out; but to get out of a sack in front of everybody, to make himself a laughingstock . . . this held him back, and he decided to wait, only groaning slightly under Choub's uncouth boots. Choub himself had no less of a wish for freedom, feeling something under him that was terribly awkward to sit on. But once he heard his daughter's decision, he calmed down and no longer wanted to get out, considering that to reach his house one would have to walk at least a hundred paces, maybe two. If he got out, he would have to straighten his clothes, button his coat, fasten his belt – so much work! And the hat with earflaps had stayed at Solokha's. Better let the girls take him on a sled. But it happened not at all as Choub expected. Just as the girls went off to fetch the sled, the skinny chum was coming out of the tavern, upset and in low spirits. The woman who kept the tavern was in no way prepared to give him credit; he had waited in hopes some pious squire might come and treat him; but, as if on purpose, all the squires stayed home like honest Christians and ate kutya in the bosom of their families. Reflecting on the corruption of morals and the wooden heart of the Jewess who sold the drink, the chum wandered into the sacks and stopped in amazement.

'Look what sacks somebody's left in the road!' he said, glancing around. 'There must be pork in them. Somebody's had real luck to get so much stuff for his caroling! What frightful sacks! Suppose they're stuffed with buckwheat loaves and lard biscuits – that's good enough. If it's nothing but flatbread, that's already something: the Jewess gives a dram of vodka for each flatbread. I'll take it quick, before anybody sees me.' Here he hauled the sack with Choub and the deacon onto his shoulders, but felt it was too heavy. 'No, it's too heavy to carry alone,' he said, 'but here, as if on purpose, comes the weaver Shapuvalenko. Good evening, Ostap!'

'Good evening,' said the weaver, stopping.

'Where are you going?'

'Dunno, wherever my legs take me.'

'Help me, good man, to carry these sacks! Somebody went caroling and then dropped them in the middle of the road. We'll divide the goods fifty-fifty.'

'Sacks? And what's in the sacks, wheat loaves or flatbread?'

'I suppose there's everything in them.'

Here they hastily pulled sticks from a wattle fence, put a sack on them, and carried it on their shoulders.

'Where are we taking it? to the tavern?' the weaver asked as they went.

'That's what I was thinking – to the tavern. But the cursed Jewess won't believe us, she'll think we stole it; besides, I just came from the tavern. We'll take it to my place. No one will be in our way: my wife isn't home.'

'You're sure she's not home?' the prudent weaver asked.

'Thank God, we've still got some wits left,' said the chum, 'the devil if I'd go where she is. I suppose she'll be dragging about with the women till dawn.'

'Who's there?' cried the chum's wife, hearing the noise in

the front hall produced by the two friends coming in with the sack, and she opened the door.

The chum was dumbfounded.

'There you go!' said the weaver, dropping his arms.

The chum's wife was a treasure of a sort not uncommon in the wide world. Like her husband, she hardly ever stayed home but spent almost all her days fawning on some cronies and wealthy old women, praised and ate with great appetite, and fought with her husband only in the mornings, which was the one time she occasionally saw him. Their cottage was twice as old as the local scrivener's balloon trousers, the roof lacked straw in some places. Only remnants of the wattle fence were to be seen, because no one ever took a stick along against dogs when leaving the house, intending to pass by the chum's kitchen garden instead and pull one out of his fence. Three days would go by without the stove being lit. Whatever the tender spouse wheedled out of good people she hid the best she could from her husband, and she often arbitrarily took his booty if he hadn't managed to drink it up in the tavern. The chum, despite his perennial sangfroid, did not like yielding to her, and therefore almost always left the house with two black eyes, and his dear better half trudged off to tell the old women about her husband's outrages and the beatings she suffered from him.

Now, you can picture to yourself how thrown off the weaver and the chum were by her unexpected appearance. Setting the sack down, they stepped in front of it, covering it with their coat skirts; but it was too late: the chum's wife, though she saw poorly with her old eyes, nevertheless noticed the sack.

'Well, that's good!' she said, with the look of an exultant hawk. 'It's good you got so much for your caroling! That's what good people always do; only, no, I suspect you picked

61

it up somewhere. Show me this minute! Do you hear? Show me your sack right this minute!'

'The hairy devil can show it to you, not us,' said the chum, assuming a dignified air.

'What business is it of yours?' said the weaver. 'We got it for caroling, not you.'

'No, you're going to show it to me, you worthless drunkard!' the wife exclaimed, hitting the tall chum on the chin with her fist and going for the sack.

But the weaver and the chum valiantly defended the sack and forced her to retreat. Before they had time to recover, the spouse came running back to the front hall, this time with a poker in her hands. She nimbly whacked her husband on the hands and the weaver on the back with the poker, and was now standing beside the sack.

'What, we let her get to it?' said the weaver, coming to his senses.

'Eh, what do you mean we let her – why did you let her?' the chum said with sangfroid.

'Your poker must be made of iron!' the weaver said after a short silence, rubbing his back. 'My wife bought a poker at the fair last year, paid twenty-five kopecks – it's nothing . . . doesn't even hurt . . .'

Meanwhile the triumphant spouse, setting a tallow lamp on the floor, untied the sack and peeked into it. But her old eyes, which had made out the sack so well, must have deceived her this time.

'Eh, there's a whole boar in there!' she cried out, clapping her hands for joy.

'A boar! do you hear, a whole boar!' the weaver nudged the chum. 'It's all your fault!'

'No help for it!' the chum said, shrugging.

'No help? Don't stand there, let's take the sack from her!

62

Come on! Away with you! away! it's our boar!' the weaver shouted, bearing down on her.

'Get out, get out, cursed woman! It's not your goods!' the chum said, coming closer.

The spouse again took hold of the poker, but just then Choub climbed out of the sack and stood in the middle of the hall, stretching, like a man who has just awakened from a long sleep.

The chum's wife gave a cry, slapping her skirts, and they all involuntarily opened their mouths.

'Why did she say a boar, the fool! That's not a boar!' said the chum, goggling his eyes.

'See what a man got thrown into the sack!' said the weaver, backing away in fear. 'Say what you like, you can even burst, but it's the doing of the unclean powers. He wouldn't even fit through the window!'

'It's my chum!' cried the chum, looking closer.

'And who did you think it was?' said Choub, smiling. 'A nice trick I pulled on you, eh? And you probably wanted to eat me as pork? Wait, I've got good news for you: there's something else in the sack – if not a boar, then surely a piglet or some other live thing. Something's been moving under me all the time.'

The weaver and the chum rushed to the sack, the mistress of the house seized it from the other side, and the fight would have started again if the deacon, seeing there was nowhere to hide, hadn't climbed out of the sack.

'Here's another one!' the weaver exclaimed in fright. 'Devil knows how this world . . . it makes your head spin . . . not sausages or biscuits, they throw people into sacks!'

'It's the deacon!' said Choub, more astonished than anyone else. 'Well, now! that's Solokha for you! putting us into sacks . . . That's why she's got a house full of sacks . . . Now

63

I see it all: she had two men sitting in each sack. And I thought I was the only one she... That's Solokha for you!'

The girls were a bit surprised to find one sack missing. 'No help for it, this one will be enough for us,' Oksana prattled. They all took hold of the sack and heaved it onto the sled.

The headman decided to keep quiet, reasoning that if he shouted for them to untie the sack and let him out, the foolish girls would run away, thinking the devil was sitting in it, and he would be left out in the street maybe till the next day.

The girls, meanwhile, all took each other's hands and flew like the wind, pulling the sled over the creaking snow. Many of them sat on the sled for fun; some got on the headman himself. The headman resolved to endure everything. They finally arrived, opened the doors to the house and the front hall wide, and with loud laughter dragged the sack inside.

'Let's see what's in it,' they all shouted and hastened to untie the sack.

Here the hiccups that had never ceased to torment the headman all the while he was sitting in the sack became so bad that he started hicking and coughing very loudly.

'Ah, somebody's in there!' they all cried and rushed out of the house in fear.

'What the devil! Why are you running around like crazy?' said Choub, coming in the door.

'Ah, Papa!' said Oksana, 'there's somebody in the sack!'

'In the sack? Where did you get this sack?'

'The blacksmith left them in the middle of the road,' they all said at once.

'Well,' Choub thought to himself, 'didn't I say so?...'

'What are you so afraid of?' he said. 'Let's see. Now, then,

my man, never mind if we don't call you by your full name
– get out of the sack!'

The headman got out.

'Ah!' cried the girls.

'The headman was in it, too,' Choub said to himself in
perplexity, looking him up and down, 'fancy that! . . . Eh! . . .'
He could say nothing more.

The headman was no less confused himself and did not
know how to begin.

'Must be cold out?' he said, addressing Choub.

'A bit nippy,' Choub replied. 'And, if I may ask, what do
you grease your boots with, mutton fat or tar?'

He had not meant to say that, he had meant to ask:
'How did you, the headman, get into this sack?' but, without
knowing why himself, he had said something completely
different.

'Tar's better!' said the headman. 'Well, good-bye, Choub!'
And, pulling down his earflaps, he walked out of the house.

'Why did I ask so stupidly what he greases his boots
with!' Choub said, looking at the door through which the
headman had gone. 'That's Solokha! putting such a man
into a sack! . . . A devil of a woman! Fool that I am . . . but
where's that cursed sack?'

'I threw it in the corner, there's nothing else in it,' said
Oksana.

'I know these tricks – nothing else in it! Give it to me;
there's another one sitting in it! Shake it out well . . . What,
nothing? . . . Cursed woman! And to look at her – just like
a saint, as if she never put anything non-lenten near her lips.'

But let us leave Choub to pour out his vexation at leisure
and go back to the blacksmith, because it must already be
past eight o'clock outside.

*   *   *

At first Vakula found it frightening when he rose to such a height that he could see nothing below and flew like a fly right under the moon, so that if he hadn't ducked slightly he would have brushed it with his hat. However, in a short while he took heart and began making fun of the devil. He was extremely amused by the way the devil sneezed and coughed whenever he took his cypress-wood cross from his neck and put it near him. He would purposely raise his hand to scratch his head, and the devil, thinking he was about to cross him, would speed up his flight. Everything was bright aloft. The air was transparent, all in a light silvery mist. Everything was visible; and he could even observe how a sorcerer, sitting in a pot, raced past them like the wind; how the stars gathered together to play blindman's buff; how a whole swarm of phantoms billowed in a cloud off to one side; how a devil dancing around the moon took his hat off on seeing the mounted blacksmith; how a broom came flying hack, having just served some witch . . . they met a lot more trash. Seeing the blacksmith, all stopped for a moment to look at him and then rushed on their way again. The blacksmith flew on, and suddenly Petersburg, all ablaze, glittered before him. (It was lit up for some occasion.) The devil, flying over the toll gate, turned into a horse, and the blacksmith saw himself on a swift racer in the middle of the street.

My God! the clatter, the thunder, the glitter; four-story walls loomed on both sides; the clatter of horses' hooves and the rumble of wheels sounded like thunder and echoed on four sides; houses grew as if rising from the ground at every step; bridges trembled; carriages flew by; cabbies and postilions shouted; snow swished under a thousand sleds flying on all sides; passers-by pressed against and huddled under houses studded with lamps, and their huge shadows flitted over the walls, their heads reaching the chimneys and roofs. The blacksmith looked about him in amazement. It seemed to him that the houses all turned their countless fiery eyes on him and stared. He saw so many gentlemen in fur-lined coats that he didn't know before whom to doff his hat. 'My God, so much nobility here!' thought the blacksmith. 'I think each one going down the street in a fur coat is another assessor, another assessor! And the ones driving around in those wonderful britzkas with windows, if they're not police chiefs, then they're surely commissars, or maybe even higher up.' His words were interrupted by a question from the devil: 'Shall we go straight to the tsaritsa?' 'No, it's scary,' thought the blacksmith. 'The Zaporozhtsy who passed through Dikanka in the fall are staying here somewhere. They were coming from the Setch with papers for the tsaritsa. I'd better talk it over with them.'

'Hey little Satan, get in my pocket and lead me to the Zaporozhtsy.'

The devil instantly shrank and became so small that he easily got into Vakula's pocket. And before Vakula had time to look around, he found himself in front of a big house, went up the stairs, himself not knowing how, opened a door, and drew back slightly from the splendor on seeing the furnished room; then he took heart somewhat, recognizing the same Cossacks who had passed through Dikanka sitting cross-legged on silk divans in their tarred boots and smoking the strongest tobacco, the kind known as root-stock.

'Good day, gentlemen! God be with you! So this is where we meet again!' said the blacksmith, going closer and bowing to the ground.

'Who's that man there?' the one sitting right in front of the blacksmith asked another sitting further away.

'You don't recognize me?' said the blacksmith. 'It's me,

Vakula, the blacksmith! When you passed through Dikanka in the fall, you stayed – God grant you all health and long life – for nearly two days. And I put a new tire on the front wheel of your kibitka then!'

'Ah,' said the first Cossack, 'this is that same blacksmith who paints so well. Greetings, landsman, what brings you here?'

'Oh, I just came for a look around. They say...'

'Well, landsman,' the Cossack said, assuming a dignified air and wishing to show that he, too, could speak Russian, 'it's a beeg city, eh?'

The blacksmith did not want to disgrace himself and look like a greenhorn; what's more, as we had occasion to see earlier, he, too, was acquainted with literate language.

'A grand province!' he replied with equanimity. 'No disputing it: the houses are plenty big, there's good paintings hanging everywhere. A lot of houses have an extremity of letters in gold leaf written on them. Wonderful proportions, there's no disputing it!'

The Zaporozhtsy, hearing the blacksmith express himself so fluently, drew very favorable conclusions about him.

'We'll talk more with you later, landsman; right now we're on our way to the tsaritsa.'

'To the tsaritsa? Be so kind, masters, as to take me with you!'

'You?' the Cossack said, with the air of a tutor talking to his four-year-old charge who is begging to be put on a real, big horse. 'What will you do there? No, impossible.' With that, his face assumed an imposing mien. 'We, brother, are going to discuss our own affairs with the tsaritsa.'

'Take me!' the blacksmith persisted. 'Beg them!' he whispered softly to the devil, hitting the pocket with his fist.

Before he got the words out, another Cossack spoke up:

'Let's take him, brothers!'

'All right, let's take him!' said the others.

'Get dressed the same as we are.'

The blacksmith was just pulling on a green jacket when the door suddenly opened, and a man with gold braid came in and said it was time to go.

Again it seemed a marvel to the blacksmith, as he raced along in the huge carriage rocking on its springs, when four-storied houses raced backward past him on both sides, and the street, rumbling, seemed to roll under the horses' hooves.

'My God, what light!' the blacksmith thought to himself. 'Back home it's not so bright at noontime.'

The carriages stopped in front of the palace. The Cossacks got out, went into the magnificent front hall, and started up the brilliantly lit stairway.

'What a stairway!' the blacksmith whispered to himself. 'It's a pity to trample it underfoot. Such ornaments! See, and they say it's all tall tales! the devil it's tall tales! my God, what a banister! such workmanship! it's fifty roubles' worth of iron alone.'

After climbing the stairs, the Cossacks passed through the first hall. The blacksmith followed them timidly, afraid of slipping on the parquet floor at every step. They passed through three halls, and the blacksmith still couldn't stop being amazed. On entering the fourth, he inadvertently went up to a painting that hung on the wall. It was of the most pure Virgin with the Child in her arms. 'What a painting! what wonderful art!' he thought. 'It seems to be speaking! it seems alive! And the holy Child! He clasps his little hands and smiles, poor thing! And the colors! oh, my God, what colors! I bet there's not a kopeck's worth of ochre; it's all verdigris and crimson, and the blue is so bright! Great workmanship! and the ground must have been done in white lead.

But, astonishing as the painting is, this brass handle,' he went on, going up to the door and feeling the latch, 'is worthy of still greater astonishment. What perfect finish! I bet German blacksmiths made it all, and for a very dear price ...'

The blacksmith would probably have gone on reasoning for a long time, if a lackey with galloons hadn't nudged his arm, reminding him not to lag behind. The Cossacks passed through two more halls and stopped. Here they were told to wait. In the hall there was a group of generals in gold-embroidered uniforms. The Cossacks bowed on all sides and stood in a cluster.

A minute later a rather stout man of majestic height, wearing a hetman's uniform and yellow boots, came in, accompanied by a whole retinue. His hair was disheveled, one eye was slightly askew, his face showed a certain haughty grandeur, all his movements betrayed a habit of command. The generals who had all been pacing up and down quite arrogantly in their golden uniforms began bustling about and bowing low and seemed to hang on his every word and even his slightest gesture, so as to rush at once and fulfill it. But the hetman did not pay any attention, barely nodded his head, and went up to the Cossacks.

The Cossacks all gave a low bow.

'Are you all here?' he asked with a drawl, pronouncing the words slightly through his nose.

'All here, father!' the Cossacks replied, bowing again.

'You won't forget to speak the way I taught you?'

'No, father, we won't forget.'

'Is that the tsar?' the blacksmith asked one of the Cossacks.

'Tsar, nothing! it's Potemkin himself,' the man replied.

Voices came from the other room, and the blacksmith did not know where to look from the multitude of ladies entering in satin dresses with long trains and the courtiers in gold-embroidered caftans and with queues behind. He saw only splendor and nothing more. Suddenly the Cossacks all fell to the ground and cried out in one voice:

'Have mercy, mother, have mercy!'

The blacksmith, seeing nothing, also zealously prostrated himself on the floor.

'Get up!' a voice imperious and at the same time pleasant sounded above them. Some of the courtiers bustled about and nudged the Cossacks.

'We won't get up, mother! we won't! we'd rather die than get up!' the Cossacks cried.

Potemkin was biting his lips. Finally he went over himself and whispered commandingly to one of the Cossacks. They got up.

Here the blacksmith also ventured to raise his head and saw standing before him a woman of small stature, even somewhat portly, powdered, with blue eyes, and with that majestically smiling air which knew so well how to make all obey and could belong only to a woman who reigns.

'His Highness promised to acquaint me today with one of my peoples whom I have not yet seen,' the lady with the blue eyes said as she studied the Cossacks with curiosity. 'Are you being kept well here?' she continued, coming nearer.

'Thank you, mother! The victuals are good, though the lamb hereabouts is not at all like in our Zaporozhye – but why not take what comes? . . .'

Potemkin winced, seeing that the Cossacks were saying something completely different from what he had taught them . . .

One of the Cossacks, assuming an air of dignity, stepped forward:

'Have mercy, mother! Why would you ruin loyal people? How have we angered you? Have we joined hands with the foul Tartar? Have we made any agreements with the Turk? Have we betrayed you in deed or in thought? Why, then, the disgrace? First we heard that you had ordered fortresses built everywhere for protection against us; then we heard that you wanted to *turn us into carabinieri*; now we hear of new calamities. In what is the Zaporozhye army at fault? that it brought your troops across the Perekop and helped your generals to cut down the Crimeans? . . .'

Potemkin kept silent and with a small brush casually cleaned the diamonds that studded his hands.

'What, then, do you want?' Catherine asked solicitously.

The Cossacks looked meaningly at one another.

'Now's the time! The tsaritsa is asking what we want!' the blacksmith said to himself and suddenly fell to the ground.

'Your Imperial Majesty, punish me not, but grant me mercy! Meaning no offense to Your Imperial Grace, but what are the booties you're wearing made of? I bet not one cobbler in any country of the world can make them like that. My God, if only my wife could wear such booties!'

The empress laughed. The courtiers also laughed. Potemkin frowned and smiled at the same time. The Cossacks began nudging the blacksmith's arm, thinking he had lost his mind.

'Get up!' the empress said benignly. 'If you want so much to have such shoes, it's not hard to do. Bring him my most expensive shoes at once, the ones with gold! Truly this simple-heartedness pleases me very much! Here,' the empress went on, directing her eyes at a middle-aged man with a plump but somewhat pale face, who was standing further off than the others and whose modest caftan with big mother-of-pearl buttons showed that he did not belong to the number of the courtiers, 'you have a subject worthy of your witty pen!'

'You are too gracious, Your Imperial Majesty. Here at

least a La Fontaine is called for,' the man with the mother-of-pearl buttons replied, bowing.

'I tell you in all honesty, I still love your *Brigadier* to distraction. You read remarkably well! However,' the empress went on, turning to the Cossacks, 'I've heard that in the Setch you never marry.'

'How so, mother! You know yourself a man can't live without a wife,' replied the same Cossack who had spoken with the blacksmith, and the blacksmith was surprised to hear this Cossack, who had such a good knowledge of literate language, talk with the tsaritsa as if on purpose in the coarsest way, usually called muzhik speech. 'Clever folk!' he thought to himself. 'He's surely doing it for a reason.'

'We're not monks,' the Cossack went on, 'but sinful people. We fall for non-lenten things, as all honest Christendom does. Not a few among us have wives, though they don't live with them in the Setch. There are some who have wives in Poland; there are some who have wives in the Ukraine; there are even some who have wives in Turkey.'

Just then the shoes were brought to the blacksmith.

'My God, what an adornment!' he cried joyfully, seizing the shoes. 'Your Imperial Majesty! If the shoes on your feet are like this, and Your Honor probably even wears them to go ice skating, then how must the feet themselves be! I bet of pure sugar, at least!'

The empress, who did in fact have very shapely and lovely feet, could not help smiling at hearing such a compliment from the lips of a simple-hearted blacksmith, who, in his Zaporozhye outfit, could be considered a handsome fellow despite his swarthy complexion.

Gladdened by such favorable attention, the blacksmith was just going to question the tsaritsa properly about everything – was it true that tsars eat only honey and lard, and so on – but feeling the Cossacks nudging him in the ribs, he decided to keep quiet. And when the empress, turning to the elders, began asking how they lived in the Setch and what their customs were, he stepped back, bent to his pocket, and said softly, 'Get me out of here, quick!' and suddenly found himself beyond the toll gate.

'He drowned! by God, he drowned! May I never leave this spot if he didn't drown!' the weaver's fat wife babbled, standing in the middle of the street amidst a crowd of Dikanka women.

'What, am I some kind of liar? did I steal anybody's cow? did I put a spell on anybody, that you don't believe me?' shouted a woman in a Cossack blouse, with a violet nose, waving her arms. 'May I never want to drink water again if old Pereperchikha didn't see the blacksmith hang himself with her own eyes!'

'The blacksmith hanged himself? just look at that!' said the headman, coming out of Choub's house, and he stopped and pushed closer to the talking women.

'Why not tell us you'll never drink vodka again, you old drunkard!' replied the weaver's wife. 'A man would have to be as crazy as you are to hang himself! He drowned! drowned in a hole in the ice! I know it as well as I know you just left the tavern.'

'The hussy! see what she reproaches me with!' the woman with the violet nose retorted angrily, 'You'd better shut up, you jade! Don't I know that the deacon comes calling on you every evening?'

The weaver's wife flared up.

'The deacon what? Calls on whom? How you lie!'

'The deacon?' sang out the deacon's wife, in a rabbitskin coat covered with blue nankeen, pushing her way toward

74

the quarreling women. 'I'll show you a deacon! who said deacon?'

'It's her the deacon comes calling on!' said the woman with the violet nose, pointing at the weaver's wife.

'So it's you, you bitch!' said the deacon's wife, accosting the weaver's wife. 'So it's you, you hellcat, who blow fog in his eyes and give him unclean potions to drink so as to make him come to you?'

'Leave me alone, you she-devil!' the weaver's wife said, backing away.

'You cursed hellcat, may you never live to see your children! Pfui!...' and the deacon's wife spat straight into the weaver's wife's eyes.

The weaver's wife wanted to respond in kind, but instead spat into the unshaven chin of the headman, who, in order to hear better, had edged right up to the quarreling women.

'Agh, nasty woman!' cried the headman, wiping his face with the skirt of his coat and raising his whip. That gesture caused everyone to disband, cursing, in all directions. 'What vileness!' he repeated, still wiping himself. 'So the black-smith is drowned! My God, and what a good painter he was! What strong knives, sickles, and plows he could forge! Such strength he had! Yes,' he went on, pondering, 'there are few such people in our village. That's why I noticed while I was still sitting in that cursed sack that the poor fellow was really in bad spirits. That's it for your blacksmith – he was, and now he's not! And I was just going to have my piebald mare shod!...'

And, filled with such Christian thoughts, the headman slowly trudged home.

Oksana was confused when the news reached her. She trusted little in Pereperchikha's eyes, or in women's talk; she knew that the blacksmith was too pious to dare destroy his soul. But what if he had left with the intention of never coming back to the village? There was hardly such a fine fellow as the blacksmith anywhere else! And he loved her so! He had put up with her caprices longest! All night under her blanket the beauty tossed from right to left, from left to right – and couldn't fall asleep. Now, sprawled in an enchanting nakedness which the dark of night concealed even from herself, she scolded herself almost aloud; then, calming down, she resolved not to think about anything – and went on thinking. And she was burning all over; and by morning she was head over heels in love with the blacksmith.

Choub expressed neither joy nor grief at Vakula's lot. His thoughts were occupied with one thing: he was simply unable to forget Solokha's perfidy and, even in his sleep, never stopped abusing her.

Morning came. Even before dawn the whole church was filled with people. Elderly women in white head scarves and white flannel blouses piously crossed themselves just at the entrance to the church. Ladies in green and yellow vests, and some even in dark blue jackets with gold curlicues behind, stood in front of them. Young girls with a whole mercer's shop of ribbons wound round their heads, and with beads, crosses, and coin necklaces on their necks, tried to make their way still closer to the iconostasis. But in front of them all stood the squires and simple muzhiks with mustaches, topknots, thick necks, and freshly shaven chins, almost all of them in hooded flannel cloaks, from under which peeked here a white and there a blue blouse. All the faces, wherever you looked, had a festive air. The headman licked his chops, imagining himself breaking his fast with sausage; the young girls' thoughts were of going ice skating with the lads; the old women whispered their prayers more zealously than ever. You could hear the Cossack Sverbyguz's bowing all over the church. Only Oksana stood as if not herself: she prayed, and did not pray. There were so many different feelings crowding in her heart, one more vexing than another, one more rueful than another, that her face expressed nothing but great confusion; tears quivered in her eyes. The girls couldn't understand the reason for it and didn't suspect that the blacksmith was to blame. However, Oksana was not the only one concerned about the black-smith. The parishioners all noticed that it was as if the feast was not a feast, as if something was lacking. As luck would have it, the deacon, after his journey in the sack, had grown hoarse and croaked in a barely audible voice; true, the visit-ing singer hit the bass notes nicely, but it would have been much better if the blacksmith had been there, who, when-ever the 'Our Father' or the 'Cherubic Hymn' was sung, always went up to the choir and sang out from there in the same way they sing in Poltava. Besides, he was the one who did the duties of the church warden. Matins were already over; after matins, the liturgy . . . Where, indeed, had the blacksmith disappeared to?

Still more swiftly in the remaining time of night did the devil race home with the blacksmith. Vakula instantly found himself by his cottage. Just then the cock crowed. 'Hold on!' he cried, snatching the devil by the tail as he was about to run away. 'Wait, friend, that's not all – I haven't thanked you yet.' Here, seizing a switch, he measured him out three strokes, and the poor devil broke into a run, like a muzhik who has just been given a roasting by an assessor. And so, instead of deceiving, seducing, and duping others, the enemy of the human race was duped himself. After which, Vakula went into the front hall, burrowed under the hay and slept until dinnertime. Waking up, he was frightened when he saw the sun already high. 'I slept through matins and the liturgy!' – and the pious blacksmith sank into dejection, reasoning that God, as a punishment for his sinful intention of destroying his soul, must have sent him a sleep that kept him from going to church on such a solemn feast day. However, having calmed himself by deciding to confess it to the priest the next week and to start that same day making fifty bows a day for a whole year, he peeked into the cottage; but no one was home. Solokha must not have come back yet. He carefully took the shoes from his bosom and again marveled at the costly workmanship and the strange adventure of the past night; he washed, dressed the best he could, putting on the clothes he got from the Cossacks, took from his trunk a new hat of Reshetilovo astrakhan with a blue top, which he had not worn even once since he bought it while he was in Poltava; he also took out a new belt of all colors; he put it all into a handkerchief along with a whip and went straight to Choub.

Choub goggled his eyes when the blacksmith came in, and didn't know which to marvel at: that the blacksmith had resurrected, or that the blacksmith had dared to come to him, or that he had got himself up so foppishly as a Zaporozhye Cossack. But he was still more amazed when Vakula untied the handkerchief and placed before him a brand-new hat and a belt such as had never been seen in the village, and himself fell at his feet and said in a pleading voice:

'Have mercy, father! don't be angry! here's a whip for you: beat me as much as your soul desires, I give myself up; I repent of everything; beat me, only don't be angry! You were once bosom friends with my late father, you ate bread and salt together and drank each other's health.'

78

Choub, not without secret pleasure, beheld the black-smith – who did not care a hoot about anyone in the village, who bent copper coins and horseshoes in his bare hands like buckwheat pancakes – this same blacksmith, lying at his feet. So as not to demean himself, Choub took the whip and struck him three times on the back.

'Well, that's enough for you, get up! Always listen to your elders! Let's forget whatever was between us! So, tell me now, what do you want?'

'Give me Oksana for my wife, father!'

Choub thought a little, looked at the hat and belt; it was a wonderful hat and the belt was no worse; he remembered the perfidious Solokha and said resolutely:

'Right-o! Send the matchmakers!'

'Aie!' Oksana cried out, stepping across the threshold and seeing the blacksmith, and with amazement and joy she fastened her eyes on him.

'Look, what booties I've brought you!' said Vakula, 'the very ones the tsaritsa wears!'

'No! no! I don't need any booties!' she said, waving her hands and not taking her eyes off him. 'Even without the booties, I . . .' She blushed and did not say any more.

The blacksmith went up to her and took her hand; the beauty looked down. Never yet had she been so wondrously pretty. The delighted blacksmith gently kissed her, her face flushed still more, and she became even prettier.

A bishop of blessed memory was driving through Dikanka, praised the location of the village, and, driving down the street, stopped in front of a new cottage.

'And to whom does this painted cottage belong?' His Reverence asked of the beautiful woman with a baby in her arms who was standing by the door.

79

'To the blacksmith Vakula,' said Oksana, bowing to him, for it was precisely she.

'Fine! fine work!' said His Reverence, studying the doors and windows. The windows were all outlined in red, and on the doors everywhere there were mounted Cossacks with pipes in their teeth.

But His Reverence praised Vakula still more when he learned that he had undergone a church penance and had painted the entire left-hand choir green with red flowers free of charge. That, however, was not all: on the wall to the right as you entered the church, Vakula had painted a devil in hell, such a nasty one that everybody spat as they went by; and the women, if a child started crying in their arms, would carry it over to the picture and say, 'See what a caca's painted there!' and the child, holding back its tears, would look askance at the picture and press against its mother's breast.

ARTHUR CONAN DOYLE

THE BLUE
CARBUNCLE

I HAD CALLED upon my friend Sherlock Holmes upon the second morning after Christmas, with the intention of wishing him the compliments of the season. He was lounging upon the sofa in a purple dressing gown, a pipe-rack within his reach upon the right, and a pile of crumpled morning papers, evidently newly studied, near at hand. Beside the couch was a wooden chair, and on the angle of the back hung a very seedy and disreputable hard felt hat, much the worse for wear, and cracked in several places. A lens and a forceps lying upon the seat of the chair suggested that the hat had been suspended in this manner for the purpose of examination.

'You are engaged,' said I; 'perhaps I interrupt you.'

'Not at all. I am glad to have a friend with whom I can discuss my results. The matter is a perfectly trivial one' (he jerked his thumb in the direction of the old hat), 'but there are points in connection with it which are not entirely devoid of interest, and even of instruction.'

I seated myself in his armchair, and warmed my hands before his crackling fire, for a sharp frost had set in, and the windows were thick with the ice crystals. 'I suppose,' I remarked, 'that, homely as it looks, this thing has some deadly story linked on to it – that it is the clue which will guide you in the solution of some mystery, and the punishment of some crime.'

'No, no. No crime,' said Sherlock Holmes, laughing. 'Only one of those whimsical little incidents which will happen when you have four million human beings all jostling each other within the space of a few square miles. Amid the action and reaction of so dense a swarm of humanity, every possible combination of events may be expected to take place, and many a little problem will be presented which may be striking and bizarre without being criminal. We have already had experience of such.'

'So much so,' I remarked, 'that, of the last six cases which I have added to my notes, three have been entirely free of any legal crime.'

'Precisely. You allude to my attempt to recover the Irene Adler papers, to the singular case of Miss Mary Suther-land, and to the adventure of the man with the twisted lip. Well, I have no doubt that this small matter will fall into the same innocent category. You know Peterson, the commissionaire?'

'Yes.'

'It is to him that this trophy belongs.'

'It is his hat.'

'No, no; he found it. Its owner is unknown. I beg that you will look upon it, not as a battered billy-cock, but as an intellectual problem. And, first, as to how it came here. It arrived upon Christmas morning, in company with a good fat goose; which is, I have no doubt, roasting at this moment in front of Peterson's fire. The facts are these. About four o'clock on Christmas morning, Peterson, who, as you know, is a very honest fellow, was returning from some small jollification and was making his way homewards down Tottenham Court Road. In front of him he saw, in the gaslight, a tallish man, walking with a slight stagger, and carrying a white goose slung over his shoulder. As he reached the corner of Goodge Street a row broke out between this stranger and a little knot of roughs. One of the latter knocked off the man's hat, on which he raised his stick to defend himself and, swinging it over his head, smashed the shop window behind him. Peterson had rushed forward to protect the stranger from his assailants, but the man, shocked at having broken the window, and seeing an official-looking person in uniform rushing towards him, dropped his goose, took to his heels and vanished amid the labyrinth of small streets which lie at the back of Tottenham Court Road. The roughs had also fled at the appearance of Peterson, so that he was left in possession of the field of battle, and also of the spoils of victory in the shape of this battered hat and a most unimpeachable Christmas goose.'

'Which surely he restored to their owner?'

'My dear fellow, there lies the problem. It is true that "For Mrs Henry Baker" was printed upon a small card which was tied to the bird's left leg, and it is also true that the initials "H. B." are legible upon the lining of this hat; but, as there are some thousands of Bakers, and some hundreds of Henry Bakers in this city of ours, it is not easy to restore lost property to any one of them.'

'What, then, did Peterson do?'

'He brought round both hat and goose to me on Christmas morning, knowing that even the smallest problems are of interest to me. The goose we retained until this morning, when there were signs that, in spite of the slight frost, it would be well that it should be eaten without unnecessary delay. Its finder has carried it off, therefore, to fulfil the ultimate destiny of a goose, while I continue to retain the hat of the unknown gentleman who lost his Christmas dinner.'

'Did he not advertise?'

'No.'

'Then, what clue could you have as to his identity?'

'Only as much as we can deduce.'

'From his hat?'

'Precisely.'

'But you are joking. What can you gather from this old battered felt?'

'Here is my lens. You know my methods. What can you gather yourself as to the individuality of the man who has worn this article?'

I took the tattered object in my hands, and turned it over rather ruefully. It was a very ordinary black hat of the usual round shape, hard and much the worse for wear. The lining had been of red silk, but was a good deal discoloured. There was no maker's name; but, as Holmes had remarked, the initials 'H. B.' were scrawled upon one side. It was pierced in the brim for a hat-securer, but the elastic was missing. For the rest, it was cracked, exceedingly dusty, and spotted in several places, although there seemed to have been some attempt to hide the discoloured patches by smearing them with ink.

'I can see nothing,' said I, handing it back to my friend.

'On the contrary, Watson, you can see everything. You fail, however, to reason from what you see. You are too timid in drawing your inferences.'

'Then, pray tell me what it is that you can infer from this hat?'

He picked it up, and gazed at it in the peculiar introspective fashion which was characteristic of him. 'It is perhaps less suggestive than it might have been,' he remarked, 'and yet there are a few inferences which are very distinct, and a few others which represent at least a strong balance of probability. That the man was highly intellectual is of course obvious upon the face of it, and also that he was fairly well-to-do within the last three years, although he has now fallen upon evil days. He had foresight, but has less now than formerly, pointing to a moral retrogression, which, when taken with the decline of his fortunes, seems to indicate some evil influence, probably drink, at work upon him. This may account also for the obvious fact that his wife has ceased to love him.'

'My dear Holmes!'

'He has, however, retained some degree of self-respect,' he continued, disregarding my remonstrance. 'He is a man who leads a sedentary life, goes out little, is out of training entirely, is middle-aged, has grizzled hair which he has had cut within the last few days, and which he anoints with lime-cream. These are the more patent facts which are to be deduced from his hat. Also, by the way, that it is extremely improbable that he has gas laid on in his house.'

'You are certainly joking, Holmes.'

'Not in the least. Is it possible that even now when I give you these results you are unable to see how they are attained?'

'I have no doubt that I am very stupid; but I must confess that I am unable to follow you. For example, how did you deduce that this man was intellectual?'

For answer Holmes clapped the hat upon his head. It came right over the forehead and settled upon the bridge of his nose. 'It is a question of cubic capacity,' said he: 'a man with so large a brain must have something in it.'

'The decline of his fortunes, then?'

'This hat is three years old. These flat brims curled at the edge came in then. It is a hat of the very best quality. Look at the band of ribbed silk, and the excellent lining. If this man could afford to buy so expensive a hat three years ago, and has had no hat since, then he has assuredly gone down in the world.'

'Well, that is clear enough, certainly. But how about the foresight, and the moral retrogression?'

Sherlock Holmes laughed. 'Here is the foresight,' said he, putting his finger upon the little disc and loop of the hat-securer. 'They are never sold upon hats. If this man ordered one, it is a sign of a certain amount of foresight, since he went out of his way to take this precaution against the wind. But since we see that he has broken the elastic, and has not troubled to replace it, it is obvious that he has less foresight now than formerly, which is a distinct proof of a weakening nature. On the other hand, he has endeavoured to conceal some of these stains upon the felt by daubing them with ink, which is a sign that he has not entirely lost his self-respect.'

'Your reasoning is certainly plausible.'

'The further points, that he is middle-aged, that his hair is grizzled, that it has been recently cut, and that he uses lime-cream, are all to be gathered from a close examination of the lower part of the lining. The lens discloses a large number of hair ends, clean cut by the scissors of the barber. They all appear to be adhesive, and there is a distinct odour of lime-cream. This dust, you will observe, is not the gritty, grey dust of the street, but the fluffy brown dust of the house, showing that it has been hung up indoors most of the time; while the marks of moisture upon the inside are proof positive that the wearer perspired very freely, and could, therefore, hardly be in the best of training.'

'But his wife – you said that she had ceased to love him.'

'This hat has not been brushed for weeks. When I see you, my dear Watson, with a week's accumulation of dust upon your hat, and when your wife allows you to go out in such a state, I shall fear that you also have been unfortunate enough to lose your wife's affection.'

'But he might be a bachelor.'

'Nay, he was bringing home the goose as a peace-offering to his wife. Remember the card upon the bird's leg.'

'You have an answer to everything. But how on earth do you deduce that the gas is not laid on in the house?'

'One tallow stain, or even two, might come by chance; but, when I see no less than five, I think that there can be little doubt that the individual must be brought into frequent contact with burning tallow – walks upstairs at night probably with his hat in one hand and a guttering candle in the other. Anyhow, he never got tallow stains from a gas jet. Are you satisfied?'

'Well, it is very ingenious,' said I, laughing; 'but since, as you said just now, there has been no crime committed, and no harm done save the loss of a goose, all this seems to be rather a waste of energy.'

Sherlock Holmes had opened his mouth to reply when the door flew open, and Peterson the commissionaire rushed into the apartment with flushed cheeks and the face of a man who is dazed with astonishment.

'The goose, Mr Holmes! The goose, sir!' he gasped.

'Eh! What of it, then? Has it returned to life, and flapped off through the kitchen window?' Holmes twisted himself round upon the sofa to get a fairer view of the man's excited face.

'See here, sir! See what my wife found in its crop!' He held out his hand, and displayed upon the centre of the palm a brilliantly scintillating blue stone, rather smaller than a bean in size, but of such purity and radiance that it twinkled like an electric point in the dark hollow of his hand.

Sherlock Holmes sat up with a whistle. 'By Jove, Peterson,' said he, 'this is treasure-trove indeed! I suppose you know what you have got?'

'A diamond, sir! A precious stone! It cuts into glass as though it were putty.'

'It's more than a precious stone. It's *the* precious stone.'

'Not the Countess of Morcar's blue carbuncle?' I ejaculated.

'Precisely so. I ought to know its size and shape, seeing that I have read the advertisement about it in *The Times* every day lately. It is absolutely unique, and its value can only be conjectured, but the reward offered of a thousand pounds is certainly not within a twentieth part of the market price.'

'A thousand pounds! Great Lord of mercy!' The commissionaire plumped down into a chair, and stared from one to the other of us.

'That is the reward, and I have reason to know that there are sentimental considerations in the background which would induce the Countess to part with half of her fortune if she could but recover the gem.'

'It was lost, if I remember aright, at the Hotel Cosmopolitan,' I remarked.

'Precisely so, on the 22nd of December, just five days ago. John Horner, a plumber, was accused of having abstracted it from the lady's jewel-case. The evidence against him was so strong that the case has been referred to the Assizes. I have some account of the matter here, I believe.' He rummaged amid his newspapers, glancing over the dates, until at last he smoothed one out, doubled it over, and read the following paragraph:

' "Hotel Cosmopolitan Jewel Robbery, John Horner, 26, plumber, was brought up upon the charge of having upon the 22nd inst., abstracted from the jewel-case of the Countess of Morcar the valuable gem known as the blue carbuncle. James Ryder, upper-attendant at the hotel, gave his evidence to the effect that he had shown Horner up to the dressing-room of the Countess of Morcar upon the day of the robbery, in order that he might solder the second bar of the grate, which was loose. He had remained with Horner some little time but had finally been called away. On returning, he found that Horner had disappeared, that the bureau had been forced open, and that the small morocco casket in which, as it afterwards transpired, the Countess was accustomed to keep her jewel, was lying empty upon the dressing-table. Ryder instantly gave the alarm, and Horner was arrested the same evening; but the stone could not be found either upon his person or in his rooms. Catherine Cusack, maid to the Countess, deposed to having heard Ryder's cry of dismay on discovering the robbery and to having rushed into the room, where she found matters were as described by the last witness. Inspector Bradstreet, B Division, gave evidence as to the arrest of Horner, who struggled frantically, and protested his innocence in the strongest terms. Evidence of a previous conviction for robbery having been given against the prisoner, the magistrate refused to deal summarily with the offence, but referred it to the Assizes. Horner, who had shown signs of intense emotion during the proceedings, fainted away at the conclusion, and was carried out of court."

'Hum! So much for the police-court,' said Holmes thoughtfully, tossing aside his paper. 'The question for us now to solve is the sequence of events from a rifled jewel-case at one end to the crop of a goose in Tottenham Court Road at the other. You see, Watson, our little deductions have suddenly assumed a much more important and less innocent aspect. Here is the stone; the stone came from the goose, and the goose came from Mr Henry Baker, the gentleman with the bad hat and all the other characteristics with which I have bored you. So now we must set ourselves very seriously to finding this gentleman, and ascertaining what part he has played in this little mystery. To do this, we must try the simplest means first, and these lie undoubtedly in an advertisement in all the evening papers. If this fail, I shall have recourse to other methods.'

'What will you say?'

'Give me a pencil, and that slip of paper. Now, then: "Found at the corner of Goodge Street, a goose and a black felt hat. Mr Henry Baker can have the same by applying at 6.30 this evening at 221B Baker Street." That is clear and concise.'

'Very. But will he see it?'

'Well, he is sure to keep an eye on the papers, since, to a poor man, the loss was a heavy one. He was clearly so scared by his mischance in breaking the window, and by the approach of Peterson, that he thought of nothing but flight; but since then he must have bitterly regretted the impulse which caused him to drop his bird. Then, again, the intro-duction of his name will cause him to see it, for every one who knows him will direct his attention to it. Here you are, Peterson, run down to the advertising agency and have this put in the evening papers.'

'In which, sir?'

'Oh, in the *Globe, Star, Pall Mall, St James's Gazette, Evening News, Standard, Echo,* and any others that occur to you.'

'Very well, sir. And this stone?'

'Ah, yes. I shall keep the stone. Thank you. And, I say, Peterson, just buy a goose on your way back, and leave it here with me, for we must have one to give to this gentleman in place of the one which your family is now devouring.'

When the commissionaire had gone, Holmes took up the stone and held it against the light. 'It's a bonny thing,' said he. 'Just see how it glints and sparkles. Of course it is a nucleus and focus of crime. Every good stone is. They are the devil's pet baits. In the larger and older jewels every facet may stand for a bloody deed. This stone is not yet twenty years old. It was found in the banks of the Amoy River in Southern China, and is remarkable in having every characteristic of the carbuncle, save that it is blue in shade, instead of ruby red. In spite of its youth, it has already a sinister history. There have been two murders, a vitriol-throwing, a suicide, and several robberies brought about for the sake of this forty-grain weight of crystallized charcoal. Who would think that so pretty a toy would be a purveyor to the gallows and the prison? I'll lock it up in my strong-box, now, and drop a line to the Countess to say that we have it.'

'Do you think this man Horner is innocent?'

'I cannot tell.'

'Well, then, do you imagine that this other one, Henry Baker, had anything to do with the matter?'

'It is, I think, much more likely that Henry Baker is an absolutely innocent man, who had no idea that the bird which he was carrying was of considerably more value than if it were made of solid gold. That, however, I shall determine by a very simple test, if we have an answer to our advertisement.'

'And you can do nothing until then?'

'Nothing.'

'In that case I shall continue my professional round. But I shall come back in the evening at the hour you have mentioned, for I should like to see the solution of so tangled a business.'

'Very glad to see you. I dine at seven. There is a woodcock, I believe. By the way, in view of recent occurrences, perhaps I ought to ask Mrs Hudson to examine its crop.'

I had been delayed at a case, and it was a little after half-past six when I found myself in Baker Street once more. As I approached the house I saw a tall man in a Scotch bonnet, with a coat which was buttoned up to his chin, waiting outside in the bright semi-circle which was thrown from the fanlight. Just as I arrived, the door was opened, and we were shown up together to Holmes's room.

'Mr Henry Baker, I believe,' said he, rising from his armchair, and greeting his visitor with the easy air of geniality which he could so readily assume. 'Pray take this chair by the fire, Mr Baker. It is a cold night, and I observe that your circulation is more adapted for summer than for winter. Ah, Watson, you have just come at the right time. Is that your hat, Mr Baker?'

'Yes, sir, that is undoubtedly my hat.'

He was a large man, with rounded shoulders, a massive head, and a broad, intelligent face, sloping down to a pointed beard of grizzled brown. A touch of red in nose and cheeks, with a slight tremor of his extended hand, recalled Holmes's surmise as to his habits. His rusty black frock-coat was buttoned right up in front, with the collar turned up, and his lank wrists protruded from his sleeves without a sign of cuff or shirt. He spoke in a low staccato fashion, choosing his words with care, and gave the impression generally of a man of learning and letters who had had ill-usage at the hands of fortune.

'We have retained these things for some days,' said Holmes, 'because we expected to see an advertisement from you giving your address. I am at a loss to know now why you did not advertise.'

Our visitor gave a rather shame-faced laugh. 'Shillings have not been so plentiful with me as they once were,' he remarked. 'I had no doubt that the gang of roughs who assaulted me had carried off both my hat and the bird. I did not care to spend more money in a hopeless attempt at recovering them.'

'Very naturally. By the way, about the bird – we were compelled to eat it.'

'To eat it!' Our visitor half rose from his chair in his excitement.

'Yes; it would have been no use to anyone had we not done so. But I presume that this other goose upon the sideboard, which is about the same weight and perfectly fresh, will answer your purpose equally well?'

'Oh, certainly, certainly!' answered Mr Baker, with a sigh of relief.

'Of course, we still have the feathers, legs, crop, and so on of your own bird, if you so wish –'

The man burst into a hearty laugh. 'They might be useful to me as relics of my adventure,' said he, 'but beyond that I can hardly see what use the *disjecta membra* of my late acquaintance are going to be to me. No, sir, I think that, with your permission, I will confine my attentions to the excellent bird which I perceive upon the sideboard.'

Sherlock Holmes glanced sharply across at me with a slight shrug of his shoulders.

'There is your hat, then, and there your bird,' said he. 'By the way, would it bore you to tell me where you got the other one from? I am somewhat of a fowl fancier, and I have seldom seen a better-grown goose.'

'Certainly sir,' said Baker, who had risen and tucked his

newly-gained property under his arm. 'There are a few of us who frequent the "Alpha" Inn near the Museum – we are to be found in the Museum itself during the day, you understand. This year our good host, Windigate by name, instituted a goose-club, by which, on consideration of some few pence every week, we were each to receive a bird at Christmas. My pence were duly paid, and the rest is familiar to you. I am much indebted to you, sir, for a Scotch bonnet is fitted neither to my years nor my gravity.' With a comical pomposity of manner he bowed solemnly to both of us, and strode off upon his way.

'So much for Mr Henry Baker,' said Holmes, when he had closed the door behind him. 'It is quite certain that he knows nothing whatever about the matter. Are you hungry, Watson?'

'Not particularly.'

'Then I suggest that we turn our dinner into a supper, and follow up this clue while it is still hot.'

'By all means.'

It was a bitter night, so we drew on our ulsters and wrapped cravats about our throats. Outside, the stars were shining coldly in a cloudless sky and the breath of the passers-by blew out into smoke like so many pistol shots. Our footfalls rang out crisply and loudly as we swung through the doctors' quarter, Wimpole Street, Harley Street, and so through Wigmore Street into Oxford Street. In a quarter of an hour we were in Bloomsbury at the 'Alpha' Inn, which is a small public-house at the corner of one of the streets which run down into Holborn. Holmes pushed open the door of the private bar, and ordered two glasses of beer from the ruddy-faced, white-aproned landlord.

'Your beer should be excellent if it is as good as your geese,' he said.

'My geese!' The man seemed surprised.

'Yes. I was speaking only half an hour ago to Mr Henry Baker, who was a member of your goose-club.'

'Ah! yes, I see. But you see, sir, them's not *our* geese.'

'Indeed! Whose, then?'

'Well, I got the two dozen from a salesman in Covent Garden.'

'Indeed! I know some of them. Which was it?'

'Breckinridge is his name.'

'Ah! I don't know him. Well, here's your good health, landlord, and prosperity to your house. Good-night!

'Now for Mr Breckinridge,' he continued, buttoning up his coat, as we came out into the frosty air. 'Remember, Watson, that though we have so homely a thing as a goose at one end of this chain, we have at the other a man who will certainly get seven years' penal servitude, unless we can establish his innocence. It is possible that our inquiry may but confirm his guilt; but, in any case, we have a line of investigation which has been missed by the police, and which a singular chance has placed in our hands. Let us follow it out to the bitter end. Faces to the south, then, and quick march!'

We passed across Holborn, down Endell Street, and so through a zigzag of slums to Covent Garden Market. One of the largest stalls bore the name of Breckinridge upon it, and the proprietor, a horsey-looking man with a sharp face and trim side-whiskers, was helping a boy to put up the shutters.

'Good evening, it's a cold night,' said Holmes.

The salesman nodded, and shot a questioning glance at my companion.

'Sold out of geese, I see,' continued Holmes, pointing at the bare slabs of marble.

'Let you have five hundred to-morrow morning.'

'That's no good.'

'Well, there are some on the stall with the gas flare.'

'Oh, but I was recommended to you.'

'Who by?'

'The landlord of the "Alpha".'

'Ah, yes; I sent him a couple of dozen.'

'Fine birds they were, too. Now where did you get them from?'

To my surprise the question provoked a burst of anger from the salesman.

'Now then, mister,' said he, with his head cocked and his arms akimbo, 'what are you driving at? Let's have it straight, now.'

'It is straight enough. I should like to know who sold you the geese which you supplied to the "Alpha".'

'Well, then, I shan't tell you. So now!'

'Oh, it is a matter of no importance; but I don't know why you should be so warm over such a trifle.'

'Warm! You'd be as warm, maybe, if you were pestered as I am. When I pay good money for a good article there should be an end of the business; but it's "Where are the geese?" and "Who did you sell the geese to?" and "What will you take for the geese?" One would think they were the only geese in the world, to hear the fuss that is made over them.'

'Well, I have no connection with any other people who have been making inquiries,' said Holmes carelessly. 'If you won't tell us the bet is off, that is all. But I'm always ready to back my opinion on a matter of fowls, and I have a fiver on it that the bird I ate is country bred.'

'Well, then, you've lost your fiver, for it's town bred,' snapped the salesman.

'It's nothing of the kind.'

'I say it is.'

'I don't believe you.'

'D'you think you know more about fowls than I, who have handled them ever since I was a nipper? I tell you, all those birds that went to the "Alpha" were town bred.'

'You'll never persuade me to believe that.'

'Will you bet, then?'

'It's merely taking your money, for I know that I am right. But I'll have a sovereign on with you, just to teach you not to be obstinate.'

The salesman chuckled grimly. 'Bring me the books, Bill,' said he.

The small boy brought round a small thin volume and a great greasy-backed one, laying them out together beneath the hanging lamp.

'Now then, Mr Cocksure,' said the salesman, 'I thought that I was out of geese, but before I finish you'll find that there is still one left in my shop. You see this little book?'

'Well?'

'That's the list of the folk from whom I buy. D'you see? Well, then, here on this page are the country folk, and the numbers after their names are where their accounts are in the big ledger. Now, then! You see this other page in red ink? Well, that is a list of my town suppliers. Now, look at that third name. Just read it out to me.'

'Mrs Oakshott, 117, Brixton Road – 249,' read Holmes.

'Quite so. Now turn that up in the ledger.'

Holmes turned to the page indicated. 'Here you are, "Mrs Oakshott, 117, Brixton Road, egg and poultry supplier."'

'Now, then, what's the last entry?'

'"December 22. Twenty-four geese at 7s 6d."'

'Quite so. There you are. And underneath?'

' "Sold to Mr Windigate of the 'Alpha' at 12*s*." '

'What have you to say now?'

Sherlock Holmes looked deeply chagrined. He drew a sovereign from his pocket and threw it down upon the slab, turning away with the air of a man whose disgust is too deep for words. A few yards off he stopped under a lamp-post, and laughed in the hearty, noiseless fashion which was peculiar to him.

'When you see a man with whiskers of that cut and the "*Pink 'Un*" protruding out of his pocket, you can always draw him by a bet,' said he. 'I dare say that if I had put a hundred pounds down in front of him, that man would not have given me such complete information as was drawn from him by the idea that he was doing me on a wager. Well, Watson, we are, I fancy, nearing the end of our quest, and the only point which remains to be determined is whether we should go on to this Mrs Oakshott tonight, or whether we should reserve it for to-morrow. It is clear from what that surly fellow said that there are others besides ourselves who are anxious about the matter, and I should –'

His remarks were suddenly cut short by a loud hubbub which broke out from the stall which we had just left. Turning round we saw a little rat-faced fellow, standing in the centre of the circle of yellow light which was thrown by the swinging lamp, while Breckinridge the salesman, framed in the door of his stall, was shaking his fists fiercely at the cringing figure.

'I've had enough of you and your geese,' he shouted. 'I wish you were all at the devil together. If you come pestering me any more with your silly talk I'll set the dog at you. You bring Mrs Oakshott here and I'll answer her, but what have you to do with it? Did I buy the geese off you?'

'No: but one of them was mine all the same,' whined the little man.

'Well, then, ask Mrs Oakshott for it.'

'She told me to ask you.'

'Well, you can ask the King of Proosia, for all I care. I've had enough of it. Get out of this!' He rushed fiercely forward, and the inquirer flitted away into the darkness.

'Ha, this may save us a visit to Brixton Road,' whispered Holmes. 'Come with me, and we will see what is to be made of this fellow.' Striding through the scattered knots of people who lounged round the flaring stalls, my companion speedily overtook the little man and touched him upon the shoulder. He sprang round, and I could see in the gaslight that every vestige of colour had been driven from his face.

'Who are you, then? What do you want?' he asked in a quavering voice.

'You will excuse me,' said Holmes, blandly, 'but I could not help overhearing the questions which you put to the salesman just now. I think that I could be of assistance to you.'

'You? Who are you? How could you know anything of the matter?'

'My name is Sherlock Holmes. It is my business to know what other people don't know.'

'But you can know nothing of this?'

'Excuse me, I know everything of it. You are endeavouring to trace some geese which were sold by Mrs Oakshott, of Brixton Road, to a salesman named Breckinridge, by him in turn to Mr Windigate, of the "Alpha", and by him to his club, of which Mr Henry Baker is a member.'

'Oh, sir, you are the very man whom I have longed to meet,' cried the little fellow, with outstretched hands and quivering fingers. 'I can hardly explain to you how interested I am in this matter.'

Sherlock Holmes hailed a four-wheeler which was passing. 'In that case we had better discuss it in a cosy room rather than in this windswept market-place,' said he. 'But pray tell me, before we go further, who it is that I have the pleasure of assisting.'

The man hesitated for an instant. 'My name is John Robinson,' he answered, with a sidelong glance.

'No, no; the real name,' said Holmes sweetly. 'It is always awkward doing business with an *alias*.'

A flush sprang to the white cheeks of the stranger. 'Well, then,' said he, 'my real name is James Ryder.'

'Precisely so. Head attendant at the Hotel Cosmopolitan. Pray step into the cab, and I shall soon be able to tell you everything which you would wish to know.'

The little man stood glancing from one to the other of us with half-frightened, half-hopeful eyes, as one who is not sure whether he is on the verge of a windfall or of a catastrophe. Then he stepped into the cab, and in half an hour we were back in the sitting-room at Baker Street. Nothing had been said during our drive, but the high, thin breathing of our new companion, and the claspings and unclaspings of his hands, spoke of the nervous tension within him.

'Here we are!' said Holmes cheerily, as we filed into the room. 'The fire looks very seasonable in this weather. You look cold, Mr Ryder. Pray take the basket chair. I will just put on my slippers before we settle this little matter of yours. Now, then! You want to know what became of those geese?'

'Yes, sir.'

'Or rather, I fancy, of that goose. It was one bird, I imagine, in which you were interested – white, with a black bar across the tail.'

Ryder quivered with emotion. 'Oh, sir,' he cried, 'can you tell me where it went to?'

'It came here.'

'Here?'

'Yes, and a most remarkable bird it proved. I don't wonder that you should take an interest in it. It laid an egg after it was dead – the bonniest, brightest little blue egg that was ever seen. I have it here in my museum.'

Our visitor staggered to his feet, and clutched the mantel-piece with his right hand. Holmes unlocked his strong-box, and held up the blue carbuncle, which shone out like a star, with a cold, brilliant, many-pointed radiance. Ryder stood glaring with a drawn face, uncertain whether to claim or to disown it.

'The game's up, Ryder,' said Holmes quietly. 'Hold up, man, or you'll be into the fire. Give him an arm back into his chair, Watson. He's not got blood enough to go in for felony with impunity. Give him a dash of brandy. So! Now he looks a little more human. What a shrimp it is, to be sure!'

For a moment he had staggered and nearly fallen, but the brandy brought a tinge of colour into his cheeks, and he sat staring with frightened eyes at his accuser.

'I have almost every link in my hands, and all the proofs which I could possibly need, so there is little which you need tell me. Still, that little may as well be cleared up to make the case complete. You had heard, Ryder, of this blue stone of the Countess of Morcar's?'

'It was Catherine Cusack who told me of it,' said he, in a crackling voice.

'I see. Her ladyship's waiting-maid. Well the temptation of sudden wealth so easily acquired was too much for you, as it has been for better men before you; but you were not very scrupulous in the means you used. It seems to me, Ryder, that there is the making of a very pretty villain in you. You knew that this man Horner, the plumber, had been concerned in some such matter before, and that suspicion would rest the more readily upon him. What did you do, then? You made some small job in my lady's room – you and your confederate Cusack – and you managed that he should be the man sent for. Then, when he had left, you rifled the jewel-case, raised the alarm, and had this unfortunate man arrested. You then –'

Ryder threw himself down suddenly upon the rug, and clutched at my companion's knees. 'For God's sake, have mercy!' he shrieked. 'Think of my father! Of my mother! It would break their hearts. I never went wrong before! I never will again. I swear it. I'll swear it on a Bible. Oh, don't bring it into court! For Christ's sake, don't!'

'Get back into your chair!' said Holmes sternly. 'It is very well to cringe and crawl now, but you thought little enough of this poor Horner in the dock for a crime of which he knew nothing.'

'I will fly, Mr Holmes. I will leave the country, sir. Then the charge against him will break down.'

'Hum! We will talk about that. And now let us hear a true account of the next act. How came the stone into the goose, and how came the goose into the open market? Tell us the truth, for there lies your only hope of safety.'

Ryder passed his tongue over his parched lips. 'I will tell you it just as it happened, sir,' said he. 'When Horner had been arrested, it seemed to me that it would be best for me to get away with the stone at once, for I did not know at what moment the police might not take it into their heads to search me and my room. There was no place about the hotel where it would be safe. I went out, as if on some commission, and I made for my sister's house. She had married a man named Oakshott, and lived in Brixton Road, where she fattened fowls for the market. All the way there every man I met seemed to me to be a policeman or a detective, and for all that it was a cold night, the sweat was pouring down my face before I came to the Brixton Road. My sister asked me what was the matter, and why I was so pale; but I told her that I had been upset by the jewel robbery at the hotel. Then I went into the backyard, and smoked a pipe, and wondered what it would be best to do.

'I had a friend once called Maudsley who went to the bad, and has just been serving his time in Pentonville. One day he had met me, and fell into talk about the ways of thieves and how they could get rid of what they stole. I knew that he would be true to me, for I knew one or two things about him, so I made up my mind to go right on to Kilburn, where he lived and take him into my confidence. He would show me how to turn the stone into money. But how to get to him in safety? I thought of the agonies I had gone through in coming from the hotel. I might at any moment be seized and searched, and there would be the stone in my waistcoat pocket. I was leaning against the wall at the time, and looking at the geese which were waddling about round my feet, and suddenly an idea came into my head which showed me how I could beat the best detective that ever lived.

'My sister had told me some weeks before that I might have the pick of her geese for a Christmas present, and I knew that she was always as good as her word. I would take my goose now, and in it I would carry my stone to Kilburn. There was a little shed in the yard, and behind this I drove one of the birds, a fine big one, white, with a barred tail. I caught it, and, prising its bill open, I thrust the stone down its throat as far as my finger could reach. The bird gave a gulp, and I felt the stone pass along its gullet and down into its crop. But the creature flapped and struggled, and out came my sister to know what was the matter. As I turned to speak to her the brute broke loose, and fluttered off among the others.

' "Whatever were you doing with that bird, Jem?" says she.

' "Well," said I, "you said you'd give me one for Christmas, and I was feeling which was the fattest."

' "Oh," says she, "we've set yours aside for you. Jem's bird, we call it. It's the big, white one over yonder. There's twenty-six of them, which makes one for you, and one for us, and two dozen for the market."

' "Thank you, Maggie," says I; "but if it is all the same to you I'd rather have that one I was handling just now."

' "The other is a good three pound heavier," she said, "and we fattened it expressly for you."

' "Never mind. I'll have the other, and I'll take it now," said I.

' "Oh, just as you like," said she, a little huffed. "Which is it you want, then?"

' "That white one, with the barred tail, right in the middle of the flock."

' "Oh, very well. Kill it and take it with you."

'Well, I did what she said, Mr Holmes, and I carried the bird all the way to Kilburn. I told my pal what I had done, for he was a man that it was easy to tell a thing like that to. He laughed until he choked, and we got a knife and opened the goose. My heart turned to water, for there was no sign of the stone, and I knew that some terrible mistake had occurred. I left the bird, rushed back to my sister's, and hurried into the backyard. There was not a bird to be seen there.

' "Where are they all, Maggie?" I cried.

' "Gone to the dealer's."

' "Which dealer's?"

' "Breckinridge, of Covent Garden."

' "But was there another with a barred tail?" I asked, "the same as the one I chose?"

' "Yes, Jem, there were two barred-tailed ones, and I could never tell them apart."

'Well, then, of course, I saw it all, and I ran off as hard as my feet would carry me to this man Breckinridge; but he had sold the lot at once, and not one word would he tell me as to where they had gone. You heard him yourselves tonight. Well, he has always answered me like that. My sister thinks that I am going mad. Sometimes I think that I am myself. And now – now I am myself a branded thief, without ever having touched the wealth for which I sold my character. God help me! God help me!' He burst into convulsive sobbing, with his face buried in his hands.

There was a long silence, broken only by his heavy breathing, and by the measured tapping of Sherlock Holmes's finger-tips upon the edge of the table. Then my friend rose, and threw open the door.

'Get out!' said he.

'What, sir! Oh, heaven bless you!'

'No more words. Get out!'

And no more words were needed. There was a rush, a clatter upon the stairs, the bang of a door, and the crisp rattle of running footfalls from the street.

'After all, Watson,' said Holmes, reaching up his hand for his clay pipe, 'I am not retained by the police to supply their deficiencies. If Horner were in danger it would be another thing, but this fellow will not appear against him, and the case must collapse. I suppose that I am committing a felony but it is just possible that I am saving a soul. This fellow will not go wrong again. He is too terribly frightened. Send him to gaol now, and you make him a gaol-bird for life. Besides, it is the season of forgiveness. Chance has put in our way a most singular and whimsical problem, and its solution is its own reward. If you will have the goodness to touch the bell, Doctor, we will begin another investigation, in which also a bird will be the chief feature.'

ANTHONY TROLLOPE

CHRISTMAS AT
THOMPSON HALL

Mrs Brown's Success

EVERYONE REMEMBERS THE severity of the Christmas of 187–. I will not designate the year more closely, lest I should enable those who are too curious to investigate the circumstances of this story, and inquire into details which I do not intend to make known. That winter, however, was especially severe, and the cold of the last ten days of December was more felt, I think, in Paris than in any part of England. It may, indeed, be doubted whether there is any town in any country in which thoroughly bad weather is more afflicting than in the French capital. Snow and hail seem to be colder there, and fires certainly are less warm, than in London. And then there is a feeling among visitors to Paris that Paris ought to be gay; that gaiety, prettiness, and liveliness are its aims, as money, commerce, and general business are the aims of London, – which with its outside sombre darkness does often seem to want an excuse for its ugliness. But on this occasion, at this Christmas of 187–, Paris was neither gay nor pretty nor lively. You could not walk the streets without being ankle deep, not in snow, but in snow that had just become slush; and there were falling throughout the day and night of the 23rd of December a succession of damp half-frozen abominations from the sky which made it almost impossible for men and women to go about their business.

It was at ten o'clock on that evening that an English lady

and gentleman arrived at the Grand Hotel on the Boulevard des Italiens. As I have reasons for concealing the names of this married couple I will call them Mr and Mrs Brown. Now I wish it to be understood that in all the general affairs of life this gentleman and this lady lived happily together, with all the amenities which should bind a husband and a wife. Mrs Brown was one of a wealthy family, and Mr Brown, when he married her, had been relieved from the necessity of earning his bread. Nevertheless she had at once yielded to him when he expressed a desire to spend the winters of their life in the South of France; and he, though he was by disposition somewhat idle, and but little prone to the energetic occupations of life, would generally allow himself, at other periods of the year, to be carried hither and thither by her, whose more robust nature delighted in the excitement of travelling. But on this occasion there had been a little difference between them.

Early in December an intimation had reached Mrs Brown at Pau that on the coming Christmas there was to be a great gathering of all the Thompsons in the Thompson family hall at Stratford-le-Bow, and that she who had been a Thompson was desired to join the party with her husband. On this occasion her only sister was desirous of introducing to the family generally a most excellent young man to whom she had recently become engaged. The Thompsons, – the real name, however, is in fact concealed, – were a numerous and a thriving people. There were uncles and cousins and brothers who had all done well in the world, and who were all likely to do better still. One had lately been returned to Parliament for the Essex Flats, and was at the time of which I am writing a conspicuous member of the gallant Conservative majority. It was partly in triumph at this success that the great Christmas gathering of the Thompsons was to be held, and an opinion had been expressed by the legislator himself that should Mrs Brown, with her husband, fail to join the family on this happy occasion she and he would be regarded as being *fainéant* Thompsons.

Since her marriage, which was an affair now nearly eight years old, Mrs Brown had never passed a Christmas in England. The desirability of doing so had often been mooted by her. Her very soul craved the festivities of holly and mince-pies. There had ever been meetings of the Thompsons at Thompson Hall, though meetings not so significant, not so important to the family, as this one which was now to be collected. More than once had she expressed a wish to see old Christmas again in the old house among the old faces. But her husband had always pleaded a certain weakness about his throat and chest as a reason for remaining among the delights of Pau. Year after year she had yielded; and now this loud summons had come.

It was not without considerable trouble that she had induced Mr Brown to come as far as Paris. Most unwillingly had he left Pau; and then, twice on his journey, – both at Bordeaux and Tours, – he had made an attempt to return. From the first moment he had pleaded his throat, and when at last he had consented to make the journey he had stipulated for sleeping at those two towns and at Paris. Mrs Brown, who, without the slightest feeling of fatigue, could have made the journey from Pau to Stratford without stopping, had assented to everything, – so that they might be at Thompson Hall on Christmas Eve. When Mr Brown uttered his unavailing complaints at the two first towns at which they stayed, she did not perhaps quite believe all that he said of his own condition. We know how prone the strong are to suspect the weakness of the weak, – as the weak are to be disgusted by the strength of the strong.

There were perhaps a few words between them on the journey, but the result had hitherto been in favour of the lady. She had succeeded in bringing Mr Brown as far as Paris.

Had the occasion been less important, no doubt she would have yielded. The weather had been bad even when they left Pau, but as they had made their way northwards it had become worse and still worse. As they left Tours Mr Brown, in a hoarse whisper, had declared his conviction that the journey would kill him. Mrs Brown, however, had unfortunately noticed half an hour before that he had scolded the waiter on the score of an over-charged franc or two with a loud and clear voice. Had she really believed that there was danger, or even suffering, she would have yielded; – but no woman is satisfied in such a matter to be taken in by false pretences. She observed that he ate a good dinner on his way to Paris, and that he took a small glass of cognac with complete relish, – which a man really suffering from bronchitis surely would not do. So she persevered, and brought him into Paris, late in the evening, in the midst of all that slush and snow. Then, as they sat down to supper, she thought that he did speak hoarsely, and her loving feminine heart began to misgive her.

But this now was at any rate clear to her, – that he could not be worse off by going on to London than he would be should he remain in Paris. If a man is to be ill he had better be ill in the bosom of his family than at a hotel. What comfort could he have, what relief, in that huge barrack? As for the cruelty of the weather, London could not be worse than Paris, and then she thought she had heard that sea air is good for a sore throat. In that bedroom which had been allotted to them *au quatrième*, they could not even get a decent fire. It would in every way be wrong now to forgo the great Christmas gathering when nothing could be gained by staying in Paris.

She had perceived that as her husband became really ill he became also more tractable and less disputatious. Immediately after that little glass of cognac he had declared that he would be _____ if he would go beyond Paris, and she began to fear that, after all, everything would have been done in vain. But as they went down to supper between ten and eleven he was more subdued, and merely remarked that this journey would, he was sure, be the death of him. It was half-past eleven when they got back to their bedroom, and then he seemed to speak with good sense, – and also with much real apprehension. 'If I can't get something to relieve me I know I shall never make my way on,' he said. It was intended that they should leave the hotel at half-past five the next morning, so as to arrive at Stratford, travelling by the tidal train, at half-past seven on Christmas Eve. The early hour, the long journey, the infamous weather, the prospect of that horrid gulf between Boulogne and Folkestone, would have been as nothing to Mrs Brown, had it not been for that settled look of anguish which had now pervaded her husband's face. 'If you don't find something to relieve me I shall never live through it,' he said again, sinking back into the questionable comfort of a Parisian hotel arm-chair.

'But, my dear, what can I do?' she asked, almost in tears, standing over him and caressing him. He was a thin, genteel-looking man, with a fine long, soft brown beard, a little bald at the top of the head, but certainly a genteel-looking man. She loved him dearly, and in her softer moods was apt to spoil him with her caresses. 'What can I do, my dearie? You know I would do anything if I could. Get into bed, my pet, and be warm, and then to-morrow morning you will be all right.' At this moment he was preparing himself for his bed, and she was assisting him. Then she tied a piece of flannel round his throat, and kissed him, and put him in beneath the bed-clothes.

'I'll tell you what you can do,' he said very hoarsely. His voice was so bad now that she could hardly hear him. So she crept close to him, and bent over him. She would do anything if he would only say what. Then he told her what was his plan. Down in the salon he had seen a large jar of mustard standing on a sideboard. As he left the room he had observed that this had not been withdrawn with the other appurtenances of the meal. If she could manage to find her way down there, taking with her a handkerchief folded for the purpose, and if she could then appropriate a part of the contents of that jar, and returning with her prize, apply it to his throat, he thought that he could get some relief, so that he might be able to leave his bed the next morning at five. 'But I am afraid it will be very disagreeable for you to go down all alone at this time of night,' he croaked out in a piteous whisper.

'Of course I'll go,' said she. 'I don't mind going in the least. Nobody will bite me,' and she at once began to fold a clean handkerchief. 'I won't be two minutes, my darling, and if there is a grain of mustard in the house I'll have it on your chest almost immediately.' She was a woman not easily cowed, and the journey down into the salon was nothing to her. Before she went she tucked the clothes carefully up to his ears, and then she started.

To run along the first corridor till she came to a flight of stairs was easy enough, and easy enough to descend them. Then there was another corridor, and another flight, and a third corridor and a third flight, and she began to think that she was wrong. She found herself in a part of the hotel which she had not hitherto visited, and soon discovered by looking through an open door or two that she had found her way among a set of private sitting-rooms which she had not seen before. Then she tried to make her way back, up the same stairs and through the same passages, so that she might start again. She was beginning to think that she had lost herself altogether, and that she would be able to find neither the salon nor her bedroom, when she happily met the night porter. She was dressed in a loose white dressing gown, with a white net over her loose hair, and with white worsted slippers. I ought perhaps to have described her personal appearance sooner. She was a large woman, with a commanding bust, thought by some to be handsome, after the manner of Juno. But with strangers there was a certain severity of manner about her, – a fortification, as it were, of her virtue against all possible attacks, – a declared determination to maintain at all points, the beautiful character of a British matron, which, much as it had been appreciated at Thompson Hall, had met with some ill-natured criticism among French men and women. At Pau she had been called La Fière Anglaise. The name had reached her own ears and those of her husband. He had been much annoyed, but she had taken it in good part, – and had endeavoured to live up to it. With her husband she could, on occasion, be soft, but she was of opinion that with other men a British matron should be stern. She was now greatly in want of assistance; but, nevertheless, when she met the porter she remembered her character. 'I have lost my way wandering through these horrid passages,' she said, in her severest tone. This was in answer to some question from him, – some question to which her reply was given very slowly. Then when he asked where Madame wished to go, she paused, again thinking what destination she would announce. No doubt the man could take her back to her bedroom, but if so, the mustard must be renounced, and with the mustard, as she now feared, all hope of reaching Thompson Hall on Christmas Eve. But she, though she was in many respects a brave woman, did not dare to tell the man that she was prowling about the hotel in order that she might make a midnight raid upon the mustard pot. She paused, therefore, for a moment, that she might collect her thoughts, erecting her head as she did so in her best Juno fashion, till the porter was lost in admiration. Thus she gained time to fabricate a tale. She had, she said, dropped her handkerchief under the supper table; would he show her the way to the salon, in order that she might pick it up. But the porter did more than that, and accompanied her to the room in which she had supped.

Here, of course, there was a prolonged, and, it need hardly be said, a vain search. The good-natured man insisted on emptying an enormous receptacle of soiled table-napkins, and on turning them over one by one, in order that the lady's property might be found. The lady stood by unhappy, but still patient, and, as the man was stooping to his work, her eye was on the mustard pot. There it was, capable of containing enough to blister the throats of a score of sufferers. She edged off a little towards it while the man was busy, trying to persuade herself that he would surely forgive her if she took the mustard, and told him her whole story. But the descent from her Juno bearing would have been so great! She must have owned, not only to the quest for mustard, but also to a fib, – and she could not do it. The porter was at last of opinion that Madame must have made a mistake, and Madame acknowledged that she was afraid it was so.

With a longing, lingering eye, with an eye turned back, oh! so sadly, to the great jar, she left the room, the porter leading the way. She assured him that she would find it by herself, but he would not leave her till he had put her on to the proper passage. The journey seemed to be longer now even than before, but as she ascended the many stairs she swore to herself that she would not even yet be baulked of her object. Should her husband want comfort for his poor throat, and the comfort be there within her reach, and he not have it? She counted every stair as she went up, and marked every turn well. She was sure now that she would know the way, and that she could return to the room without fault. She would go back to the salon. Even though the man should encounter her again, she would go boldly forward and seize the remedy which her poor husband so grievously required.

'Ah, yes,' she said, when the porter told her that her room, No. 333, was in the corridor which they had then reached, 'I know it all now. I am so much obliged. Do not come a step further.' He was anxious to accompany her up to the very door, but she stood in the passage and prevailed. He lingered awhile – naturally. Unluckily she had brought no money with her, and could not give him the two-franc piece which he had earned. Nor could she fetch it from her room, feeling that were she to return to her husband without the mustard no second attempt would be possible. The disappointed man turned on his heel at last, and made his way down the stairs and along the passage. It seemed to her to be almost an eternity while she listened to his still audible footsteps. She had gone on, creeping noiselessly up to the very door of her room, and there she stood, shading the candle in her hand, till she thought that the man must have wandered away into some furthest corner of that endless building. Then she turned once more and retraced her steps.

There was no difficulty now as to the way. She knew it, every stair. At the head of each flight she stood and listened, but not a sound was to be heard, and then she went on again. Her heart beat high with anxious desire to achieve her object, and at the same time with fear. What might have been explained so easily at first would now be as difficult of explanation. At last she was in the great public vestibule, which she was now visiting for the third time, and of which, at her last visit, she had taken the bearings accurately. The door was there – closed, indeed, but it opened easily to the hand. In the hall, and on the stairs, and along the passages, there had been gas, but here there was no light beyond that given by the little taper which she carried. When accompanied by the porter she had not feared the darkness, but now there was something in the obscurity which made her dread to walk the length of the room up to the mustard jar. She paused, and listened, and trembled. Then she thought of the glories of Thompson Hall, of the genial warmth of a British Christmas, of that proud legislator who was her first cousin, and with a rush she made good the distance, and laid her hand upon the copious delft. She looked round, but there was no one there; no sound was heard; not the distant creak of a shoe, not a rattle from one of those doors. As she paused with her fair hand upon the top of the jar, while the other held the white cloth on which the medicinal compound was to be placed, she looked like Lady Macbeth as she listened at Duncan's chamber door.

There was no doubt as to the sufficiency of the contents. The jar was full nearly up to the lips. The mixture was, no doubt, very different from that good wholesome English mustard which your cook makes fresh for you, with a little water, in two minutes. It was impregnated with a sour odour, and was, to English eyes, unwholesome of colour. But still it was mustard. She seized the horn spoon, and without further delay spread an ample sufficiency on the folded square of the handkerchief. Then she commenced to hurry her return.

But still there was a difficulty, no thought of which had occurred to her before. The candle occupied one hand, so that she had but the other for the sustenance of her treasure. Had she brought a plate or saucer from the salon, it would have been all well. As it was she was obliged to keep her eye intent on her right hand, and to proceed very slowly on her return journey. She was surprised to find what an aptitude the thing had to slip from her grasp. But still she progressed slowly, and was careful not to miss a turning. At last she was safe at her chamber door. There it was, No. 333.

Mrs Brown's Failure

With her eye still fixed upon her burden, she glanced up at the number of the door – 333. She had been determined all through not to forget that. Then she turned the latch and crept in. The chamber also was dark after the gaslight on the stairs, but that was so much the better. She herself had put out the two candles on the dressing-table before she had left her husband. As she was closing the door behind her she paused, and could hear that he was sleeping. She was well aware that she had been long absent, – quite long enough for a man to fall into slumber who was given that way. She must have been gone, she thought, fully an hour. There had been no end to that turning over of napkins which she had so well known to be altogether vain. She paused at the centre table of the room, still looking at the mustard, which she now delicately dried from off her hand. She had had no idea that it would have been so difficult to carry so light and so small an affair. But there it was, and nothing had been lost. She took some small instrument from the washing-stand, and with the handle collected the flowing fragments into the centre. Then the question occurred to her whether, as her husband was sleeping so sweetly, it would be well to disturb him. She listened again, and felt that the slight murmur of a snore with which her ears were regaled was altogether free from any real malady in the throat. Then it occurred to her, that after all, fatigue perhaps had only made him cross. She bethought herself how, during the whole journey, she had failed to believe in his illness. What meals he had eaten! How thoroughly he had been able to enjoy his full complement of cigars! And then that glass of brandy, against which she had raised her voice slightly in feminine opposition. And now he was sleeping there like an infant, with full, round, perfected, almost sonorous workings of the throat. Who does not know that sound, almost of two rusty bits of iron scratching against each other, which comes from a suffering windpipe? There was no semblance of that here. Why disturb him when he was so thoroughly enjoying that rest which, more certainly than anything else, would fit him for the fatigue of the morrow's journey?

I think that, after all her labour, she would have left the pungent cataplasm on the table, and have crept gently into bed beside him, had not a thought suddenly struck her of the great injury he had been doing her if he were not really ill. To send her down there, in a strange hotel, wandering among the passages, in the middle of the night, subject to the contumely of any one who might meet her, on a commission which, if it were not sanctified by absolute necessity, would be so thoroughly objectionable! At this moment she hardly did believe that he had ever really been ill. Let him have the cataplasm; if not as a remedy, then as a punishment. It could, at any rate, do him no harm. It was with an idea of avenging rather than of justifying the past labours of the night that she proceeded at once to quick action.

Leaving the candle on the table so that she might steady her right hand with the left, she hurried stealthily to the bed-side. Even though he was behaving badly to her, she would not cause him discomfort by waking him roughly. She would do a wife's duty to him as a British matron should. She would not only put the warm mixture on his neck, but would sit carefully by him for twenty minutes, so that she might relieve him from it when the proper period should have come for removing the counter irritation from his throat. There would doubtless be some little difficulty in this, – in collecting the mustard after it had served her purpose. Had she been at home, surrounded by her own comforts, the application would have been made with some delicate linen bag, through which the pungency of the spice would have penetrated with strength sufficient for the purpose. But the circumstance of the occasion had not admitted this. She had, she felt, done wonders in achieving so much success as this which she had obtained. If there should be anything disagreeable in the operation he must submit to it. He had asked for mustard for his throat, and mustard he should have.

As these thoughts passed quickly through her mind, lean-ing over him in the dark, with her eye fixed on the mixture lest it should slip, she gently raised his flowing beard with her left hand, and with her other inverted rapidly, steadily but very softly fixed the handkerchief on his throat. From the bottom of his chin to the spot at which the collar bones meeting together form the orifice of the chest it covered the whole noble expanse. There was barely time for a glance, but never had she been more conscious of the grand propor-tions of that manly throat. A sweet feeling of pity came upon her, causing her to determine to relieve his sufferings in the shorter space of fifteen minutes. He had been lying on his back, with his lips apart, and as she held back his beard, that and her hand nearly covered the features of his face. But he made no violent effort to free himself from the encounter. He did not even move an arm or a leg. He simply emitted a snore louder than any that had come before. She was aware that it was not his wont to be so loud – that there was generally something more delicate and perhaps more querulous in his nocturnal voice, but then the present circumstances were exceptional. She dropped the beard very softly – and there on the pillow before her lay the face of a stranger. She had put the mustard plaster on the wrong man.

Not Priam wakened in the dead of night, not Dido when first she learned that Æneas had fled, not Othello when he learned that Desdemona had been chaste, not Medea when she became conscious of her slaughtered children, could have been more struck with horror than was this British matron as she stood for a moment gazing with awe on that stranger's bed. One vain, half-completed, snatching grasp she made at the handkerchief, and then drew back her hand. If she were to touch him would he not wake at once, and find her standing there in his bedroom? And then how could she explain it? By what words could she so quickly make him know the circumstances of that strange occurrence that he should accept it all before he had said a word that might offend her? For a moment she stood all but paralysed after that faint ineffectual movement of her arm. Then he stirred his head uneasily on the pillow, opened wider his lips, and twice in rapid succession snored louder than before. She started back a couple of paces, and with her body placed between him and the candle, with her face averted, but with her hand still resting on the foot of the bed, she endeavoured to think what duty required of her.

She had injured the man. Though she had done it most unwittingly, there could be no doubt but that she had injured him. If for a moment she could be brave, the injury might in truth be little; but how disastrous might be the consequences if she were now in her cowardice to leave him, who could tell? Applied for fifteen or twenty minutes a mustard plaster may be the salvation of a throat ill at ease, but if left there throughout the night upon the neck of a strong man, ailing nothing, only too prone in his strength to slumber soundly, how sad, how painful, for aught she knew how dangerous might be the effects! And surely it was an error which any man with a heart in his bosom would pardon! Judging from what little she had seen of him she thought that he must have a heart in his bosom. Was it not her duty to wake him, and then quietly to extricate him from the embarrassment which she had brought upon him?

But in doing this what words should she use? How should she wake him? How should she make him understand her goodness, her beneficence, her sense of duty, before he should have jumped from the bed and rushed to the bell, and have summoned all above and all below to the rescue? 'Sir, do not move, do not stir, do not scream. I have put a mustard plaster on your throat, thinking that you were my husband. As yet no harm has been done. Let me take it off, and then hold your peace for ever.' Where is the man of such native constancy and grace of spirit that, at the first moment of waking with a shock, he could hear these words from the mouth of an unknown woman by his bed-side, and at once obey them to the letter? Would he not surely jump from his bed, with that horrid compound falling about him, – from which there could be no complete relief unless he would keep his present attitude without a motion. The picture which presented itself to her mind as to his probable conduct was so terrible that she found herself unable to incur the risk.

Then an idea presented itself to her mind. We all know how in a moment quick thoughts will course through the subtle brain. She would find that porter and send him to explain it all. There should be no concealment now. She would tell the story and would bid him to find the necessary aid. Alas! as she told herself that she would do so, she knew well that she was only running from the danger which it was her duty to encounter. Once again she put out her hand as though to return along the bed. Then thrice he snorted louder than before, and moved up his knee uneasily beneath the clothes as though the sharpness of the mustard were already working upon his skin. She watched him for a moment longer, and then, with the candle in her hand, she fled.

Poor human nature! Had he been an old man, even a middle-aged man, she would not have left him to his un-merited sufferings. As it was, though she completely recog-nized her duty, and knew what justice and goodness demanded of her, she could not do it. But there was still left to her that plan of sending the night-porter to him. It was not till she was out of the room and had gently closed the door behind her, that she began to bethink herself how she had made the mistake. With a glance of her eye she looked up, and then saw the number on the door: 353. Remarking to herself, with a Briton's natural criticism on things French, that those horrid foreigners do not know how to make their figures, she scudded rather than ran along the corridor, and then down some stairs and along another passage, – so that she might not be found in the neighbourhood should the poor man in his agony rush rapidly from his bed.

In the confusion of her first escape she hardly ventured to look for her own passage, – nor did she in the least know how she had lost her way when she came upstairs with the mustard in her hand. But at the present moment her chief object was the night-porter. She went on descending till she came again to that vestibule, and looking up at the clock saw that it was now past one. It was not yet midnight when she left her husband, but she was not at all astonished at the lapse of time. It seemed to her as though she had passed a night among these miseries. And, oh, what a night! But there was yet much to be done. She must find that porter, and then return to her own suffering husband. Ah, – what now should she say to him! If he should really be ill, how should she assuage him? And yet how more than ever necessary was it that they should leave that hotel early in the morning, – that they should leave Paris by the very earliest and quickest train that would take them as fugitives from their present dangers! The door of the salon was open, but she had no courage to go in search of a second supply. She would have lacked strength to carry it up the stairs. Where now, oh, where, was that man? From the vestibule she made her way into the hall, but everything seemed to be deserted. Through the glass she could see a light in the court beyond, but she could not bring herself to endeavour even to open the hall doors.

And now she was very cold, – chilled to her very bones. All this had been done at Christmas, and during such severity of weather as had never before been experienced by living Parisians. A feeling of great pity for herself gradually came upon her. What wrong had she done that she should be so grievously punished? Why should she be driven to wander about in this way till her limbs were failing her? And then, so absolutely important as it was that her strength should support her in the morning! The man would not die even though he were left there without aid, to rid himself of the cataplasm as best he might. Was it absolutely necessary that she should disgrace herself?

But she could not even procure the means of disgracing herself, if that telling her story to the night-porter would have been, a disgrace. She did not find him, and at last resolved to make her way back to her own room without further quest. She began to think that she had done all that she could do. No man was ever killed by a mustard plaster on his throat. His discomfort at the worst would not be worse than hers had been – or too probably than that of her poor husband. So she went back up the stairs and along the passages, and made her way on this occasion to the door of her room without any difficulty. The way was so well known to her that she could not but wonder that she had failed before. But now her hands had been empty, and her eyes had been at her full command. She looked up, and there was the number, very manifest on this occasion, – 333. She opened the door most gently, thinking that her husband might be sleeping as soundly as that other man had slept, and she crept into the room.

Mrs Brown Attempts to Escape

But her husband was not sleeping. He was not even in bed, as she had left him. She found him sitting there before the fireplace, on which one half-burned log still retained a spark of what had once pretended to be a fire. Nothing more wretched than his appearance could be imagined. There was a single lighted candle on the table, on which he was leaning with his two elbows, while his head rested between his hands. He had on a dressing-gown over his night-shirt, but otherwise was not clothed. He shivered audibly, or rather shook himself with the cold, and made the table to chatter as she entered the room. Then he groaned, and let his head fall from his hands on to the table. It occurred to her at the moment as she recognized the tone of his querulous voice, and as she saw the form of his neck, that she must have been deaf and blind when she had mistaken that stalwart stranger for her husband. 'Oh, my dear,' she said, 'why are you not in bed?' He answered nothing in words, but only groaned again. 'Why did you get up? I left you warm and comfortable.'

'Where have you been all night?' he half whispered, half croaked, with an agonizing effort.

'I have been looking for the mustard.'

'Have been looking all night and haven't found it? Where have you been?'

She refused to speak a word to him till she had got him into bed, and then she told her story. But, alas, that which she told was not the true story! As she was persuading him to go back to his rest, and while she arranged the clothes again around him, she with difficulty made up her mind as to what she would do and what she would say. Living or dying he must be made to start for Thompson Hall at half-past five on the next morning. It was no longer a question of the amenities of Christmas, no longer a mere desire to satisfy the family ambition of her own people, no longer an anxiety to see her new brother-in-law. She was conscious that there was in that house one whom she had deeply injured, and from whose vengeance, even from whose aspect, she must fly. How could she endure to see that face which she was so well sure that she would recognize, or to hear the slightest sound of that voice which would be quite familiar to her ears, though it had never spoken a word in her hearing? She must certainly fly on the wings of the earliest train which would carry her towards the old house; but in order that she might do so she must propitiate her husband.

So she told her story. She had gone forth, as he had bade her, in search of the mustard, and then had suddenly lost her way. Up and down the house she had wandered, perhaps nearly a dozen times. 'Had she met no one?' he asked in that raspy, husky whisper. 'Surely there must have been some one about the hotel! Nor was it possible that she could have been roaming about all those hours.' 'Only one hour, my dear,' she said. Then there was a question about the duration of time, in which both of them waxed angry, and as she became angry her husband waxed stronger, and as he became violent beneath the clothes the comfortable idea returned to her that he was not perhaps so ill as he would seem to be. She found herself driven to tell him something about the porter, having to account for that lapse of time by explaining how she had driven the poor man to search for the handkerchief which she had never lost.

'Why did you not tell him you wanted the mustard?'

'My dear!'

'Why not? There is nothing to be ashamed of in wanting mustard.'

'At one o'clock in the morning! I couldn't do it. To tell you the truth, he wasn't very civil, and I thought that he was, – perhaps a little tipsy. Now, my dear, do go to sleep.'

'Why didn't you get the mustard?'

'There was none there, – nowhere at all about the room. I went down again and searched everywhere. That's what took me so long. They always lock up those kind of things at these French hotels. They are too close-fisted to leave anything out. When you first spoke of it I knew that it would be gone when I got there. Now, my dear, do go to sleep, because we positively must start in the morning.'

'That is impossible,' said he, jumping up in the bed.

'We must go, my dear. I say that we must go. After all that has passed I wouldn't not be with Uncle John and my cousin Robert to-morrow evening for more, – more, – more than I would venture to say.'

'Bother!' he exclaimed.

'It's all very well for you to say that, Charles, but you don't know. I say that we must go to-morrow, and we will.'

'I do believe you want to kill me, Mary.'

'That is very cruel, Charles, and most false, and most unjust. As for making you ill, nothing could be so bad for you as this wretched place, where nobody can get warm either day or night. If anything will cure your throat for you at once it will be the sea air. And only think how much more comfortable they can make you at Thompson Hall than anywhere in this country. I have so set my heart upon it, Charles, that I will do it. If we are not there to-morrow night Uncle John won't consider us as belonging to the family.'

'I don't believe a word of it.'

'Jane told me so in her letter. I wouldn't let you know before because I thought it so unjust. But that has been the reason why I've been so earnest about it all through.'

It was a thousand pities that so good a woman should have been driven by the sad stress of circumstances to tell so many fibs. One after another she was compelled to invent them, that there might be a way open to her of escaping the horrors of a prolonged sojourn in that hotel. At length, after much grumbling, he became silent, and she trusted that he was sleeping. He had not as yet said that he would start at the required hour in the morning, but she was perfectly determined in her own mind that he should be made to do so. As he lay there motionless, and as she wandered about the room pretending to pack her things, she more than once almost resolved that she would tell him everything. Surely then he would be ready to make any effort. But there came upon her an idea that he might perhaps fail to see all the circumstances, and that, so failing, he would insist on remaining that he might tender some apology to the injured gentleman. An apology might have been very well had she not left him there in his misery – but what apology would be possible now? She would have to see him and speak to him, and everyone in the hotel would know every detail of the story. Everyone in France would know that it was she who had gone to the strange man's bed-side, and put the mustard plaster on the strange man's throat in the dead of night! She could not tell the story even to her husband, lest even her husband should betray her.

Her own sufferings at the present moment were not light. In her perturbation of mind she had foolishly resolved that she would not herself go to bed. The tragedy of the night had seemed to her too deep for personal comfort. And then how would it be were she to sleep, and have no one to call her? It was imperative that she should have all her powers ready for thoroughly arousing him. It occurred to her that the servant of the hotel would certainly run her too short of time. She had to work for herself and for him too, and therefore she would not sleep. But she was very cold, and she put on first a shawl over her dressing-gown and then a cloak. She could not consume all the remaining hours of the night in packing one bag and one portmanteau, so that at last she sat down on the narrow red cotton velvet sofa, and, looking at her watch, perceived that as yet it was not much past two o'clock. How was she to get through those other three long, tedious, chilly hours?

Then there came a voice from the bed – 'Ain't you coming?'

'I hoped you were asleep, my dear.'

'I haven't been asleep at all. You'd better come, if you don't mean to make yourself as ill as I am.'

'You are not so very bad, are you, darling?'

'I don't know what you call bad. I never felt my throat so choked in my life before!' Still as she listened she thought that she remembered his throat to have been more choked. If the husband of her bosom could play with her feelings and deceive her on such an occasion as this, – then, then, – then she thought that she would rather not have any husband of her bosom at all. But she did creep into bed, and lay down beside him without saying another word.

Of course she slept, but her sleep was not the sleep of the blest. At every striking of the clock in the quadrangle she would start up in alarm, fearing that she had let the time go by. Though the night was so short it was very long to her. But he slept like an infant. She could hear from his breathing that he was not quite so well as she could wish him to be, but still he was resting in beautiful tranquillity. Not once did he move when she started up, as she did so frequently. Orders had been given and repeated over and over again that they should be called at five. The man in the office had almost been angry as he assured Mrs Brown for the fourth time that Monsieur and Madame would most assuredly be wakened at the appointed time. But still she would trust no one, and was up and about the room before the clock had struck half-past four.

In her heart of hearts she was very tender towards her

husband. Now, in order that he might feel a gleam of warmth while he was dressing himself, she collected together the fragments of half-burned wood, and endeavoured to make a little fire. Then she took out from her bag a small pot, and a patent lamp, and some chocolate, and prepared for him a warm drink, so that he might have it instantly as he was awakened. She would do anything for him in the way of ministering to his comfort – only he must go! Yes, he certainly must go!

And then she wondered how that strange man was bearing himself at the present moment. She would fain have ministered to him too had it been possible; but ah! – it was so impossible! Probably before this he would have been aroused from his troubled slumbers. But then – how aroused? At what time in the night would the burning heat upon his chest have awakened him to a sense of torture which must have been so altogether incomprehensible to him? Her strong imagination showed to her a clear picture of the scene, – clear, though it must have been done in the dark. How he must have tossed and hurled himself under the clothes; how those strong knees must have worked themselves up and down before the potent god of sleep would allow him to return to perfect consciousness; how his fingers, restrained by no reason, would have trampled over his feverish throat, scattering everywhere that unhappy poultice! Then when he should have sat up wide awake, but still in the dark – with her mind's eye she saw it all – feeling that some fire as from the infernal regions had fallen upon him but whence he would know not, how fiercely wild would be the working of his spirit! Ah, now she knew, now she felt, now she acknowledged how bound she had been to awaken him at the moment, whatever might have been the personal inconvenience to herself! In such a position what would he do – or rather what had he done? She could follow much of it in her own thoughts; – how he would scramble madly from his bed, and with one hand still on his throat, would snatch hurriedly at the matches with the other. How the light would come, and how then he would rush to the mirror. Ah, what a sight he would behold! She could see it all to the last widespread daub.

But she could not see, she could not tell herself, what in such a position a man would do; – at any rate, not what that man would do. Her husband, she thought, would tell his wife, and then the two of them, between them, would – put up with it. There are misfortunes which, if they be published, are simply aggravated by ridicule. But she remembered the features of the stranger as she had seen them at that instant in which she had dropped his beard, and she thought that there was a ferocity in them, a certain tenacity of self-importance, which would not permit their owner to endure such treatment in silence. Would he not storm and rage, and ring the bell, and call all Paris to witness his revenge?

But the storming and the raging had not reached her yet, and now it wanted but a quarter to five. In three-quarters of an hour they would be in that demi-omnibus which they had ordered for themselves, and in half-an-hour after that they would be flying towards Thompson Hall. Then she allowed herself to think of those coming comforts, – of those comforts so sweet, if only they would come! That very day now present to her was the 24th December, and on that very evening she would be sitting in Christmas joy among all her uncles and cousins, holding her new brother-in-law affectionately by the hand. Oh, what a change from Pandemonium to Paradise; – from that wretched room, from that miserable house in which there was such ample cause for fear, to all the domestic Christmas bliss of the home of the Thompsons! She resolved that she would not, at any rate, be deterred by any light opposition on the part of her husband. 'It wants just a quarter to five,' she said, putting her hand steadily upon his shoulder, 'and I'll get a cup of chocolate for you, so that you may get up comfortably.'

'I've been thinking about it,' he said, rubbing his eyes with the back of his hands. 'It will be so much better to go over by the mail train to-night. We should be in time for Christmas just the same.'

'That will not do at all,' she answered, energetically. 'Come, Charles, after all the trouble do not disappoint me.'

'It is such a horrid grind.'

'Think what I have gone through, – what I have done for you! In twelve hours we shall be there, among them all. You won't be so little like a man as not to go on now.' He threw himself back upon the bed, and tried to readjust the clothes round his neck. 'No, Charles, no,' she continued; 'not if I know it. Take your chocolate and get up. There is not a moment to be lost.' With that she laid her hand upon his shoulder, and made him clearly understand that he would not be allowed to take further rest in that bed.

Grumbling, sulky, coughing continually, and declaring that life under such circumstances was not worth having, he did at last get up and dress himself. When once she saw that he was obeying her she became again tender to him, and certainly took much more than her own share of the trouble of the proceedings. Long before the time was up she was ready, and the porter had been summoned to take the luggage down stairs. When the man came she was rejoiced to see that it was not he whom she had met among the passages during her nocturnal rambles. He shouldered the box, and told them that they would find coffee and bread and butter in the small *salle-à-manger* below.

'I told you that it would be so, when you would boil that stuff,' said the ungrateful man, who had nevertheless swallowed the hot chocolate when it was given to him.

They followed their luggage down into the hall; but as she went, at every step, the lady looked around her. She dreaded the sight of that porter of the night; she feared lest some potential authority of the hotel should come to her and ask her some horrid question; but of all her fears her greatest fear was that there should arise before her an apparition of that face which she had seen recumbent on its pillow.

As they passed the door of the great salon, Mr Brown looked in. 'Why, there it is still!' said he.

'What?' said she, trembling in every limb.

'The mustard-pot!'

'They have put it in there since,' she exclaimed energetically, in her despair. 'But never mind. The omnibus is here. Come away.' And she absolutely took him by the arm.

But at that moment a door behind them opened, and Mrs Brown heard herself called by her name. And there was the night-porter, – with a handkerchief in his hand. But the further doings of that morning must be told in a further chapter.

Mrs Brown Does Escape

It had been visible to Mrs Brown from the first moment of her arrival on the ground floor that 'something was the matter', if we may be allowed to use such a phrase; and she felt all but convinced that this something had reference to her. She fancied that the people of the hotel were looking at her as she swallowed, or tried to swallow, her coffee.

When her husband was paying the bill there was something disagreeable in the eye of the man who was taking the money. Her sufferings were very great, and no one sympathized with her. Her husband was quite at his ease, except that he was complaining of the cold. When she was anxious to get him out into the carriage, he still stood there leisurely, arranging shawl after shawl around his throat. 'You can do that quite as well in the omnibus,' she had just said to him very crossly, when there appeared upon the scene through a side door that very porter whom she dreaded, with a soiled pocket-handkerchief in his hand.

Even before the sound of her own name met her ears Mrs Brown knew it all. She understood the full horror of her position from that man's hostile face, and from the little article which he held in his hand. If during the watches of the night she had had money in her pocket, if she had made a friend of this greedy fellow by well-timed liberality, all might have been so different! But she reflected that she had allowed him to go unfee'd after all his trouble, and she knew that he was her enemy. It was the handkerchief that she feared. She thought that she might have brazened out anything but that. No one had seen her enter or leave that strange man's room. No one had seen her dip her hands in that jar. She had, no doubt, been found wandering about the house while the slumberer had been made to suffer so strangely, and there might have been suspicion, and perhaps accusation. But she would have been ready with frequent protestations to deny all charges made against her, and, though no one might have believed her, no one could have convicted her. Here, however, was evidence against which she would be unable to stand for a moment. At the first glance she acknowledged the potency of that damning morsel of linen.

During all the horrors of the night she had never given a thought to the handkerchief, and yet she ought to have known that the evidence it would bring against her was palpable and certain. Her name, 'M. Brown', was plainly written on the corner. What a fool she had been not to have thought of this! Had she but remembered the plain marking which she, as a careful, well-conducted, British matron, had put upon all her clothes, she would at any hazard have recovered the article. Oh that she had waked the man, or bribed the porter, or even told her husband! But now she was, as it were, friendless, without support, without a word that she could say in her own defence, convicted of having committed this assault upon a strange man as he slept in his own bedroom, and then of having left him! The thing must be explained by the truth; but how to explain such truth, how to tell such story in a way to satisfy injured folk, and she with barely time sufficient to catch the train! Then it occurred to her that they could have no legal right to stop her because the pocket-handkerchief had been found in a strange gentleman's bedroom. 'Yes, it is mine,' she said, turning to her husband, as the porter, with a loud voice, asked if she were not Madame Brown. 'Take it, Charles, and come on.' Mr Brown naturally stood still in astonishment. He did put out his hand, but the porter would not allow the evidence to pass so readily out of his custody.

'What does it all mean?' asked Mr Brown.

'A gentleman has been – eh – eh –. Something has been done to a gentleman in his bedroom,' said the clerk.

'Something done to a gentleman!' repeated Mr Brown.

'Something very bad indeed,' said the porter. 'Look here,' and he showed the condition of the handkerchief.

'Charles, we shall lose the train,' said the affrighted wife.

'What the mischief does it all mean?' demanded the husband.

'Did Madame go into the gentleman's room?' asked the clerk. Then there was an awful silence, and all eyes were fixed upon the lady.

'What does it all mean?' demanded the husband. 'Did you go into anybody's room?'

'I did,' said Mrs Brown with much dignity, looking round upon her enemies as a stag at bay will look upon the hounds which are attacking him. 'Give me the handkerchief.' But the night-porter quickly put it behind his back. 'Charles, we cannot allow ourselves to be delayed. You shall write a letter to the keeper of the hotel, explaining it all.' Then she essayed to swim out, through the front door, into the courtyard in which the vehicle was waiting for them. But three or four men and women interposed themselves, and even her husband did not seem quite ready to continue his journey. 'To-night is Christmas Eve,' said Mrs Brown, 'and we shall not be at Thompson Hall! Think of my sister!'

'Why did you go into the man's bedroom, my dear?' whispered Mr Brown in English.

But the porter heard the whisper, and understood the language; – the porter who had not been 'tipped'. 'Ye'es; – vy?' asked the porter.

'It was a mistake, Charles; there is not a moment to lose. I can explain it all to you in the carriage.' Then the clerk suggested that Madame had better postpone her journey a little. The gentleman upstairs had certainly been very badly treated, and had demanded to know why so great an outrage had been perpetrated. The clerk said that he did not wish to send for the police – here Mrs Brown gasped terribly and threw herself on her husband's shoulder, – but he did not think he could allow the party to go till the gentleman upstairs had received some satisfaction. It had now become clearly impossible that the journey could be made by the early train. Even Mrs Brown gave it up herself, and demanded of her husband that she should be taken back to her bedroom.

'But what is to be said to the gentleman?' asked the porter.

Of course it was impossible that Mrs Brown should be made to tell her story there in the presence of them all. The clerk, when he found he had succeeded in preventing her from leaving the house, was satisfied with a promise from Mr Brown that he would inquire from his wife what were these mysterious circumstances, and would then come down to the office and give some explanation. If it were necessary, he would see the strange gentleman, – whom he now ascertained to be a certain Mr Jones returning from the east of Europe. He learned also that this Mr Jones had been most anxious to travel by that very morning train which he and his wife had intended to use, – that Mr Jones had been most particular in giving his orders accordingly, but that at the last moment he had declared himself to be unable even to dress himself, because of the injury which had been done him during the night. When Mr Brown heard this from the clerk just before he was allowed to take his wife upstairs, while she was sitting on a sofa in a corner with her face hidden, a look of awful gloom came over his own countenance. What could it be that his wife had done to the gentleman of so terrible a nature? 'You had better come up with me,' he said to her with marital severity, and the poor cowed woman went with him tamely as might have done some patient Grizel. Not a word was spoken till they were in the room and the door was locked. 'Now,' said he, 'what does it all mean?'

It was not till nearly two hours had passed that Mr Brown came down the stairs very slowly, – turning it all over in his mind. He had now gradually heard the absolute and exact truth, and had very gradually learned to believe it. It was first necessary that he should understand that his wife had told him many fibs during the night; but, as she constantly alleged to him when he complained of her conduct in this respect, they had all been told on his behalf. Had she not struggled to get the mustard for his comfort, and when she had secured the prize had she not hurried to put it on, – as she had fondly thought, – his throat? And though she had fibbed to him afterwards, had she not done so in order that he might not be troubled? 'You are not angry with me because I was in that man's room?' she asked, looking full into his eyes, but not quite without a sob. He paused a moment, and then declared, with something of a true husband's confidence in his tone, that he was not in the least angry with her on that account. Then she kissed him, and bade him remember that after all no one could really injure them. 'What harm has been done, Charles? The gentleman won't die because he has had a mustard plaster on his throat. The worst is about Uncle John and dear Jane. They do think so much of Christmas Eve at Thompson Hall!'

Mr Brown, when he again found himself in the clerk's office, requested that his card might be taken up to Mr Jones. Mr Jones had sent down his own card, which was handed to Mr Brown: 'Mr Barnaby Jones.' 'And how was it all, sir?' asked the clerk, in a whisper – a whisper which had at the same time something of authoritative demand and something also of submissive respect. The clerk of course was anxious to know the mystery. It is hardly too much to say that every one in that vast hotel was by this time anxious to have the mystery unravelled. But Mr Brown would tell nothing to any one. 'It is merely a matter to be explained between me and Mr Jones,' he said. The card was taken upstairs, and after a while he was ushered into Mr Jones' room. It was, of course, that very 353 with which the reader is already acquainted. There was a fire burning, and the remains of Mr Jones' breakfast were on the table. He was sitting in his dressing-gown and slippers, with his shirt open in the front, and a silk handkerchief very loosely covering his throat. Mr Brown, as he entered the room, of course looked with considerable anxiety at the gentleman of whose condition he had heard so sad an account; but he could only observe some considerable stiffness of movement and demeanour as Mr Jones turned his head round to greet him.

'This has been a very disagreeable accident, Mr Jones,' said the husband of the lady.

'Accident! I don't know how it could have been an accident. It has been a most – most – most – a most monstrous, – er, – er, – I must say, interference with a gentleman's privacy, and personal comfort.'

'Quite so, Mr Jones, but, – on the part of the lady, who is my wife—'

'So I understand. I myself am about to become a married man, and I can understand what your feelings must be. I wish to say as little as possible to harrow them.' Here Mr Brown bowed. 'But, – there's the fact. She did do it.'

'She thought it was – me!'

'What!'

'I give you my word as a gentleman, Mr Jones. When she was putting that mess upon you she thought it was me! She did, indeed.'

Mr Jones looked at his new acquaintance and shook his head. He did not think it possible that any woman would make such a mistake as that.

'I had a very bad sore throat,' continued Mr Brown, 'and indeed you may perceive it still,' – in saying this, he perhaps aggravated a little sign of his distemper, 'and I asked Mrs Brown to go down and get one, – just what she put on you.'

'I wish you'd had it,' said Mr Jones, putting his hand up to his neck.

'I wish I had, – for your sake as well as mine, – and for hers, poor woman. I don't know when she will get over the shock.'

'I don't know when I shall. And it has stopped me on my journey. I was to have been to-night, this very night, this Christmas Eve, with the young lady I am engaged to marry. Of course I couldn't travel. The extent of the injury done nobody can imagine at present.'

'It has been just as bad to me, sir. We were to have been with our family this Christmas Eve. There were particular reasons, – most particular. We were only hindered from going by hearing of your condition.'

'Why did she come into my room at all? I can't under-stand that. A lady always knows her own room at an hotel.'

'353 – that's yours; 333 – that's ours. Don't you see how easy it was? She had lost her way, and she was a little afraid lest the thing should fall down.'

'I wish it had, with all my heart.'

'That's how it was. Now I'm sure, Mr Jones, you'll take a lady's apology. It was a most unfortunate mistake, – most unfortunate; but what more can be said?'

Mr Jones gave himself up to reflection for a few moments before he replied to this. He supposed that he was bound to believe the story as far as it went. At any rate, he did not know how he could say that he did not believe it. It seemed to him to be almost incredible, – especially incredible in regard to that personal mistake, for, except that they both had long beards and brown beards, Mr Jones thought that there was no point of resemblance between himself and Mr

Brown. But still, even that, he felt, must be accepted. But then why had he been left, deserted, to undergo all those torments? 'She found out her mistake at last, I suppose?' he said.

'Oh, yes.'

'Why didn't she wake a fellow and take it off again?'

'Ah!'

'She can't have cared very much for a man's comfort when she went away and left him like that.'

'Ah! there was the difficulty, Mr Jones.'

'Difficulty! Who was it that had done it? To come to me, in my bedroom, in the middle of the night and put that thing on me, and then leave it there and say nothing about it! It seems to me deuced like a practical joke.'

'No, Mr Jones!'

'That's the way I look at it,' said Mr Jones, plucking up his courage.

'There isn't a woman in all England, or in all France, less likely to do such a thing than my wife. She's as steady as a rock, Mr Jones, and would no more go into another gentle-man's bedroom in joke than — Oh dear no! You're going to be a married man yourself.'

'Unless all this makes a difference,' said Mr Jones, almost in tears. 'I had sworn that I would be with her this Christmas Eve.'

'Oh, Mr Jones, I cannot believe that will interfere with your happiness. How could you think that your wife, as is to be, would do such a thing as that in joke?'

'She wouldn't do it at all; – joke or anyway.'

'How can you tell what accident might happen to any one?'

'She'd have wakened the man then afterwards. I'm sure she would. She would never have left him to suffer in that way. Her heart is too soft. Why didn't she send you to wake me, and explain it all. That's what my Jane would have done; and I should have gone and wakened him. But the whole thing is impossible,' he said, shaking his head as he remembered that he and his Jane were not in a condition as yet to undergo any such mutual trouble. At last Mr Jones was brought to acknowledge that nothing more could be done. The lady sent her apology, and told her story, and he must bear the trouble and inconvenience to which she had subjected him. He still, however, had his own opinion about her conduct generally, and could not be brought to give any sign of amity. He simply bowed when Mr Brown was hoping to induce him to shake hands, and sent no word of pardon to the great offender.

The matter, however, was so far concluded that there was no further question of police interference, nor any doubt but that the lady with her husband was to be allowed to leave Paris by the night train. The nature of the accident probably became known to all. Mr Brown was interrogated by many, and though he professed to declare that he would answer no question, nevertheless he found it better to tell the clerk something of the truth than to allow the matter to be shrouded in mystery. It is to be feared that Mr Jones, who did not once show himself through the day, but who employed the hours in endeavouring to assuage the injury done him, still lived in the conviction that the lady had played a practical joke on him. But the subject of such a joke never talks about it, and Mr Jones could not be induced to speak even by friendly adherence of the night-porter.

Mrs Brown also clung to the seclusion of her own bed-room, never once stirring from it till the time came in which she was to be taken down to the omnibus. Upstairs she ate her meals, and upstairs she passed her time in packing and unpacking, and in requesting that telegrams might be sent repeatedly to Thompson Hall. In the course of the day two such telegrams were sent, in the latter of which the Thompson family were assured that the Browns would arrive, probably in time for breakfast on Christmas Day, certainly in time for church. She asked more than once tenderly after Mr Jones' welfare, but could obtain no information. 'He was very cross, and that's all I know about it,' said Mr Brown. Then she made a remark as to the gentleman's Christian name, which appeared on the card as 'Barnaby'. 'My sister's husband's name will be Burnaby,' she said. 'And this man's Christian name is Barnaby; that's all the difference,' said her husband, with ill-timed jocularity.

We all know how people under a cloud are apt to fail in asserting their personal dignity. On the former day a separate vehicle had been ordered by Mr Brown to take himself and his wife to the station, but now, after his misfortunes, he contented himself with such provision as the people at the hotel might make for him. At the appointed hour he brought his wife down, thickly veiled. There were many strangers as she passed through the hall, ready to look at the lady who had done that wonderful thing in the dead of night, but none could see a feature of her face as she stepped across the hall, and was hurried into the omnibus. And there were many eyes also on Mr Jones, who followed her very quickly, for he also, in spite of his sufferings, was leaving Paris on the evening in order that he might be with his English friends on Christmas Day. He, as he went through the crowd, assumed an air of great dignity, to which, perhaps, something was added by his endeavours, as he walked, to save his poor throat from irritation. He, too, got into the same omnibus, stumbling over the feet of his enemy in the dark. At the station they got their tickets, one close after the other, and then were brought into each other's presence in the waiting-room. I think it must be acknowledged that here Mr Jones was conscious not only of her presence, but of her consciousness of his presence, and that he assumed an attitude, as though he should have said, 'Now do you think it possible for me to believe that you mistook me for your husband?' She was perfectly quiet, but sat through that quarter of an hour with her face continually veiled. Mr Brown made some little overture of conversation to Mr Jones, but Mr Jones, though he did mutter some reply, showed plainly enough that he had no desire for further intercourse. Then came the accustomed stampede, the awful rush, the internecine struggle in which seats had to be found. Seats, I fancy, are regularly found, even by the most tardy, but it always appears that every British father and every British husband is actuated at these stormy moments by a conviction that unless he prove himself a very Hercules he and his daughters and his wife will be left desolate in Paris. Mr Brown was quite Herculean, carrying two bags and a hat-box in his own hands, besides the cloaks, the coats, the rugs, the sticks, and the umbrellas. But when he had got himself and his wife well seated, with their faces to the engine, with a corner seat for her, – there was Mr Jones immediately opposite to her. Mr Jones, as soon as he perceived the inconvenience of his position, made a scramble for another place, but he was too late. In that contiguity the journey as far as Dover had to be made. She, poor woman, never once took up her veil. There he sat, without closing an eye, stiff as a ramrod, sometimes showing by little uneasy gestures that the trouble at his neck was still there, but never speaking a word, and hardly moving a limb.

Crossing from Calais to Dover the lady was, of course, separated from her victim. The passage was very bad, and she more than once reminded her husband how well it would have been with them now had they pursued their journey as she had intended, – as though they had been detained in Paris by his fault! Mr Jones, as he laid himself down on his back, gave himself up to wondering whether any man before him had ever been made subject to such absolute injustice. Now and again he put his hand up to his own beard, and began to doubt whether it could have been moved, as it must have been moved, without waking him. What if chloroform had been used? Many such suspicions crossed his mind during the misery of that passage.

They were again together in the same railway carriage from Dover to London. They had now got used to the close neighbourhood, and knew how to endure each the presence of the other. But as yet Mr Jones had never seen the lady's face. He longed to know what were the features of the woman who had been so blind – if indeed that story were true. Or if it were not true, of what like was the woman who would dare in the middle of the night to play such a trick as that. But still she kept her veil close over her face.

From Cannon Street the Browns took their departure in a cab for the Liverpool Street Station, whence they would be conveyed by the Eastern Counties Railway to Stratford. Now at any rate their troubles were over. They would be in ample time, not only for Christmas Day church, but for Christmas Day breakfast. 'It will be just the same as getting in there last night,' said Mr Brown, as he walked across the platform to place his wife in the carriage for Stratford. She entered it first, and as she did so there she saw Mr Jones seated in the corner! Hitherto she had borne his presence well, but now she could not restrain herself from a little start and a little scream. He bowed his head very slightly, as though acknowledging the compliment, and then down she dropped her veil. When they arrived at Stratford, the journey being over in a quarter of an hour, Jones was out of the carriage even before the Browns.

'There is Uncle John's carriage,' said Mrs Brown, thinking that now, at any rate, she would be able to free herself from the presence of this terrible stranger. No doubt he was a handsome man to look at, but on no face so sternly hostile had she ever before fixed her eyes. She did not, perhaps, reflect that the owner of no other face had ever been so deeply injured by herself.

Mrs Brown at Thompson Hall

'Please, sir, we were to ask for Mr Jones,' said the servant, putting his head into the carriage after both Mr and Mrs Brown had seated themselves.

'Mr Jones!' exclaimed the husband.

'Why ask for Mr Jones?' demanded the wife. The servant was about to tender some explanation when Mr Jones stepped up and said that he was Mr Jones. 'We are going to Thompson Hall,' said the lady with great vigour.

'So am I,' said Mr Jones, with much dignity. It was, however, arranged that he should sit with the coachman, as there was a rumble behind for the other servant. The luggage was put into a cart, and away all went for Thompson Hall.

'What do you think about it, Mary,' whispered Mr Brown, after a pause. He was evidently awe-struck by the horror of the occasion.

'I cannot make it out at all. What do you think?'

'I don't know what to think. Jones going to Thompson Hall!'

'He's a very good-looking young man,' said Mrs Brown.

'Well; – that's as people think. A stiff, stuck-up fellow,

I should say. Up to this moment he has never forgiven you for what you did to him.'

'Would you have forgiven his wife, Charles, if she'd done it to you?'

'He hasn't got a wife, – yet.'

'How do you know?'

'He is coming home now to be married,' said Mr Brown. 'He expects to meet the young lady this very Christmas Day. He told me so. That was one of the reasons why he was so angry at being stopped by what you did last night.'

'I suppose he knows Uncle John, or he wouldn't be going to the Hall,' said Mrs Brown.

'I can't make it out,' said Mr Brown, shaking his head.

'He looks quite like a gentleman,' said Mrs Brown, 'though he has been so stiff. Jones! Barnaby Jones! You're sure it was Barnaby?'

'That was the name on the card.'

'Not Burnaby?' asked Mrs Brown.

'It was Barnaby Jones on the card, – just the same as "Barnaby Rudge", and as for looking like a gentleman, I'm by no means quite so sure. A gentleman takes an apology when it's offered.'

'Perhaps, my dear, that depends on the condition of his throat. If you had had a mustard plaster on all night, you might not have liked it. But here we are at Thompson Hall at last.'

Thompson Hall was an old brick mansion, standing within a huge iron gate, with a gravel sweep before it. It had stood there before Stratford was a town, or even a suburb, and had then been known by the name Bow Place. But it had been in the hands of the present family for the last thirty years, and was now known far and wide as Thompson Hall, – a comfortable, roomy, old-fashioned place, perhaps a little dark and dull to look at, but much more substantially built than most of our modern villas. Mrs Brown jumped with alacrity from the carriage, and with a quick step entered the home of her forefathers. Her husband followed her more leisurely, but he, too, felt that he was at home at Thompson Hall. Then Mr Jones walked in also; – but he looked as though he were not at all at home. It was still very early, and no one of the family was as yet down. In these circumstances it was almost necessary that something should be said to Mr Jones.

'Do you know Mr Thompson?' asked Mr Brown.

'I never had the pleasure of seeing him, – as yet,' answered Mr Jones, very stiffly.

'Oh, – I didn't know; – because you said you were coming here.'

'And I have come here. Are you friends of Mr. Thompson?'

'Oh, dear, yes,' said Mrs Brown. 'I was a Thompson myself before I married.'

'Oh, – indeed!' said Mr Jones. 'How very odd; – very odd indeed.'

During this time the luggage was being brought into the house, and two old family servants were offering them assistance. Would the new comers like to go up to their bedrooms? Then the housekeeper, Mrs Green, intimated with a wink that Miss Jane would, she was sure, be down quite immediately. The present moment, however, was still very unpleasant. The lady probably had made her guess as to the mystery; but the two gentlemen were still altogether in the dark. Mrs Brown had no doubt declared her parentage, but Mr Jones, with such a multitude of strange facts crowding on his mind, had been slow to understand her. Being somewhat suspicious by nature he was beginning to

152

think whether possibly the mustard had been put by this lady on his throat with some reference to his connection with Thompson Hall. Could it be that she, for some reason of her own, had wished to prevent his coming, and had contrived this untoward stratagem out of her brain? or had she wished to make him ridiculous to the Thompson family, – to whom, as a family, he was at present unknown? It was becoming more and more improbable to him that the whole thing should have been an accident. When, after the first horrid torments of that morning in which he had in his agony invoked the assistance of the night-porter, he had begun to reflect on his situation, he had determined that it would be better that nothing further should be said about it. What would life be worth to him if he were to be known wherever he went as the man who had been mustard-plastered in the middle of the night by a strange lady? The worst of a practical joke is that the remembrance of the absurd condition sticks so long to the sufferer! At the hotel that night-porter, who had possessed himself of the handkerchief and had read the name and had connected that name with the occupant of 333 whom he had found wandering about the house with some strange purpose, had not permitted the thing to sleep. The porter had pressed the matter home against the Browns, and had produced the interview which has been recorded. But during the whole of that day Mr Jones had been resolving that he would never again either think of the Browns or speak of them. A great injury had been done to him, – a most outrageous injustice; – but it was a thing which had to be endured. A horrid woman had come across him like a nightmare. All he could do was to endeavour to forget the terrible visitation. Such had been his resolve, – in making which he had passed that long day in Paris. And now the Browns had stuck to him from the moment of his leaving his room! He had been forced to travel with them, but had travelled with them as a stranger. He had tried to comfort himself with the reflection that at every fresh stage he would shake them off. In one railway after another the vicinity had been bad, – but still they were strangers. Now he found himself in the same house with them, – where of course the story would be told. Had not the thing been done on purpose that the story might be told there at Thompson Hall?

Mrs Brown had acceded to the proposition of the house-keeper, and was about to be taken to her room when there was heard a sound of footsteps along the passage above and on the stairs, and a young lady came bounding on to the scene. 'You have all of you come a quarter of an hour earlier than we thought possible,' said the young lady. 'I did so mean to be up to receive you!' With that she passed her sister on the stairs, – for the young lady was Miss Jane Thompson, sister to our Mrs Brown, – and hurried down into the hall. Here Mr Brown, who had ever been on affec-tionate terms with his sister-in-law, put himself forward to receive her embraces; but she, apparently not noticing him in her ardour, rushed on and threw herself on to the breast of the other gentleman. 'This is my Charles,' she said. 'Oh, Charles, I thought you never would be here.'

Mr Charles Burnaby Jones, for such was his name since he had inherited the Jones property in Pembrokeshire, received into his arms the ardent girl of his heart with all that love, and devotion to which she was entitled, but could not do so without some external shrinking from her embrace. 'Oh, Charles, what is it?' she said.

'Nothing, dearest – only – only –.' Then he looked piteously up into Mrs Brown's face, as though imploring her not to tell the story.

'Perhaps, Jane, you had better introduce us,' said Mrs Brown.

'Introduce you! I thought you had been travelling together, and staying at the same hotel – and all that.'

'So we have; but people may be in the same hotel without knowing each other. And we have travelled all the way home with Mr Jones without in the least knowing who he was.'

'How very odd! Do you mean you have never spoken?'

'Not a word,' said Mrs Brown.

'I do so hope you'll love each other,' said Jane.

'It shan't be my fault if we don't,' said Mrs Brown.

'I'm sure it shan't be mine,' said Mr Brown, tendering his hand to the other gentleman. The various feelings of the moment were too much for Mr Jones, and he could not respond quite as he should have done. But as he was taken upstairs to his room he determined that he would make the best of it.

The owner of the house was old Uncle John. He was a bachelor, and with him lived various members of the family. There was the great Thompson of them all, Cousin Robert, who was now member of Parliament for the Essex Flats, and young John, as a certain enterprising Thompson of the age of forty was usually called, and then there was old Aunt Bess, and among other young branches there was Miss Jane Thompson who was now engaged to marry Mr Charles Burnaby Jones. As it happened, no other member of the family had as yet seen Mr Burnaby Jones, and he, being by nature of a retiring disposition, felt himself to be ill at ease when he came into the breakfast parlour among all the Thompsons. He was known to be a gentleman of good family and ample means, and all the Thompsons had approved of the match, but during that first Christmas breakfast he did not seem to accept his condition jovially. His own Jane sat beside him, but then on the other side sat Mrs Brown. She assumed an immediate intimacy, – as women know how to do on such occasions, – being determined from the very first to regard her sister's husband as a brother; but he still feared her. She was still to him the woman who had come to him in the dead of night with that horrid mixture, – and had then left him.

'It was so odd that both of you should have been detained on the very same day,' said Jane.

'Yes, it was odd,' said Mrs Brown, with a smile, looking round upon her neighbour.

'It was abominably bad weather, you know,' said Brown.

'But you were both so determined to come,' said the old gentleman. 'When we got the two telegrams at the same moment, we were sure that there had been some agreement between you.'

'Not exactly an agreement,' said Mrs Brown; whereupon Mr Jones looked as grim as death.

'I'm sure there is something more than we understand yet,' said the member of Parliament.

Then they all went to church, as a united family ought to do on Christmas Day, and came home to a fine old English early dinner at three o'clock, – a sirloin of beef a foot-and-a-half broad, a turkey as big as an ostrich, a plum pudding bigger than the turkey, and two or three dozen mince-pies. 'That's a very large bit of beef,' said Mr Jones, who had not lived much in England latterly. 'It won't look so large,' said the old gentleman, 'when all our friends downstairs have had their say to it.' 'A plum-pudding on Christmas Day can't be too big,' he said again, 'if the cook will but take time enough over it. I never knew a bit go to waste yet.'

By this time there had been some explanation as to past events between the two sisters. Mrs Brown had indeed told Jane all about it, how ill her husband had been, how she had been forced to go down and look for the mustard, and then what she had done with the mustard. 'I don't think they are a bit alike you know, Mary, if you mean that,' said Jane.

'Well, no; perhaps not quite alike. I only saw his beard, you know. No doubt it was stupid, but I did it.'

'Why didn't you take it off again?' asked the sister.

'Oh, Jane, if you'd only think of it? Could you!' Then of course all that occurred was explained, how they had been stopped on their journey, how Brown had made the best apology in his power, and how Jones had travelled with them and had never spoken a word. The gentleman had only taken his new name a week since but of course had had his new card printed immediately. 'I'm sure I should have thought of it if they hadn't made a mistake with the first name. Charles said it was like Barnaby Rudge.'

'Not at all like Barnaby Rudge,' said Jane; 'Charles Burnaby Jones is a very good name.'

'Very good indeed, – and I'm sure that after a little bit he won't be at all the worse for the accident.'

Before dinner the secret had been told no further, but still there had crept about among the Thompsons, and, indeed, downstairs also, among the retainers, a feeling that there was a secret. The old housekeeper was sure that Miss Mary, as she still called Mrs Brown, had something to tell if she could only be induced to tell it, and that this something had reference to Mr Jones' personal comfort. The head of the family, who was a sharp old gentleman, felt this also, and the member of Parliament, who had an idea that he specially should never be kept in the dark, was almost angry. Mr Jones, suffering from some kindred feeling throughout the dinner, remained silent and unhappy. When two or three toasts had been drunk, – the Queen's health, the old gentleman's health, the young couple's health, Brown's health, and the general health of all the Thompsons, then tongues were loosened and a question was asked, 'I know that there has been something doing in Paris between these young people that we haven't heard as yet,' said the uncle. Then Mrs Brown laughed, and Jane, laughing too, gave Mr Jones to understand that she at any rate knew all about it.

'If there is a mystery I hope it will be told at once,' said the member of Parliament, angrily.

'Come, Brown, what is it?' asked another male cousin.

'Well, there was an accident. I'd rather Jones should tell,' said he.

Jones' brow became blacker than thunder, but he did not say a word. 'You mustn't be angry with Mary,' Jane whispered into her lover's ear.

'Come, Mary, you never were slow at talking,' said the uncle.

'I do hate this kind of thing,' said the member of Parliament.

'I will tell it all,' said Mrs Brown, very nearly in tears, or else pretending to be very nearly in tears. 'I know I was very wrong, and I do beg his pardon, and if he won't say that he forgives me I never shall be happy again.' Then she clasped her hands, and, turning round, looked him piteously in the face.

'Oh yes; I do forgive you,' said Mr Jones.

'My brother,' said she, throwing her arms round him and kissing him. He recoiled from the embrace, but I think that he attempted to return the kiss. 'And now I will tell the

158

whole story,' said Mrs Brown. And she told it, acknowledging her fault with true contrition, and swearing that she would atone for it by life-long sisterly devotion.

'And you mustard-plastered the wrong man!' said the old gentleman, almost rolling off his chair with delight.

'I did,' said Mrs Brown, sobbing, 'and I think that no woman ever suffered as I suffered.'

'And Jones wouldn't let you leave the hotel?'

'It was the handkerchief stopped us,' said Brown.

'If it had turned out to be anybody else,' said the member of Parliament, 'the results might have been most serious, – not to say discreditable.'

'That's nonsense, Robert,' said Mrs Brown, who was disposed to resent the use of so severe a word, even from the legislator cousin.

'In a strange gentleman's bedroom!' he continued. 'It only shows that what I have always said is quite true. You should never go to bed in a strange house without locking your door.'

Nevertheless it was a very jovial meeting, and before the evening was over Mr Jones was happy, and had been brought to acknowledge that the mustard plaster would probably not do him any permanent injury.

LEO TOLSTOY

WHERE LOVE IS, GOD IS

Translated by Louise and Aylmer Maude

IN A CERTAIN TOWN there lived a cobbler, Martin Avdéitch by name. He had a tiny room in a basement, the one window of which looked out on to the street. Through it one could only see the feet of those who passed by, but Martin recognized the people by their boots. He had lived long in the place and had many acquaintances. There was hardly a pair of boots in the neighbourhood that had not been once or twice through his hands, so he often saw his own handiwork through the window. Some he had re-soled, some patched, some stitched up, and to some he had even put fresh uppers. He had plenty to do, for he worked well, used good material, did not charge too much, and could be relied on. If he could do a job by the day required, he undertook it; if not, he told the truth and gave no false promises; so he was well known and never short of work.

Martin had always been a good man; but in his old age he began to think more about his soul and to draw nearer to God. While he still worked for a master, before he set up on his own account, his wife had died, leaving him with a three-year-old son. None of his elder children had lived, they had all died in infancy. At first Martin thought of sending his little son to his sister's in the country, but then he felt sorry to part with the boy, thinking: 'It would be hard for my little Kapitón to have to grow up in a strange family; I will keep him with me.'

Martin left his master and went into lodgings with his

163

little son. But he had no luck with his children. No sooner had the boy reached an age when he could help his father and be a support as well as a joy to him, than he fell ill and, after being laid up for a week with a burning fever, died. Martin buried his son, and gave way to despair so great and overwhelming that he murmured against God. In his sorrow he prayed again and again that he too might die, reproaching God for having taken the son he loved, his only son, while he, old as he was, remained alive. After that Martin left off going to church.

One day an old man from Martin's native village, who had been a pilgrim for the last eight years, called in on his way from Tróitsa Monastery. Martin opened his heart to him, and told him of his sorrow.

'I no longer even wish to live, holy man,' he said. 'All I ask of God is that I soon may die. I am now quite without hope in the world.'

The old man replied: 'You have no right to say such things, Martin. We cannot judge God's ways. Not our reasoning, but God's will, decides. If God willed that your son should die and you should live, it must be best so. As to your despair – that comes because you wish to live for your own happiness.'

'What else should one live for?' asked Martin.

'For God, Martin,' said the old man. 'He gives you life, and you must live for Him. When you have learnt to live for Him, you will grieve no more, and all will seem easy to you.'

Martin was silent awhile, and then asked: 'But how is one to live for God?'

The old man answered: 'How one may live for God has been shown us by Christ. Can you read? Then buy the Gospels, and read them: there you will see how God would have you live. You have it all there.'

These words sank deep into Martin's heart, and that same day he went and bought himself a Testament in large print, and began to read.

At first he meant only to read on holidays, but having once begun he found it made his heart so light that he read every day. Sometimes he was so absorbed in his reading that the oil in his lamp burnt out before he could tear himself away from the book. He continued to read every night, and the more he read the more clearly he understood what God required of him, and how he might live for God. And his heart grew lighter and lighter. Before, when he went to bed he used to lie with a heavy heart, moaning as he thought of his little Kapitón; but now he only repeated again and again: 'Glory to Thee, glory to Thee, O Lord! Thy will be done!'

From that time Martin's whole life changed. Formerly, on holidays he used to go and have tea at the public-house, and did not even refuse a glass or two of vodka. Sometimes, after having had a drop with a friend, he left the public-house not drunk, but rather merry, and would say foolish things: shout at a man, or abuse him. Now, all that sort of thing passed away from him. His life became peaceful and joyful. He sat down to his work in the morning, and when he had finished his day's work he took the lamp down from the wall, stood it on the table, fetched his book from the shelf, opened it, and sat down to read. The more he read the better he understood, and the clearer and happier he felt in his mind.

It happened once that Martin sat up late, absorbed in his book. He was reading Luke's Gospel; and in the sixth chapter he came upon the verses:

'To him that smiteth thee on the one cheek offer also the other; and from him that taketh away thy cloak withhold not thy coat also. Give to every man that asketh thee; and of him that taketh away thy goods ask them not again. And as ye would that men should do to you, do ye also to them likewise.'

He also read the verses where our Lord says:

'And why call ye me, Lord, Lord, and do not the things which I say? Whosoever cometh to me, and heareth my sayings, and doeth them, I will shew you to whom he is like: He is like a man which built an house, and digged deep, and laid the foundation on a rock: and when the flood arose, the stream beat vehemently upon that house, and could not shake it: for it was founded upon a rock. But he that heareth, and doeth not, is like a man that without a foundation built an house upon the earth, against which the stream did beat vehemently, and immediately it fell; and the ruin of that house was great.'

When Martin read these words his soul was glad within him. He took off his spectacles and laid them on the book, and leaning his elbows on the table pondered over what he had read. He tried his own life by the standard of those words, asking himself:

'Is my house built on the rock, or on sand? If it stands on the rock, it is well. It seems easy enough while one sits here alone, and one thinks one has done all that God commands; but as soon as I cease to be on my guard, I sin again. Still I will persevere. It brings such joy. Help me, O Lord!'

He thought all this, and was about to go to bed, but was loth to leave his book. So he went on reading the seventh chapter – about the centurion, the widow's son, and the answer to John's disciples – and he came to the part where a rich Pharisee invited the Lord to his house; and he read how the woman who was a sinner, anointed his feet and washed them with her tears, and how he justified her. Coming to the forty-fourth verse, he read:

'And turning to the woman, he said unto Simon, Seest thou this woman? I entered into thine house, thou gavest me no water for my feet: but she hath wetted my feet with her tears, and wiped them with her hair. Thou gavest me no kiss; but she, since the time I came in, hath not ceased to kiss my feet. My head with oil thou didst not anoint: but she hath anointed my feet with ointment.'

He read these verses and thought: 'He gave no water for his feet, gave no kiss, his head with oil he did not anoint. . . .' And Martin took off his spectacles once more, laid them on his book, and pondered.

'He must have been like me, that Pharisee. He too thought only of himself – how to get a cup of tea, how to keep warm and comfortable; never a thought of his guest. He took care of himself, but for his guest he cared nothing at all. Yet who was the guest? The Lord himself! If he came to me, should I behave like that?'

Then Martin laid his head upon both his arms and, before he was aware of it, he fell asleep.

'Martin!' he suddenly heard a voice, as if someone had breathed the word above his ear.

He started from his sleep. 'Who's there?' he asked.

He turned round and looked at the door; no one was there. He called again. Then he heard quite distinctly: 'Martin, Martin! Look out into the street to-morrow, for I shall come.'

Martin roused himself, rose from his chair and rubbed his eyes, but did not know whether he had heard these words in a dream or awake. He put out the lamp and lay down to sleep.

Next morning he rose before daylight, and after saying his prayers he lit the fire and prepared his cabbage soup and buckwheat porridge. Then he lit the samovar, put on his apron, and sat down by the window to his work. As he sat working Martin thought over what had happened the night before. At times it seemed to him like a dream, and at times he thought that he had really heard the voice. 'Such things have happened before now,' thought he.

So he sat by the window, looking out into the street more than he worked, and whenever anyone passed in unfamiliar boots he would stoop and look up, so as to see not the feet only but the face of the passer-by as well. A house-porter passed in new felt boots; then a water-carrier. Presently an old soldier of Nicholas's reign came near the window spade in hand. Martin knew him by his boots, which were shabby old felt ones, goloshed with leather. The old man was called Stepánitch: a neighbouring tradesman kept him in his house for charity, and his duty was to help the house-porter. He began to clear away the snow before Martin's window. Martin glanced at him and then went on with his work.

'I must be growing crazy with age,' said Martin, laughing at his fancy. 'Stepánitch comes to clear away the snow, and I must needs imagine it's Christ coming to visit me. Old dotard that I am!'

Yet after he had made a dozen stitches he felt drawn to look out of the window again. He saw that Stepánitch had leaned his spade against the wall, and was either resting himself or trying to get warm. The man was old and broken down, and had evidently not enough strength even to clear away the snow.

'What if I called him in and gave him some tea?' thought Martin. 'The samovar is just on the boil.'

He stuck his awl in its place, and rose; and putting the samovar on the table, made tea. Then he tapped the window with his fingers. Stepánitch turned and came to the window. Martin beckoned to him to come in, and went himself to open the door.

'Come in,' he said, 'and warm yourself a bit. I'm sure you must be cold.'

'May God bless you!' Stepánitch answered. 'My bones do ache to be sure.' He came in, first shaking off the snow, and lest he should leave marks on the floor he began wiping his feet; but as he did so he tottered and nearly fell.

'Don't trouble to wipe your feet,' said Martin; 'I'll wipe up the floor – it's all in the day's work. Come, friend, sit down and have some tea.'

Filling two tumblers, he passed one to his visitor, and pouring his own out into the saucer, began to blow on it.

Stepánitch emptied his glass, and, turning it upside down, put the remains of his piece of sugar on the top. He began to express his thanks, but it was plain that he would be glad of some more.

'Have another glass,' said Martin, refilling the visitor's tumbler and his own. But while he drank his tea Martin kept looking out into the street.

'Are you expecting anyone?' asked the visitor.

'Am I expecting anyone? Well, now, I'm ashamed to tell you. It isn't that I really expect anyone; but I heard something last night which I can't get out of my mind. Whether it was a vision, or only a fancy, I can't tell. You see, friend, last night I was reading the Gospel, about Christ the Lord, how he suffered, and how he walked on earth. You have heard tell of it, I dare say.'

'I have heard tell of it,' answered Stepánitch; 'but I'm an ignorant man and not able to read.'

'Well, you see, I was reading of how he walked on earth. I came to that part, you know, where he went to a Pharisee who did not receive him well. Well, friend, as I read about it, I thought how that man did not receive Christ the Lord with proper honour. Suppose such a thing could happen to such a man as myself, I thought, what would I not do to receive him! But that man gave him no reception at all. Well, friend, as I was thinking of this, I began to doze, and as I dozed I heard someone call me by name. I got up, and thought I heard someone whispering, "Expect me; I will come to-morrow." This happened twice over. And to tell you the truth, it sank so into my mind that, though I am ashamed of it myself, I keep on expecting him, the dear Lord!'

Stepánitch shook his head in silence, finished his tumbler and laid it on its side; but Martin stood it up again and refilled it for him.

'Here, drink another glass, bless you! And I was thinking, too, how he walked on earth and despised no one, but went mostly among common folk. He went with plain people, and chose his disciples from among the likes of us, from workmen like us, sinners that we are. "He who raises himself," he said, "shall be humbled; and he who humbles himself shall be raised." "You call me Lord," he said, "and I will wash your feet." "He who would be first," he said, "let him be the servant of all; because," he said, "blessed are the poor, the humble, the meek, and the merciful." '

Stepánitch forgot his tea. He was an old man, easily moved to tears, and as he sat and listened the tears ran down his cheeks.

'Come, drink some more,' said Martin. But Stepánitch crossed himself, thanked him, moved away his tumbler, and rose.

'Thank you, Martin Avdéitch,' he said, 'you have given me food and comfort both for soul and body.'

'You're very welcome. Come again another time. I am glad to have a guest,' said Martin.

Stepánitch went away; and Martin poured out the last of the tea and drank it up. Then he put away the tea things and sat down to his work, stitching the back seam of a boot. And as he stitched he kept looking out of the window, waiting for Christ, and thinking about him and his doings. And his head was full of Christ's sayings.

Two soldiers went by: one in Government boots, the other in boots of his own; then the master of a neighbouring house, in shining goloshes; then a baker carrying a basket. All these passed on. Then a woman came up in worsted stockings and peasant-made shoes. She passed the window, but stopped by the wall. Martin glanced up at her through the window, and saw that she was a stranger, poorly dressed, and with a baby in her arms. She stopped by the wall with her back to the wind, trying to wrap the baby up though she had hardly anything to wrap it in. The woman had only summer clothes on, and even they were shabby and worn. Through the window Martin heard the baby crying, and the woman trying to soothe it, but unable to do so. Martin rose, and going out of the door and up the steps he called to her.

'My dear, I say, my dear!'

The woman heard, and turned round.

'Why do you stand out there with the baby in the cold? Come inside. You can wrap him up better in a warm place. Come this way!'

The woman was surprised to see an old man in an apron, with spectacles on his nose, calling to her, but she followed him in.

They went down the steps, entered the little room, and the old man led her to the bed.

'There, sit down, my dear, near the stove. Warm yourself, and feed the baby.'

'Haven't any milk. I have eaten nothing myself since early morning,' said the woman, but still she took the baby to her breast.

Martin shook his head. He brought out a basin and some bread. Then he opened the oven door and poured some cabbage soup into the basin. He took out the porridge pot also, but the porridge was not yet ready, so he spread a cloth on the table and served only the soup and bread.

'Sit down and eat, my dear, and I'll mind the baby. Why, bless me, I've had children of my own; I know how to manage them.'

The woman crossed herself, and sitting down at the table began to eat, while Martin put the baby on the bed and sat down by it. He chucked and chucked, but having no teeth he could not do it well and the baby continued to cry. Then Martin tried poking at him with his finger; he drove his finger straight at the baby's mouth and then quickly drew it back, and did this again and again. He did not let the baby take his finger in its mouth, because it was all black with cobbler's wax. But the baby first grew quiet watching the finger, and then began to laugh. And Martin felt quite pleased.

The woman sat eating and talking, and told him who she was, and where she had been.

'I'm a soldier's wife,' said she. 'They sent my husband somewhere, far away, eight months ago, and I have heard nothing of him since. I had a place as cook till my baby was born, but then they would not keep me with a child. For three months now I have been struggling, unable to find a place, and I've had to sell all I had for food. I tried to go as a wet-nurse, but no one would have me; they said I was too starved-looking and thin. Now I have just been to see a tradesman's wife (a woman from our village is in service with her) and she has promised to take me. I thought it was all settled at last, but she tells me not to come till next week. It is far to her place, and I am fagged out, and baby is quite starved, poor mite. Fortunately our landlady has pity on us, and lets us lodge free, else I don't know what we should do.'

Martin sighed. 'Haven't you any warmer clothing?' he asked.

'How could I get warm clothing?' said she. 'Why, I pawned my last shawl for sixpence yesterday.'

Then the woman came and took the child, and Martin got up. He went and looked among some things that were hanging on the wall, and brought back an old cloak.

'Here,' he said, 'though it's a worn-out old thing, it will do to wrap him up in.'

The woman looked at the cloak, then at the old man, and taking it, burst into tears. Martin turned away, and groping under the bed brought out a small trunk. He fumbled about in it, and again sat down opposite the woman. And the woman said:

'The Lord bless you, friend. Surely Christ must have sent me to your window, else the child would have frozen. It was mild when I started, but now see how cold it has turned. Surely it must have been Christ who made you look out of your window and take pity on me, poor wretch!'

Martin smiled and said, 'It is quite true; it was he made me do it. It was no mere chance made me look out.'

And he told the woman his dream, and how he had heard the Lord's voice promising to visit him that day.

'Who knows? All things are possible,' said the woman. And she got up and threw the cloak over her shoulders, wrapping it round herself and round the baby. Then she bowed, and thanked Martin once more.

'Take this for Christ's sake,' said Martin, and gave her

173

sixpence to get her shawl out of pawn. The woman crossed herself, and Martin did the same, and then he saw her out.

After the woman had gone, Martin ate some cabbage soup, cleared the things away, and sat down to work again. He sat and worked, but did not forget the window, and every time a shadow fell on it he looked up at once to see who was passing. People he knew and strangers passed by, but no one remarkable.

After a while Martin saw an apple-woman stop just in front of his window. She had a large basket, but there did not seem to be many apples left in it; she had evidently sold most of her stock. On her back she had a sack full of chips, which she was taking home. No doubt she had gathered them at some place where building was going on. The sack evidently hurt her, and she wanted to shift it from one shoulder to the other, so she put it down on the footpath and, placing her basket on a post, began to shake down the chips in the sack. While she was doing this a boy in a tattered cap ran up, snatched an apple out of the basket, and tried to slip away; but the old woman noticed it, and turning, caught the boy by his sleeve. He began to struggle, trying to free himself, but the old woman held on with both hands, knocked his cap off his head, and seized hold of his hair. The boy screamed and the old woman scolded. Martin dropped his awl, not waiting to stick it in its place, and rushed out of the door. Stumbling up the steps, and dropping his spectacles in his hurry, he ran out into the street. The old woman was pulling the boy's hair and scolding him, and threatening to take him to the police. The lad was struggling and protesting, saying, 'I did not take it. What are you beating me for? Let me go!'

Martin separated them. He took the boy by the hand and said, 'Let him go, Granny. Forgive him for Christ's sake.'

'I'll pay him out, so that he won't forget it for a year! I'll take the rascal to the police!'

Martin began entreating the old woman.

'Let him go, Granny. He won't do it again. Let him go for Christ's sake!'

The old woman let go, and the boy wished to run away, but Martin stopped him

'Ask the Granny's forgiveness!' said he. 'And don't do it another time. I saw you take the apple.'

The boy began to cry and to beg pardon.

'That's right. And now here's an apple for you,' and Martin took an apple from the basket and gave it to the boy, saying, 'I will pay you, Granny.'

'You will spoil them that way, the young rascals,' said the old woman. 'He ought to be whipped so that he should remember it for a week.'

'Oh, Granny, Granny,' said Martin, 'that's our way – but it's not God's way. If he should be whipped for stealing an apple, what should be done to us for our sins?'

The old woman was silent.

And Martin told her the parable of the lord who forgave his servant a large debt, and how the servant went out and seized his debtor by the throat. The old woman listened to it all, and the boy, too, stood by and listened.

'God bids us forgive,' said Martin, 'or else we shall not be forgiven. Forgive everyone; and a thoughtless youngster most of all.'

The old woman wagged her head and sighed.

'It's true enough,' said she, 'but they are getting terribly spoilt.'

'Then we old ones must show them better ways,' Martin replied.

'That's just what I say,' said the old woman. 'I have had

seven of them myself, and only one daughter is left.' And the old woman began to tell how and where she was living with her daughter, and how many grandchildren she had. 'There now,' she said, 'I have but little strength left, yet I work hard for the sake of my grandchildren; and nice children they are, too. No one comes out to meet me but the children. Little Annie, now, won't leave me for anyone. "It's grandmother, dear grandmother, darling grandmother."' And the old woman completely softened at the thought.

'Of course, it was only his childishness, God help him,' said she, referring to the boy.

As the old woman was about to hoist her sack on her back, the lad sprang forward to her, saying, 'Let me carry it for you, Granny. I'm going that way.'

The old woman nodded her head, and put the sack on the boy's back, and they went down the street together, the old woman quite forgetting to ask Martin to pay for the apple. Martin stood and watched them as they went along talking to each other.

When they were out of sight Martin went back to the house. Having found his spectacles unbroken on the steps, he picked up his awl and sat down again to work. He worked a little, but could soon not see to pass the bristle through the holes in the leather; and presently he noticed the lamplighter passing on his way to light the street lamps.

'Seems it's time to light up,' thought he. So he trimmed his lamp, hung it up, and sat down again to work. He finished off one boot and, turning it about, examined it. It was all right. Then he gathered his tools together, swept up the cuttings, put away the bristles and the thread and the awls, and, taking down the lamp, placed it on the table. Then he took the Gospels from the shelf. He meant to open them at

176

the place he had marked the day before with a bit of morocco, but the book opened at another place. As Martin opened it, his yesterday's dream came back to his mind, and no sooner had he thought of it than he seemed to hear footsteps, as though someone were moving behind him. Martin turned round, and it seemed to him as if people were standing in the dark corner, but he could not make out who they were. And a voice whispered in his ear: 'Martin, Martin, don't you know me?'

'Who is it?' muttered Martin.

'It is I,' said the voice. And out of the dark corner stepped Stepánitch, who smiled and vanishing like a cloud was seen no more.

'It is I,' said the voice again. And out of the darkness stepped the woman with the baby in her arms, and the woman smiled and the baby laughed, and they too vanished.

'It is I,' said the voice once more. And the old woman and the boy with the apple stepped out and both smiled, and then they too vanished.

And Martin's soul grew glad. He crossed himself, put on his spectacles, and began reading the Gospel just where it had opened; and at the top of the page he read:

'I was an hungred, and ye gave me meat: I was thirsty, and ye gave me drink: I was a stranger, and ye took me in.'

And at the bottom of the page he read:

'Inasmuch as ye did it unto one of these my brethren, even these least, ye did it unto me' (*Matt.* xxv).

And Martin understood that his dream had come true; and that the Saviour had really come to him that day, and he had welcomed him.

ANTON CHEKHOV

VANKA

Translated by Constance Garnett

VANKA ZHUKOV, a boy of nine, who had been for three months apprenticed to Alyahin the shoemaker, was sitting up on Christmas Eve. Waiting till his master and mistress and their workmen had gone to the midnight service, he took out of his master's cupboard a bottle of ink and a pen with a rusty nib, and, spreading out a crumpled sheet of paper in front of him, began writing. Before forming the first letter he several times looked round fearfully at the door and the windows, stole a glance at the dark ikon, on both sides of which stretched shelves full of lasts, and heaved a broken sigh. The paper lay on the bench while he knelt before it.

'Dear grandfather, Konstantin Makaritch,' he wrote, 'I am writing you a letter. I wish you a happy Christmas, and all blessings from God Almighty. I have neither father nor mother, you are the only one left me.'

Vanka raised his eyes to the dark ikon on which the light of his candle was reflected, and vividly recalled his grandfather, Konstantin Makaritch, who was night watchman to a family called Zhivarev. He was a thin but extraordinarily nimble and lively little old man of sixty-five, with an everlastingly laughing face and drunken eyes. By day he slept in the servants' kitchen, or made jokes with the cooks; at night, wrapped in an ample sheepskin, he walked round the grounds and tapped with his little mallet. Old Kashtanka and Eel, so-called on account of his dark colour and his long body like a weasel's, followed him with hanging heads. This Eel was exceptionally polite and affectionate, and looked with equal kindness on strangers and his own masters, but had not a very good reputation. Under his politeness and meekness was hidden the most Jesuitical cunning. No one knew better how to creep up on occasion and snap at one's legs, to slip into the storeroom, or steal a hen from a peasant. His hind legs had been nearly pulled off more than once, twice he had been hanged, every week he was thrashed till he was half dead, but he always revived.

At this moment grandfather was, no doubt, standing at the gate, screwing up his eyes at the red windows of the church, stamping with his high felt boots, and joking with the servants. His little mallet was hanging on his belt. He was clasping his hands, shrugging with the cold, and, with an aged chuckle, pinching first the housemaid, then the cook.

'How about a pinch of snuff?' he was saying, offering the women his snuff-box.

The women would take a sniff and sneeze. Grandfather would be indescribably delighted, go off into a merry chuckle, and cry:

'Tear it off, it has frozen on!'

They give the dogs a sniff of snuff too. Kashtanka sneezes, wriggles her head, and walks away offended. Eel does not sneeze, from politeness, but wags his tail. And the weather is glorious. The air is still, fresh, and transparent. The night is dark, but one can see the whole village with its white roofs and coils of smoke coming from the chimneys, the trees silvered with hoar frost, the snowdrifts. The whole sky spangled with gay twinkling stars, and the Milky Way is as distinct as though it had been washed and rubbed with snow for a holiday. . . .

Vanka sighed, dipped his pen, and went on writing:

'And yesterday I had a wigging. The master pulled me out into the yard by my hair, and whacked me with a boot-stretcher because I accidentally fell asleep while I was rocking their brat in the cradle. And a week ago the mistress told me to clean a herring, and I began from the tail end, and she took the herring and thrust its head in my face. The workmen laugh at me and send me to the tavern for vodka, and tell me to steal the master's cucumbers for them, and the master beats me with anything that comes to hand. And there is nothing to eat. In the morning they give me bread, for dinner, porridge, and in the evening, bread again; but as for tea, or soup, the master and mistress gobble it all up themselves. And I am put to sleep in the passage, and when their wretched brat cries I get no sleep at all, but have to rock the cradle. Dear grandfather, show the divine mercy, take me away from here, home to the village. It's more than I can bear. I bow down to your feet, and will pray to God for you for ever, take me away from here or I shall die.'

Vanka's mouth worked, he rubbed his eyes with his black fist, and gave a sob.

'I will powder your snuff for you,' he went on. 'I will pray for you, and if I do anything you can thrash me like Sidor's goat. And if you think I've no job, then I will beg the steward for Christ's sake to let me clean his boots, or I'll go for a shepherd-boy instead of Fedka. Dear grandfather, it is more than I can bear, it's simply no life at all. I wanted to run away to the village, but I have no boots, and I am afraid of the frost. When I grow up big I will take care of you for this, and not let anyone annoy you, and when you die I will pray for the rest of your soul, just as for my mammy's.

'Moscow is a big town. It's all gentlemen's houses, and there are lots of horses, but there are no sheep, and the dogs are not spiteful. The lads here don't go out with the star, and they don't let anyone go into the choir, and once I saw in a shop window fishing-hooks for sale, fitted ready with the line and for all sorts of fish, awfully good ones, there was even one hook that would hold a forty-pound sheat-fish. And I have seen shops where there are guns of all sorts, after the pattern of the master's guns at home, so that I shouldn't wonder if they are a hundred roubles each. . . . And in the butchers' shops there are grouse and woodcocks and fish and hares, but the shopmen don't say where they shoot them.

'Dear grandfather, when they have the Christmas tree at the big house, get me a gilt walnut, and put it away in the green trunk. Ask the young lady Olga Ignatyevna, say it's for Vanka.'

Vanka gave a tremulous sigh, and again stared at the window. He remembered how his grandfather always went into the forest to get the Christmas tree for his master's family, and took his grandson with him. It was a merry time! Grandfather made a noise in his throat, the forest crackled with the frost, and looking at them Vanka chortled too. Before chopping down the Christmas tree, grandfather would smoke a pipe, slowly take a pinch of snuff, and laugh at frozen Vanka. . . . The young fir trees, covered with hoar frost, stood motionless, waiting to see which of them was to die. Wherever one looked, a hare flew like an arrow over the snowdrifts. . . . Grandfather could not refrain from shouting: 'Hold him, hold him . . . hold him! Ah, the bob-tailed devil!'

When he had cut down the Christmas tree, grandfather used to drag it to the big house, and there set to work to decorate it. . . . The young lady, who was Vanka's favourite, Olga Ignatyevna, was the busiest of all. When Vanka's mother Pelageya was alive, and a servant in the big house,

Olga Ignatyevna used to give him goodies, and having nothing better to do, taught him to read and write, to count up to a hundred, and even to dance a quadrille. When Pelageya died, Vanka had been transferred to the servants' kitchen to be with his grandfather, and from the kitchen to the shoemaker's in Moscow.

'Do come, dear grandfather,' Vanka went on with his letter. 'For Christ's sake, I beg you, take me away. Have pity on an unhappy orphan like me; here everyone knocks me about, and I am fearfully hungry; I can't tell you what misery it is, I am always crying. And the other day the master hit me on the head with a last, so that I fell down. My life is wretched, worse than any dog's. . . . I send greetings to Alyona, one-eyed Yegorka, and the coachman, and don't give my concertina to anyone. I remain, your grandson, Ivan Zhukov. Dear grandfather, do come.'

Vanka folded the sheet of writing-paper twice, and put it into an envelope he had bought the day before for a kopeck. . . . After thinking a little, he dipped the pen and wrote the address:

To grandfather in the village.

Then he scratched his head, thought a little, and added: *Konstantin Makaritch.* Glad that he had not been prevented from writing, he put on his cap and, without putting on his little greatcoat, ran out into the street as he was in his shirt. . . .

The shopmen at the butcher's, whom he had questioned the day before, told him that letters were put in post-boxes, and from the boxes were carried about all over the earth in mailcarts with drunken drivers and ringing bells. Vanka ran to the nearest post-box, and thrust the precious letter in the slit. . . .

An hour later, lulled by sweet hopes, he was sound asleep.... He dreamed of the stove. On the stove was sitting his grandfather, swinging his bare legs, and reading the letter to the cooks....

By the stove was Eel, wagging his tail.

WILLA CATHER

THE BURGLAR'S CHRISTMAS

TWO VERY SHABBY-LOOKING young men stood at the corner of Prairie Avenue and Eightieth Street, looking despondently at the carriages that whirled by. It was Christmas Eve, and the streets were full of vehicles; florists' wagons, grocers' carts and carriages. The streets were in that half-liquid, half-congealed condition peculiar to the streets of Chicago at that season of the year. The swift wheels that spun by sometimes threw the slush of mud and snow over the two young men who were talking on the corner.

'Well,' remarked the elder of the two, 'I guess we are at our rope's end, sure enough. How do you feel?'

'Pretty shaky. The wind's sharp tonight. If I had had anything to eat I mightn't mind it so much. There is simply no show. I'm sick of the whole business. Looks like there's nothing for it but the lake.'

'O, nonsense, I thought you had more grit. Got anything left you can hock?'

'Nothing but my beard, and I am afraid they wouldn't find it worth a pawn ticket,' said the younger man ruefully, rubbing the week's growth of stubble on his face.

'Got any folks anywhere? Now's your time to strike 'em if you have.'

'Never mind if I have, they're out of the question.'

'Well, you'll be out of it before many hours if you don't make a move of some sort. A man's got to eat. See here, I am going down to Longtin's saloon. I used to play the banjo in there with a couple of coons, and I'll bone him for some of his free-lunch stuff. You'd better come along, perhaps they'll fill an order for two.'

'How far down is it?'

'Well, it's clear downtown, of course, way down on Michigan Avenue.'

'Thanks, I guess I'll loaf around here. I don't feel equal to the walk, and the cars – well, the cars are crowded.' His features drew themselves into what might have been a smile under happier circumstances.

'No, you never did like street cars, you're too aristocratic. See here, Crawford, I don't like leaving you here. You ain't good company for yourself tonight.'

'Crawford? O, yes, that's the last one. There have been so many I forget them.'

'Have you got a real name, anyway?'

'O, yes, but it's one of the ones I've forgotten. Don't you worry about me. You go along and get your free lunch. I think I had a row in Longtin's place once. I'd better not show myself there again.' As he spoke the young man nodded and turned slowly up the avenue.

He was miserable enough to want to be quite alone. Even the crowd that jostled by him annoyed him. He wanted to think about himself. He had avoided this final reckoning with himself for a year now. He had laughed it off and drunk it off. But now, when all those artificial devices which are employed to turn our thoughts into other channels and shield us from ourselves had failed him, it must come. Hunger is a powerful incentive to introspection.

It is a tragic hour, that hour when we are finally driven to reckon with ourselves, when every avenue of mental distraction has been cut off and our own life and all its ineffaceable failures closes about us like the walls of that old torture chamber of the Inquisition. Tonight, as this man stood stranded in the streets of the city, his hour came. It was not the first time he had been hungry and desperate and alone. But always before there had been some outlook, some chance ahead, some pleasure yet untasted that seemed worth the effort, some face that he fancied was, or would be, dear. But it was not so tonight. The unyielding conviction was upon him that he had failed in everything, had outlived everything. It had been near him for a long time, that Pale Spectre. He had caught its shadow at the bottom of his glass many a time, at the head of his bed when he was sleepless at night, in the twilight shadows when some great sunset broke upon him. It had made life hateful to him when he awoke in the morning before now. But now it settled slowly over him, like night, the endless Northern nights that bid the sun a long farewell. It rose up before him like granite. From this brilliant city with its glad bustle of Yuletide he was shut off as completely as though he were a creature of another species. His days seemed numbered and done, sealed over like the little coral cells at the bottom of the sea. Involuntarily he drew that cold air through his lungs slowly, as though he were tasting it for the last time.

Yet he was but four and twenty, this man – he looked even younger – and he had a father some place down East who had been very proud of him once. Well, he had taken his life into his own hands, and this was what he had made of it. That was all there was to be said. He could remember the hopeful things they used to say about him at college in the old days, before he had cut away and begun to live by his wits, and he found courage to smile at them now. They had read him wrongly. He knew now that he never had the essentials of success, only the superficial agility that is often mistaken for it. He was tow without the tinder, and he had burnt himself out at other people's fires. He had helped other people to make it win, but he himself – he had never touched an enterprise that had not failed eventually. Or, if it survived his connection with it, it left him behind.

His last venture had been with some ten-cent specialty company, a little lower than all the others, that had gone to pieces in Buffalo, and he had worked his way to Chicago by boat. When the boat made up its crew for the outward voyage, he was dispensed with as usual. He was used to that. The reason for it? O, there are so many reasons for failure! His was a very common one.

As he stood there in the wet under the street light he drew up his reckoning with the world and decided that it had treated him as well as he deserved. He had overdrawn his account once too often. There had been a day when he thought otherwise; when he had said he was unjustly handled, that his failure was merely the lack of proper adjustment between himself and other men, that some day he would be recognized and it would all come right. But he knew better than that now, and he was still man enough to bear no grudge against any one – man or woman.

Tonight was his birthday, too. There seemed something particularly amusing in that. He turned up a limp little coat collar to try to keep a little of the wet chill from his throat, and instinctively began to remember all the birthday parties he used to have. He was so cold and empty that his mind seemed unable to grapple with any serious question. He kept thinking about gingerbread and frosted cakes like a child. He could remember the splendid birthday parties his mother used to give him, when all the other little boys in the block came in their Sunday clothes and creaking shoes, with their ears still red from their mother's towel, and the pink and white birthday cake, and the stuffed olives and all the dishes of which he had been particularly fond, and how he would eat and eat and then go to bed and dream of Santa Claus. And in the morning he would awaken and eat again, until by night the family doctor arrived with his castor oil, and poor William used to dolefully say that it was altogether too much to have your birthday and Christmas all at once. He could remember, too, the royal birthday suppers he had given at college, and the stag dinners, and the toasts, and the music, and the good fellows who had wished him happiness and really meant what they said.

And since then there were other birthday suppers that he could not remember so clearly; the memory of them was heavy and flat, like cigarette smoke that has been shut in a room all night, like champagne that has been a day opened, a song that has been too often sung, an acute sensation that has been overstrained. They seemed tawdry and garish, discordant to him now. He rather wished he could forget them altogether.

Whichever way his mind now turned there was one thought that it could not escape, and that was the idea of food. He caught the scent of a cigar suddenly, and felt a sharp pain in the pit of his abdomen and a sudden moisture in his mouth. His cold hands clenched angrily, and for a moment he felt that bitter hatred of wealth, of ease, of everything that is well fed and well housed that is common to starving men. At any rate he had a right to eat! He had demanded great things from the world once: fame and wealth and admiration. Now it was simply bread – and he would have it! He looked about him quickly and felt the blood begin to stir in his veins. In all his straits he had never stolen anything, his tastes were above it. But tonight there would be no tomorrow. He was amused at the way in which the idea excited him. Was it possible there was yet one more experience that would distract him, one thing that had power to excite his jaded interest? Good! he had failed at everything else, now he would see what his chances would be as a common thief. It would be amusing to watch the beautiful consistency of his destiny work itself out even in that role. It would be interesting to add another study to his gallery of futile attempts, and then label them all: 'the failure as a journalist', 'the failure as a lecturer', 'the failure as a business man', 'the failure as a thief', and so on, like the titles under the pictures of the Dance of Death. It was time that Childe Roland came to the dark tower.

A girl hastened by him with her arms full of packages. She walked quickly and nervously, keeping well within the shadow, as if she were not accustomed to carrying bundles and did not care to meet any of her friends. As she crossed the muddy street, she made an effort to lift her skirt a little, and as she did so one of the packages slipped unnoticed from beneath her arm. He caught it up and overtook her. 'Excuse me, but I think you dropped something.'

She started, 'O, yes, thank you, I would rather have lost anything than that.'

The young man turned angrily upon himself. The package must have contained something of value. Why had he not kept it? Was this the sort of thief he would make? He ground his teeth together. There is nothing more maddening than to have morally consented to crime and then lack the nerve force to carry it out.

A carriage drove up to the house before which he stood. Several richly dressed women alighted and went in. It was a new house, and must have been built since he was in Chicago last. The front door was open and he could see down the hallway and up the staircase. The servant had left the door and gone with the guests. The first floor was brilliantly lighted, but the windows upstairs were dark. It looked very easy, just to slip upstairs to the darkened chambers where the jewels and trinkets of the fashionable occupants were kept.

Still burning with impatience against himself he entered quickly. Instinctively he removed his mud-stained hat as he passed quickly and quietly up the staircase. It struck him as being a rather superfluous courtesy in a burglar, but he had done it before he had thought. His way was clear enough, he met no one on the stairway or in the upper hall. The gas was lit in the upper hall. He passed the first chamber door through sheer cowardice. The second he entered quickly, thinking of something else lest his courage should fail him, and closed the door behind him. The light from the hall shone into the room through the transom. The apartment was furnished richly enough to justify his expectations. He went at once to the dressing case. A number of rings and small trinkets lay in a silver tray. These he put hastily in his pocket. He opened the upper drawer and found, as he expected, several leather cases. In the first he opened was a lady's watch, in the second a pair of old-fashioned bracelets; he seemed to dimly remember having seen bracelets like them before, somewhere. The third case was heavier, the spring was much worn, and it opened easily. It held a cup of some kind. He held it up to the light and then his strained nerves gave way and he uttered a sharp exclamation. It was the silver mug he used to drink from when he was a little boy.

The door opened, and a woman stood in the doorway facing him. She was a tall woman, with white hair, in even-ing dress. The light from the hall streamed in upon him, but she was not afraid. She stood looking at him a moment, then she threw out her hand and went quickly toward him.

'Willie, Willie! Is it you?'

He struggled to loose her arms from him, to keep her

lips from his cheek. 'Mother – you must not! You do not understand! O, my God, this is worst of all!' Hunger, weakness, cold, shame, all came back to him, and shook his self-control completely. Physically he was too weak to stand a shock like this. Why could it not have been an ordinary discovery, arrest, the station house and all the rest of it. Anything but this! A hard dry sob broke from him. Again he strove to disengage himself.

'Who is it says I shall not kiss my son? O, my boy, we have waited so long for this! You have been so long in coming, even I almost gave you up.'

Her lips upon his cheek burnt him like fire. He put his hand to his throat, and spoke thickly and incoherently: 'You do not understand. I did not know you were here. I came here to rob – it is the first time – I swear it – but I am a common thief. My pockets are full of your jewels now. Can't you hear me? I am a common thief!'

'Hush, my boy, those are ugly words. How could you rob your own house? How could you take what is your own? They are all yours, my son, as wholly yours as my great love – and you can't doubt that, Will, do you?'

That soft voice, the warmth and fragrance of her person stole through his chill, empty veins like a gentle stimulant. He felt as though all his strength were leaving him and even consciousness. He held fast to her and bowed his head on her strong shoulder, and groaned aloud.

'O, mother, life is hard, hard!'

She said nothing, but held him closer. And O, the strength of those white arms that held him! O, the assurance of safety in that warm bosom that rose and fell under his cheek! For a moment they stood so, silently. Then they heard a heavy step upon the stair. She led him to a chair and went out and closed the door. At the top of the staircase she met a tall, broad-shouldered man, with iron-gray hair, and a face alert and stern. Her eyes were shining and her cheeks on fire, her whole face was one expression of intense determination.

'James, it is William in there, come home. You must keep him at any cost. If he goes this time, I go with him. O, James, be easy with him, he has suffered so.' She broke from a command to an entreaty, and laid her hand on his shoulder. He looked questioningly at her a moment, then went in the room and quietly shut the door.

She stood leaning against the wall, clasping her temples with her hands and listening to the low indistinct sound of the voices within. Her own lips moved silently. She waited a long time, scarcely breathing. At last the door opened, and her husband came out. He stopped to say in a shaken voice, 'You go to him now, he will stay. I will go to my room. I will see him again in the morning.'

She put her arm about his neck. 'O, James, I thank you, I thank you! This is the night he came so long ago, you remember? I gave him to you then, and now you give him back to me!'

'Don't, Helen,' he muttered. 'He is my son, I have never forgotten that. I failed with him. I don't like to fail, it cuts my pride. Take him and make a man of him.' He passed on down the hall.

She flew into the room where the young man sat with his head bowed upon his knee. She dropped upon her knees beside him. Ah, it was so good to him to feel those arms again!

'He is so glad, Willie, so glad! He may not show it, but he is as happy as I. He never was demonstrative with either of us, you know.'

'O, my God, he was good enough,' groaned the man.

197

'I told him everything, and he was good enough. I don't see how either of you can look at me, speak to me, touch me.' He shivered under her clasp again as when she had first touched him, and tried weakly to throw her off. But she whispered softly, 'This is my right, my son.'

Presently, when he was calmer, she rose. 'Now, come with me into the library, and I will have your dinner brought there.'

As they went downstairs she remarked apologetically, 'I will not call Ellen tonight; she has a number of guests to attend to. She is a big girl now, you know, and came out last winter. Besides, I want you all to myself tonight.'

When the dinner came, and it came very soon, he fell upon it savagely. As he ate she told him all that had transpired during the years of his absence, and how his father's business had brought them there. 'I was glad when we came. I thought you would drift West. I seemed a good deal nearer to you here.'

There was a gentle unobtrusive sadness in her tone that was too soft for a reproach.

'Have you everything you want? It is a comfort to see you eat.'

He smiled grimly. 'It is certainly a comfort to me. I have not indulged in this frivolous habit for some thirty-five hours.'

She caught his hand and pressed it sharply, uttering a quick remonstrance.

'Don't say that! I know, but I can't hear you say it – it's too terrible! My boy, food has choked me many a time when I have thought of the possibility of that. Now take the old lounging chair by the fire, and if you are too tired to talk, we will just sit and rest together.'

He sank into the depths of the big leather chair with the

lions' heads on the arms, where he had sat so often in the days when his feet did not touch the floor and he was half afraid of the grim monsters cut in the polished wood. That chair seemed to speak to him of things long forgotten. It was like the touch of an old familiar friend. He felt a sudden yearning tenderness for the happy little boy who had sat there and dreamed of the big world so long ago. Alas, he had been dead many a summer, that little boy!

He sat looking up at the magnificent woman beside him. He had almost forgotten how handsome she was; how lustrous and sad were the eyes that were set under that serene brow, how impetuous and wayward the mouth even now, how superb the white throat and shoulders! Ah, the wit and grace and fineness of this woman! He remembered how proud he had been of her as a boy when she came to see him at school. Then in the deep red coals of the grate he saw the faces of other women who had come since then into his vexed, disordered life. Laughing faces, with eyes artificially bright, eyes without depth or meaning, features without the stamp of high sensibilities. And he had left this face for such as those!

He sighed restlessly and laid his hand on hers. There seemed refuge and protection in the touch of her, as in the old days when he was afraid of the dark. He had been in the dark so long now, his confidence was so thoroughly shaken, and he was bitterly afraid of the night and of himself.

'Ah, mother, you make other things seem so false. You must feel that I owe you an explanation, but I can't make any, even to myself. Ah, but we make poor exchanges in life. I can't make out the riddle of it all. Yet there are things I ought to tell you before I accept your confidence like this.'

'I'd rather you wouldn't, Will. Listen: Between you and

me there can be no secrets. We are more alike than other people. Dear boy, I know all about it. I am a woman, and circumstances were different with me, but we are of one blood. I have lived all your life before you. You have never had an impulse that I have not known, you have never touched a brink that my feet have not trod. This is your birthday night. Twenty-four years ago I foresaw all this. I was a young woman then and I had hot battles of my own, and I felt your likeness to me. You were not like other babies. From the hour you were born you were restless and discontented, as I had been before you. You used to brace your strong little limbs against mine and try to throw me off as you did tonight. Tonight you have come back to me, just as you always did after you ran away to swim in the river that was forbidden you, the river you loved because it was forbidden. You are tired and sleepy, just as you used to be then, only a little older and a little paler and a little more foolish. I never asked you where you had been then, nor will I now. You have come back to me, that's all in all to me. I know your every possibility and limitation, as a composer knows his instrument.'

He found no answer that was worthy to give to talk like this. He had not found life easy since he had lived by his wits. He had come to know poverty at close quarters. He had known what it was to be gay with an empty pocket, to wear violets in his buttonhole when he had not breakfasted, and all the hateful shams of the poverty of idleness. He had been a reporter on a big metropolitan daily, where men grind out their brains on paper until they have not one idea left – and still grind on. He had worked in a real estate office, where ignorant men were swindled. He had sung in a comic opera chorus and played Harris in an Uncle Tom's Cabin company, and edited a socialist weekly. He had been dogged by debt and hunger and grinding poverty, until to sit here by a warm fire without concern as to how it would be paid for seemed unnatural.

He looked up at her questioningly. 'I wonder if you know how much you pardon?'

'O, my poor boy, much or little, what does it matter? Have you wandered so far and paid such a bitter price for knowledge and not yet learned that love has nothing to do with pardon or forgiveness, that it only loves, and loves – and loves? They have not taught you well, the women of your world.' She leaned over and kissed him, as no woman had kissed him since he left her.

He drew a long sigh of rich content. The old life, with all its bitterness and useless antagonism and flimsy sophistries, its brief delights that were always tinged with fear and distrust and unfaith, that whole miserable, futile, swindled world of Bohemia seemed immeasurably distant and far away, like a dream that is over and done. And as the chimes rang joyfully outside and sleep pressed heavily upon his eyelids, he wondered dimly if the Author of this sad little riddle of ours were not able to solve it after all, and if the Potter would not finally mete out his all comprehensive justice, such as none but he could have, to his Things of Clay, which are made in his own patterns, weak or strong, for his own ends; and if some day we will not awaken and find that all evil is a dream, a mental distortion that will pass when the dawn shall break.

O. HENRY

A CHAPARRAL
CHRISTMAS GIFT

THE ORIGINAL CAUSE of the trouble was about twenty years in growing. At the end of that time it was worth it.

Had you lived anywhere within fifty miles of Sundown Ranch you would have heard of it. It possessed a quantity of jet-black hair, a pair of extremely frank, deep-brown eyes and a laugh that rippled across the prairie like the sound of a hidden brook. The name of it was Rosita McMullen; and she was the daughter of old man McMullen of the Sundown Sheep Ranch.

There came riding on red roan steeds – or, to be more explicit, on a paint and a flea-bitten sorrel – two wooers. One was Madison Lane, and the other was the Frio Kid. But at that time they did not call him the Frio Kid, for he had not earned the honours of special nomenclature. His name was simply Johnny McRoy.

It must not be supposed that these two were the sum of the agreeable Rosita's admirers. The broncos of a dozen others champed their bits at the long hitching rack of the Sundown Ranch. Many were the sheeps'-eyes that were cast in those savannas that did not belong to the flocks of Dan McMullen. But of all the cavaliers, Madison Lane and Johnny McRoy galloped far ahead, wherefore they are to be chronicled.

Madison Lane, a young cattleman from the Nueces country, won the race. He and Rosita were married one Christmas Day. Armed, hilarious, vociferous, magnanimous, the cowmen and the sheepmen, laying aside their hereditary hatred, joined forces to celebrate the occasion.

Sundown Ranch was sonorous with the cracking of jokes and sixshooters, the shine of buckles and bright eyes, the outspoken congratulations of the herders of kine.

But while the wedding feast was at its liveliest there descended upon it Johnny McRoy, bitten by jealousy, like one possessed.

'I'll give you a Christmas present,' he yelled, shrilly, at the door, with his .45 in his hand. Even then he had some reputation as an offhand shot.

His first bullet cut a neat underbit in Madison Lane's right ear. The barrel of his gun moved an inch. The next shot would have been the bride's had not Carson, a sheepman, possessed a mind with triggers somewhat well oiled and in repair. The guns of the wedding party had been hung, in their belts, upon nails in the wall when they sat at table, as a concession to good taste. But Carson, with great promptness, hurled his plate of roast venison and frijoles at McRoy, spoiling his aim. The second bullet, then, only shattered the white petals of a Spanish dagger flower suspended two feet above Rosita's head.

The guests spurned their chairs and jumped for their weapons. It was considered an improper act to shoot the bride and groom at a wedding. In about six seconds there were twenty or so bullets due to be whizzing in the direction of Mr McRoy.

'I'll shoot better next time,' yelled Johnny; 'and there'll be a next time.' He backed rapidly out the door.

Carson, the sheepman, spurred on to attempt further exploits by the success of his plate-throwing, was first to reach the door. McRoy's bullet from the darkness laid him low.

The cattlemen then swept out upon him, calling for

vengeance, for, while the slaughter of a sheepman has not always lacked condonement, it was a decided misdemeanour in this instance. Carson was innocent; he was no accomplice at the matrimonial proceedings; nor had any one heard him quote the line 'Christmas comes but once a year' to the guests.

But the sortie failed in its vengeance. McRoy was on his horse and away, shouting back curses and threats as he galloped into the concealing chaparral.

That night was the birthnight of the Frio Kid. He became the 'bad man' of that portion of the State. The rejection of his suit by Miss McMullen turned him to a dangerous man. When officers went after him for the shooting of Carson, he killed two of them, and entered upon the life of an outlaw. He became a marvellous shot with either hand. He would turn up in towns and settlements, raise a quarrel at the slightest opportunity, pick off his man and laugh at the officers of the law. He was so cool, so deadly, so rapid, so inhumanly blood-thirsty that none but faint attempts were ever made to capture him. When he was at last shot and killed by a little one-armed Mexican who was nearly dead himself from fright, the Frio Kid had the deaths of eighteen men on his head. About half of these were killed in fair duds depending upon the quickness of the draw. The other half were men whom he assassinated from absolute wantonness and cruelty.

Many tales are told along the border of his impudent courage and daring. But he was not one of the breed of desperadoes who have seasons of generosity and even of softness. They say he never had mercy on the object of his anger. Yet at this and every Christmastide it is well to give each one credit, if it can be done, for whatever speck of good he may have possessed. If the Frio Kid ever did a kindly act or felt a throb of generosity in his heart it was once at such a time and season, and this is the way it happened.

One who has been crossed in love should never breathe the odour from the blossoms of the ratama tree. It stirs the memory to a dangerous degree.

One December in the Frio country there was a ratama tree in full bloom, for the winter had been as warm as springtime. That way rode the Frio Kid and his satellite and co-murderer, Mexican Frank. The Kid reined in his mustang, and sat in his saddle, thoughtful and grim, with dangerously narrowing eyes. The rich, sweet scent touched him somewhere beneath his ice and iron.

'I don't know what I've been thinking about, Mex,' he remarked in his usual mild drawl, 'to have forgot all about a Christmas present I got to give. I'm going to ride over to-morrow night and shoot Madison Lane in his own house. He got my girl – Rosita would have had me if he hadn't cut into the game. I wonder why I happened to overlook it up to now?'

'Ah, shucks, Kid,' said Mexican, 'don't talk foolishness. You know you can't get within a mile of Mad Lane's house to-morrow night. I see old man Allen day before yesterday, and he says Mad is going to have Christmas doings at his house. You remember how you shot up the festivities when Mad was married, and about the threats you made? Don't you suppose Mad Lane'll kind of keep his eye open for a certain Mr Kid? You plumb make me tired, Kid, with such remarks.'

'I'm going,' repeated the Frio Kid, without heat, 'to go to Madison Lane's Christmas doings, and kill him. I ought to have done it a long time ago. Why, Mex, just two weeks ago I dreamed me and Rosita was married instead of her and him: and we was living in a house, and I could see her smiling

208

at me, and – oh! h—l, Mex, he got her: and I'll get him – yes, sir, on Christmas Eve he got her, and then's when I'll get him.'

'There's other ways of committing suicide,' advised the Mexican. 'Why don't you go and surrender to the sheriff?'

'I'll get him,' said the Kid.

Christmas Eve fell as balmy as April. Perhaps there was a hint of faraway frostiness in the air, but it tingled like seltzer, perfumed faintly with late prairie blossoms and the mesquite grass.

When night came the five or six rooms of the ranch-house were brightly lit. In one room was a Christmas tree, for the Lanes had a boy of three, and a dozen or more guests were expected from the nearer ranches.

At nightfall Madison Lane called aside Jim Belcher and three other cowboys employed on his ranch.

'Now, boys,' said Lane, 'keep your eyes open. Walk around the house and watch the road well. All of you know the "Frio Kid", as they call him now, and if you see him, open fire on him without asking any questions. I'm not afraid of his coming around, but Rosita is. She's been afraid he'd come in on us every Christmas since we were married.'

The guests had arrived in buckboards and on horseback, and were making themselves comfortable inside.

The evening went along pleasantly. The guests enjoyed and praised Rosita's excellent supper, and afterward the men scattered in groups about the rooms or on the broad 'gallery', smoking and chatting.

The Christmas tree, of course, delighted the youngsters, and above all were they pleased when Santa Claus himself in magnificent white beard and furs appeared and began to distribute the toys.

'It's my papa,' announced Billy Sampson, aged six. 'I've seen him wear 'em before.'

Berkly, a sheepman, an old friend of Lane, stopped Rosita as she was passing by him on the gallery, where he was sitting smoking.

'Well, Mrs Lane,' said he, 'I suppose by this Christmas you've gotten over being afraid of that fellow McRoy, haven't you? Madison and I have talked about it, you know.'

'Very nearly,' said Rosita, smiling, 'but I am still nervous sometimes. I shall never forget that awful time when he came so near to killing us.'

'He's the most cold-hearted villain in the world,' said Berkly. 'The citizens all along the border ought to turn out and hunt him down like a wolf.'

'He has committed awful crimes,' said Rosita, 'but – I – don't – know. I think there is a spot of good somewhere in everybody. He was not always bad – that I know.'

Rosita turned into the hallway between the rooms. Santa Claus, in muffling whiskers and furs, was just coming through.

'I heard what you said through the window, Mrs Lane,' he said. 'I was just going down in my pocket for a Christmas present for your husband. But I've left one for you, instead. It's in the room to your right.'

'Oh, thank you, kind Santa Claus,' said Rosita, brightly.

Rosita went into the room, while Santa Claus stepped into the cooler air of the yard.

She found no one in the room but Madison.

'Where is my present that Santa said he left for me in here?' she asked.

'Haven't seen anything in the way of a present,' said her husband, laughing, 'unless he could have meant me.'

The next day Gabriel Radd, the foreman of the XO Ranch, dropped into the post-office at Loma Alta.

'Well, the Frio Kid's got his dose of lead at last,' he remarked to the postmaster.

'That so? How'd it happen?'

'One of old Sanchez's Mexican sheep herders did it! – think of it! the Frio Kid killed by a sheep herder! The Greaser saw him riding along past his camp about twelve o'clock last night, and was so skeered that he up with a Winchester and let him have it. Funniest part of it was that the Kid was dressed all up with white Angora-skin whiskers and a regular Santy Claus rig-out from head to foot. Think of the Frio Kid playing Santy!'

SAKI

REGINALD'S
CHRISTMAS REVEL

THEY SAY (said Reginald) that there's nothing sadder than victory except defeat. If you've ever stayed with dull people during what is alleged to be the festive season you can probably revise that saying. I shall never forget putting in a Christmas at the Babwolds'. Mrs Babwold is some relation of my father's – a sort of to-be-left-till-called-for cousin – and that was considered sufficient reason for my having to accept her invitation at about the sixth time of asking; though why the sins of the father should be visited by the children – you won't find any notepaper in that drawer; that's where I keep old menus and first-night programmes.

Mrs Babwold wears a rather solemn personality, and has never been known to smile even when saying disagreeable things to her friends or making out the Stores list. She takes her pleasures sadly. A state elephant at a Durbar gives one a very similar impression. Her husband gardens in all weathers. When a man goes out in the pouring rain to brush caterpillars off rose trees, I generally imagine his life indoors leaves something to be desired; anyway, it must be very unsettling for the caterpillars.

Of course there were other people there. There was a Major Somebody who had shot things in Lapland, or somewhere of that sort; I forget what they were, but it wasn't for want of reminding. We had them cold with every meal almost, and he was continually giving us details of what they measured from tip to tip, as though he thought we were going to make them warm under-things for the winter. I used to listen to him with a rapt attention that I thought rather suited me, and then one day I quite modestly gave the dimensions of an okapi I had shot in the Lincolnshire fens. The Major turned a beautiful Tyrian scarlet (I remember thinking at the time that I should like my bathroom hung in that colour), and I think that at that moment he almost found it in his heart to dislike me. Mrs Babwold put on a first-aid-to-the-injured expression, and asked him why he didn't publish a book of his sporting reminiscences; it would be so interesting She didn't remember till afterwards that he had given her two fat volumes on the subject, with his portrait and autograph as a frontispiece and an appendix on the habits of the Arctic mussel.

It was in the evening that we cast aside the cares and distractions of the day and really lived. Cards were thought to be too frivolous and empty a way of passing the time, so most of them played what they called a book game. You went out into the hall – to get an inspiration, I suppose – then you came in again with a muffler tied round your neck and looked silly, and the others were supposed to guess that you were *Wee MacGreegor*. I held out against the inanity as long as I decently could, but at last, in a lapse of good-nature, I consented to masquerade as a book, only I warned them that it would take some time to carry out. They waited for the best part of forty minutes while I went and played wineglass skittles with the page-boy in the pantry; you play it with a champagne cork, you know, and the one who knocks down the most glasses without breaking them wins. I won, with four unbroken out of seven; I think William suffered from over-anxiousness. They were rather mad in the drawing-room at my not having come back, and they weren't a bit pacified when I told them afterwards that I was *At the end of the passage.*

'I never did like Kipling,' was Mrs Babwold's comment, when the situation dawned upon her. 'I couldn't see anything clever in *Earthworms out of Tuscany* – or is that by Darwin?'

Of course these games are very educational, but, personally, I prefer bridge.

On Christmas evening we were supposed to be specially festive in the Old English fashion. The hall was horribly draughty, but it seemed to be the proper place to revel in, and it was decorated with Japanese fans and Chinese lanterns, which gave it a very Old English effect. A young lady with a confidential voice favoured us with a long recitation about a little girl who died or did something equally hackneyed, and then the Major gave us a graphic account of a struggle he had with a wounded bear. I privately wished that the bears would win sometimes on these occasions; at least they wouldn't go vapouring about it afterwards. Before we had time to recover our spirits, we were indulged with some thought-reading by a young man whom one knew instinctively had a good mother and an indifferent tailor – the sort of young man who talks unflaggingly through the thickest soup, and smooths his hair dubiously as though he thought it might hit back. The thought-reading was rather a success; he announced that the hostess was thinking about poetry, and she admitted that her mind was dwelling on one of Austin's odes. Which was near enough. I fancy she had been really wondering whether a scrag-end of mutton and some cold plum-pudding would do for the kitchen dinner next day. As a crowning dissipation, they all sat down to play progressive halma, with milk-chocolate for prizes. I've been carefully brought up, and I don't like to play games of skill for milk-chocolate, so I invented a headache and retired from the scene. I had been preceded a few minutes earlier by Miss Langshan-Smith, a rather formidable lady, who always got up at some uncomfortable hour in the morning, and gave you the impression that she had been in communication with most of the European Governments before breakfast. There was a paper pinned on her door with a signed request that she might be called particularly early on the morrow. Such an opportunity does not come twice in a lifetime. I covered up everything except the signature with another notice, to the effect that before these words should meet the eye she would have ended a misspent life, was sorry for the trouble she was giving, and would like a military funeral. A few minutes later I violently exploded an air-filled paper bag on the landing, and gave a stage moan that could have been heard in the cellars. Then I pursued my original intention and went to bed. The noise those people made in forcing open the good lady's door was positively indecorous; she resisted gallantly, but I believe they searched her for bullets for about a quarter of an hour, as if she had been a historic battlefield.

I hate travelling on Boxing Day, but one must occasionally do things that one dislikes.

VLADIMIR NABOKOV

CHRISTMAS

AFTER WALKING BACK from the village to his manor across the dimming snows, Sleptsov sat down in a corner, on a plush-covered chair which he never remembered using before. It was the kind of thing that happens after some great calamity. Not your brother but a chance acquaintance, a vague country neighbor to whom you never paid much attention, with whom in normal times you exchange scarcely a word, is the one who comforts you wisely and gently, and hands you your dropped hat after the funeral service is over, and you are reeling from grief, your teeth chattering, your eyes blinded by tears. The same can be said of inanimate objects. Any room, even the coziest and the most absurdly small, in the little-used wing of a great country house has an unlived-in corner. And it was such a corner in which Sleptsov sat.

The wing was connected by a wooden gallery, now encumbered with our huge north Russian snowdrifts, to the master house, used only in summer. There was no need to awaken it, to heat it: the master had come from Petersburg for only a couple of days and had settled in the annex where it was a simple matter to get the stoves of white Dutch tile going.

The master sat in his corner, on that plush chair, as in a doctor's waiting room. The room floated in darkness; the dense blue of early evening filtered through the crystal feathers of frost on the windowpane. Ivan, the quiet, portly valet, who had recently shaved off his mustache and now looked like his late father, the family butler, brought in a kerosene lamp, all trimmed and brimming with light. He set it on a small table, and noiselessly caged it within its pink silk shade. For an instant a tilted mirror reflected his lit ear and cropped gray hair. Then he withdrew and the door gave a subdued creak.

Sleptsov raised his hand from his knee and slowly examined it. A drop of candle wax had stuck and hardened in the thin fold of skin between two fingers. He spread his fingers and the little white scale cracked.

2

The following morning, after a night spent in nonsensical, fragmentary dreams totally unrelated to his grief, as Sleptsov stepped out into the cold veranda, a floorboard emitted a merry pistol crack underfoot, and the reflections of the many-colored panes formed paradisal lozenges on the white-washed cushionless window seats. The outer door resisted at first, then opened with a luscious crunch, and the dazzling frost hit his face. The reddish sand providently sprinkled on the ice coating the porch steps resembled cinnamon, and thick icicles shot with greenish blue hung from the eaves. The snowdrifts reached all the way to the windows of the annex, tightly gripping the snug little wooden structure in their frosty clutches. The creamy white mounds of what were flower beds in summer swelled slightly above the level snow in front of the porch, and farther off loomed the radiance of the park, where every black branchlet was rimmed with silver, and the firs seemed to draw in their green paws under their bright plump load.

Wearing high felt boots and a short fur-lined coat with a karakul collar, Sleptsov strode off slowly along a straight path, the only one cleared of snow, into that blinding distant landscape. He was amazed to be still alive, and able to perceive the brilliance of the snow and feel his front teeth ache from the cold. He even noticed that a snow-covered bush resembled a fountain and that a dog had left a series of saffron marks on the slope of a snowdrift, which had burned through its crust. A little farther, the supports of a footbridge stuck out of the snow, and there Sleptsov stopped. Bitterly, angrily, he pushed the thick, fluffy covering off the parapet. He vividly recalled how this bridge looked in summer. There was his son walking along the slippery planks, flecked with aments, and deftly plucking off with his net a butterfly that had settled on the railing. Now the boy sees his father. Forever-lost laughter plays on his face, under the turned-down brim of a straw hat burned dark by the sun; his hand toys with the chainlet of the leather purse attached to his belt, his dear, smooth, suntanned legs in their serge shorts and soaked sandals assume their usual cheerful widespread stance. Just recently, in Petersburg, after having babbled in his delirium about school, about his bicycle, about some great Oriental moth, he died, and yesterday Sleptsov had taken the coffin – weighed down, it seemed, with an entire lifetime – to the country, into the family vault near the village church.

It was quiet as it can only be on a bright, frosty day. Sleptsov raised his leg high, stepped off the path and, leaving blue pits behind him in the snow, made his way among the trunks of amazingly white trees to the spot where the park dropped off toward the river. Far below, ice blocks sparkled near a hole cut in the smooth expanse of white and, on the opposite bank, very straight columns of pink smoke stood above the snowy roofs of log cabins. Sleptsov took off his karakul cap and leaned against a tree trunk. Somewhere far away peasants were chopping wood – every blow bounced resonantly skyward – and beyond the light silver mist of trees, high above the squat isbas, the sun caught the equanimous radiance of the cross on the church.

3

That was where he headed after lunch, in an old sleigh with a high straight back. The cod of the black stallion clacked strongly in the frosty air, the white plumes of low branches glided overhead, and the ruts in front gave off a silvery blue sheen. When he arrived he sat for an hour or so by the grave, resting a heavy, woolen-gloved hand on the iron of the railing that burned his hand through the wool. He came home with a slight sense of disappointment, as if there, in the burial vault, he had been even further removed from his son than here, where the countless summer tracks of his rapid sandals were preserved beneath the snow.

In the evening, overcome by a fit of intense sadness, he had the main house unlocked. When the door swung open with a weighty wail, and a whiff of special, unwintery coolness came from the sonorous iron-barred vestibule, Sleptsov took the lamp with its tin reflector from the watchman's hand and entered the house alone. The parquet floors crackled eerily under his step. Room after room filled with yellow light, and the shrouded furniture seemed unfamiliar; instead of a tinkling chandelier, a soundless bag hung from the ceiling; and Sleptsov's enormous shadow, slowly extending one arm, floated across the wall and over the gray squares of curtained paintings.

He went into the room which had been his son's study in summer, set the lamp on the window ledge, and, breaking his fingernails as he did so, opened the folding shutters, even

224

though all was darkness outside. In the blue glass the yellow flame of the slightly smoky lamp appeared, and his large, bearded face showed momentarily.

He sat down at the bare desk and sternly, from under bent brows, examined the pale wallpaper with its garlands of bluish roses; a narrow office-like cabinet, with sliding drawers from top to bottom; the couch and armchairs under slipcovers; and suddenly, dropping his head onto the desk, he started to shake, passionately, noisily, pressing first his lips, then his wet cheek, to the cold, dusty wood and clutching at its far corners.

In the desk he found a notebook, spreading boards, supplies of black pins, and an English biscuit tin that contained a large exotic cocoon which had cost three rubles. It was papery to the touch and seemed made of a brown folded leaf. His son had remembered it during his sickness, regretting that he had left it behind, but consoling himself with the thought that the chrysalid inside was probably dead. He also found a torn net: a tarlatan bag on a collapsible hoop (and the muslin still smelled of summer and sun-hot grass).

Then, bending lower and lower and sobbing with his whole body, he began pulling out one by one the glass-topped drawers of the cabinet. In the dim lamplight the even files of specimens shone silk-like under the glass. Here, in this room, on that very desk, his son had spread the wings of his captures. He would first pin the carefully killed insect in the cork-bottomed groove of the setting board, between the adjustable strips of wood, and fasten down flat with pinned strips of paper the still fresh, soft wings. They had now dried long ago and been transferred to the cabinet – those spectacular Swallowtails, those dazzling Coppers and Blues, and the various Fritillaries, some mounted in a supine position to display the mother-of-pearl undersides. His son used to pronounce their Latin names with a moan of triumph or in an arch aside of disdain. And the moths, the moths, the first Aspen Hawk of five summers ago!

4

The night was smoke-blue and moonlit; thin clouds were scattered about the sky but did not touch the delicate, icy moon. The trees, masses of gray frost, cast dark shadows on the drifts, which scintillated here and there with metallic sparks. In the plush-upholstered, well-heated room of the annex Ivan had placed a two-foot fir tree in a clay pot on the table, and was just attaching a candle to its cruciform tip when Sleptsov returned from the main house, chilled, red-eyed, with gray dust smears on his cheek, carrying a wooden case under his arm. Seeing the Christmas tree on the table, he asked absently: 'What's that?'

Relieving him of the case, Ivan answered in a low, mellow voice: 'There's a holiday coming up tomorrow.'

'No, take it away,' said Sleptsov with a frown, while thinking, Can this be Christmas Eve? How could I have forgotten?

Ivan gently insisted: 'It's nice and green. Let it stand for a while.'

'Please take it away,' repeated Sleptsov, and bent over the case he had brought. In it he had gathered his son's belongings – the folding butterfly net, the biscuit tin with the pear-shaped cocoon, the spreading board, the pins in their lacquered box, the blue notebook. Half of the first page had been torn out, and its remaining fragment contained part of a French dictation. There followed daily entries, names of captured butterflies, and other notes:

'Walked across the bog as far as Borovichi, . . .'

'Raining today. Played checkers with Father, then read Goncharov's Frigate, *a deadly bore.'*

'Marvelous hot day. Rode my bike in the evening. A midge got in my eye. Deliberately rode by her dacha twice, but didn't see her...'

Sleptsov raised his head, swallowed something hot and huge. Of whom was his son writing?

'Rode my bike as usual,' he read on, *'Our eyes nearly met. My darling, my love...'*

'This is unthinkable,' whispered Sleptsov. 'I'll never know....'

He bent over again, avidly deciphering the childish handwriting that slanted up then curved down in the margin.

'Saw a fresh specimen of the Camberwell Beauty today. That means autumn is here. Rain in the evening. She has probably left, and we didn't even get acquainted. Farewell, my darling. I feel terribly sad....'

'He never said anything to me....' Sleptsov tried to remember, rubbing his forehead with his palm.

On the last page there was an ink drawing: the hind view of an elephant – two thick pillars, the corners of two ears, and a tiny tail.

Sleptsov got up. He shook his head, restraining yet another onrush of hideous sobs.

'I-can't-bear-it-any-longer,' he drawled between groans, repeating even more slowly, 'I – can't – bear – it – any – longer....'

'It's Christmas tomorrow,' came the abrupt reminder, 'and I'm going to die. Of course. It's so simple. This very night...'

He pulled out a handkerchief and dried his eyes, his beard, his cheeks. Dark streaks remained on the handkerchief.

'... death,' Sleptsov said softly, as if concluding a long sentence.

227

The clock ticked. Frost patterns overlapped on the blue glass of the window. The open notebook shone radiantly on the table; next to it the light went through the muslin of the butterfly net, and glistened on a corner of the open tin. Sleptsov pressed his eyes shut, and had a fleeting sensation that earthly life lay before him, totally bared and comprehensible – and ghastly in its sadness, humiliatingly pointless, sterile, devoid of miracles. . . .

At that instant there was a sudden snap – a thin sound like that of an overstretched rubber band breaking. Sleptsov opened his eyes. The cocoon in the biscuit tin had burst at its tip, and a black, wrinkled creature the size of a mouse was crawling up the wall above the table. It stopped, holding on to the surface with six black furry feet, and started palpitating strangely. It had emerged from the chrysalid because a man overcome with grief had transferred a tin box to his warm room, and the warmth had penetrated its taut leaf-and-silk envelope; it had awaited this moment so long, had collected its strength so tensely, and now, having broken out, it was slowly and miraculously expanding. Gradually the wrinkled tissues, the velvety fringes, unfurled; the fan-pleated veins grew firmer as they filled with air. It became a winged thing imperceptibly, as a maturing face imperceptibly becomes beautiful. And its wings – still feeble, still moist – kept growing and unfolding, and now they were developed to the limit set for them by God, and there, on the wall, instead of a little lump of life, instead of a dark mouse, was a great *Attacus* moth like those that fly, birdlike, around lamps in the Indian dusk.

And then those thick black wings, with a glazy eyespot on each and a purplish bloom dusting their hooked foretips, took a full breath under the impulse of tender, ravishing, almost human happiness.

DAMON RUNYON

DANCING DAN'S
CHRISTMAS

NOW ONE TIME it comes on Christmas, and in fact it is the evening before Christmas, and I am in Good Time Charley Bernstein's little speakeasy in West Forty-seventh Street, wishing Charley a Merry Christmas and having a few hot Tom and Jerrys with him.

This hot Tom and Jerry is an old-time drink that is once used by one and all in this country to celebrate Christmas with, and in fact it is once so popular that many people think Christmas is invented only to furnish an excuse for hot Tom and Jerry, although of course this is by no means true.

But anybody will tell you that there is nothing that brings out the true holiday spirit like hot Tom and Jerry, and I hear that since Tom and Jerry goes out of style in the United States, the holiday spirit is never quite the same.

Well, as Good Time Charley and I are expressing our holiday sentiments to each other over our hot Tom and Jerry, and I am trying to think up the poem about the night before Christmas and all through the house, which I know will interest Charley no little, all of a sudden there is a big knock at the front door, and when Charley opens the door, who comes in carrying a large package under one arm but a guy by the name of Dancing Dan.

This Dancing Dan is a good-looking young guy, who always seems well-dressed, and he is called by the name of

231

Dancing Dan because he is a great hand for dancing around and about with dolls in night clubs, and other spots where there is any dancing. In fact, Dan never seems to be doing anything else, although I hear rumors that when he is not dancing he is carrying on in a most illegal manner at one thing and another. But of course you can always hear rumors in this town about anybody, and personally I am rather fond of Dancing Dan as he always seems to be getting a great belt out of life.

Anybody in town will tell you that Dancing Dan is a guy with no Barnaby whatever in him, and in fact he has about as much gizzard as anybody around, although I wish to say I always question his judgment in dancing so much with Miss Muriel O'Neill, who works in the Half Moon night club. And the reason I question his judgment in this respect is because everybody knows that Miss Muriel O'Neill is a doll who is very well thought of by Heine Schmitz, and Heine Schmitz is not such a guy as will take kindly to anybody dancing more than once and a half with a doll that he thinks well of.

Well, anyway, as Dancing Dan comes in, he weighs up the joint in one quick peek, and then he tosses the package he is carrying into a corner where it goes plunk, as if there is something very heavy in it, and then he steps up to the bar alongside of Charley and me and wishes to know what we are drinking.

Naturally we start boosting hot Tom and Jerry to Dancing Dan, and he says he will take a crack at it with us, and after one crack, Dancing Dan says he will have another crack, and Merry Christmas to us with it, and the first thing anybody knows it is a couple of hours later and we are still having cracks at the hot Tom and Jerry with Dancing Dan, and Dan says he never drinks anything so soothing in his life. In fact, Dancing Dan says he will recommend Tom and Jerry to everybody he knows, only he does not know anybody good enough for Tom and Jerry, except maybe Miss Muriel O'Neill, and she does not drink anything with drugstore rye in it.

Well, several times while we are drinking this Tom and Jerry, customers come to the door of Good Time Charley's little speakeasy and knock, but by now Charley is commencing to be afraid they will wish Tom and Jerry, too, and he does not feel we will have enough for ourselves, so he hangs out a sign which says 'Closed on Account of Christmas', and the only one he will let in is a guy by the name of Ooky, who is nothing but an old rum-dum, and who is going around all week dressed like Santa Claus and carrying a sign advertising Moe Lewinsky's clothing joint around in Sixth Avenue.

This Ooky is still wearing his Santa Claus outfit when Charley lets him in, and the reason Charley permits such a character as Ooky in his joint is because Ooky does the porter work for Charley when he is not Santa Claus for Moe Lewinsky, such as sweeping out, and washing the glasses, and one thing and another.

Well, it is about nine-thirty when Ooky comes in, and his puppies are aching, and he is all petered out generally from walking up and down and here and there with his sign, for any time a guy is Santa Claus for Moe Lewinsky he must earn his dough. In fact, Ooky is so fatigued, and his puppies hurt him so much that Dancing Dan and Good Time Charley and I all feel very sorry for him, and invite him to have a few mugs of hot Tom and Jerry with us, and wish him plenty of Merry Christmas.

But old Ooky is not accustomed to Tom and Jerry and after about the fifth mug he folds up in a chair, and goes right to sleep on us. He is wearing a pretty good Santa Claus make-up, what with a nice red suit trimmed with white cotton, and a wig, and false nose, and long white whiskers, and a big sack stuffed with excelsior on his back, and if I do not know Santa Claus is not apt to be such a guy as will snore loud enough to rattle the windows, I will think Ooky is Santa Claus sure enough.

Well, we forget Ooky and let him sleep, and go on with our hot Tom and Jerry, and in the meantime we try to think up a few songs appropriate to Christmas, and Dancing Dan finally renders *My Dad's Dinner Pail* in a nice baritone and very loud, while I do first rate with *Will You Love Me in December As You Do in May?*

About midnight Dancing Dan wishes to see how he looks as Santa Claus.

So Good Time Charley and I help Dancing Dan pull off Ooky's outfit and put it on Dan, and this is easy as Ooky only has this Santa Claus outfit on over his ordinary clothes, and he does not even wake up when we are undressing him of the Santa Claus uniform.

Well, I wish to say I see many a Santa Claus in my time, but I never see a better looking Santa Claus than Dancing Dan, especially after he gets the wig and white whiskers fixed just right, and we put a sofa pillow that Good Time Charley happens to have around the joint for the cat to sleep on down his pants to give Dancing Dan a nice fat stomach such as Santa Claus is bound to have.

'Well,' Charley finally says, 'it is a great pity we do not know where there are some stockings hung up somewhere, because then,' he says, 'you can go around and stuff things in these stockings, as I always hear this is the main idea of a Santa Claus. But,' Charley says, 'I do not suppose anybody in this section has any stockings hung up, or if they have,' he says, 'the chances are they are so full of holes they will not hold anything. Anyway,' Charley says, 'even if there are any stockings hung up we do not have anything to stuff in them, although personally,' he says, 'I will gladly donate a few pints of Scotch.'

Well, I am pointing out that we have no reindeer and that a Santa Claus is bound to look like a terrible sap if he goes around without any reindeer, but Charley's remarks seem to give Dancing Dan an idea, for all of a sudden he speaks as follows:

'Why,' Dancing Dan says, 'I know where a stocking is hung up. It is hung up at Miss Muriel O'Neill's flat over here in West Forty-ninth Street. This stocking is hung up by nobody but a party by the name of Gammer O'Neill, who is Miss Muriel O'Neill's grandmamma,' Dancing Dan says. 'Gammer O'Neill is going on ninety-odd,' he says, 'and Miss Muriel O'Neill tells me she cannot hold out much longer, what with one thing and another, including being a little childish in spots.

'Now,' Dancing Dan says, 'I remember Miss Muriel O'Neill is telling me just the other night how Gammer O'Neill hangs up her stocking on Christmas Eve all her life, and,' he says, 'I judge from what Miss Muriel O'Neill says that the old doll always believes Santa Claus will come along some Christmas and fill the stocking full of beautiful gifts. But,' Dancing Dan says, 'Miss Muriel O'Neill tells me Santa Claus never does this, although Miss Muriel O'Neill personally always takes a few gifts home and pops them into the stocking to make Gammer O'Neill feel better.

'But, of course,' Dancing Dan says, 'these gifts are nothing much because Miss Muriel O'Neill is very poor, and proud, and also good, and will not take a dime off of anybody and I can lick the guy who says she will.

'Now,' Dancing Dan goes on, 'it seems that while Gammer O'Neill is very happy to get whatever she finds in her stocking on Christmas morning, she does not understand why Santa Claus is not more liberal, and,' he says, 'Miss Muriel O'Neill is saying to me that she only wishes she can give Gammer O'Neill one real big Christmas before the old doll puts her checks back in the rack.

'So,' Dancing Dan states, 'here is a job for us. Miss Muriel O'Neill and her grandmamma live all alone in this flat over in West Forty-ninth Street, and,' he says, 'at such an hour as this Miss Muriel O'Neill is bound to be working, and the chances are Gammer O'Neill is sound asleep, and we will just hop over there and Santa Claus will fill up her stocking with beautiful gifts.'

Well, I say, I do not see where we are going to get any beautiful gifts at this time of night, what with all the stores being closed, unless we dash into an all-night drug store and buy a few bottles of perfume and a bum toilet set as guys always do when they forget about their ever-loving wives until after store hours on Christmas Eve, but Dancing Dan says never mind about this, but let us have a few more Tom and Jerrys first.

So we have a few more Tom and Jerrys, and then Dancing Dan picks up the package he heaves into the corner, and dumps most of the excelsior out of Ooky's Santa Claus sack, and puts the bundle in, and Good Time Charley turns out all the lights, but one, and leaves a bottle of Scotch on the table in front of Ooky for a Christmas gift, and away we go.

Personally, I regret very much leaving the hot Tom and Jerry, but then I am also very enthusiastic about going along to help Dancing Dan play Santa Claus, while Good Time Charley is practically overjoyed, as it is the first time in his life Charley is ever mixed up in so much holiday spirit.

As we go up Broadway, headed for Forty-ninth Street, Charley and I see many citizens we know and give them a large hello, and wish them Merry Christmas, and some of these citizens shake hands with Santa Claus, not knowing he is nobody but Dancing Dan, although later I understand there is some gossip among these citizens because they claim a Santa Claus with such a breath on him as our Santa Claus has is a little out of line.

And once we are somewhat embarrassed when a lot of little kids going home with their parents from a late Christmas party somewhere gather about Santa Claus with shouts of childish glee, and some of them wish to climb up Santa Claus' legs. Naturally, Santa Claus gets a little peevish, and calls them a few names, and one of the parents comes up and wishes to know what is the idea of Santa Claus using such language, and Santa Claus takes a punch at the parent, all of which is no doubt astonishing to the little kids who have an idea of Santa Claus as a very kindly old guy.

Well, finally we arrive in front of the place where Dancing Dan says Miss Muriel O'Neill and her grandmamma live, and it is nothing but a tenement house not far back of Madison Square Garden, and furthermore it is a walkup, and at this time there are no lights burning in the joint except a gas jet in the main hall, and by the light of this jet we look at the names on the letter boxes, such as you always find in the hall of these joints, and we see that Miss Muriel O'Neill and her grandmamma live on the fifth floor.

This is the top floor, and personally I do not like the idea of walking up five flights of stairs, and I am willing to let Dancing Dan and Good Time Charley go, but Dancing Dan insists we must all go, and finally I agree because Charley is commencing to argue that the right way for us to do is to get on the roof and let Santa Claus go down a chimney, and is making so much noise I am afraid he will wake somebody up.

So up the stairs we climb and finally we come to a door on the top floor that has a little card in a slot that says O'Neill, so we know we reach our destination. Dancing Dan first tries the knob, and right away the door opens, and we are in a little two- or three-room flat, with not much furniture in it, and what furniture there is, is very poor. One single gas jet is burning near a bed in a room just off the one the door opens into, and by this light we see a very old doll is sleeping on the bed, so we judge this is nobody but Gammer O'Neill.

On her face is a large smile, as if she is dreaming of something very pleasant. On a chair at the head of the bed is hung a long black stocking, and it seems to be such a stocking as is often patched and mended, so I can see that what Miss Muriel O'Neill tells Dancing Dan about her grandmamma hanging up her stocking is really true, although up to this time I have my doubts.

Finally Dancing Dan unslings the sack on his back, and takes out his package, and unties this package, and all of a sudden out pops a raft of big diamond bracelets, and diamond rings, and diamond brooches, and diamond necklaces, and I do not know what else in the way of diamonds, and Dancing Dan and I begin stuffing these diamonds into the stocking and Good Time Charley pitches in and helps us.

There are enough diamonds to fill the stocking to the muzzle, and it is no small stocking, at that, and I judge that Gammer O'Neill has a pretty fair set of bunting sticks when she is young. In fact, there are so many diamonds that we have enough left over to make a nice little pile on the chair after we fill the stocking plumb up, leaving a nice

238

diamond-studded vanity case sticking out the top where we figure it will hit Gammer O'Neill's eye when she wakes up.

And it is not until I get out in the fresh air again that all of a sudden I remember seeing large headlines in the afternoon papers about a five-hundred-G's stickup in the afternoon of one of the biggest diamond merchants in Maiden Lane while he is sitting in his office, and I also recall once hearing rumors that Dancing Dan is one of the best lonehand git-'em-up guys in the world.

Naturally, I commence to wonder if I am in the proper company when I am with Dancing Dan, even if he is Santa Claus. So I leave him on the next corner arguing with Good Time Charley about whether they ought to go and find some more presents somewhere, and look for other stockings to stuff, and I hasten on home and go to bed.

The next day I find I have such a noggin that I do not care to stir around, and in fact I do not stir around much for a couple of weeks.

Then one night I drop around to Good Time Charley's little speakeasy, and ask Charley what is doing.

'Well,' Charley says, 'many things are doing, and personally,' he says, 'I'm greatly surprised I do not see you at Gammer O'Neill's wake. You know Gammer O'Neill leaves this wicked old world a couple of days after Christmas,' Good Time Charley says, 'and,' he says, 'Miss Muriel O'Neill states that Doc Moggs claims it is at least a day after she is entitled to go, but she is sustained,' Charley says, 'by great happiness in finding her stocking filled with beautiful gifts on Christmas morning.

'According to Miss Muriel O'Neill,' Charley says, 'Gammer O'Neill dies practically convinced that there is a Santa Claus, although of course,' he says, 'Miss Muriel O'Neill does not tell her the real owner of the gifts, an all-right guy by the name of Shapiro leaves the gifts with her after Miss Muriel O'Neill notifies him of the finding of same.

'It seems,' Charley says, 'this Shapiro is a tender-hearted guy, who is willing to help keep Gammer O'Neill with us a little longer when Doc Moggs says leaving the gifts with her will do it.

'So,' Charley says, 'everything is quite all right, as the coppers cannot figure anything except that maybe the rascal who takes the gifts from Shapiro gets conscience-stricken, and leaves them the first place he can, and Miss Muriel O'Neill receives a ten-G's reward for finding the gifts and returning them. And,' Charley says, 'I hear Dancing Dan is in San Francisco and is figuring on reforming and becoming a dancing teacher, so he can marry Miss Muriel O'Neill, and of course,' he says, 'we all hope and trust she never learn any details of Dancing Dan's career.'

Well, it is Christmas Eve a year later that I run into a guy by the name of Shotgun Sam, who is mobbed up with Heine Schmitz in Harlem, and who is a very, very obnoxious character indeed.

'Well, well, well,' Shotgun says, 'the last time I see you is another Christmas Eve like this, and you are coming out of Good Time Charley's joint, and,' he says, 'you certainly have your pots on.'

'Well, Shotgun,' I says, 'I am sorry you get such a wrong impression of me, but the truth is,' I say, 'on the occasion you speak of, I am suffering from a dizzy feeling in my head.'

'It is all right with me,' Shotgun says. 'I have a tip this guy Dancing Dan is in Good Time Charley's the night I see you, and Mockie Morgan, and Gunner Jack and me are casing the joint, because,' he says, 'Heine Schmitz is all sored up at Dan over some doll, although of course,' Shotgun says, 'it is all right now as Heine has another doll.

'Anyway,' he says, 'we never get to see Dancing Dan. We watch the joint from six-thirty in the evening until daylight Christmas morning, and nobody goes in all night but old Ooky the Santa Claus guy in his Santa Claus makeup, and,' Shotgun says, 'nobody comes out except you and Good Time Charley and Ooky.

'Well,' Shotgun says, 'it is a great break for Dancing Dan he never goes in or comes out of Good Time Charley's, at that, because,' he says, 'we are waiting for him on the second-floor front of the building across the way with some nice little sawed-offs, and are under orders from Heine not to miss.'

'Well, Shotgun,' I say, 'Merry Christmas.'

'Well, all right,' Shotgun says, 'Merry Christmas.'

EVELYN WAUGH

BELLA FLEACE GAVE A PARTY

BALLINGAR IS FOUR and a half hours from Dublin if you catch the early train from Broadstone Station and five and a quarter if you wait until the afternoon. It is the market town of a large and comparatively well-populated district. There is a pretty Protestant Church in 1820 Gothic on one side of the square and a vast, unfinished Catholic cathedral opposite it, conceived in that irresponsible medley of architectural orders that is so dear to the hearts of transmontane pietists. Celtic lettering of a sort is beginning to take the place of the Latin alphabet on the shop fronts that complete the square. These all deal in identical goods in varying degrees of dilapidation; Mulligan's Store, Flannigan's Store, Riley's Store, each sells thick black boots, hanging in bundles, soapy colonial cheese, hardware and haberdashery, oil and saddlery, and each is licensed to sell ale and porter for consumption on or off the premises. The shell of the barracks stands with empty window frames and blackened interior as a monument to emancipation. Someone has written *The Pope is a Traitor* in tar on the green pillar box. A typical Irish town.

Fleacetown is fifteen miles from Ballingar, on a direct uneven road through typical Irish country; vague purple hills in the far distance and towards them, on one side of the road, fitfully visible among drifting patches of white mist, unbroken miles of bog, dotted with occasional stacks of cut peat. On the other side the ground slopes up to the north, divided irregularly into spare fields by banks and stone walls over which the Ballingar hounds have some of their most eventful hunting. Moss lies on everything; in a rough green rug on the walls and banks, soft green velvet on the timber – blurring the transitions so that there is no knowing where the ground ends and trunk and masonry begin. All the way from Ballingar there is a succession of whitewashed cabins and a dozen or so fair-size farmhouses; but there is no gentleman's house, for all this was Fleace property in the days before the Land Commission. The demesne land is all that belongs to Fleacetown now, and this is let for pasture to neighbouring farmers. Only a few beds are cultivated in the walled kitchen garden; the rest has run to rot, thorned bushes barren of edible fruit spreading everywhere among weedy flowers reverting rankly to type. The hot-houses have been draughty skeletons for ten years. The great gates set in their Georgian arch are permanently padlocked, the lodges are derelict, and the line of the main drive is only just discernible through the meadows. Access to the house is half a mile further up through a farm gate, along a track befouled by cattle.

But the house itself, at the date with which we are dealing, was in a condition of comparatively good repair; compared, that is to say, with Ballingar House or Castle Boycott or Knode Hall. It did not, of course, set up to rival Gordontown, where the American Lady Gordon had installed electric light, central heating and a lift, or Mock House or Newhill, which were leased to sporting Englishmen, or Castle Mockstock, since Lord Mockstock married beneath him. These four houses with their neatly raked gravel, bathrooms and dynamos, were the wonder and ridicule of the country. But Fleacetown, in fair competition with the essentially Irish houses of the Free State, was unusually habitable.

Its roof was intact; and it is the roof which makes the difference between the second and third grade of Irish country houses. Once that goes you have moss in the bedrooms, ferns on the stairs and cows in the library, and in a very few years you have to move into the dairy or one of the lodges. But so long as he has, literally, a roof over his head, an Irishman's house is still his castle. There were weak bits in Fleacetown, but general opinion held that the leads were good for another twenty years and would certainly survive the present owner.

Miss Annabel Rochfort-Doyle-Fleace, to give her the full name under which she appeared in books of reference, though she was known to the entire countryside as Bella Fleace, was the last of her family. There had been Fleces and Fleysers living about Ballingar since the days of Strongbow, and farm buildings marked the spot where they had inhabited a stockaded fort two centuries before the immigration of the Boycotts or Gordons or Mockstocks. A family tree emblazed by a nineteenth-century genealogist, showing how the original stock had merged with the equally ancient Rochforts and the respectable though more recent Doyles, hung in the billiard-room. The present home had been built on extravagant lines in the middle of the eighteenth century, when the family, though enervated, was still wealthy and influential. It would be tedious to trace its gradual decline from fortune; enough to say that it was due to no heroic debauchery. The Fleaces just got unobtrusively poorer in the way that families do who make no effort to help themselves. In the last generations, too, there had been marked traces of eccentricity. Bella Fleace's mother – an O'Hara of Newhill – had from the day of her marriage until her death suffered from the delusion that she was a negress. Her brother, from whom she had inherited, devoted himself to oil painting; his mind ran on the simple subject of assassination and before his death he had executed pictures of practically every such incident in history from Julius Caesar to General Wilson. He was at work on a painting, his own murder, at the time of the troubles, when he was, in fact, ambushed and done to death with a shot-gun on his own drive.

It was under one of her brother's paintings – Abraham Lincoln in his box at the theatre – that Miss Fleace was sitting one colourless morning in November when the idea came to her to give a Christmas party. It would be unnecessary to describe her appearance closely, and somewhat confusing, because it seemed in contradiction to much of her character. She was over eighty, very untidy and very red; streaky grey hair was twisted behind her head into a horsy bun, wisps hung round her cheeks; her nose was prominent and blue veined; her eyes pale blue, blank and mad; she had a lively smile and spoke with a marked Irish intonation. She walked with the aid of a stick, having been lamed many years back when her horse rolled her among loose stones late in a long day with the Ballingar Hounds; a tipsy sporting doctor had completed the mischief, and she had not been able to ride again. She would appear on foot when hounds drew the Fleacetown coverts and loudly criticize the conduct of the huntsman, but every year fewer of her old friends turned out; strange faces appeared.

They knew Bella, though she did not know them. She had become a by-word in the neighbourhood, a much-valued joke.

'A rotten day,' they would report. 'We found our fox, but lost again almost at once. But we saw Bella. Wonder how long the old girl will last. She must be nearly ninety. My father remembers when she used to hunt – went like smoke, too.'

Indeed, Bella herself was becoming increasingly occupied with the prospect of death. In the winter before the one we are talking of, she had been extremely ill. She emerged in April, rosy cheeked as ever, but slower in her movements and mind. She gave instructions that better attention must be paid to her father's and brother's graves, and in June took the unprecedented step of inviting her heir to visit her. She had always refused to see this young man up till now. He was an Englishman, a very distant cousin, named Banks. He lived in South Kensington and occupied himself in the Museum. He arrived in August and wrote long and very amusing letters to all his friends describing his visit, and later translated his experiences into a short story for the *Spectator*. Bella disliked him from the moment he arrived. He had horn-rimmed spectacles and a B.B.C. voice. He spent most of his time photographing the Fleacetown chimney-pieces and the moulding of the doors. One day he came to Bella bearing a pile of calf-bound volumes from the library.

'I say, did you know you had these?' he asked.

'I did,' Bella lied.

'All first editions. They must be extremely valuable.'

'You put them back where you found them.'

Later, when he wrote to thank her for his visit – enclosing prints of some of his photographs – he mentioned the books again. This set Bella thinking. Why should that young puppy go poking round the house putting a price on every-thing? She wasn't dead yet, Bella thought. And the more she thought of it, the more repugnant it became to think of Archie Banks carrying off her books to South Kensington and removing the chimney-pieces and, as he threatened, writing an essay about the house for the *Architectural Review*. She had often heard that the books were valuable. Well, there were plenty of books in the library and she did not see why Archie Banks should profit by them. So she wrote a letter to a Dublin bookseller. He came to look through the library, and after a while he offered her twelve hundred pounds for the lot, or a thousand for the six books which had attracted Archie Banks's attention. Bella was not sure that she had the right to sell things out of the house; a wholesale clearance would be noticed. So she kept the sermons and military history which made up most of the collection, the Dublin bookseller went off with the first editions, which eventually fetched rather less than he had given, and Bella was left with winter coming on and a thousand pounds in hand.

It was then that it occurred to her to give a party. There were always several parties given round Ballingar at Christmas time, but of late years Bella had not been invited to any, partly because many of her neighbours had never spoken to her, partly because they did not think she would want to come, and partly because they would not have known what to do with her if she had. As a matter of fact she loved parties. She liked sitting down to supper in a noisy room, she liked dance music and gossip about which of the girls was pretty and who was in love with them, and she liked drink and having things brought to her by men in pink evening coats. And though she tried to console herself with contemptuous reflections about the ancestry of the hostesses, it annoyed her very much whenever she heard of a party being given in the neighbourhood to which she was not asked.

And so it came about that, sitting with the *Irish Times* under the picture of Abraham Lincoln and gazing across the bare trees of the park to the hills beyond, Bella took it into her head to give a party. She rose immediately and hobbled across the room to the bell-rope. Presently her butler came into the morning-room; he wore the green baize apron in which he cleaned the silver and in his hand he carried the plate brush to emphasize the irregularity of the summons.

'Was it yourself ringing?' he asked.

'It was, who else?'

'And I at the silver!'

'Riley,' said Bella with some solemnity, 'I propose to give a ball at Christmas.'

'Indeed!' said her butler. 'And for what would you want to be dancing at your age?' But as Bella adumbrated her idea, a sympathetic light began to glitter in Riley's eye.

'There's not been such a ball in the country for twenty-five years. It will cost a fortune.'

'It will cost a thousand pounds,' said Bella proudly.

The preparations were necessarily stupendous. Seven new servants were recruited in the village and set to work dusting and cleaning and polishing, clearing out furniture and pulling up carpets. Their industry served only to reveal fresh requirements; plaster mouldings, long rotten, crumbled under the feather brooms, worm-eaten mahogany floor-boards came up with the tin tacks; bare brick was disclosed behind the cabinets in the great drawing-room. A second wave of the invasion brought painters, paperhangers and plumbers, and in a moment of enthusiasm Bella had the cornice and the capitals of the pillars in the hall regilded; windows were reglazed, banisters fitted into gaping sockets, and the stair carpet shifted so that the worn strips were less noticeable.

In all these works Bella was indefatigable. She trotted from drawing-room to hall, down the long gallery, up the staircase, admonishing the hireling servants, lending a hand with the lighter objects of furniture, sliding, when the time came, up and down the mahogany floor of the drawing-room to work in the French chalk. She unloaded chests of silver in the attics, found long-forgotten services of china, went down with Riley into the cellars to count the few remaining and now flat and acid bottles of champagne. And in the evenings when the manual labourers had retired exhausted to their gross recreations, Bella sat up far into the night turning the pages of cookery books, comparing the estimates of rival caterers, inditing long and detailed letters to the agents for dance bands and, most important of all, drawing up her list of guests and addressing the high double piles of engraved cards that stood in her escritoire.

Distance counts for little in Ireland. People will readily drive three hours to pay an afternoon call, and for a dance of such importance no journey was too great. Bella had her list painfully compiled from works of reference, Riley's more up-to-date social knowledge and her own suddenly animated memory. Cheerfully, in a steady childish hand-writing, she transferred the names to the cards and addressed the envelopes. It was the work of several late sittings. Many of those whose names were transcribed were dead or bed-ridden; some whom she just remembered seeing as small children were reaching retiring age in remote corners of the globe; many of the houses she wrote down were blackened shells, burned during the troubles and never rebuilt; some had 'no one living in them, only farmers'. But at last, none too early, the last envelope was addressed. A final lap with the stamps and then later than usual she rose from the desk. Her limbs were stiff, her eyes dazzled, her tongue cloyed with the gum of the Free State post office; she felt a little dizzy, but she locked her desk that evening with the know-ledge that the most serious part of the work of the party was over. There had been several notable and deliberate omissions from that list.

* * *

'What's all this I hear about Bella giving a party?' said Lady Gordon to Lady Mockstock. 'I haven't had a card.'

'Neither have I yet. I hope the old thing hasn't forgotten me. I certainly intend to go. I've never been inside the house. I believe she's got some lovely things.'

With true English reserve the lady whose husband had leased Mock Hall never betrayed the knowledge that any party was in the air at all at Fleacetown.

As the last days approached Bella concentrated more upon her own appearance. She had bought few clothes of recent years, and the Dublin dressmaker with whom she used to deal had shut up shop. For a delirious instant she played with the idea of a journey to London and even Paris, and considerations of time alone obliged her to abandon it. In the end she discovered a shop to suit her, and purchased a very magnificent gown of crimson satin; to this she added long white gloves and satin shoes. There was no tiara, alas! among her jewels, but she unearthed large numbers of bright, nondescript Victorian rings, some chains and lockets, pearl brooches, turquoise earrings, and a collar of garnets. She ordered a coiffeur down from Dublin to dress her hair.

On the day of the ball she woke early, slightly feverish with nervous excitement, and wriggled in bed till she was called, restlessly rehearsing in her mind every detail of the arrangements. Before noon she had been to supervise the setting of hundreds of candles in the sconces round the ball-room and supper-room; and in the three great chandeliers of cut Waterford glass; she had seen the supper tables laid out with silver and glass and stood the massive wine coolers by the buffet; she had helped bank the staircase and hall with chrysanthemums. She had no luncheon that day, though Riley urged her with samples of the delicacies already arrived from the caterer's. She felt a little faint; lay down for a short time, but soon rallied to sew with her own hands the crested buttons on to the liveries of the hired servants.

The invitations were timed for eight o'clock. She wondered whether that were too early – she had heard tales of parties that began very late – but as the afternoon dragged on unendurably, and rich twilight enveloped the house, Bella became glad that she had set a short term on this exhausting wait.

At six she went up to dress. The hairdresser was there with a bag full of tongs and combs. He brushed and coiled her hair and whiffed it up and generally manipulated it until it became orderly and formal and apparently far more copious. She put on all her jewellery and, standing before the cheval glass in her room, could not forbear a gasp of surprise. Then she limped downstairs.

The house looked magnificent in the candle-light. The band was there, the twelve hired footmen, Riley in knee breeches and black silk stockings.

It struck eight. Bella waited. Nobody came.

She sat down on a gilt chair at the head of the stairs, looked steadily before her with her blank, blue eyes. In the hall, in the cloakroom, in the supper-room, the hired footmen looked at one another with knowing winks. 'What does the old girl expect? No one'll have finished dinner before ten.'

The linkmen on the steps stamped and chafed their hands.

At half-past twelve Bella rose from her chair. Her face gave no indication of what she was thinking.

'Riley, I think I will have some supper. I am not feeling altogether well.'

She hobbled slowly to the dining-room.

'Give me a stuffed quail and a glass of wine. Tell the band to start playing.'

The *Blue Danube* waltz flooded the house. Bella smiled approval and swayed her head a little to the rhythm.

'Riley, I am really quite hungry. I've had nothing all day. Give me another quail and some more champagne.'

Alone among the candles and the hired footmen, Riley served his mistress with an immense supper. She enjoyed every mouthful.

Presently she rose. 'I am afraid there must be some mistake. No one seems to be coming to the ball. It is very disappointing after all our trouble. You may tell the band to go home.'

But just as she was leaving the dining-room there was a stir in the hall. Guests were arriving. With wild resolution Bella swung herself up the stairs. She must get to the top before the guests were announced. One hand on the banister, one on her stick, pounding heart, two steps at a time. At last she reached the landing and turned to face the company. There was a mist before her eyes and a singing in her ears. She breathed with effort, but dimly she saw four figures advancing and saw Riley meet them and heard him announce:

'Lord and Lady Mockstock, Sir Samuel and Lady Gordon.'

Suddenly the daze in which she had been moving cleared. Here on the stairs were the two women she had not invited – Lady Mockstock the draper's daughter, Lady Gordon the American.

She drew herself up and fixed them with her blank, blue eyes.

'I had not expected this honour,' she said. 'Please forgive me if I am unable to entertain you.'

The Mockstocks and the Gordons stood aghast; saw the

mad blue eyes of their hostess, her crimson dress; the ball-room beyond, looking immense in its emptiness; heard the dance music echoing through the empty house. The air was charged with the scent of chrysanthemums. And then the drama and unreality of the scene were dispelled. Miss Fleace suddenly sat down, and holding out her hands to her butler, said, 'I don't quite know what's happening.'

He and two of the hired footmen carried the old lady to a sofa. She spoke only once more. Her mind was still on the same subject. 'They came uninvited, those two . . . and nobody else.'

A day later she died.

Mr Banks arrived for the funeral and spent a week sorting out her effects. Among them he found in her escritoire, stamped, addressed, but unposted, the invitations to the ball.

ELIZABETH BOWEN

GREEN HOLLY

MR RANKSTOCK ENTERED the room with a dragging tread: nobody looked up or took any notice. With a muted groan, he dropped into an armchair – out of which he shot with a sharp yelp. He searched the seat of the chair, and extracted something. '*Your* holly, I think, Miss Bates,' he said, holding it out to her.

Miss Bates took a second or two to look up from her magazine. 'What?' she said. 'Oh, it must have fallen down from that picture. Put it back, please; we haven't got very much.'

'I regret,' interposed Mr Winterslow, 'that we have any: it makes scratchy noises against the walls.'

'It is seasonable,' said Miss Bates firmly.

'You didn't do this to us last Christmas.'

'Last Christmas,' she said, 'I had Christmas leave. This year there seems to be none with berries: the birds have eaten them. If there were not a draught, the leaves would not scratch the walls. I cannot control the forces of nature, can I?'

'How should I know?' said Mr Rankstock, lighting his pipe.

These three by now felt that, like Chevalier and his Old Dutch, they had been together for forty years: and to them it did seem a year too much. Actually, their confinement dated from 1940. They were Experts – in what, the Censor would not permit me to say. They were accounted for by their friends in London as 'being somewhere off in the country, nobody knows where, doing something frightfully hush-hush, nobody knows what'. That is, they were accounted for in this manner if there were still anybody who still cared to ask; but on the whole they had dropped out of human memory. Their reappearances in their former circles were infrequent, ghostly and unsuccessful: their friends could hardly disguise their pity, and for their own part they had not a word to say. They had come to prefer to spend leaves with their families, who at least showed a flattering pleasure in their importance.

This Christmas, it so worked out that there was no question of leave for Mr Rankstock, Mr Winterslow or Miss Bates: with four others (now playing or watching ping-pong in the next room) they composed in their high-grade way a skeleton staff. It may be wondered why, after years of proximity, they should continue to address one another so formally. They did not continue; they had begun again; in the matter of appellations, as in that of intimacy, they had by now, in fact by some time ago, completed the full circle. For some months, they could not recall in which year, Miss Bates had been engaged to Mr Winterslow; before that, she had been extremely friendly with Mr Rankstock. Mr Rankstock's deviation towards one Carla (now at her ping-pong in the next room) had been totally uninteresting to everybody; including, apparently, himself. If the war lasted, Carla might next year be called Miss Tongue; at present, Miss Bates was foremost in keeping her in her place by going on addressing her by her Christian name.

If this felt like their fortieth Christmas in each other's society, it was their first in these particular quarters. You would not have thought, as Mr Rankstock said, that one country house could be much worse than any other; but this had proved, and was still proving, untrue. The Army, for reasons it failed to justify, wanted the house they had been in since 1940; so they – lock, stock and barrel and files and all – had been bundled into another one, six miles away. Since the move, tentative exploration (for they were none of them walkers) had established that they were now surrounded by rather more mud but fewer trees. What they did know was, their already sufficient distance from the market town with its bars and movies had now been added to by six miles. On the other side of their new home, which was called Mopsam Grange, there appeared to be nothing; unless, as Miss Bates suggested, swineherds, keeping their swine. Mopsam village contained villagers, evacuees, a church, a public-house on whose never-open door was chalked 'No Beer, No Matches, No Teas Served', and a vicar. The vicar had sent up a nice note, saying he was not clear whether security regulations would allow him to call; and the doctor had been up once to lance one of Carla's boils.

Mopsam Grange was neither old nor new. It replaced – unnecessarily, they all felt – a house on this site that had been burned down. It had a Gothic porch and gables, french windows, bow windows, a conservatory, a veranda, a hall which, puce-and-buff tiled and pitch-pine-panelled, rose to a gallery: in fact, every advantage. Jackdaws fidgeted in its many chimneys – for it had, till the war, stood empty: one had not to ask why. The hot-water system made what Carla called rude noises, and was capricious in its supplies to the (only) two mahogany-rimmed baths. The electric light ran from a plant in the yard; if the batteries were not kept charged the light turned brown.

The three now sat in the drawing-room, on whose walls, mirrors and fitments, long since removed, left traces. There were, however, some pictures: General Montgomery (who

261

had just shed his holly) and some Landseer engravings that had been found in an attic. Three electric bulbs, naked, shed light manfully; and in the grate the coal fire was doing far from badly. Miss Bates rose and stood twiddling the bit of holly. 'Something,' she said, 'has got to be done about this.' Mr Winterslow and Mr Rankstock, the latter sucking in his pipe, sank lower, between their shoulder-blades, in their respective armchairs. Miss Bates, having drawn a breath, took a running jump at a table, which she propelled across the floor with a grating sound. '*Achtung!*' she shouted, at Mr Rankstock, who, with an oath, withdrew his chair from her route. Having got the table under General Montgomery, Miss Bates – with a display of long, slender leg, clad in ribbed scarlet sports stockings, that was of interest to no one – mounted it, then proceeded to tuck the holly back into position over the General's frame. Meanwhile, Mr Winterslow, choosing his moment, stealthily reached across her empty chair and possessed himself of her magazine.

What a hope! – Miss Bates was known to have eyes all the way down her spine. 'Damn you, Mr Winterslow,' she said, 'put that down! Mr Rankstock, interfere with Mr Winterslow: Mr Winterslow has taken my magazine!' She ran up and down the table like something in a cage; Mr Rankstock removed his pipe from his mouth, dropped his head back, gazed up and said: 'Gad, Miss Bates; you look fine . . .'

'It's a pretty *old* magazine,' murmured Mr Winterslow flicking the pages over.

'Well, *you're* pretty old,' she said. 'I hope Carla gets you!'

'Oh, I can do better, thank you; I've got a ghost.'

This confidence, however, was cut off by Mr Rankstock's having burst into song. Holding his pipe at arm's length, rocking on his bottom in his armchair, he led them:

' "Heigh-ho! sing Heigh-ho! unto the green holly:
Most friendship is feigning, most loving mere folly –" '

' "*Mere folly, mere folly*," ' contributed Mr Winterslow, picking up, joining in. Both sang:

' "*Then, heigh ho, the holly!
This life is most jolly.*" '

'Now – *all*!' said Mr Rankstock, jerking his pipe at Miss Bates. So all three went through it once more, with degrees of passion: Miss Bates, when others desisted, being left singing 'Heigh-ho! sing heigh-ho! sing –' all by herself. Next door, the ping-pong came to an awe-struck stop. 'At any rate,' said Mr Rankstock, 'we all like Shakespeare.' Miss Bates, whose intelligence, like her singing, tonight seemed some way at the tail of the hunt, looked blank, began to get off the table, and said, 'But I thought that was a Christmas carol?'

Her companions shrugged and glanced at each other. Having taken her magazine away from Mr Winterslow, she was once more settling down to it when she seemed struck. 'What was that you said, about you had got a ghost?'

Mr Winterslow looked down his nose. 'At this early stage, I don't like to say very much. In fact, on the whole, forget it; if you don't mind –'

'Look,' Mr Rankstock said, 'if you've started seeing things –'

'I am only sorry,' his colleague said, 'that I've spoke.'

'Oh no, you're not,' said Miss Bates, 'and we'd better know. Just what *is* fishy about this Grange?'

'There is nothing "fishy",' said Mr Winterslow in a fastidious tone. It was hard, indeed, to tell from his manner whether he did or did not regret having made a start. He had reddened – but not, perhaps, wholly painfully – his eyes, now fixed on the fire, were at once bright and vacant; with unheeding, fumbling movements he got out a cigarette, lit it and dropped the match on the floor, to slowly burn one more hole in the fibre mat. Gripping the cigarette between tense lips, he first flung his arms out, as though casting off a cloak; then pressed both hands, clasped firmly, to the nerve-centre in the nape of his neck, as though to contain the sensation there. 'She was marvellous,' he brought out – 'what I could see of her.'

'Don't talk with your cigarette in your mouth,' Miss Bates said. '– Young?'

'Adorably, not so very. At the same time, quite – oh well, you know what I mean.'

'Uh-hu,' said Miss Bates. 'And wearing –?'

'I am certain she had a feather boa.'

'You mean,' Mr Rankstock said, 'that this brushed your face?'

'And when and where did this happen?' said Miss Bates with legal coldness.

Cross-examination, clearly, became more and more repugnant to Mr Winterslow in his present mood. He shut his eyes, sighed bitterly, heaved himself from his chair, said: 'Oh, well –' and stood indecisively looking towards the door. 'Don't let us keep you,' said Miss Bates. 'But one thing I don't see is: if you're being fed with beautiful thoughts, why you wanted to keep on taking my magazine?'

'I wanted to be distracted.'

'?'

'There *are* moments when I don't quite know where I am.'

'You surprise me,' said Mr Rankstock. – 'Good *God* man, what is the matter?' For Mr Winterslow, like a man being swooped around by a bat, was revolving, staring from place

264

to place high up round the walls of the gaunt, lit room. Miss Bates observed: 'Well, now we *have* started something.' Mr Rankstock, considerably kinder, said: 'That is only Miss Bates's holly, flittering in the wind.'

Mr Winterslow gulped. He walked to the inch of mirror propped on the mantelpiece and, as nonchalantly as possible, straightened his tie. Having done this, he said: 'But there isn't a wind tonight.'

The ghost hesitated in the familiar corridor. Her visibleness, even on Christmas Eve, was not under her own control; and now she had fallen in love again her dependence upon it began to dissolve in patches. This was a concentration of every feeling of the woman prepared to sail downstairs *en grande tenue*. Flamboyance and agitation were both present. But between these, because of her years of death, there cut an extreme anxiety: it was not merely a matter of, how was she? but of, *was* she – tonight – at all? Death had left her to be her own mirror; for into no other was she able to see.

For tonight, she had discarded the feather boa; it had been dropped into the limbo that was her wardrobe now. Her shoulders, she knew, were bare. Round their bareness shimmered a thousand evenings. Her own person haunted her – above her forehead, the crisped springy weight of her pompadour; round her feet the frou-frou of her skirts on a thick carpet; in her nostrils the scent from her corsage; up and down her forearm the glittery slipping of bracelets warmed by her own blood. It is the haunted who haunt.

There were lights in the house again. She had heard laughter, and there had been singing. From those few dim lights and untrue notes her senses, after their starvation, set going the whole old grand opera. She smiled, and moved down the corridor to the gallery, where she stood looking down into the hall. The tiles of the hall floor were as pretty as ever, as cold as ever, and bore, as always on Christmas Eve, the trickling pattern of dark blood. The figure of the man with the side of his head blown out lay as always, one foot just touching the lowest step of the stairs. It was too bad. She had been silly, but it could not be helped. They should not have shut her up in the country. How could she not make hay while the sun shone? The year round, no man except her husband, his uninteresting jealousy, his dull passion. Then, at Christmas, so many men that one did not know where to turn. The ghost, leaning further over the gallery, pouted down at the suicide. She said: 'You should have let me explain.' The man made no answer: he never had.

Behind a door somewhere downstairs, a racket was going on: the house sounded funny, there were no carpets. The morning-room door was flung open and four flushed people, headed by a young woman, charged out. They clattered across the man and the trickling pattern as though there were nothing there but the tiles. In the morning-room she saw one small white ball trembling to stillness upon the floor. As the people rushed the stairs and fought for place in the gallery the ghost drew back – a purest act of repugnance, for this was not necessary. The young woman, to one of whose temples was strapped a cotton-wool pad, held her place and disappeared round a corner exulting: '*My* bath, *my* bath!' 'Then may you freeze in it, Carla!' returned the scrawniest of the defeated ones. The words pierced the ghost, who trembled – they did not know!

Who were they? She did not ask. She did not care. She never had been inquisitive: information had bored her. Her schooled lips had framed one set of questions, her eyes a consuming other. Now the mills of death with their catching wheels had stripped her of semblance, cast her forth on an everlasting holiday from pretence. She was left with – nay, had become – her obsession. Thus is it to be a ghost. The ghost fixed her eyes on the other, the drawing-room door. He had gone in there. He would have to come out again.

The handle turned; the door opened; Winterslow came out. He shut the door behind him, with the sedulous slowness of an uncertain man. He had been humming, and now, squaring his shoulders, began to sing, '... *Mere folly, mere folly* –' as he crossed the hall towards the foot of the staircase, obstinately never raising his eyes. 'So it is you,' breathed the ghost, with unheard softness. She gathered about her, with a gesture not less proud for being tormentedly uncertain, the total of her visibility – was it possible diamonds should not glitter now, on her rising-and-falling breast – and swept from the gallery to the head of the stairs.

Winterslow shivered violently, and looked up. He licked his lips. He said: 'This cannot go on.'

The ghost's eyes, with tender impartiality and mockery, from above swept Winterslow's face. The hair receding, the furrowed forehead, the tired sag of the jowl, the strain-reddened eyelids, the blue-shaved chin – nothing was lost on her, nothing broke the spell. With untroubled wonder she saw his handwoven tie, his coat pockets shapeless as saddle-bags, the bulging knees of his flannel trousers. Wonder went up in rhapsody: so much chaff in the fire. She never had had illusions: *the* illusion was all. Lovers cannot be choosers. He'd do. He would have to do. – 'I know!' she agreed, with rapture, casting her hands together. 'We are mad – you and I. Oh, what is going to happen? I entreat you to leave this house tonight!'

Winterslow, in a dank, unresounding voice, said: 'And anyhow, what made you pick on me?'

267

'It's Kismet,' wailed the ghost zestfully. 'Why did you have to come here? Why you? I had been so peaceful, just like a little girl. People spoke of love, but I never knew what they meant. Oh, I could wish we had never met, you and I!'

Winterslow said: 'I have been here for three months; we have all of us been here, as a matter of fact. Why all this all of a sudden?'

She said: 'There's a Christmas Eve party, isn't there, going on? One Christmas Eve party, there was a terrible accident. Oh, comfort me! No one has understood. – Don't stand *there*; I can't bear it – not just *there*!'

Winterslow, whether he heard or not, cast a scared glance down at his feet, which were in slippers, then shifted a pace or two to the left. 'Let me up,' he said wildly. 'I tell you, I want my spectacles! I just want to get my spectacles. Let me by!'

'*Let* you up!' the ghost marvelled. 'But I am only waiting...'

She was more than waiting: she set up a sort of suction, an icy indrawing draught. Nor was this wholly psychic, for an isolated holly leaf of Miss Bates's, dropped at a turn of the staircase, twitched. And not, you could think, by chance did the electric light choose this moment for one of its brown fade-outs: gradually, the scene – the hall, the stairs and the gallery – faded under this fog-dark but glass-clear veil of hallucination. The feet of Winterslow, under remote control, began with knocking unsureness to mount the stairs. At their turn he staggered, steadied himself, and then stamped derisively upon the holly leaf. 'Bah,' he neighed – '*spectacles*!'

By the ghost now putting out everything, not a word could be dared.

'Where are you?'

Weakly, her dress rustled, three steps down: the rings on her hand knocked weakly over the panelling. 'Here, oh here,' she sobbed. 'Where I was before . . .'

'Hell,' said Miss Bates, who had opened the drawing-room door and was looking resentfully round the hall. 'This electric light.'

Mr Rankstock, from inside the drawing-room, said: 'Find the man.'

'The man has gone to the village. Mr Rankstock, if *you* were half a man –. Mr Winterslow, what are you doing, kneeling down on the stairs? Have you come over funny? Really, this is the end.'

At the other side of a baize door, one of the installations began ringing. 'Mr Rankstock,' Miss Bates yelled implacably, 'yours, this time.' Mr Rankstock, with an expression of hatred, whipped out a pencil and pad and shambled across the hall. Under cover of this Mr Winterslow pushed himself upright, brushed his knees and began to descend the stairs, to confront his colleague's narrow but not unkind look. Weeks of exile from any hairdresser had driven Miss Bates to the Alice-in-Wonderland style: her snood, tied at the top, was now thrust back, adding inches to her pale, polished brow. Nicotine stained the fingers she closed upon Mr Winterslow's elbow, propelling him back to the drawing-room. 'There is always drink,' she said. 'Come along.'

He said hopelessly: 'If you mean the bottle between the filing cabinets, I finished that when I had to work last night. – Look here, Miss Bates, why should she have picked on *me*?'

'It has been broken off, then?' said Miss Bates. 'I'm sorry for you, but I don't like your tone. I resent your attitude to my sex. For that matter, why did you pick on her? Romantic, nostalgic Blue-Danube-fixated – hein? There's Carla, an understanding girl, unselfish, getting over her boils; there are Avice and Lettice, due back on Boxing Day. There is me, as you have ceased to observe. But oh dear no; *we* do not trail feather boas –'

'– She only wore that in the afternoon.'

'Now let me tell you something,' said Miss Bates. 'When I opened the door, just now, to have a look at the lights, what do you think *I* first saw there in the hall?'

'Me,' replied Mr Winterslow, with returning assurance.

'O-*oh* no; oh indeed no,' said Miss Bates. 'You – why should I think twice of that, if you *were* striking attitudes on the stairs? You? – no, I saw your enchanting inverse. Extended, and it is true stone dead, I saw the man of my dreams. From his attitude, it was clear he had died for love. There were three pearl studs in his boiled shirt, and his white tie must have been tied in heaven. And the hand that had dropped the pistol had dropped a white rose; it lay beside him brown and crushed from having been often kissed. The ideality of those kisses, for the last of which I arrived too late –' here Miss Bates beat her fist against the bow of her snood – 'will haunt, and by haunting satisfy me. The destruction of his features, before I saw them, made their former perfection certain, where I am concerned. – And here I am, left, left, left, to watch dust gather on Mr Rankstock and you; to watch – yes, I who saw in a flash the ink-black perfection of *his* tailoring – mildew form on those clothes that you never change; to remember how both of you had in common that way of blowing your noses before you kissed me. He had been deceived – hence the shot, hence the fall. But who was *she*, your feathered friend, to deceive him? Who could have deceived him more superbly than I? – *I* could be fatal,' moaned Miss Bates, pacing the drawing-room. '*I* could be fatal – only give me a break!'

'Well, I'm sorry,' said Mr Winterslow, 'but really, what can I do, or poor Rankstock do? We are just ourselves.'

'You put the thing in a nutshell,' said Miss Bates. 'Perhaps I could bear it if you just got your hairs cut.'

'If it comes to that, Miss Bates, you might get yours set.'

Mr Rankstock's re-entry into the drawing-room – this time with brisker step, for a nice little lot of new trouble was brewing up – synchronized with the fall of the piece of holly, again, from the General's frame to the Rankstock chair. This time he saw it in time, '*Your* holly, I think, Miss Bates,' he said, holding it out to her.

'We must put it back,' said Miss Bates. 'We haven't got very much.'

'I cannot see,' said Mr Winterslow, 'why we should have any. I don't see the point of holly without berries.'

'The birds have eaten them,' said Miss Bates. 'I cannot control the forces of nature, can I?'

'*Then heigh-ho! sing heigh-ho! –*' Mr Rankstock led off.

'Yes,' she said, 'let us have that pretty carol again.'

JOHN CHEEVER

CHRISTMAS IS A SAD SEASON FOR THE POOR

CHRISTMAS IS A sad season. The phrase came to Charlie an instant after the alarm clock had waked him, and named for him an amorphous depression that had troubled him all the previous evening. The sky outside his window was black. He sat up in bed and pulled the light chain that hung in front of his nose. Christmas is a very sad day of the year, he thought. Of all the millions of people in New York, I am practically the only one who has to get up in the cold black of 6 a.m. on Christmas Day in the morning; I am practically the only one.

He dressed, and when he went downstairs from the top floor of the rooming house in which he lived, the only sounds he heard were the coarse sounds of sleep; the only lights burning were lights that had been forgotten. Charlie ate some breakfast in an all-night lunchwagon and took an Elevated train uptown. From Third Avenue, he walked over to Park. Park Avenue was dark. House after house put into the shine of the street lights a wall of black windows. Millions and millions were sleeping, and this general loss of consciousness generated an impression of abandonment, as if this were the fall of the city, the end of time. He opened the iron-and-glass doors of the apartment building where he had been working for six months as an elevator operator, and went through the elegant lobby to a locker room at the back. He put on a striped vest with brass buttons, a false ascot, a pair of pants with a light-blue stripe on the seam,

275

and a coat. The night elevator man was dozing on the little bench in the car. Charlie woke him. The night elevator man told him thickly that the day doorman had been taken sick and wouldn't be in that day. With the doorman sick, Charlie wouldn't have any relief for lunch, and a lot of people would expect him to whistle for cabs.

Charlie had been on duty a few minutes when 14 rang – a Mrs Hewing, who, he happened to know, was kind of immoral. Mrs Hewing hadn't been to bed yet, and she got into the elevator wearing a long dress under her fur coat. She was followed by her two funny-looking dogs. He took her down and watched her go out into the dark and take her dogs to the curb. She was outside for only a few minutes. Then she came in and he took her up to 14 again. When she got off the elevator, she said, 'Merry Christmas, Charlie.'

'Well, it isn't much of a holiday for me, Mrs Hewing,' he said. 'I think Christmas is a very sad season of the year. It isn't that people around here ain't generous – I mean I got plenty of tips – but, you see, I live alone in a furnished room and I don't have any family or anything, and Christmas isn't much of a holiday for me.'

'I'm sorry, Charlie,' Mrs Hewing said. 'I don't have any family myself. It is kind of sad when you're alone, isn't it?' She called her dogs and followed them into her apartment. He went down.

It was quiet then, and Charlie lighted a cigarette. The heating plant in the basement encompassed the building at that hour in a regular and profound vibration, and the sullen noises of arriving steam heat began to resound, first in the lobby and then to reverberate up through all the sixteen stories, but this was a mechanical awakening, and it didn't lighten his loneliness or his petulance. The black air outside the glass doors had begun to turn blue, but the blue light seemed to have no source; it appeared in the middle of the air. It was a tearful light, and as it picked out the empty street and the long file of Christmas trees, he wanted to cry. Then a cab drove up, and the Walsers got out, drunk and dressed in evening clothes, and he took them up to their penthouse. The Walsers got him to brooding about the difference between his life in a furnished room and the lives of the people overhead. It was terrible.

Then the early churchgoers began to ring, but there were only three of these that morning. A few more went off to church at eight o'clock, but the majority of the building remained unconscious, although the smell of bacon and coffee had begun to drift into the elevator shaft.

At a little after nine, a nursemaid came down with a child. Both the nursemaid and the child had a deep tan and had just returned, he knew, from Bermuda. He had never been to Bermuda. He, Charlie, was a prisoner, confined eight hours a day to a six-by-eight elevator cage, which was confined, in turn, to a sixteen-story shaft. In one building or another, he had made his living as an elevator operator for ten years. He estimated the average trip at about an eighth of a mile, and when he thought of the thousands of miles he had travelled, when he thought that he might have driven the car through the mists above the Caribbean and set it down on some coral beach in Bermuda, he held the narrowness of his travels against his passengers, as if it were not the nature of the elevator but the pressure of their lives that confined him, as if they had clipped his wings.

He was thinking about this when the DePauls, on 9, rang. They wished him a merry Christmas.

'Well, it's nice of you to think of me,' he said as they descended, 'but it isn't much of a holiday for me. Christmas is a sad season when you're poor. I live alone in a furnished room. I don't have any family.'

'Who do you have dinner with, Charlie?' Mrs DePaul asked.

'I don't have any Christmas dinner,' Charlie said. 'I just get a sandwich.'

'Oh, Charlie!' Mrs DePaul was a stout woman with an impulsive heart, and Charlie's plaint struck at her holiday mood as if she had been caught in a cloudburst. 'I do wish we could share our Christmas dinner with you, you know,' she said. 'I come from Vermont, you know, and when I was a child, you know, we always used to have a great many people at our table. The mailman, you know, and the school-teacher, and just anybody who didn't have any family of their own, you know, and I wish we could share our dinner with you the way we used to, you know, and I don't see any reason why we can't. We can't have you at the table, you know, because you couldn't leave the elevator – could you? – but just as soon as Mr DePaul has carved the goose, I'll give you a ring, and I'll arrange a tray for you, you know, and I want you to come up and at least share our Christmas dinner.'

Charlie thanked them, and their generosity surprised him, but he wondered if, with the arrival of friends and relatives, they wouldn't forget their offer.

Then old Mrs Gadshill rang, and when she wished him a merry Christmas, he hung his head.

'It isn't much of a holiday for me, Mrs Gadshill,' he said. 'Christmas is a sad season if you're poor. You see, I don't have any family. I live alone in a furnished room.'

'I don't have any family either, Charlie,' Mrs Gadshill said. She spoke with a pointed lack of petulance, but her grace was forced. 'That is, I don't have any children with me today. I have three children and seven grandchildren,

278

but none of them can see their way to coming East for Christmas with me. Of course, I understand their problems. I know that it's difficult to travel with children during the holidays, although I always seemed to manage it when I was their age, but people feel differently, and we mustn't condemn them for the things we can't understand. But I know how you feel, Charlie. I haven't any family either. I'm just as lonely as you.'

Mrs Gadshill's speech didn't move him. Maybe she was lonely, but she had a ten-room apartment and three servants and bucks and bucks and diamonds and diamonds, and there were plenty of poor kids in the slums who would be happy at a chance at the food her cook threw away. Then he thought about poor kids. He sat down on a chair in the lobby and thought about them.

They got the worst of it. Beginning in the fall, there was all this excitement about Christmas and how it was a day for them. After Thanksgiving, they couldn't miss it. It was fixed so they couldn't miss it. The wreaths and decorations everywhere, and bells ringing, and trees in the park, and Santa Clauses on every corner and pictures in the magazines and newspapers and on every wall and window in the city told them that if they were good, they would get what they wanted. Even if they couldn't read, they couldn't miss it. They couldn't miss it even if they were blind. It got into the air the poor kids inhaled. Every time they took a walk, they'd see all the expensive toys in the store windows, and they'd write letters to Santa Claus, and their mothers and fathers would promise to mail them, and after the kids had gone to sleep, they'd burn the letters in the stove. And when it came Christmas morning, how could you explain it, how could you tell them that Santa Claus only visited the rich, that he didn't know about the good? How could you face them when all you had to give them was a balloon or a lollipop?

On the way home from work a few nights earlier, Charlie had seen a woman and a little girl going down Fifty-ninth Street. The little girl was crying. He guessed she was crying, he knew she was crying, because she'd seen all the things in the toy-store windows and couldn't understand why none of them were for her. Her mother did housework, he guessed, or maybe was a waitress, and he saw them going back to a room like his, with green walls and no heat, on Christmas Eve, to eat a can of soup. And he saw the little girl hang up her ragged stocking and fall asleep, and he saw the mother looking through her purse for something to put into the stocking – This reverie was interrupted by a bell on 11. He went up, and Mr and Mrs Fuller were waiting. When they wished him a merry Christmas, he said, 'Well, it isn't much of a holiday for me, Mrs Fuller. Christmas is a sad season when you're poor.'

'Do you have any children, Charlie?' Mrs Fuller asked.

'Four living,' he said. 'Two in the grave.' The majesty of his lie overwhelmed him. 'Mrs Leary's a cripple,' he added.

'How sad, Charlie,' Mrs Fuller said. She started out of the elevator when it reached the lobby, and then she turned. 'I want to give your children some presents, Charlie,' she said. 'Mr Fuller and I are going to pay a call now, but when we come back, I want to give you some things for your children.'

He thanked her. Then the bell rang on 4, and he went up to get the Westons.

'It isn't much of a holiday for me,' he told them when they wished him a merry Christmas. 'Christmas is a sad season when you're poor. You see, I live alone in a furnished room.'

'Poor Charlie,' Mrs Weston said. 'I know just how you feel. During the war, when Mr Weston was away, I was all alone at Christmas. I didn't have any Christmas dinner or a tree or anything. I just scrambled myself some eggs and sat there and cried.' Mr Weston, who had gone into the lobby, called impatiently to his wife. 'I know just how you feel, Charlie,' Mrs Weston said.

By noon, the climate in the elevator shaft had changed from bacon and coffee to poultry and game, and the house, like an enormous and complex homestead, was absorbed in the preparations for a domestic feast. The children and their nursemaids had all returned from the Park. Grandmothers and aunts were arriving in limousines. Most of the people who came through the lobby were carrying packages wrapped in colored paper, and were wearing their best furs and new clothes. Charlie continued to complain to most of the tenants when they wished him a merry Christmas, changing his story from the lonely bachelor to the poor father, and back again, as his mood changed, but this outpouring of melancholy, and the sympathy it aroused, didn't make him feel any better.

At half past one, 9 rang, and when he went up, Mr DePaul was standing in the door of their apartment holding a cocktail shaker and a glass. 'Here's a little Christmas cheer, Charlie,' he said, and he poured Charlie a drink. Then a maid appeared with a tray of covered dishes, and Mrs DePaul came out of the living room. 'Merry Christmas, Charlie,' she said. 'I had Mr DePaul carve the goose early, so that you could have some, you know. I didn't want to put the dessert on the tray, because I was afraid it would melt, you know, so when we have our dessert, we'll call you.'

'And what is Christmas without presents?' Mr DePaul

said, and he brought a large, flat box from the hall and laid it on top of the covered dishes.

'You people make it seem like a real Christmas to me,' Charlie said. Tears started into his eyes. 'Thank you, thank you.'

'Merry Christmas! Merry Christmas!' they called, and they watched him carry his dinner and his present into the elevator. He took the tray and the box into the locker room when he got down. On the tray, there was a soup, some kind of creamed fish, and a serving of goose. The bell rang again, but before he answered it, he tore open the DePauls' box and saw that it held a dressing gown. Their generosity and their cocktail had begun to work on his brain, and he went jubilantly up to 12. Mrs Gadshill's maid was standing in the door with a tray, and Mrs Gadshill stood behind her. 'Merry Christmas, Charlie!' she said. He thanked her, and tears came into his eyes again. On the way down, he drank off the glass of sherry on Mrs Gadshill's tray. Mrs Gadshill's contribution was a mixed grill. He ate the lamb chop with his fingers. The bell was ringing again, and he wiped his face with a paper towel and went up to 11. 'Merry Christmas, Charlie,' Mrs Fuller said, and she was standing in the door with her arms full of packages wrapped in silver paper, just like a picture in an advertisement, and Mr Fuller was beside her with an arm around her, and they both looked as if they were going to cry. 'Here are some things I want you to take home to your children,' Mrs Fuller said. 'And here's something for Mrs Leary and here's something for you. And if you want to take these things out to the elevator, we'll have your dinner ready for you in a minute.' He carried the things into the elevator and came back for the tray. 'Merry Christmas, Charlie!' both of the Fullers called after him as he closed the door. He took their dinner and their presents

282

into the locker room and tore open the box that was marked for him. There was an alligator wallet in it, with Mr Fuller's initials in the corner. Their dinner was also goose, and he ate a piece of the meat with his fingers and was washing it down with a cocktail when the bell rang. He went up again. This time it was the Westons. 'Merry Christmas, Charlie!' they said, and they gave him a cup of eggnog, a turkey dinner, and a present. Their gift was also a dressing gown. Then 7 rang, and when he went up, there was another dinner and some more toys. Then 14 rang, and when he went up, Mrs Hewing was standing in the hall, in a kind of negligee, holding a pair of riding boots in one hand and some neckties in the other. She had been crying and drinking. 'Merry Christmas, Charlie,' she said tenderly. 'I wanted to give you something, and I've been thinking about you all morning, and I've been all over the apartment, and these are the only things I could find that a man might want. These are the only things that Mr Brewer left. I don't suppose you'd have any use for the riding boots, but wouldn't you like the neckties?' Charlie took the neckties and thanked her and hurried back to the car, for the elevator bell had rung three times.

By three o'clock, Charlie had fourteen dinners spread on the table and the floor of the locker room, and the bell kept ringing. Just as he started to eat one, he would have to go up and get another, and he was in the middle of the Parsons' roast beef when he had to go up and get the DePauls' dessert. He kept the door of the locker room closed, for he sensed that the quality of charity is exclusive and that his friends would have been disappointed to find that they were not the only ones to try to lessen his loneliness. There were goose, turkey, chicken, pheasant, grouse, and pigeon. There were trout and salmon, creamed scallops

283

and oysters, lobster, crabmeat, whitebait, and clams. There were plum puddings, mince pies, mousses, puddles of melted ice cream, layer cakes, *Torten*, éclairs, and two slices of Bavarian cream. He had dressing gowns, neckties, cuff links, socks, and handkerchiefs, and one of the tenants had asked for his neck size and then given him three green shirts. There were a glass teapot filled, the label said, with jasmine honey, four bottles of aftershave lotion, some alabaster bookends, and a dozen steak knives. The avalanche of charity he had precipitated filled the locker room and made him hesitant, now and then, as if he had touched some wellspring in the female heart that would bury him alive in food and dressing gowns. He had made almost no headway on the food, for all the servings were preternaturally large, as if loneliness had been counted on to generate in him a brutish appetite. Nor had he opened any of the presents that had been given to him for his imaginary children, but he had drunk everything they sent down, and around him were the dregs of Martinis, Manhattans, Old-Fashioneds, champagne-and-raspberry shrub cocktails, eggnogs, Bronxes, and Side Cars.

His face was blazing. He loved the world, and the world loved him. When he thought back over his life, it appeared to him in a rich and wonderful light, full of astonishing experiences and unusual friends. He thought that his job as an elevator operator — cruising up and down through hundreds of feet of perilous space — demanded the nerve and the intellect of a birdman. All the constraints of his life — the green walls of his room and the months of unemployment — dissolved. No one was ringing, but he got into the elevator and shot it at full speed up to the penthouse and down again, up and down, to test his wonderful mastery of space.

A bell rang on 12 while he was cruising, and he stopped in his flight long enough to pick up Mrs Gadshill. As the car started to fall, he took his hands off the controls in a paroxysm of joy and shouted, 'Strap on your safety belt, Mrs Gadshill! We're going to make a loop-the-loop!' Mrs Gadshill shrieked. Then, for some reason, she sat down on the floor of the elevator. Why was her face so pale, he wondered; why was she sitting on the floor? She shrieked again. He grounded the car gently, and cleverly, he thought, and opened the door. 'I'm sorry if I scared you, Mrs Gadshill,' he said meekly. 'I was only fooling.' She shrieked again. Then she ran out into the lobby, screaming for the superintendent.

The superintendent fired Charlie and took over the elevator himself. The news that he was out of work stung Charlie for a minute. It was his first contact with human meanness that day. He sat down in the locker room and gnawed on a drumstick. His drinks were beginning to let him down, and while it had not reached him yet, he felt a miserable soberness in the offing. The excess of food and presents around him began to make him feel guilty and unworthy. He regretted bitterly the lie he had told about his children. He was a single man with simple needs. He had abused the goodness of the people upstairs. He was unworthy.

Then up through this drunken train of thought surged the sharp figure of his landlady and her three skinny children. He thought of them sitting in their basement room. The cheer of Christmas had passed them by. This image got him to his feet. The realization that he was in a position to give, that he could bring happiness easily to someone else, sobered him. He took a big burlap sack, which was used for collecting waste, and began to stuff it, first with his presents and then with the presents for his imaginary

285

children. He worked with the haste of a man whose train is approaching the station, for he could hardly wait to see those long faces light up when he came in the door. He changed his clothes, and, fired by a wonderful and unfamiliar sense of power, he slung his bag over his shoulder like a regular Santa Claus, went out the back way, and took a taxi to the lower East Side.

The landlady and her children had just finished off a turkey, which had been sent to them by the local Democratic Club, and they were stuffed and uncomfortable when Charlie began pounding on the door, shouting 'Merry Christmas!' He dragged the bag in after him and dumped the presents for the children onto the floor. There were dolls and musical toys, blocks, sewing kits, an Indian suit, and a loom, and it appeared to him that, as he had hoped, his arrival in the basement dispelled its gloom. When half the presents had been opened, he gave the landlady a bathrobe and went upstairs to look over the things he had been given for himself.

Now, the landlady's children had already received so many presents by the time Charlie arrived that they were confused with receiving, and it was only the landlady's intuitive grasp of the nature of charity that made her allow the children to open some of the presents while Charlie was still in the room, but as soon as he had gone, she stood between the children and the presents that were still unopened. 'Now, you kids have had enough already,' she said. 'You kids have got your share. Just look at the things you got there. Why, you ain't even played with the half of them. Mary Anne, you ain't even looked at that doll the Fire Department give you. Now, a nice thing to do would be to take all this stuff that's left over to those poor people on Hudson Street – them Deckkers.

286

They ain't got nothing.' A beatific light came into her face when she realized that she could give, that she could bring cheer, that she could put a healing finger on a case needier than hers, and – like Mrs DePaul and Mrs Weston, like Charlie himself and like Mrs Deckker, when Mrs Deckker was to think, subsequently, of the poor Shannons – first love, then charity, and then a sense of power drove her. 'Now, you kids help me get all this stuff together. Hurry, hurry, hurry,' she said, for it was dark then, and she knew that we are bound, one to another, in licentious benevolence for only a single day, and that day was nearly over. She was tired, but she couldn't rest, she couldn't rest.

TRUMAN CAPOTE

A CHRISTMAS
MEMORY

IMAGINE A MORNING in late November. A coming of winter morning more than twenty years ago. Consider the kitchen of a spreading old house in a country town. A great black stove is its main feature; but there is also a big round table and a fireplace with two rocking chairs placed in front of it. Just today the fireplace commenced its seasonal roar.

A woman with shorn white hair is standing at the kitchen window. She is wearing tennis shoes and a shapeless gray sweater over a summery calico dress. She is small and sprightly, like a bantam hen; but, due to a long youthful illness, her shoulders are pitifully hunched. Her face is remarkable – not unlike Lincoln's, craggy like that, and tinted by sun and wind; but it is delicate too, finely boned, and her eyes are sherry-colored and timid. 'Oh my,' she exclaims, her breath smoking the windowpane, 'it's fruitcake weather!'

The person to whom she is speaking is myself. I am seven; she is sixty-something. We are cousins, very distant ones, and we have lived together – well, as long as I can remember. Other people inhabit the house, relatives; and though they have power over us, and frequently make us cry, we are not, on the whole, too much aware of them. We are each other's best friend. She calls me Buddy, in memory of a boy who was formerly her best friend. The other Buddy died in the 1880's, when she was still a child. She is still a child.

'I knew it before I got out of bed,' she says, turning away from the window with a purposeful excitement in her eyes. 'The courthouse bell sounded so cold and clear. And there were no birds singing; they've gone to warmer country, yes indeed. Oh, Buddy, stop stuffing biscuit and fetch our buggy. Help me find my hat. We've thirty cakes to bake.'

It's always the same: a morning arrives in November, and my friend, as though officially inaugurating the Christmas time of year that exhilarates her imagination and fuels the blaze of her heart, announces: 'It's fruitcake weather! Fetch our buggy. Help me find my hat.'

The hat is found, a straw cartwheel corsaged with velvet roses out-of-doors has faded: it once belonged to a more fashionable relative. Together, we guide our buggy, a dilapidated baby carriage, out to the garden and into a grove of pecan trees. The buggy is mine; that is, it was bought for me when I was born. It is made of wicker, rather unraveled, and the wheels wobble like a drunkard's legs. But it is a faithful object; springtimes, we take it to the woods and fill it with flowers, herbs, wild fern for our porch pots; in the summer, we pile it with picnic paraphernalia and sugar-cane fishing poles and roll it down to the edge of a creek; it has its winter uses, too: as a truck for hauling firewood from the yard to the kitchen, as a warm bed for Queenie, our tough little orange and white rat terrier who has survived distemper and two rattlesnake bites. Queenie is trotting beside it now.

Three hours later we are back in the kitchen hulling a heaping buggyload of windfall pecans. Our backs hurt from gathering them: how hard they were to find (the main crop having been shaken off the trees and sold by the orchard's owners, who are not us) among the concealing leaves, the frosted, deceiving grass. Caarackle! A cheery crunch, scraps of miniature thunder sound as the shells collapse and the golden mound of sweet oily ivory meat mounts in the milk-glass bowl. Queenie begs to taste, and now and again my friend sneaks her a mite, though insisting we deprive ourselves. 'We mustn't, Buddy. If we start, we won't stop. And there's scarcely enough as there is. For thirty cakes.' The kitchen is growing dark. Dusk turns the window into a mirror: our reflections mingle with the rising moon as we work by the fireside in the firelight. At last, when the moon is quite high, we toss the final hull into the fire and, with joined sighs, watch it catch flame. The buggy is empty, the bowl is brimful.

We eat our supper (cold biscuits, bacon, blackberry jam) and discuss tomorrow. Tomorrow the kind of work I like best begins: buying. Cherries and citron, ginger and vanilla and canned Hawaiian pineapple, rinds and raisins and walnuts and whiskey and oh, so much flour, butter, so many eggs, spices, flavorings: why, we'll need a pony to pull the buggy home.

But before these purchases can be made, there is the question of money. Neither of us has any. Except for skinflint sums persons in the house occasionally provide (a dime is considered very big money); or what we earn ourselves from various activities: holding rummage sales, selling buckets of hand-picked blackberries, jars of homemade jam and apple jelly and peach preserves, rounding up flowers for funerals and weddings. Once we won seventy-ninth prize, five dollars, in a national football contest. Not that we know a fool thing about football. It's just that we enter any contest we hear about: at the moment our hopes are centered on the fifty-thousand-dollar Grand Prize being offered to name a new brand of coffee (we suggested 'A.M.'; and, after some hesitation, for my friend thought it perhaps sacrilegious,

293

the slogan 'A.M.! Amen!'). To tell the truth, our only *really* profitable enterprise was the Fun and Freak Museum we conducted in a back-yard woodshed two summers ago. The Fun was a stereopticon with slide views of Washington and New York lent us by a relative who had been to those places (she was furious when she discovered why we'd borrowed it); the Freak was a three-legged biddy chicken hatched by one of our own hens. Everybody hereabouts wanted to see that biddy: we charged grownups a nickel, kids two cents. And took in a good twenty dollars before the museum shut down due to the decease of the main attraction.

But one way and another we do each year accumulate Christmas savings, a Fruitcake Fund. These moneys we keep hidden in an ancient bead purse under a loose board under the floor under a chamber pot under my friend's bed. The purse is seldom removed from this safe location except to make a deposit, or, as happens every Saturday, a withdrawal; for on Saturdays I am allowed ten cents to go to the picture show. My friend has never been to a picture show, nor does she intend to: 'I'd rather hear you tell the story, Buddy. That way I can imagine it more. Besides, a person my age shouldn't squander their eyes. When the Lord comes, let me see him clear.' In addition to never having seen a movie, she has never: eaten in a restaurant, traveled more than five miles from home, received or sent a telegram, read anything except funny papers and the Bible, worn cosmetics, cursed, wished someone harm, told a lie on purpose, let a hungry dog go hungry. Here are a few things she has done, does do: killed with a hoe the biggest rattlesnake ever seen in this county (sixteen rattles), dip snuff (secretly), tame humming-birds (just try it) till they balance on her finger, tell ghost stories (we both believe in ghosts) so tingling they chill you in July, talk to herself, take walks in the rain, grow the prettiest japonicas in town, know the recipe for every sort of old-time Indian cure, including a magical wart-remover.

Now, with supper finished, we retire to the room in a faraway part of the house where my friend sleeps in a scrap-quilt-covered iron bed painted rose pink, her favorite color. Silently, wallowing in the pleasures of conspiracy, we take the bead purse from its secret place and spill its contents on the scrap quilt. Dollar bills, tightly rolled and green as May buds. Somber fifty-cent pieces, heavy enough to weight a dead man's eyes. Lovely dimes, the liveliest coin, the one that really jingles. Nickels and quarters, worn smooth as creek pebbles. But mostly a hateful heap of bitter-odored pennies. Last summer others in the house contracted to pay us a penny for every twenty-five flies we killed. Oh, the carnage of August: the flies that flew to heaven! Yet it was not work in which we took pride. And, as we sit counting pennies, it is as though we were back tabulating dead flies. Neither of us has a head for figures; we count slowly, lose track, start again. According to her calculations we have $12.73. According to mine, exactly $13. 'I do hope you're wrong, Buddy. We can't mess around with thirteen. The cakes will fall. Or put somebody in the cemetery. Why, I wouldn't dream of getting out of bed on the thirteenth.' This is true: she always spends thirteenths in bed. So, to be on the safe side, we subtract a penny and toss it out the window.

Of the ingredients that go into our fruitcakes, whiskey is the most expensive, as well as the hardest to obtain: State laws forbid its sale. But everybody knows you can buy a bottle from Mr Haha Jones And the next day, having completed our more prosaic shopping, we set out for Mr Haha's business address, a 'sinful' (to quote public opinion) fish-fry and dancing café down by the river. We've been there before, and on the same errand; but in previous years our dealings have been with Haha's wife, an iodine-dark Indian woman with brazzy peroxided hair and a dead-tired disposition. Actually, we've never laid eyes on her husband, though we've heard that he's an Indian too. A giant with razor scars across his cheeks. They call him Haha because he's so gloomy, a man who never laughs. As we approach his café (a large log cabin festooned inside and out with chains of garish-gay naked lightbulbs and standing by the river's muddy edge under the shade of river trees where moss drifts through the branches like gray mist) our steps slow down. Even Queenie stops prancing and sticks close by. People have been murdered in Haha's café. Cut to pieces. Hit on the head. There's a case coming up in court next month. Naturally these goings-on happen at night when the colored lights cast crazy patterns and the victrola wails. In the daytime Haha's is shabby and deserted. I knock at the door, Queenie barks, my friend calls: 'Mrs Haha, ma'am? Anyone to home?'

Footsteps. The door opens. Our hearts overturn. It's Mr Haha Jones himself! And he *is* a giant; he *does* have scars; he *doesn't* smile. No, he glowers at us through Satan-tilted eyes and demands to know: 'What you want with Haha?'

For a moment we are too paralyzed to tell. Presently my friend half-finds her voice, a whispery voice at best: 'If you please, Mr Haha, we'd like a quart of your finest whiskey.'

His eyes tilt more. Would you believe it? Haha is smiling! Laughing, too. 'Which one of you is a drinkin' man?'

'It's for making fruitcakes, Mr Haha. Cooking.'

This sobers him. He frowns. 'That's no way to waste good whiskey.' Nevertheless, he retreats into the shadowed café and seconds later appears carrying a bottle of daisy yellow unlabeled liquor. He demonstrates its sparkle in the sunlight and says: 'Two dollars.'

We pay him with nickels and dimes and pennies. Suddenly, jangling the coins in his hand like a fistful of dice, his face softens. 'Tell you what,' he proposes, pouring the money back into our bead purse, 'just send me one of them fruitcakes instead.'

'Well,' my friend remarks on our way home, 'there's a lovely man. We'll put an extra cup of raisins in *his* cake.'

The black stove, stoked with coal and firewood, glows like a lighted pumpkin. Eggbeaters whirl, spoons spin round in bowls of butter and sugar, vanilla sweetens the air, ginger spices it; melting, nose-tingling odors saturate the kitchen, suffuse the house, drift out to the world on puffs of chimney smoke. In four days our work is done. Thirty-one cakes, dampened with whiskey, bask on window sills and shelves.

Who are they for?

Friends. Not necessarily neighbor friends: indeed, the larger share are intended for persons we've met maybe once, perhaps not at all. People who've struck our fancy. Like President Roosevelt. Like the Reverend and Mrs J. C. Lucey, Baptist missionaries to Borneo who lectured here last winter. Or the little knife grinder who comes through town twice a year. Or Abner Packer, the driver of the six o'clock bus from Mobile, who exchanges waves with us every day as he passes in a dust-cloud whoosh. Or the young Wistons, a California couple whose car one afternoon broke down outside the house and who spent a pleasant hour chatting with us on the porch (young Mr Wiston snapped our picture, the only one we've ever had taken). Is it because my friend is shy with everyone *except* strangers that these strangers, and merest acquaintances, seem to us our truest friends? I think yes. Also, the scrapbooks we keep of thank-you's on White House stationery, time-to-time communications from California and Borneo, the knife grinder's penny post cards, make us feel connected to eventful worlds beyond the kitchen with its view of a sky that stops.

Now a nude December fig branch grates against the window. The kitchen is empty, the cakes are gone; yesterday we carted the last of them to the post office, where the cost of stamps turned our purse inside out. We're broke. That rather depresses me, but my friend insists on celebrating with two inches of whiskey left in Haha's bottle. Queenie has a spoonful in a bowl of coffee (she likes her coffee chicory-flavored and strong). The rest we divide between a pair of jelly glasses. We're both quite awed at the prospect of drinking straight whiskey; the taste of it brings screwed-up expressions and sour shudders. But by and by we begin to sing, the two of us singing different songs simultaneously. I don't know the words to mine, just: *Come on along, come on along, to the dark-town strutters' ball.* But I can dance: that's what I mean to be, a tap dancer in the movies. My dancing shadow rollicks on the walls; our voices rock the chinaware; we giggle: as if unseen hands were tickling us. Queenie rolls on her back, her paws plow the air, something like a grin stretches her black lips. Inside myself I feel warm and sparky as those crumbling logs, carefree as the wind in the chimney. My friend waltzes round the stove, the hem of her poor calico skirt pinched between her fingers as though it were a party dress: *Show me the way to go home*, she sings, her tennis shoes squeaking on the floor. *Show me the way to go home.*

Enter: two relatives. Very angry. Potent with eyes that scold, tongues that scald. Listen to what they have to say, the words tumbling together into a wrathful tune: 'A child of seven! whiskey on his breath! are you out of your mind? feeding a child of seven! must be loony! road to ruination! remember Cousin Kate? Uncle Charlie? Uncle Charlie's brother-in-law? shame! scandal! humiliation! kneel, pray, beg the Lord!'

Queenie sneaks under the stove. My friend gazes at her shoes, her chin quivers, she lifts her skirt and blows her nose and runs to her room. Long after the town has gone to sleep and the house is silent except for the chimings of clocks and the sputter of fading fires, she is weeping into a pillow already as wet as a widow's handkerchief.

'Don't cry,' I say, sitting at the bottom of her bed and shivering despite my flannel nightgown that smells of last winter's cough syrup, 'don't cry,' I beg, teasing her toes, tickling her feet, 'you're too old for that.'

'It's because,' she hiccups, 'I *am* too old. Old and funny.'

'Not funny. Fun. More fun than anybody. Listen. If you don't stop crying you'll be so tired tomorrow we can't go cut a tree.'

She straightens up. Queenie jumps on the bed (where Queenie is not allowed) to lick her cheeks. 'I know where we'll find pretty trees, Buddy. And holly, too. With berries big as your eyes. It's way off in the woods. Farther than we've ever been. Papa used to bring us Christmas trees from there: carry them on his shoulder. That's fifty years ago. Well, now: I can't wait for morning.'

Morning. Frozen rime lusters the grass; the sun, round as an orange and orange as hot-weather moons, balances on the horizon, burnishes the silvered winter woods. A wild turkey calls. A renegade hog grunts in the undergrowth. Soon, by the edge of knee-deep, rapid-running water, we have to abandon the buggy. Queenie wades the stream first, paddles across barking complaints at the swiftness of the current, the pneumonia-making coldness of it. We follow, holding our shoes and equipment (a hatchet, a burlap sack) above our heads. A mile more: of chastising thorns, burs and briers that catch at our clothes; of rusty pine needles brilliant with gaudy fungus and molted feathers. Here, there, a flash, a flutter, an ecstasy of shrillings remind us that not all the birds have flown south. Always, the path unwinds through lemony sun pools and pitch vine tunnels. Another creek to cross: a disturbed armada of speckled trout froths the water round us, and frogs the size of plates practice belly flops; beaver workmen are building a dam. On the farther shore, Queenie shakes herself and trembles. My friend shivers, too: not with cold but enthusiasm. One of her hat's ragged roses sheds a petal as she lifts her head and inhales the pine-heavy air. 'We're almost there; can you smell it, Buddy?' she says, as though we were approaching an ocean.

And, indeed, it is a kind of ocean. Scented acres of holi-day trees, prickly-leafed holly. Red berries shiny as Chinese bells: black crows swoop upon them screaming. Having stuffed our burlap sacks with enough greenery and crimson to garland a dozen windows, we set about choosing a tree. 'It should be,' muses my friend, 'twice as tall as a boy. So a boy can't steal the star.' The one we pick is twice as tall as me. A brave handsome brute that survives thirty hatchet strokes before it keels with a creaking rending cry. Lugging it like a kill, we commence the long trek out. Every few yards we abandon the struggle, sit down and pant. But we have the strength of triumphant huntsmen; that and the tree's virile, icy perfume revive us, goad us on. Many compli-ments accompany our sunset return along the red clay road to town; but my friend is sly and noncommittal when passers-by praise the treasure perched on our buggy: what a fine tree and where did it come from? 'Yonderways,' she murmurs vaguely. Once a car stops and the rich mill owner's lazy wife leans out and whines: 'Giveya two-bits cash for that ol tree.' Ordinarily my friend is afraid of saying no; but on this occasion she promptly shakes her head: 'We wouldn't take a dollar.' The mill owner's wife persists. 'A dollar, my foot! Fifty cents. That's my last offer. Goodness, woman, you can get another one.' In answer, my friend gently reflects: 'I doubt it. There's never two of anything.'

Home: Queenie slumps by the fire and sleeps till tomorrow, snoring loud as a human.

A trunk in the attic contains: a shoebox of ermine tails (off the opera cape of a curious lady who once rented a room in the house), coils of frazzled tinsel gone gold with age, one silver star, a brief rope of dilapidated, undoubtedly dangerous candy-like light bulbs. Excellent decorations, as far as they go, which isn't far enough: my friend wants our tree to blaze 'like a Baptist window', droop with weighty snows of ornament. But we can't afford the made-in-Japan splendors at the five-and-dime. So we do what we've always done: sit for days at the kitchen table with scissors and crayons and stacks of colored paper. I make sketches and my friend cuts them out: lots of cats, fish too (because they're easy to draw), some apples, some watermelons, a few winged angels devised from saved-up sheets of Hershey-bar tin foil. We use safety pins to attach these creations to the tree; as a final touch, we sprinkle the branches with shredded cotton (picked in August for this purpose). My friend, surveying the effect, clasps her hands together. 'Now honest, Buddy. Doesn't it look good enough to eat?' Queenie tries to eat an angel.

After weaving and ribboning holly wreaths for all the front windows, our next project is the fashioning of family gifts. Tie-dye scarves for the ladies, for the men a home-brewed lemon and licorice and aspirin syrup to be taken 'at the first Symptoms of a Cold and after Hunting'. But when it comes

301

time for making each other's gift, my friend and I separate to work secretly. I would like to buy her a pearl-handled knife, a radio, a whole pound of chocolate-covered cherries (we tasted some once, and she always swears: 'I could live on them, Buddy, Lord yes I could – and that's not taking His name in vain'). Instead, I am building her a kite. She would like to give me a bicycle (she's said so on several million occasions: 'If only I could, Buddy. It's bad enough in life to do without something *you* want; but confound it, what gets my goat is not being able to give somebody something you want *them* to have. Only one of these days I will, Buddy. Locate you a bike. Don't ask how. Steal it, maybe'). Instead, I'm fairly certain that she is building me a kite – the same as last year, and the year before: the year before that we exchanged slingshots. All of which is fine by me. For we are champion kite-fliers who study the wind like sailors; my friend, more accomplished than I, can get a kite aloft when there isn't enough breeze to carry clouds.

Christmas Eve afternoon we scrape together a nickel and go to the butcher's to buy Queenie's traditional gift, a good gnawable beef bone. The bone, wrapped in funny paper, is placed high in the tree near the silver star. Queenie knows it's there. She squats at the foot of the tree staring up in a trance of greed: when bedtime arrives she refuses to budge. Her excitement is equaled by my own. I kick the covers and turn my pillow as though it were a scorching summer's night. Somewhere a rooster crows: falsely, for the sun is still on the other side of the world.

'Buddy, are you awake?' It is my friend, calling from her room, which is next to mine; and an instant later she is sitting on my bed holding a candle. 'Well, I can't sleep a hoot,' she declares. 'My mind's jumping like a jack rabbit. Buddy, do you think Mrs Roosevelt will serve our cake at dinner?' We huddle in the bed, and she squeezes my hand I-love-you. 'Seems like your hand used to be so much smaller. I guess I hate to see you grow up. When you're grown up, will we still be friends?' I say always. 'But I feel so bad, Buddy. I wanted so bad to give you a bike. I tried to sell my cameo Papa gave me. Buddy' – she hesitates, as though embarrassed – 'I made you another kite.' Then I confess that I made her one, too; and we laugh. The candle burns too short to hold. Out it goes, exposing the starlight, the stars spinning at the window like a visible caroling that slowly, slowly daybreak silences. Possibly we doze; but the beginnings of dawn splash us like cold water: we're up, wide-eyed and wandering while we wait for others to waken. Quite deliberately my friend drops a kettle on the kitchen floor. I tap-dance in front of closed doors. One by one the household emerges, looking as though they'd like to kill us both; but it's Christmas, so they can't. First, a gorgeous breakfast: just everything you can imagine – from flapjacks and fried squirrel to hominy grits and honey-in-the-comb. Which puts everyone in a good humor except my friend and I. Frankly, we're so impatient to get at the presents we can't eat a mouthful.

Well, I'm disappointed. Who wouldn't be? With socks, a Sunday school shirt, some handkerchiefs, a hand-me-down sweater and a year's subscription to a religious magazine for children. *The Little Shepherd*. It makes me boil. It really does.

My friend has a better haul. A sack of Satsumas, that's her best present. She is proudest, however, of a white wool shawl knitted by her married sister. But she *says* her favorite gift is the kite I built her. And it *is* very beautiful; though not as beautiful as the one she made me, which is blue and scattered with gold and green Good Conduct stars; moreover, my name is painted on it, 'Buddy'.

'Buddy, the wind is blowing.'

The wind is blowing, and nothing will do till we've run to a pasture below the house where Queenie has scooted to bury her bone (and where, a winter hence, Queenie will be buried, too). There, plunging through the healthy waist-high grass, we unreel our kites, feel them twitching at the string like sky fish as they swim into the wind. Satisfied, sun-warmed, we sprawl in the grass and peel Satsumas and watch our kites cavort. Soon I forget the socks and hand-me-down sweater. I'm as happy as if we'd already won the fifty-thousand-dollar Grand Prize in that coffee-naming contest.

'My, how foolish I am!' my friend cries, suddenly alert, like a woman remembering too late she has biscuits in the oven. 'You know what I've always thought?' she asks in a tone of discovery, and not smiling at me but a point beyond. 'I've always thought a body would have to be sick and dying before they saw the Lord. And I imagined that when He came it would be like looking at the Baptist window: pretty as colored glass with the sun pouring through, such a shine you don't know it's getting dark. And it's been a comfort: to think of that shine taking away all the spooky feeling. But I'll wager it never happens. I'll wager at the very end a body realizes the Lord has already shown Himself. That things as they are' – her hand circles in a gesture that gathers clouds and kites and grass and Queenie pawing earth over her bone – 'just what they've always seen, was seeing Him. As for me, I could leave the world with today in my eyes.'

This is our last Christmas together.

Life separates us. Those who Know Best decide that I belong in a military school. And so follows a miserable succession of bugle-blowing prisons, grim reveille-ridden summer camps. I have a new home too. But it doesn't count. Home is where my friend is, and there I never go.

And there she remains, puttering around the kitchen. Alone with Queenie. Then alone. ('Buddy dear,' she writes in her wild hard-to-read script, 'yesterday Jim Macy's horse kicked Queenie bad. Be thankful she didn't feel much. I wrapped her in a Fine Linen sheet and rode her in the buggy down to Simpson's pasture where she can be with all her Bones...') For a few Novembers she continues to bake her fruitcakes single-handed; not as many, but some: and, of course, she always sends me 'the best of the batch'. Also, in every letter she encloses a dime wadded in toilet paper: 'See a picture show and write me the story.' But gradually in her letters she tends to confuse me with her other friend, the Buddy who died in the 1880's; more and more thirteenths are not the only days she stays in bed: a morning arrives in November, a leafless birdless coming of winter morning, when she cannot rouse herself to exclaim: 'Oh my, it's fruitcake weather!'

And when that happens, I know it. A message saying so merely confirms a piece of news some secret vein had already received, severing from me an irreplaceable part of myself, letting it loose like a kite on a broken string. That is why, walking across a school campus on this particular December morning, I keep searching the sky. As if I expected to see, rather like hearts, a lost pair of kites hurrying toward heaven.

JOHN UPDIKE

THE CAROL SING

SURELY ONE OF the natural wonders of Tarbox was Mr Burley at the Town Hall carol sing. How he would jubilate, how he would God-rest those merry gentlemen, how he would boom out when the male voices became Good King Wenceslas:

> *Mark my footsteps, good my page;*
> *Tread thou in them boldly:*
> *Thou shalt find the winter's rage*
> *Freeze thy blood less co-oh-ldly.*

When he hit a good 'oh', standing beside him was like being inside a great transparent Christmas ball. He had what you'd have to call a God-given bass. This year, we other male voices just peck at the tunes: Wendell Huddlestone, whose hardware store has become the pizza place where the drop-outs collect after dark; Squire Wentworth, who is still getting up petitions to protect the marsh birds from the atomic power plant; Lionel Merson, lighter this year by about three pounds of gallstones; and that selectman whose freckled bald head looks like the belly of a trout; and that fireman whose face is bright brown all the year round from clamming; and the widow Covode's bearded son, who went into divinity school to avoid the draft; and the Bisbee boy, who no sooner was back from Vietnam than he grew a beard and painted his car every color of the rainbow; and the husband of the new couple that moved this September into the

Whitman place on the beach road. He wears thick glasses above a little mumble of a mouth tight as a keyhole, but his wife appears perky enough.

> The-ey lookèd up and saw a star,
> Shining in the east, beyond them far;
> And to the earth it ga-ave great light,
> And so it continued both da-ay and night.

She is wearing a flouncy little Christmassy number, red with white polka dots, one of those dresses so short that when she sits down on the old plush deacon's bench she has to help it with her hand to tuck under her bottom, otherwise it wouldn't. A bright bit of a girl with long thighs glossy as pond ice. She smiles nervously up over her cup of cinnamon-stick punch, wondering why she is here, in this dusty drafty public place. We must look monstrous to her, we Tarbox old-timers. And she has never heard Mr Burley sing, but she knows something is missing this year; there is something failed, something hollow. Hester Hartner sweeps wrong notes into every chord: arthritis – arthritis and indifference.

> The first good joy that Mary had,
> It was the joy of one;
> To see the blessèd Jesus Christ
> When he was first her son.

The old upright, a Pickering, for most of the year has its keyboard turned to the wall, beneath the town zoning map, its top piled high with rolled-up plot plans filing for variances. The Town Hall was built, strange to say, as a Unitarian church, around 1830, but it didn't take around here, Unitarianism; the sea air killed it. You need big trees for a shady mystic mood, or at least a lake to see yourself in like they have in Concord. So the town took over the shell and ran a second floor through the air of the sanctuary, between the balconies: offices and the courtroom below, more offices and this hall above. You can still see the Doric pilasters along the walls, the top halves. They used to use it more; there were the Tarbox Theatricals twice a year, and political rallies with placards and straw hats and tambourines, and get-togethers under this or that local auspice, and town meetings until we went representative. But now not even the holly the ladies of the Grange have hung around can cheer it up, can chase away the smell of dust and must, of cobwebs too high to reach and rats' nests in the piano, that faint sour tang of blueprints. And Hester lately has taken to chewing eucalyptus drops.

> *And him to serve God give us grace,*
>   O lux beata Trinitas.

The little wife in polka dots is laughing now: maybe the punch is getting to her, maybe she's getting used to the look of us. Strange people look ugly only for a while, until you begin to fill in those tufty monkey features with a little history and stop seeing their faces and start seeing their lives. Regardless, it does us good, to see her here, to see young people at the carol sing. We need new blood.

> *This time of the year is spent in good cheer,*
>   *And neighbors together do meet,*
> *To sit by the fire, with friendly desire,*
>   *Each other in love to greet.*
> *Old grudges forgot are put in the pot,*
>   *All sorrows aside they lay;*
> *The old and the young doth carol this song,*
>   *To drive the cold winter away.*

At bottom it's a woman's affair, a chance in the darkest of months to put on some gaudy clothes and get out of the house. Those old holidays weren't scattered around the calendar by chance. Harvest and seedtime, seedtime and harvest, the elbows of the year. The women do enjoy it; they enjoy jostle of most any kind, in my limited experience. The widow Covode as full of rouge and purple as an old-time Scollay Square tart, when her best hope is burial on a sunny day, with no frost in the ground. Mrs Hortense broad as a barn door, yet her hands putting on a duchess's airs. Mamie Nevins sporting a sprig of mistletoe in her neck brace. They miss Mr Burley. He never married and was everybody's gallant for this occasion. He was the one to spike the punch and this year they let young Covode do it, maybe that's why Little Polka Dots can't keep a straight face and giggles across the music like a pruning saw.

Adeste, fideles,
Laeti triumphantes;
Venite, venite
In Bethlehem.

Still that old tussle, 'v' versus 'wenite', the 'th' as hard or soft. Education is what divides us. People used to actually resent it, the way Burley, with his education, didn't go to some city, didn't get out. Exeter, Dartmouth, a year at the Sorbonne, then thirty years of Tarbox. By the time he hit fifty he was fat and fussy. Arrogant, too. Last sing, he two or three times told Hester to pick up her tempo. 'Presto, Hester, not andante!' Never married, and never really worked. Burley Hosiery that his grandfather had founded, was shut down and the machines sold South before Burley got his manhood. He built himself a laboratory instead

312

and was always about to come up with something perfect: the perfect synthetic substitute for leather, the harmless insecticide, the beer can that turned itself into mulch. Some said at the end he was looking for a way to turn lead into gold. That was just malice. Anything high attracts lightning, anybody with a name attracts malice. When it happened, the papers in Boston gave him six inches and a photograph ten years old. 'After a long illness.' It wasn't a long illness, it was cyanide, the Friday after Thanksgiving.

> *The holly bears a prickle,*
> *As sharp as any thorn,*
> *And Mary bore sweet Jesus Christ*
> *On Christmas day in the morn.*

They said the cyanide ate out his throat worse than a blow-torch. Such a detail is satisfying but doesn't clear up the mystery. Why? Health, money, hobbies, that voice. Not having that voice makes a big hole here. Without his lead, no man dares take the lower parts; we just wheeze away at the melody with the women. It's as if the floor they put in has been taken away and we're standing in air, halfway up that old sanctuary. We peek around guiltily, missing Burley's voice. The absent seem to outnumber the present. We feel insulted, slighted. The dead flee us. The older you get, the more of them snub you. He was rude enough last year, Burley, correcting Hester's tempo. At one point, he even reached over, his face black with impatience, and slapped her hands that were still trying to make sense of the keys.

> *Rise, and bake your Christmas bread:*
> *Christians, rise! The world is bare,*
> *And blank, and dark with want and care,*
> *Yet Christmas comes in the morning.*

Well, why anything? Why do *we*? Come every year sure as the solstice to carol these antiquities that if you listened to the words would break your heart. Silence, darkness, Jesus, angels. Better, I suppose, to sing than to listen.

MURIEL SPARK

CHRISTMAS FUGUE

AS A GROWING schoolgirl Cynthia had been a nature-lover; in those days she had thought of herself in those terms. She would love to go for solitary walks beside a river, feel the rain on her face, lean over old walls, gazing into dark pools. She was dreamy, wrote nature poetry. It was part of a home-counties culture of the nineteen-seventies, and she had left all but the memories behind her when she left England to join her cousin Moira, a girl slightly older than herself, in Sydney, where Moira ran a random boutique of youthful clothes, handbags, hand-made slippers, ceramics, cushions, decorated writing paper, and many other art-like objects. Moira married a successful lawyer and moved to Adelaide. Beautiful Sydney suddenly became empty for Cynthia. She had a boyfriend. He, too, suddenly became empty. At twenty-four she wanted a new life. She had never really known the old life.

So many friends had invited her to spend Christmas day with them that she couldn't remember how many. Kind faces, smiling, 'You'll be lonely without Moira. . . . What are your plans for Christmas?' Georgie (her so-called boyfriend) 'Look, you must come to us. We'd love you to come to us for Christmas. My kid brother and sister. . . .'

Cynthia felt terribly empty. 'Actually, I'm going back to England.' 'So soon? Before Christmas?'

She packed her things, gave away all the stuff she didn't want. She had a one-way air ticket, Sydney–London, precisely on Christmas day. She would spend Christmas day on the plane. She thought all the time of all the beauty and blossoming life-style she was leaving behind her, the sea, the beaches, the shops, the mountains, but now it was like leaning over an old wall, dreaming. England was her destination, and really her destiny. She had never had a full adult life in England. Georgie saw her off on the plane. He was going for a new life, too, to the blue hills and wonderful colours of Brisbane, where his only uncle needed him on his Queensland sheep farm. For someone else, Cynthia thought, he won't be empty. Far from it. But he is empty for me.

She would not be alone in England. Her parents, divorced, were in their early fifties. Her brother, still unmarried, was a city accountant. An aunt had died recently; Cynthia was the executor of her will. She would not be alone in England, or in any way wondering what to do.

The plane was practically empty.

'Nobody flies on Christmas day,' said the hostess who served the preliminary drinks. 'At least, very few. The rush is always before Christmas, and then there's always a full flight after Boxing day till New Year when things begin to normalize.' She was talking to a young man who had remarked on the number of empty seats. 'I'm spending Christmas on the plane because I'd nowhere else to go. I thought it might be amusing.'

'It will be amusing,' said the pretty hostess. 'We'll make it fun.'

The young man looked pleased. He was a few seats in front of Cynthia. He looked around, saw Cynthia and smiled. In the course of the next hour he made it known to this small world in the air that he was a teacher returning from an exchange programme.

The plane had left Sydney at after three in the afternoon

of Christmas day. There remained over nine hours to Bang-kok, their refuelling stop.

Luxuriously occupying two vacant front seats of the compartment was a middle-aged couple fully intent on their reading; he, a copy of *Time* Magazine, she, a tattered paper-back of Agatha Christie's: *The Mysterious Affair at Styles*.

A thin, tall man with glasses passed the couple on the way to the lavatories. On his emergence he stopped, pointed at the paperback and said, 'Agatha Christie! You're reading Agatha Christie. She's a serial killer. On your dark side you yourself are a serial killer.' The man beamed triumphantly and made his way to a seat behind the couple.

A steward appeared and was called by the couple, both together. 'Who's that man?' – 'Did you hear what he said? He said I am a serial killer.'

'Excuse me sir is there something wrong?' the steward demanded of the man with glasses.

'Just making an observation,' the man replied.

The steward disappeared into the front of the plane, and reappeared with a uniformed officer, a co-pilot, who had in his hand a sheet of paper, evidently a list of passengers. He glanced at the seat number of the bespectacled offender, then at him: 'Professor Sygmund Schatt?' 'Sygmund spelt with a y,' precised the professor. 'Nothing wrong. I was merely making a professional observation.'

'Keep them to yourself in future.'

'I will not be silenced,' said Sygmund Schatt. 'Plot and scheme against me as you may.'

The co-pilot went to the couple, bent towards them, and whispered something reassuring.

'You see!' said Schatt.

The pilot walked up the aisle towards Cynthia. He sat down beside her.

'A complete nut. They do cause anxiety on planes. But maybe he's harmless. He'd better be. Are you feeling lonely?'

Cynthia looked at the officer. He was good-looking, fairly young, young enough. 'Just a bit,' she said.

'First class is empty,' said the officer. 'Like to come there?'

'I don't want to –'

'Come with me,' he said. 'What's your name?'

'Cynthia. What's yours?'

'Tom. I'm one of the pilots. There are three of us today so far. Another's coming on at Bangkok.'

'That makes me feel safe.'

It fell about that at Bangkok, when everyone else had got off the plane to stretch their legs for an hour and a half; the passengers had gone to walk around the departments of the Duty Free shop, buy presents 'from Bangkok' of a useless nature such as dolls and silk ties, to drink coffee and other beverages with biscuits and pastries; Tom and Cynthia stayed on. They made love in a beautifully appointed cabin with real curtains in the windows – unrealistic yellow flowers on a white background. Then they talked about each other, and made love again.

'Christmas day,' he said. 'I'll never forget this one.'

'Nor me,' she said.

They had half an hour before the crew and passengers would rejoin them. One of the tankers which had refuelled the plane could be seen moving off.

Cynthia luxuriated in the washroom with its toilet waters and toothbrushes. She made herself fresh and pretty, combed her well-cut casque of dark hair. When she got back to the cabin he was returning from somewhere, looking young, smiling. He gave her a box. 'Christmas present.'

It contained a set of plaster Christmas crib figures, 'made

in China'. A kneeling Virgin and St Joseph, the baby Jesus and a shoemaker with his bench, a woodcutter, an unidentifiable monk, two shepherds and two angels.

Cynthia arranged them on the table in front of her.

'Do you believe in it?' she said.

'Well, I believe in Christmas.'

'Yes, I, too. It means a new life. I don't see any mother and father really kneeling beside the baby's cot worshipping it, do you?'

'No, that part's symbolic.'

'These are simply lovely,' she said touching her presents. 'Made of real stuff, not plastic.'

'Let's celebrate,' he said. He disappeared and returned with a bottle of champagne.

'How expensive . . .'

'Don't worry. It flows on First.'

'Will you be going on duty?'

'No,' he said. 'I clock in tomorrow.'

They made love again, high up in the air.

After that, Cynthia walked back to her former compartment. Professor Sygmund Schatt was having an argument with a hostess about his food which had apparently been pre-ordered, and now, in some way, did not come up to scratch. Cynthia sat in her old seat, and taking a postcard from the pocket in front of her, wrote to her cousin Moira. 'Having a lovely time at 35,000 feet. I have started a new life. Love XX Cynthia.' She then felt this former seat was part of the old life, and went back again to First.

In the night Tom came and sat beside her.

'You didn't eat much,' he said.

'How did you know?'

'I noticed.'

'I didn't feel up to the Christmas dinner,' she said.

'Would you like something now?'

'A turkey sandwich. Let me go and ask the hostess.'

'Leave it to me.'

Tom told her he was now in the final stages of a divorce. His wife had no doubt had a hard time of it, his job taking him away so much. But she could have studied something. She wouldn't learn, hated to learn.

And he was lonely. He asked her to marry him, and she wasn't in the least surprised. But she said, 'Oh, Tom, you don't know me.'

'I think I do.'

'We don't know each other.'

'Well, I think we should do.'

She said she would think about it. She said she would cancel her plans and come to spend some time in his flat in London at Camden Town.

'I'll have my time off within three days – by the end of the week,' he said.

'God, is he all right, is he reliable?' she said to herself. 'Am I safe with him? Who is he?' But she was really carried away.

Around 4 a.m. she woke and found him beside her. He said, 'It's Boxing day now. You're a lovely girl.'

She had always imagined she was, but had always, so far, fallen timid when with men. She had experienced two brief love affairs in Australia, neither memorable. All alone in the first class compartment with Tom, high in the air – this was reality, something to be remembered, the start of a new life.

'I'll give you the key of the flat,' he said. 'Go straight there. Nobody will disturb you. I've been sharing it with my young brother. But he's away for about six weeks I should say. In fact he's doing time. He got mixed up in a football row and he's in for grievous bodily harm and affray. Only, the bodily harm wasn't so grievous. He was just in the wrong place at the wrong time. Anyway, the flat's free for at least six weeks.'

At the airport, despite the early hour of ten past five in the morning, there was quite a crowd to meet the plane. Having retrieved her luggage, Cynthia pushed her trolley towards the exit. She had no expectation whatsoever that anyone would be there to meet her.

Instead, there was her father and his wife Elaine; there was her mother with her husband Bill; crowding behind them at the barrier were her brother and his girlfriend, her cousin Moira's cousin by marriage, and a few other men and women whom she did not identify, accompanied, too, by some children of about 10 to 14. In fact her whole family, known and unknown, had turned out to meet Cynthia. How had they known the hour of her arrival? She had promised, only, to ring them when she got to England. 'Your cousin Moira,' said her father, 'told us your flight. We wanted you home, you know that.'

She went first to her mother's house. It was now Boxing day but they had saved Christmas day for her arrival. All the Christmas rituals were fully observed. The tree and the presents – dozens of presents for Cynthia. Her brother and his girl with some other cousins came over for Christmas dinner.

When they came to open the presents, Cynthia brought out from her luggage a number of packages she had brought from Australia for the occasion. Among them, labelled for her brother, was a plaster Nativity set, made in China.

'What a nice one,' said her brother. 'One of the best I've seen, and not plastic.'

'I got it in Moira's boutique,' Cynthia said. 'She has very special things.'

She talked a lot about Australia, its marvels. Then, at tea-time, they got down to her aunt's will, of which Cynthia was an executor. Cynthia felt happy, in her element, as an executor to a will, for she was normally dreamy, not legally minded at all and now she felt the flattery of her aunt's confidence in her. The executorship gave her some sort of authority in the family. She was now arranging, too, to spend New Year with her father and his second clan.

Her brother had set out the Nativity figures on a table. 'I don't know,' she said, 'why the mother and the father are kneeling beside the child; it seems so unreal.' She didn't hear what the others said, if anything, in response to this observa-tion. She only felt a strange stirring of memory. There was to be a flat in Camden Town, but she had no idea of the address.

'The plane stopped at Bangkok,' she told them.

'Did you get off?'

'Yes, but you know you can't get out of the airport. There was a coffee bar and a lovely shop.'

It was later that day when she was alone, unpacking, in her room, that she rang the airline.

'No,' said a girl's voice, 'I don't think there are curtains with yellow flowers in the first-class cabins. I'll have to ask. Was there any particular reason ... ?'

'There was a co-pilot called Tom. Can you give me his full name please? I have an urgent message for him.'

'What flight did you say?'

Cynthia told her not only the flight but her name and original seat number in Business Class.

After a long wait, the voice spoke again, 'Yes, you are one of the arrivals.'

'I know that,' said Cynthia.

'I can't give you information about our pilots, I'm afraid. But there was no pilot on the plane called Tom . . . Thomas, no. The stewards in Business were Bob, Andrew, Sheila and Lilian.'

'No pilot called Tom? About thirty-five, tall, brown hair. I met him. He lives in Camden Town.' Cynthia gripped the phone. She looked round at the reality of the room.

'The pilots are Australian; I can tell you that but no more. I'm sorry. They're our personnel.'

'It was a memorable flight. Christmas day. I'll never forget that one,' said Cynthia.

'Thank you. We appreciate that,' said the voice. It seemed thousands of miles away.

GRACE PALEY

THE LOUDEST
VOICE

THERE IS A certain place where dumbwaiters boom, doors slam, dishes crash; every window is a mother's mouth bidding the street shut up, go skate somewhere else, come home. My voice is the loudest.

There, my own mother is still as full of breathing as me and the grocer stands up to speak to her. 'Mrs Abramowitz,' he says, 'people should not be afraid of their children.'

'Ah, Mr Bialik,' my mother replies, 'if you say to her or her father "Ssh," they say, "In the grave it will be quiet." '

'From Coney Island to the cemetery,' says my papa. 'It's the same subway; it's the same fare.'

I am right next to the pickle barrel. My pinky is making tiny whirlpools in the brine. I stop a moment to announce: 'Campbell's Tomato Soup. Campbell's Vegetable Beef Soup. Campbell's S-c-otch Broth...'

'Be quiet,' the grocer says, 'the labels are coming off.'

'Please, Shirley, be a little quiet,' my mother begs me.

In that place the whole street groans: Be quiet! Be quiet! but steals from the happy chorus of my inside self not a tittle or a jot.

There, too, but just around the corner, is a red brick building that has been old for many years. Every morning the children stand before it in double lines which must be straight. They are not insulted. They are waiting anyway.

I am usually among them. I am, in fact, the first, since I begin with 'A'.

One cold morning the monitor tapped me on the shoulder. 'Go to Room 409, Shirley Abramowitz,' he said. I did as I was told. I went in a hurry up a down staircase to Room 409, which contained sixth-graders. I had to wait at the desk without wiggling until Mr Hilton, their teacher, had time to speak.

After five minutes he said, 'Shirley?'

'What?' I whispered.

He said, 'My! My! Shirley Abramowitz! They told me you had a particularly loud, clear voice and read with lots of expression. Could that be true?'

'Oh yes,' I whispered.

'In that case, don't be silly; I might very well be your teacher someday. Speak up, speak up.'

'Yes,' I shouted.

'More like it,' he said. 'Now, Shirley, can you put a ribbon in your hair or a bobby pin? It's too messy.'

'Yes!' I bawled.

'Now, now, calm down.' He turned to the class. 'Children, not a sound. Open at page 39. Read till 52. When you finish, start again.' He looked me over once more. 'Now, Shirley, you know, I suppose, that Christmas is coming. We are preparing a beautiful play. Most of the parts have been given out. But I still need a child with a strong voice, lots of stamina. Do you know what stamina is? You do? Smart kid. You know, I heard you read "The Lord is my shepherd" in Assembly yesterday. I was very impressed. Wonderful delivery. Mrs Jordan, your teacher, speaks highly of you. Now listen to me, Shirley Abramowitz, if you want to take the part and be in the play, repeat after me, "I swear to work harder than I ever did before." '

I looked to heaven and said at once, 'Oh, I swear.' I kissed my pinky and looked at God.

'That is an actor's life, my dear,' he explained. 'Like a soldier's, never tardy or disobedient to his general, the director. Everything,' he said, 'absolutely everything will depend on you.'

That afternoon, all over the building, children scraped and scrubbed the turkeys and the sheaves of corn off the schoolroom windows. Goodbye Thanksgiving. The next morning a monitor brought red paper and green paper from the office. We made new shapes and hung them on the walls and glued them to the doors.

The teachers became happier and happier. Their heads were ringing like the bells of childhood. My best friend, Evie, was prone to evil, but she did not get a single demerit for whispering. We learned 'Holy Night' without an error. 'How wonderful!' said Miss Glacé, the student teacher. 'To think that some of you don't even speak the language!' We learned 'Deck the Halls' and 'Hark! The Herald Angels'... They weren't ashamed and we weren't embarrassed.

Oh, but when my mother heard about it all, she said to my father: 'Misha, you don't know what's going on there. Cramer is the head of the Tickets Committee.'

'Who?' asked my father. 'Cramer? Oh yes, an active woman.'

'Active? Active has to have a reason. Listen,' she said sadly, 'I'm surprised to see my neighbors making tra-la-la for Christmas.'

My father couldn't think of what to say to that. Then he decided: 'You're in America! Clara, you wanted to come here. In Palestine the Arabs would be eating you alive. Europe you had pogroms. Argentina is full of Indians. Here you got Christmas... Some joke, ha?'

'Very funny, Misha. What is becoming of you? If we came to a new country a long time ago to run away from tyrants, and instead we fall into a creeping pogrom, that our children learn a lot of lies, so what's the joke? Ach, Misha, your idealism is going away.'

'So is your sense of humor.'

'That I never had, but idealism you had a lot of.'

'I'm the same Misha Abramovitch, I didn't change an iota. Ask anyone.'

'Only ask me,' says my mama, may she rest in peace. 'I got the answer.'

Meanwhile the neighbors had to think of what to say too.

Marty's father said: 'You know, he has a very important part, my boy.'

'Mine also,' said Mr Sauerfeld.

'Not my boy!' said Mrs Klieg. 'I said to him no. The answer is no. When I say no! I mean no!'

The rabbi's wife said, 'It's disgusting!' But no one listened to her. Under the narrow sky of God's great wisdom she wore a strawberry-blond wig.

Every day was noisy and full of experience. I was Right-hand Man. Mr Hilton said: 'How could I get along without you, Shirley?'

He said: 'Your mother and father ought to get down on their knees every night and thank God for giving them a child like you.'

He also said: 'You're absolutely a pleasure to work with, my dear, dear child.'

Sometimes he said: 'For godsakes, what did I do with the script? Shirley! Shirley! Find it.'

Then I answered quietly: 'Here it is, Mr Hilton.'

Once in a while, when he was very tired, he would cry out: 'Shirley, I'm just tired of screaming at those kids. Will you tell Ira Pushkov not to come in till Lester points to that star the second time?'

Then I roared: 'Ira Pushkov, what's the matter with you? Dope! Mr Hilton told you five times already, don't come in till Lester points to that star the second time.'

'Ach, Clara,' my father asked, 'what does she do there till six o'clock she can't even put the plates on the table?'

'Christmas,' said my mother coldly.

'Ho! Ho!' my father said. 'Christmas. What's the harm? After all, history teaches everyone. We learn from reading this is a holiday from pagan times also, candles, lights, even Hanukkah. So we learn it's not altogether Christian. So if they think it's a private holiday, they're only ignorant, not patriotic. What belongs to history belongs to all men. You want to go back to the Middle Ages? Is it better to shave your head with a second-hand razor? Does it hurt Shirley to learn to speak up? It does not. So maybe someday she won't live between the kitchen and the shop. She's not a fool.'

I thank you, Papa, for your kindness. It is true about me to this day. I am foolish but I am not a fool.

That night my father kissed me and said with great interest in my career, 'Shirley, tomorrow's your big day. Congrats.'

'Save it,' my mother said. Then she shut all the windows in order to prevent tonsillitis.

In the morning it snowed. On the street corner a tree had been decorated for us by a kind city administration. In order to miss its chilly shadow our neighbors walked three blocks east to buy a loaf of bread. The butcher pulled down black window shades to keep the colored lights from shining on his chickens. Oh, not me. On the way to school, with both my hands I tossed it a kiss of tolerance. Poor thing, it was a stranger in Egypt.

I walked straight into the auditorium past the staring children. 'Go ahead, Shirley!' said the monitors. Four boys,

333

big for their age, had already started work as propmen and stagehands.

Mr Hilton was very nervous. He was not even happy. Whatever he started to say ended in a sideward look of sadness. He sat slumped in the middle of the first row and asked me to help Miss Glacé. I did this, although she thought my voice too resonant and said, 'Show-off!'

Parents began to arrive long before we were ready. They wanted to make a good impression. From among the yards of drapes I peeked out at the audience. I saw my embarrassed mother.

Ira, Lester, and Meyer were pasted to their beards by Miss Glacé. She almost forgot to thread the star on its wire, but I reminded her. I coughed a few times to clear my throat. Miss Glacé looked around and saw that everyone was in costume and on line waiting to play his part. She whispered, 'All right...' Then:

Jackie Sauerfeld, the prettiest boy in first grade, parted the curtains with his skinny elbow and in a high voice sang out:

> *Parents dear*
> *We are here*
> *To make a Christmas play in time.*
> *It we give*
> *In narrative*
> *And illustrate with pantomime.*

He disappeared.

My voice burst immediately from the wings to the great shock of Ira Lester, and Meyer, who were waiting for it but were surprised all the same.

'I remember, I remember, the house where I was born...'

Miss Glacé yanked the curtain open and there it was, the house – an old hayloft, where Celia Kornbluh lay in the straw with Cindy Lou, her favorite doll. Ira, Lester, and Meyer moved slowly from the wings toward her, sometimes pointing to a moving star and sometimes ahead to Cindy Lou.

It was a long story and it was a sad story. I carefully pronounced all the words about my lonesome childhood, while little Eddie Braunstein wandered upstage and down with his shepherd's stick, looking for sheep. I brought up lonesomeness again, and not being understood at all except by some women everybody hated. Eddie was too small for that and Marty Groff took his place, wearing his father's prayer shawl. I announced twelve friends, and half the boys in the fourth grade gathered round Marty, who stood on an orange crate while my voice harangued. Sorrowful and loud, I declaimed about love and God and Man, but because of the terrible deceit of Abie Stock we came suddenly to a famous moment. Marty, whose remembering tongue I was, waited at the foot of the cross. He stared desperately at the audience. I groaned, 'My God, my God, why hast thou forsaken me?' The soldiers who were sheiks grabbed poor Marty to pin him up to die, but he wrenched free, turned again to the audience, and spread his arms aloft to show despair and the end. I murmured at the top of my voice, 'The rest is silence, but as everyone in this room, in this city – in this world – now knows, I shall have life eternal.'

That night Mrs Kornbluh visited our kitchen for a glass of tea.

'How's the virgin?' asked my father with a look of concern.

'For a man with a daughter, you got a fresh mouth, Abramovitch.'

'Here,' said my father kindly, 'have some lemon, it'll sweeten your disposition.'

They debated a little in Yiddish, then fell in a puddle of

335

Russian and Polish. What I understood next was my father, who said, 'Still and all, it was certainly a beautiful affair, you have to admit, introducing us to the beliefs of a different culture.'

'Well, yes,' said Mrs Kornbluh. 'The only thing... you know Charlie Turner – that cute boy in Celia's class – a couple others? They got very small parts or no part at all. In very bad taste, it seemed to me. After all, it's their religion.'

'Ach,' explained my mother, 'what could Mr Hilton do? They got very small voices; after all, why should they holler? The English language they know from the beginning by heart. They're blond like angels. You think it's so important they should get in the play? Christmas... the whole piece of goods... they own it.'

I listened and listened until I couldn't listen anymore. Too sleepy, I climbed out of bed and kneeled. I made a little church of my hands and said, 'Hear, O Israel...' Then I called out in Yiddish, 'Please, good night, good night. Ssh.' My father said, 'Ssh yourself,' and slammed the kitchen door.

I was happy. I fell asleep at once. I had prayed for everybody: my talking family, cousins far away, passersby, and all the lonesome Christians. I expected to be heard. My voice was certainly the loudest.

ALICE MUNRO

THE TURKEY SEASON

To Joe Radford

WHEN I WAS fourteen I got a job at the Turkey Barn for the Christmas season. I was still too young to get a job working in a store or as a part-time waitress; I was also too nervous.

I was a turkey gutter. The other people who worked at the Turkey Barn were Lily and Marjorie and Gladys, who were also gutters; Irene and Henry, who were pluckers; Herb Abbott, the foreman, who superintended the whole operation and filled in wherever he was needed. Morgan Elliott was the owner and boss. He and his son, Morgy, did the killing.

Morgy I knew from school. I thought him stupid and despicable and was uneasy about having to consider him in a new and possibly superior guise, as the boss's son. But his father treated him so roughly, yelling and swearing at him, that he seemed no more than the lowest of the workers. The other person related to the boss was Gladys. She was his sister, and in her case there did seem to be some privilege of position. She worked slowly and went home if she was not feeling well, and was not friendly to Lily and Marjorie, although she was, a little, to me. She had come back to live with Morgan and his family after working for many years in Toronto, in a bank. This was not the sort of job she was used to. Lily and Marjorie, talking about her when she wasn't there, said she had had a nervous breakdown. They said Morgan made her work in the Turkey Barn to pay for her keep. They also said, with no worry about the contradiction, that she had taken the job because she was after a man, and that the man was Herb Abbott.

All I could see when I closed my eyes, the first few nights after working there, was turkeys. I saw them hanging upside down, plucked and stiffened, pale and cold, with the heads and necks limp, the eyes and nostrils clotted with dark blood; the remaining bits of feathers – those dark and bloody too – seemed to form a crown. I saw them not with aversion but with a sense of endless work to be done.

Herb Abbott showed me what to do. You put the turkey down on the table and cut its head off with a cleaver. Then you took the loose skin around the neck and stripped it back to reveal the crop, nestled in the cleft between the gullet and the windpipe.

'Feel the gravel,' said Herb encouragingly. He made me close my fingers around the crop. Then he showed me how to work my hand down behind it to cut it out, and the gullet and windpipe as well. He used shears to cut the vertebrae.

'Scrunch, scrunch,' he said soothingly. 'Now, put your hand in.'

I did. It was deathly cold in there, in the turkey's dark insides.

'Watch out for bone splinters.'

Working cautiously in the dark, I had to pull the connecting tissues loose.

'Ups-a-daisy.' Herb turned the bird over and flexed each leg. 'Knees up, Mother Brown. Now.' He took a heavy knife and placed it directly on the knee knuckle joints and cut off the shank.

'Have a look at the worms.'

Pearly-white strings, pulled out of the shank, were creeping about on their own.

'That's just the tendons shrinking. Now comes the nice part!'

He slit the bird at its bottom end, letting out a rotten smell.

'Are you educated?'

I did not know what to say.

'What's that smell?'

'Hydrogen sulfide.'

'Educated,' said Herb, sighing. 'All right. Work your fingers around and get the guts loose. Easy. Easy. Keep your fingers together. Keep the palm inwards. Feel the ribs with the back of your hand. Feel the guts fit into your palm. Feel that? Keep going. Break the strings – as many as you can. Keep going. Feel a hard lump? That's the gizzard. Feel a soft lump? That's the heart. Okay? Okay. Get your fingers around the gizzard. Easy. Start pulling this way. That's right. That's right. Start to pull her out.'

It was not easy at all. I wasn't even sure what I had was the gizzard. My hand was full of cold pulp.

'Pull,' he said, and I brought out a glistening, liverish mass.

'Got it. There's the lights. You know what they are? Lungs. There's the heart. There's the gizzard. There's the gall. Now, you don't ever want to break that gall inside or it will taste the entire turkey.' Tactfully, he scraped out what I had missed, including the testicles, which were like a pair of white grapes.

'Nice pair of earrings,' Herb said.

Herb Abbott was a tall, firm, plump man. His hair was dark and thin, combed straight back from a widow's peak, and his eyes seemed to be slightly slanted, so that he looked like a pale Chinese or like pictures of the Devil, except that he was smooth-faced and benign. Whatever he did around the Turkey Barn – gutting, as he was now, or loading the truck, or hanging the carcasses – was done with efficient, economical movements, quickly and buoyantly. 'Notice about Herb – he always walks like he had a boat moving underneath him,' Marjorie said, and it was true. Herb worked on the lake boats, during the season, as a cook. Then he worked for Morgan until after Christmas. The rest of the time he helped around the poolroom, making hamburgers, sweeping up, stopping fights before they got started. That was where he lived: he had a room above the poolroom on the main street.

In all the operations at the Turkey Barn it seemed to be Herb who had the efficiency and honor of the business continually on his mind; it was he who kept everything under control. Seeing him in the yard talking to Morgan, who was a thick, short man, red in the face, an unpredictable bully, you would be sure that it was Herb who was the boss and Morgan the hired help. But it was not so.

If I had not had Herb to show me, I don't think I could have learned turkey gutting at all. I was clumsy with my hands and had been shamed for it so often that the least show of impatience on the part of the person instructing me could have brought on a dithering paralysis. I could not stand to be watched by anybody but Herb. Particularly, I couldn't stand to be watched by Lily and Marjorie, two middle-aged sisters, who were very fast and thorough and competitive gutters. They sang at their work and talked abusively and intimately to the turkey carcasses.

'Don't you nick me, you old bugger!'

'Aren't you the old crap factory!'

I had never heard women talk like that.

Gladys was not a fast gutter, though she must have been thorough; Herb would have talked to her otherwise. She never sang and certainly she never swore. I thought her rather old, though she was not as old as Lily and Marjorie; she must have been over thirty. She seemed offended by everything that went on and had the air of keeping plenty of bitter judgments to herself. I never tried to talk to her, but she spoke to me one day in the cold little washroom off the gutting shed. She was putting pancake makeup on her face. The color of the makeup was so distinct from the color of her skin that it was as if she were slapping orange paint over a whitewashed, bumpy wall.

She asked me if my hair was naturally curly.

I said yes.

'You don't have to get a permanent?'

'No.'

'You're lucky. I have to do mine up every night. The chemicals in my system won't allow me to get a permanent.'

There are different ways women have of talking about their looks. Some women make it clear that what they do to keep themselves up is for the sake of sex, for men. Others, like Gladys, make the job out to be a kind of housekeeping, whose very difficulties they pride themselves on. Gladys was genteel. I could see her in the bank, in a navy-blue dress with the kind of detachable white collar you can wash at night. She would be grumpy and correct.

Another time, she spoke to me about her periods, which were profuse and painful. She wanted to know about mine. There was an uneasy, prudish, agitated expression on her face. I was saved by Irene, who was using the toilet and called out, 'Do like me, and you'll be rid of all your problems for a while.' Irene was only a few years older than I was, but she was recently – tardily – married, and heavily pregnant.

Gladys ignored her, running cold water on her hands. The hands of all of us were red and sore-looking from the

343

work. 'I can't use that soap. If I use it, I break out in a rash,' Gladys said. 'If I bring my own soap in here, I can't afford to have other people using it, because I pay a lot for it – it's a special anti-allergy soap.'

I think the idea that Lily and Marjorie promoted – that Gladys was after Herb Abbott – sprang from their belief that single people ought to be teased and embarrassed whenever possible, and from their interest in Herb, which led to the feeling that somebody ought to be after him. They wondered about him. What they wondered was, How can a man want so little? No wife, no family, no house. The details of his daily life, the small preferences, were of interest. Where had he been brought up? (Here and there and all over.) How far had he gone in school? (Far enough.) Where was his girlfriend? (Never tell.) Did he drink coffee or tea if he got the choice? (Coffee.)

When they talked about Gladys's being after him they must have really wanted to talk about sex – what he wanted and what he got. They must have felt a voluptuous curiosity about him, as I did. He aroused this feeling by being circumspect and not making the jokes some men did, and at the same time by not being squeamish or gentlemanly. Some men, showing me the testicles from the turkey, would have acted as if the very existence of testicles were somehow a bad joke on me, something a girl could be taunted about; another sort of man would have been embarrassed and would have thought he had to protect me from embarrassment. A man who didn't seem to feel one way or the other was an oddity – as much to older women, probably, as to me. But what was so welcome to me may have been disturbing to them. They wanted to jolt him. They even wanted Gladys to jolt him, if she could.

There wasn't any idea then – at least in Logan, Ontario,

344

in the late forties – about homosexuality's going beyond very narrow confines. Women, certainly, believed in its rarity and in definite boundaries. There were homosexuals in town, and we knew who they were: an elegant, light-voiced, wavy-haired paperhanger who called himself an interior decorator; the minister's widow's fat, spoiled only son, who went so far as to enter baking contests and had crocheted a table-cloth; a hypochondriacal church organist and music teacher who kept the choir and his pupils in line with screaming tantrums. Once the label was fixed, there was a good deal of tolerance for these people, and their talents for deco-rating, for crocheting, and for music were appreciated – especially by women. 'The poor fellow,' they said. 'He doesn't do any harm.' They really seemed to believe – the women did – that it was the penchant for baking or music that was the determining factor, and that it was this activity that made the man what he was – not any other detours he might take, or wish to take. A desire to play the violin would be taken as more a deviation from manliness than would a wish to shun women. Indeed, the idea was that any manly man would wish to shun women but most of them were caught off guard, and for good.

I don't want to go into the question of whether Herb was homosexual or not, because the definition is of no use to me. I think that probably he was, but maybe he was not. (Even considering what happened later, I think that.) He is not a puzzle so arbitrarily solved.

The other plucker, who worked with Irene, was Henry Streets, a neighbor of ours. There was nothing remarkable about him except that he was eighty-six years old and still, as he said of himself, a devil for work. He had whisky in his thermos, and drank it from time to time through the day.

It was Henry who said to me, in our kitchen, 'You ought to get yourself a job at the Turkey Barn. They need another gutter.' Then my father said at once, 'Not her, Henry. She's got ten thumbs,' and Henry said he was just joking – it was dirty work. But I was already determined to try it – I had great need to be successful in a job like that. I was almost in the condition of a grown-up person who is ashamed of never having learned to read, so much did I feel my ineptness at manual work. Work, to everybody I knew, meant doing things I was no good at doing, and work was what people prided themselves on and measured each other by. (It goes without saying that the things I was good at, like schoolwork, were suspect or held in plain contempt.) So it was a surprise and then a triumph for me not to get fired, and to be able to turn out clean turkeys at a rate that was not disgraceful. I don't know if I really understood how much Herb Abbott was responsible for this, but he would sometimes say, 'Good girl,' or pat my waist and say, 'You're getting to be a good gutter – you'll go a long ways in the world,' and when I felt his quick, kind touch through the heavy sweater and bloody smock I wore, I felt my face glow and I wanted to lean back against him as he stood behind me. I wanted to rest my head against his wide, fleshy shoulder. When I went to sleep at night, lying on my side, I would run my cheek against the pillow and think of that as Herb's shoulder.

I was interested in how he talked to Gladys, how he looked at her or noticed her. This interest was not jealousy. I think I wanted something to happen with them. I quivered in curious expectation, as Lily and Marjorie did. We all wanted to see the flicker of sexuality in him, hear it in his voice, not because we thought it would make him seem more like other men but because we knew that with him it would be entirely different. He was kinder and more patient than most women, and as stern and remote, in some ways, as any man. We wanted to see how he could be moved.

If Gladys wanted this too, she didn't give any signs of it. It is impossible for me to tell with women like her whether they are as thick and deadly as they seem, not wanting anything much but opportunities for irritation and contempt, or if they are all choked up with gloomy fires and useless passions.

Marjorie and Lily talked about marriage. They did not have much good to say about it, in spite of their feeling that it was a state nobody should be allowed to stay out of. Marjorie said that shortly after her marriage she had gone into the woodshed with the intention of swallowing Paris green.

'I'd have done it,' she said. 'But the man came along in the grocery truck and I had to go out and buy the groceries. This was when we lived on the farm.'

Her husband was cruel to her in those days, but later he suffered an accident – he rolled the tractor and was so badly hurt he would be an invalid all his life. They moved to town, and Marjorie was the boss now.

'He starts to sulk the other night and say he don't want his supper. Well, I just picked up his wrist and held it. He was scared I was going to twist his arm. He could see I'd do it. So I say, "You *what*?" And he says, "I'll eat it." '

They talked about their father. He was a man of the old school. He had a noose in the woodshed (not the Paris green woodshed – this would be an earlier one, on another farm), and when they got on his nerves he used to line them up and threaten to hang them. Lily, who was the younger, would shake till she fell down. This same father had arranged to marry Marjorie off to a crony of his when she was just sixteen. That was the husband who had driven her to the Paris green. Their father did it because he wanted to be sure she wouldn't get into trouble.

'Hot blood,' Lily said.

I was horrified, and asked, 'Why didn't you run away?'

'His word was law,' Marjorie said.

They said that was what was the matter with kids nowadays – it was the kids that ruled the roost. A father's word should be law. They brought up their own kids strictly, and none had turned out bad yet. When Marjorie's son wet the bed she threatened to cut off his dingy with the butcher knife. That cured him.

They said ninety percent of the young girls nowadays drank, and swore, and took it lying down. They did not have daughters, but if they did and caught them at anything like that they would beat them raw. Irene, they said, used to go to the hockey games with her ski pants slit and nothing under them, for convenience in the snowdrifts afterward. Terrible.

I wanted to point out some contradictions. Marjorie and Lily themselves drank and swore, and what was so wonderful about the strong will of a father who would insure you a lifetime of unhappiness? (What I did not see was that Marjorie and Lily were not unhappy altogether – could not be, because of their sense of consequence, their pride and style.) I could be enraged then at the lack of logic in most adults' talk – the way they held to their pronouncements no matter what evidence might be presented to them. How could these women's hands be so gifted, so delicate and clever – for I knew they would be as good at dozens of other jobs as they were at gutting; they would be good at quilting and darning and painting and papering and kneading dough and setting out seedlings – and their thinking so slapdash, clumsy, infuriating?

Lily said she never let her husband come near her if he had been drinking. Marjorie said since the time she nearly died with a hemorrhage she never let her husband come near her, period. Lily said quickly that it was only when he'd been drinking that he tried anything. I could see that it was a matter of pride not to let your husband come near you, but I couldn't quite believe that 'come near' meant 'have sex'. The idea of Marjorie and Lily being sought out for such purposes seemed grotesque. They had bad teeth, their stomachs sagged, their faces were dull and spotty. I decided to take 'come near' literally.

The two weeks before Christmas was a frantic time at the Turkey Barn. I began to go in for an hour before school as well as after school and on weekends. In the morning, when I walked to work, the streetlights would still be on and the morning stars shining. There was the Turkey Barn, on the edge of a white field, with a row of big pine trees behind it, and always, no matter how cold and still it was, these trees were lifting their branches and sighing and straining. It seems unlikely that on my way to the Turkey Barn, for an hour of gutting turkeys, I should have experienced such a sense of promise and at the same time of perfect, impenetrable mystery in the universe, but I did. Herb had something to do with that, and so did the cold snap – the series of hard, clear mornings. The truth is, such feelings weren't hard to come by then. I would get them but not know how they were to be connected with anything in real life.

One morning at the Turkey Barn there was a new gutter. This was a boy eighteen or nineteen years old, a stranger named Brian. It seemed he was a relative, or perhaps just a friend, of Herb Abbott's. He was staying with Herb. He had worked on a lake boat last summer. He said he had got sick of it, though, and quit.

What he said was 'Yeah, fuckin' boats, I got sick of that.'

Language at the Turkey Barn was coarse and free, but this was one word never heard there. And Brian's use of it seemed not careless but flaunting, mixing insult and provocation. Perhaps it was his general style that made it so. He had amazing good looks: taffy hair, bright blue eyes, ruddy skin, well-shaped body – the sort of good looks nobody disagrees about for a moment. But a single, relentless notion had got such a hold on him that he could not keep from turning all his assets into parody. His mouth was wet-looking and slightly open most of the time, his eyes were half shut, his expression a hopeful leer, his movements indolent, exaggerated, inviting. Perhaps if he had been put on a stage with a microphone and a guitar and let grunt and howl and wriggle and excite, he would have seemed a true celebrant. Lacking a stage, he was unconvincing. After a while he seemed just like somebody with a bad case of hiccups – his insistent sexuality was that monotonous and meaningless.

If he had toned down a bit, Marjorie and Lily would probably have enjoyed him. They could have kept up a game of telling him to shut his filthy mouth and keep his hands to himself. As it was, they said they were sick of him, and meant it. Once, Marjorie took up her gutting knife. 'Keep your distance,' she said. 'I mean from me and my sister and that kid.'

She did not tell him to keep his distance from Gladys, because Gladys wasn't there at the time and Marjorie would probably not have felt like protecting her anyway. But it was Gladys Brian particularly liked to bother. She would throw down her knife and go into the washroom and stay there ten minutes and come out with a stony face. She didn't say she was sick anymore and go home, the way she used to. Marjorie said Morgan was mad at Gladys for sponging and she couldn't get away with it any longer.

Gladys said to me, 'I can't stand that kind of thing. I can't stand people mentioning that kind of thing and that kind of – gestures. It makes me sick to my stomach.'

I believed her. She was terribly white. But why, in that case, did she not complain to Morgan? Perhaps relations between them were too uneasy, perhaps she could not bring herself to repeat or describe such things. Why did none of us complain – if not to Morgan, at least to Herb? I never thought of it. Brian seemed just something to put up with, like the freezing cold in the gutting shed and the smell of blood and waste. When Marjorie and Lily did threaten to complain, it was about Brian's laziness.

He was not a good gutter. He said his hands were too big. So Herb took him off gutting, told him he was to sweep and clean up, make packages of giblets, and help load the truck. This meant that he did not have to be in any one place or doing any one job at a given time, so much of the time he did nothing. He would start sweeping up, leave that and mop the tables, leave that and have a cigarette, lounge against the table bothering us until Herb called him to help load. Herb was very busy now and spent a lot of time making deliveries, so it was possible he did not know the extent of Brian's idleness.

'I don't know why Herb don't fire you,' Marjorie said. 'I guess the answer is he don't want you hanging around sponging on him, with no place to go.'

'I know where to go,' said Brian.

'Keep your sloppy mouth shut,' said Marjorie. 'I pity Herb. Getting saddled.'

* * *

On the last school day before Christmas we got out early in the afternoon. I went home and changed my clothes and came in to work at about three o'clock. Nobody was working. Everybody was in the gutting shed, where Morgan Elliott was swinging a cleaver over the gutting table and yelling. I couldn't make out what the yelling was about, and thought someone must have made a terrible mistake in his work; perhaps it had been me. Then I saw Brian on the other side of the table, looking very sulky and mean, and standing well back. The sexual leer was not altogether gone from his face, but it was flattened out and mixed with a look of impotent bad temper and some fear. That's it, I thought, Brian is getting fired for being so sloppy and lazy. Even when I made out Morgan saying 'pervert' and 'filthy' and 'maniac', I still thought that was what was happening. Marjorie and Lily, and even brassy Irene, were standing around with downcast, rather pious looks, such as children get when somebody is suffering a terrible bawling out at school. Only old Henry seemed able to keep a cautious grin on his face. Gladys was not to be seen. Herb was standing closer to Morgan than anybody else. He was not interfering but was keeping an eye on the cleaver. Morgy was blubbering, though he didn't seem to be in any immediate danger.

Morgan was yelling at Brian to get out. 'And out of this town – I mean it – and don't you wait till tomorrow if you still want your arse in one piece! Out!' he shouted, and the cleaver swung dramatically towards the door. Brian started in that direction but, whether he meant to or not, he made a swaggering, taunting motion of the buttocks. This made Morgan break into a roar and run after him, swinging the cleaver in a stagy way. Brian ran, and Morgan ran after him, and Irene screamed and grabbed her stomach. Morgan was too heavy to run any distance and probably could not have thrown the cleaver very far, either. Herb watched from the doorway. Soon Morgan came back and flung the cleaver down on the table.

'All back to work! No more gawking around here! You don't get paid for gawking! What are you getting under way at?' he said, with a hard look at Irene.

'Nothing,' Irene said meekly.

'If you're getting under way get out of here.'

'I'm not.'

'All right, then!'

We got to work. Herb took off his blood-smeared smock and put on his jacket and went off, probably to see that Brian got ready to go on the suppertime bus. He did not say a word. Morgan and his son went out to the yard, and Irene and Henry went back to the adjoining shed, where they did the plucking, working knee-deep in the feathers Brian was supposed to keep swept up.

'Where's Gladys?' I said softly.

'Recuperating,' said Marjorie. She too spoke in a quieter voice than usual, and *recuperating* was not the sort of word she and Lily normally used. It was a word to be used about Gladys, with a mocking intent.

They didn't want to talk about what had happened, because they were afraid Morgan might come in and catch them at it and fire them. Good workers as they were, they were afraid of that. Besides, they hadn't seen anything. They must have been annoyed that they hadn't. All I ever found out was that Brian had either done something or shown something to Gladys as she came out of the washroom and she had started screaming and having hysterics.

Now she'll likely be laid up with another nervous breakdown, they said. And he'll be on his way out of town. And good riddance, they said, to both of them.

353

I have a picture of the Turkey Barn crew taken on Christmas Eve. It was taken with a flash camera that was someone's Christmas extravagance. I think it was Irene's. But Herb Abbott must have been the one who took the picture. He was the one who could be trusted to know or to learn immediately how to manage anything new, and flash cameras were fairly new at the time. The picture was taken about ten o'clock on Christmas Eve, after Herb and Morgy had come back from making the last delivery and we had washed off the gutting table and swept and mopped the cement floor. We had taken off our bloody smocks and heavy sweaters and gone into the little room called the lunchroom, where there was a table and a heater. We still wore our working clothes: overalls and shirts. The men wore caps and the women kerchiefs, tied in the wartime style. I am stout and cheerful and comradely in the picture, transformed into someone I don't ever remember being or pretending to be. I look years older than fourteen. Irene is the only one who has taken off her kerchief, freeing her long red hair. She peers out from it with a meek, sluttish, inviting look, which would match her reputation but is not like any look of hers I remember. Yes, it must have been her camera; she is posing for it, with that look, more deliberately than anyone else is. Marjorie and Lily are smiling, true to form, but their smiles are sour and reckless. With their hair hidden, and such figures as they have bundled up, they look like a couple of tough and jovial but testy workmen. Their kerchiefs look misplaced; caps would be better. Henry is in high spirits, glad to be part of the work force, grinning and looking twenty years younger than his age. Then Morgy, with his hangdog look, not trusting the occasion's bounty, and Morgan very flushed and bosslike and satisfied. He has just given each of us our bonus turkey. Each of these turkeys has a leg or a wing missing, or a malformation of some kind, so none of them are salable at the full price. But Morgan has been at pains to tell us that you often get the best meat off the gimpy ones, and he has shown us that he's taking one home himself.

We are all holding mugs or large, thick china cups, which contain not the usual tea but rye whisky. Morgan and Henry have been drinking since suppertime. Marjorie and Lily say they only want a little, and only take it at all because it's Christmas Eve and they are dead on their feet. Irene says she's dead on her feet as well but that doesn't mean she only wants a little. Herb has poured quite generously not just for her but for Lily and Marjorie too, and they do not object. He has measured mine and Morgy's out at the same time, very stingily, and poured in Coca-Cola. This is the first drink I have ever had, and as a result I will believe for years that rye-and-Coca-Cola is a standard sort of drink and will always ask for it, until I notice that few other people drink it and that it makes me sick. I didn't get sick that Christmas Eve, though; Herb had not given me enough. Except for an odd taste, and my own feeling of consequence, it was like drinking Coca-Cola.

I don't need Herb in the picture to remember what he looked like. That is, if he looked like himself, as he did all the time at the Turkey Barn and the few times I saw him on the street – as he did all the times in my life when I saw him except one.

The time he looked somewhat unlike himself was when Morgan was cursing out Brian and, later, when Brian had run off down the road. What was this different look? I've tried to remember, because I studied it hard at the time. It wasn't much different. His face looked softer and heavier then, and if you had to describe the expression on it you would have to say it was an expression of shame. But what would he be ashamed of? Ashamed of Brian, for the way he had behaved? Surely that would be late in the day; when had Brian ever behaved otherwise? Ashamed of Morgan, for carrying on so ferociously and theatrically? Or of himself, because he was famous for nipping fights and displays of this sort in the bud and hadn't been able to do it here? Would he be ashamed that he hadn't stood up for Brian? Would he have expected himself to do that, to stand up for Brian?

All this was what I wondered at the time. Later, when I knew more, at least about sex, I decided that Brian was Herb's lover, and that Gladys really was trying to get attention from Herb, and that that was why Brian had humiliated her – with or without Herb's connivance and consent. Isn't it true that people like Herb – dignified, secretive, honorable people – will often choose somebody like Brian, will waste their helpless love on some vicious, silly person who is not even evil, or a monster, but just some importunate nuisance? I decided that Herb, with all his gentleness and carefulness, was avenging himself on us all – not just on Gladys but on us all – with Brian, and that what he was feeling when I studied his face must have been a savage and gleeful scorn. But embarrassment as well – embarrassment for Brian and for himself and for Gladys, and to some degree for all of us. Shame for all of us – that is what I thought then.

Later still, I backed off from this explanation. I got to a stage of backing off from the things I couldn't really know. It's enough for me now just to think of Herb's face with that peculiar, stricken look; to think of Brian monkeying in the shade of Herb's dignity; to think of my own mystified concentration on Herb, my need to catch him out, if I could ever get the chance, and then move in and stay close to him.

How attractive, how delectable, the prospect of intimacy is, with the very person who will never grant it. I can still feel the pull of a man like that, of his promising and refusing. I would still like to know things. Never mind facts. Never mind theories, either.

When I finished my drink I wanted to say something to Herb. I stood beside him and waited for a moment when he was not listening to or talking with anyone else and when the increasingly rowdy conversation of the others would cover what I had to say.

'I'm sorry your friend had to go away.'

'That's all right.'

Herb spoke kindly and with amusement, and so shut me off from any further right to look at or speak about his life. He knew what I was up to. He must have known it before, with lots of women. He knew how to deal with it.

Lily had a little more whisky in her mug and told how she and her best girlfriend (dead now, of liver trouble) had dressed up as men one time and gone into the men's side of the beer parlor, the side where it said MEN ONLY, because they wanted to see what it was like. They sat in a corner drinking beer and keeping their eyes and ears open, and nobody looked twice or thought a thing about them, but soon a problem arose.

'Where were we going to go? If we went around to the other side and anybody seen us going into the ladies', they would scream bloody murder. And if we went into the men's somebody'd be sure to notice we didn't do it the right way. Meanwhile the beer was going through us like a bugger!'

'What you don't do when you're young!' Marjorie said.

Several people gave me and Morgy advice. They told us to enjoy ourselves while we could. They told us to stay out of trouble. They said they had all been young once. Herb said we were a good crew and had done a good job but he didn't want to get in bad with any of the women's husbands by keeping them there too late. Marjorie and Lily expressed indifference to their husbands, but Irene announced that she loved hers and that it was not true that he had been dragged back from Detroit to marry her, no matter what people said. Henry said it was a good life if you didn't weaken. Morgan said he wished us all the most sincere Merry Christmas.

When we came out of the Turkey Barn it was snowing. Lily said it was like a Christmas card, and so it was, with the snow whirling around the streetlights in town and around the colored lights people had put up outside their doorways. Morgan was giving Henry and Irene a ride home in the truck, acknowledging age and pregnancy and Christmas. Morgy took a shortcut through the field, and Herb walked off by himself, head down and hands in his pockets, rolling slightly, as if he were on the deck of a lake boat. Marjorie and Lily linked arms with me as if we were old comrades.

'Let's sing,' Lily said. 'What'll we sing?'

' "We Three Kings"?' said Marjorie. ' "We Three Turkey Gutters"?'

' "I'm Dreaming of a White Christmas".'

'Why dream? You got it!'

So we sang.

RICHARD FORD

CRÈCHE

FAITH IS NOT driving them, her mother, Esther, is. In the car it's the five of them. The family. On their way to Snow Mountain Highlands – Sandusky, Ohio, to northern Michigan – to ski. It's Christmas, or nearly. No one wants to spend Christmas alone.

The five include Faith, who's the motion picture lawyer, arrived from California; her mother, who's sixty-four and who's thoughtfully volunteered to drive. Roger, Faith's sister's husband, a guidance counsellor at Sandusky J.F.K. And Roger's two girls: Jane and Marjorie, ages eight and six. Daisy, the girls' mom, Faith's younger sister, Roger's estranged wife, is a presence but not along. She is in rehab in a large Midwestern city that is not Chicago or Detroit.

Outside, beyond a long, treeless expanse of frozen white winterscape, Lake Michigan suddenly becomes visible. It is pale blue with a thin fog hovering just above its metallic surface. The girls are chatting chirpily in the back seat. Roger is beside them reading *Skier* magazine. No one is arguing.

Florida would've been a much nicer holiday alternative, Faith thinks. Epcot for the girls. The Space Center. Satellite Beach. Fresh fish. The ocean. She is paying for everything and does not even like to ski. But it has been a hard year for everyone, and someone has had to take charge. If they'd all gone to Florida, she'd have ended up broke.

Her basic character strength, Faith believes, watching what seems to be a nuclear power plant coming up on the left, is the feature that makes her a first-rate lawyer: an undeterrable willingness to see things as capable of being made better. If someone at the studio, a V.P. in marketing, for example, wishes a quick exit from a totally binding yet surprisingly uncomfortable obligation – say, a legal contract – then Faith's your girl. Faith the doer. Your very own optimist. Faith the blond beauty with smarts. A client's dream with great tits. Her own tits. Just give her a day on your problem.

Her sister is a perfect case in point. Daisy has been able to admit her serious methamphetamine problems, but only after her biker boyfriend, Vince, has been made a guest of the State of Ohio. And here Faith has had a role to play, beginning with phone calls, then attorneys, a restraining order, then later the state police and handcuffs. Going through Daisy's apartment with their mother, in search of clothes Daisy could wear with dignity into rehab, Faith found dildos; six, in all – one, for some reason, under the kitchen sink. These she put into a black plastic grocery bag and left in the neighbor's street garbage just so her mother wouldn't know. Her mother is up-to-date, she feels, but not necessarily interested in dildos. For Daisy's going-in outfit they decided on a dark jersey shift and some new white Adidas.

The downside on the character issue, Faith understands, is the fact that, at almost thirty-seven, nothing's particularly solid in her life. She is very patient (with assholes), very ready to forgive (assholes), very good to help behind the scenes (with assholes). Her glass is always half full. Stand and ameliorate, her motto. Anticipate change. The skills of the law once again only partly in synch with the requirements of life.

A tall silver smokestack with blinking silver lights on top

and several gray megaphone-shaped cooling pots around it all come into view on the frozen lakefront. Dense chalky smoke drifts out the top of each.

'What's that big thing?' Jane or possibly Marjorie says, peering out the back-seat window. It is too warm in the cranberry-colored Suburban Faith rented at the Cleveland airport, plus the girls are chewing watermelon-smelling gum. Everyone could get carsick.

'That's a rocket ship ready to blast off to outer space. Would you girls like to hitch a ride on it?' Roger says. Roger, the brother-in-law, is the friendly-funny neighbor in a family sitcom, although he isn't funny. He is small and blandly not-quite-handsome and wears a brush cut and black horn-rimmed glasses. And he is loathsome – though only in subtle ways, like TV actors Faith has known. He is also thirty-seven and likes pastel cardigans and suède shoes. Faith has noticed he is, oddly enough, quite tanned.

'It is not a rocket ship,' Jane, the older child, says and puts her forehead to the foggy window then pulls back and considers the smudge mark she's left.

'It's a pickle,' Marjorie says.

'And shut up,' Jane says. 'That's a nasty expression.'

'It isn't,' Marjorie says.

'Is that a new word your mother taught you?' Roger asks and smirks. 'I bet it is. That'll be her legacy.' On the cover of *Skier* is a photograph of Alberto Tomba wearing an electric-red outfit, running the giant slalom at Kitzbühel. The headline says, 'GOING TO EXTREMES'.

'It better not be,' Faith's mother says from behind the wheel. Faith's mother is unusually thin. Over the years she has actually shrunk from a regular, plump size 12 to the point that she now swims inside her clothes, and, on occasion, can resemble a species of testy bird. There are problems with her veins and her digestion. But nothing is medically wrong. She eats.

'It's an atom plant where they make electricity,' Faith says, and smiles back approvingly at the nieces, who are staring out the car window, losing interest. 'We use it to heat our houses.'

'We don't like that kind of heat, though,' Faith's mother says. Her seat is pushed up, seemingly to accommodate her diminished size. Even her seat belt hangs on her. Esther was once a science teacher and has been Green since before it was chic.

'Why not?' Jane says.

'Don't you girls learn anything in school?' Roger says, flipping pages in his *Skier*.

'Their father could always instruct them,' Esther says. 'He's in education.'

'Guidance,' Roger says. 'But touché.'

'What's "touché"?' Jane says and wrinkles her nose.

'It's a term used in fencing,' Faith says. She likes both little girls immensely, would like to punish Roger for ever speaking sarcastically to them.

'What's fencing?' Marjorie asks.

'It's a town in Michigan where they make fences,' Roger says. 'Fencing, Michigan. It's near Lansing.'

'No, it's not,' Faith says.

'Then, you tell them,' Roger says. 'You know everything. You're the lawyer.'

'It's a game you play with swords,' Faith says. 'Only no one gets killed or hurt.' In every way, she despises Roger and wishes he'd stayed in Sandusky. Though she couldn't bring the girls without him. Letting her pay for everything is Roger's way of saying thanks.

'Now, all your lives you'll remember where you heard

364

fencing explained first and by whom,' Roger says in a nice-nasty voice. 'When you're at Harvard –'

'You didn't know,' Jane says.

'That's wrong. I did know. I absolutely knew,' Roger says. 'I was just having some fun. Christmas is a fun time.'

Faith's love life has not been going well. She has always wanted children-with-marriage, but neither of these things has quite happened. Either the men she's liked haven't liked children, or else the men who've loved her and wanted to give her all she longed for haven't seemed worth it. Practicing law for a movie studio has accordingly become extremely engrossing. Time has gone by. A series of mostly courteous men has entered but then departed, all for one reason or another unworkable: married, frightened, divorced, all three together. Lucky is how she has chiefly seen herself. She goes to the gym every day, leases an expensive car, lives alone at the beach in a rental owned by an ex-teen-age movie star who is a friend's brother and has H.I.V. A deal.

Late last spring she met a man. A stock-market hotsy-totsy with a house on Block Island. Jack. Jack flew to Block Island from the city in his own plane, had never been married at age roughly forty-six. She flew out a few times with him, met his stern-looking sisters, the pretty, social mom. There was a big blue rambling beach house facing the sea. Rose hedges, sandy pathways to secret dunes where you could swim naked – something she especially liked, though the sisters were astounded. The father was there, but was sick and would soon die, so that things were generally on hold. Jack did beaucoup business in London. Money was not a problem. Maybe when the father departed they could be married, Jack had almost suggested. But until then she could travel with him whenever she could get away. Scale back a little on the expectation side. He wanted children, would get to California often. It could work.

One night a woman called. Greta she said her name was. Greta was in love with Jack. She and Jack had had a fight, but Jack still loved her. It turned out Greta had pictures of Faith and Jack in New York together. Who knew who took them? A little bird. One was a picture of Faith and Jack exiting Jack's apartment building. Another was of Jack helping Faith out of a yellow taxi. One was of Faith, all alone, at the Park Avenue Café, eating seared swordfish. One was of Jack and Faith kissing in the front seat of an unrecognizable car – also in New York.

Jack liked particular kinds of sex in very particular kinds of ways, Greta said. She guessed Faith knew all about that by now. But 'best not to make long-range plans' was somehow the message.

When asked, Jack conceded there was a problem. But he would solve it. Tout de suite (though he was preoccupied with his father's approaching death). Jack was a tall, smooth-faced, handsome man with a shock of lustrous, mahogany-colored hair. Like a clothing model. He smiled, and everyone felt better. He'd gone to Harvard, played squash, rowed, debated, looked good in a brown suit and oldish shoes. He was trustworthy. It still seemed workable.

But Greta called more times. She sent pictures of herself and Jack together. Recent pictures, since Faith had come on board. It was harder than he thought to get untangled, Jack admitted. Faith would need to be patient. Greta was someone he'd once 'cared about very much'. Might've even married. But she had problems, yes. And he wouldn't just throw her over. He wasn't that kind of man, something she, Faith, would be glad about in the long run. Meanwhile there was his sick father. The patriarch. And his mother. And the sisters.

That had been plenty.

Snow Mountain Highlands is a small ski resort, but nice. Family, not flash. Faith's mother found it as a 'Holiday Getaway' in the Sandusky *Pennysaver*. The getaway involves a condo, weekend lift tickets, coupons for three days of Swedish smorgasbord in the Bavarian-style inn. Although the deal is for two people only. The rest have to pay. Faith will sleep with her mother in the 'Master Suite'. Roger can share the twin bedroom with the girls.

When Faith's sister Daisy began to be interested in Vince the biker, Roger had simply 'receded'. Her and Roger's sex life had lost its effervescence, Daisy confided. They had started life as a model couple in a suburb of Sandusky, but eventually – after some time and two kids – happiness ended and Daisy had been won over by Vince, who did amphetamines and, more significantly, sold them. That – Vince's arrival – was when sex had gotten really good, Daisy said. Faith silently believes Daisy envied her movie connections and movie life and her Jaguar convertible, and basically threw her life away (at least until rehab) as a way of simulating Faith's – only with a biker. Eventually Daisy left home and gained forty-five pounds on a body that was already voluptuous, if short. Last summer, at the beach at Middle Bass Island, Daisy in a rage actually punched Faith in the chest when she suggested that Daisy might lose some weight, ditch Vince, and consider coming home. 'I'm not like you,' Daisy screamed, right out on the sand. 'I fuck for pleasure. Not for business.' Then she'd waddled into the tepid surf of Lake Erie, wearing a pink one-piece that boasted a frilly skirtlet. By then, Roger had the girls, courtesy of a court order.

* * *

367

Faith has had a sauna and is now thinking about phoning Jack wherever Jack is. Block Island. New York. London. She has no particular message to leave. Later she plans to go cross-country skiing under the moonlight. Just to be a full participant. Set a good example. For this she has brought her L.A. purchases: loden knickers, a green-brown-and-red sweater made in the Himalayas, and socks from Norway. No way does she plan to get cold.

In the living room her mother is having a glass of red wine and playing solitaire with two decks by the big picture window that looks down toward the crowded ski slope and ice rink. Roger is there on the bunny slope with Jane and Marjorie, but it's impossible to distinguish them. Red suits. Yellow suits. Lots of dads with kids. All of it soundless.

Her mother plays cards at high speed, flipping cards and snapping them down as if she hates the game and wants it to be over. Her eyes are intent. She has put on a cream-colored neck brace. (The tension of driving has aggravated an old work-related injury.) And she is now wearing a Hawaii-print orange muumuu, which engulfs her. How long, Faith wonders, has her mother been shrinking? Twenty years, at least. Since Faith's father kicked the bucket.

'Maybe I'll go to Europe,' her mother says, flicking cards ferociously with bony fingers. 'That'd be adventurous, wouldn't it?'

Faith is at the window observing the expert slope. Smooth, wide pastures of snow framed by copses of beautiful spruces. Several skiers are zigzagging their way down, doing their best to be stylish. Years ago she came here with her high-school boyfriend. Eddie, a.k.a. Fast Eddie, which in some ways he was. Neither of them liked to ski, nor did they get out of bed to try. Now skiing reminds her of golf – a golf course made of snow.

'Maybe I'd take the girls out of school and treat us all to Venice,' Esther goes on. 'I'm sure Roger would be relieved.'

Faith has spotted Roger and the girls on the bunny slope. Blue, green, yellow suits, respectively. Roger is pointing, giving detailed instructions to his daughters about ski etiquette. Just like any dad. She thinks she sees him laughing. It is hard to think of Roger as an average parent.

'They're too young for Venice,' Faith says. From outside, she hears the rasp of a snow shovel and muffled voices.

'I'll take you, then,' her mother says. 'When Daisy clears rehab we can all three take in Europe. I always planned that.'

Faith likes her mother. Her mother is no fool, yet still seeks ways to be generous. But Faith cannot complete a picture that includes herself, her diminished mother, and Daisy on the Champs-Élysées or the Grand Canal. 'That's a nice idea,' Faith says. She is standing beside her mother's chair, looking down at the top of her head. Her mother's head is small. Its hair is dark gray and not especially clean, but short and sparse. She has affected a very wide part straight down the middle. Her mother looks like a homeless woman, only with a neck brace.

'I was reading what it takes to get to a hundred,' Esther says, neatening the cards on the glass tabletop in front of her. Faith has begun thinking of Jack again and what a peculiar species of creep he is. Jack Matthews still wears the Lobb captoe shoes he had made for him in college. Ugly, pretentious English shoes. 'You have to be physically active,' her mother continues. 'You have to be an optimist, which I am. You have to stay interested in things, which I more or less do. And you have to handle loss well.'

With all her concentration Faith tries not to wonder how she ranks on this scale. 'Do you want to live to a hundred?' she asks her mother.

'Oh yes,' Esther says. 'Of course. You can't imagine it, that's all. You're too young. And beautiful. And talented.' No irony. Irony is not her mother's specialty.

Outside, the men shovelling snow can be heard to say, 'Hi, we're the Weather Channel.' They are speaking to someone watching them out another window from another condo. 'In winter the most innocent places can turn lethal,' the same man says and laughs. 'Colder'n a well-digger's dick, you bet,' a second man's voice says. 'That's today's forecast.'

'The male appliance,' her mother says pleasantly, fiddling with her cards. 'That's it, isn't it? The whole mystery.'

'So I'm told,' Faith says.

'They were all women, though.'

'Who was?'

'All the people who lived to be a hundred. You could do all the other things right. But you still needed to be a woman to survive.'

'Lucky us,' Faith says.

'Right. The lucky few.'

This will be the girls' first Christmas without a tree or their mother. And Faith has attempted to improvise around this by arranging presents at the base of the large, plastic rubber-tree plant stationed against one of the empty white walls in the living room. She has brought a few red Christmas balls, a gold star, and a string of lights that promise to blink. 'Christmas in Manila' could be a possible theme.

Outside, the day is growing dim. Faith's mother is napping. Roger has gone down to the Warming Shed for a mulled wine following his ski lesson. The girls are seated on the couch side by side, wearing their Lanz of Salzburg flannel nighties with matching smiling-bunny slippers. Green and yellow again, but with printed snowflakes. They have taken their baths together, with Faith present to supervise, then insisted on putting on their nighties early for their nap. To her, these two seem perfect angels and perfectly wasted on their parents.

'We know how to ski now,' Jane says primly. They're watching Faith trim the rubber-tree plant. First the blinking lights (though there's no plug-in close enough), then the six red balls (one for each family member). Last will be the gold star. Possibly, Faith thinks, she is trying for too much. Though why not try for too much? It's Christmas.

'Would you two care to help me?' Faith smiles up at both of them from the floor where she is on her knees fiddling with the fragile green strand of tiny peaked bulbs she already knows will not light up.

'No,' Jane says.

'I don't blame you,' Faith says.

'Is Mommy coming here?' Marjorie says and blinks, crosses her tiny, pale ankles. She is sleepy and might possibly cry, Faith realizes.

'No, sweet,' Faith says. 'This Christmas Mommy is doing herself a big favor. So she can't do us one.'

'What about Vince?' Jane says authoritatively. Vince is a subject that's been gone over before. Mrs Argenbright, the girls' therapist, has taken special pains with the Vince issue. The girls have the skinny on Mr Vince but wish to be given it again, since they like him more than their father.

'Vince is a guest of the State of Ohio right now,' Faith says. 'You remember that? It's like he's in college.'

'He's not in college,' Jane says.

'Does he have a tree where he is?' Marjorie asks.

'Not *in* his house, like you do,' Faith says. 'Let's talk about happier things than Mr Vince, OK?'

What furniture the room contains conforms to the Danish

style. A raised, metal-hooded, red-enamel-painted fireplace has a paper message from the condo owners taped to it, advising that smoke damage will cause renters to lose their security deposit. The owners are residents of Grosse Pointe Farms, and are people of Russian extraction. Of course, there's no fireplace wood except for what the furniture could offer.

'I think you two should guess what you're getting for Christmas,' Faith says, carefully draping lightless lights on the stiff plastic branches. Taking pains.

'In-lines. I already know,' Jane says and crosses her ankles like her sister. They are a jury disguised as an audience. 'I don't have to wear a helmet, though.'

'But are you sure of that?' Faith glances over her shoulder and gives them a smile she has seen movie stars give to strangers. 'You could always be wrong.'

'I'd better be right,' Jane says unpleasantly, with a frown very much like one her mom uses.

'Santa's bringing me a disk player,' Marjorie says. 'It'll come in a small box. I won't even recognize it.'

'You two're too smart for your britches,' Faith says. She is quickly finished stringing Christmas lights. 'But you don't know what *I* brought you.' Among other things, she, too, has brought a disk player and an expensive pair of in-line skates. They are in the Suburban and will be returned in L.A. She has also brought movie videos. Twenty in all, including 'Star Wars' and 'Sleeping Beauty'. Daisy has sent them each fifty dollars.

'You know,' Faith says, 'I remember once a long, long time ago, my dad and I and your mom went out in the woods and cut a tree for Christmas. We didn't buy a tree, we cut it down with an axe.'

Jane and Marjorie stare at her as if they already know this story. The TV is not turned on in the room. Perhaps, Faith thinks, they don't understand someone actually talking to them – live action presenting its own unique problems.

'Do you want to hear the story?'

'Yes,' Marjorie, the younger sister, says. Jane sits watchful and silent on the orange Danish sofa. Behind her on the white wall is a framed print of Brueghel's 'Return of the Hunters', which after all is Christmassy.

'Well,' Faith says. 'Your mother and I – we were only nine and ten – we picked out the tree we desperately wanted to be our tree, but our dad said no, that that tree was too tall to fit inside our house. We should choose another one. But we both said, "No, this one's perfect. This is the best one." It was green and pretty and had a perfect shape. So our dad cut it down with his axe, and we dragged it through the woods and tied it on top of our car and brought it back to Sandusky.' Both girls have now become sleepy. There has been too much excitement, or else not enough. Their mother is in rehab. Their dad is an asshole. They're in Michigan. Who wouldn't be sleepy? 'Do you want to know what happened after that?' Faith asks. 'When we got the tree inside?'

'Yes,' Marjorie says politely.

'It was too big,' Faith says. 'It was much, much too tall. It couldn't even stand up in our living room. And it was too wide. And our dad got really mad at us because we'd killed a beautiful living tree for a bad reason, and because we hadn't listened to him and thought we knew everything just because we knew what we wanted.'

Faith suddenly doesn't know why she's telling this particular story to these innocent sweeties who do not particularly need an object lesson. So she simply stops. In the real story, of course, her father took the tree and threw it out the door into the back yard, where it stayed for weeks and turned brown. There was crying and accusations. Her father went straight to a bar and got drunk. And later their mother went to the Safeway and bought a small tree that fit and which the three of them trimmed without the aid of their father. It was waiting, trimmed, when he came home smashed. The story had usually been one others found humor in. This time all the humor seemed lacking.

'Do you want to know how the story turned out?' Faith says, smiling brightly for the girls' benefit, but feeling completely defeated.

'I do,' Marjorie says.

'We put it outside in the yard and put lights on it so our neighbors could share our big tree with us. And we bought a smaller tree for the house at the Safeway. It was a sad story that turned out good.'

'I don't believe it,' Jane says.

'Well, you should believe it,' Faith says, 'because it's true. Christmases are special. They always turn out wonderfully if you give them a chance and use your imagination.'

Jane shakes her head as Marjorie nods hers. Marjorie wants to believe. Jane, Faith thinks, is a classic older child. Like herself.

'Did you know' – this was one of Greta the girlfriend's cute messages left for her on her voice mail in Los Angeles – 'did you know that Jack hates – hates – to have his dick sucked? Hates it with a passion. Of course you didn't. How could you? He always lies about it. Oh, well. But if you're wondering why he never comes, that's why. It's a big turnoff for him. I personally think it's his mother's fault, not that she ever did it to him, of course. I don't mean that. By the way, that was a nice dress last Friday. You're very pretty. And really great tits. I can see why Jack likes you. Take care.'

* * *

374

At seven, the girls wake up from their naps and everyone is hungry at once. Faith's mother offers to take the two hostile Indians for a pizza, then on to the skating rink, while Roger and Faith share the smorgasbord coupons.

At seven-thirty, few diners have chosen the long, harshly lit, sour-smelling Tyrol Room. Most guests are outside awaiting the nightly Pageant of the Lights, in which members of the ski patrol ski down the expert slope holding lighted torches. It is a thing of beauty but takes time getting started. At the very top of the hill, a great Norway spruce has been lighted in the Yuletide tradition just as in the untrue version of Faith's story. All is viewable from the Tyrol Room through a big picture window.

Faith does not want to eat with Roger, who is slightly hung over from his gluhwein and a nap. Conversation that she would find offensive could easily occur; something on the subject of her sister, the girls' mother – Roger's (still) wife. But she is trying to keep up a Christmas spirit. Do for others, etc.

Roger, she knows, dislikes her, possibly envies her, and is also attracted to her. Once, several years ago, he confided to her that he'd very much like to fuck her ears flat. He was drunk, and Daisy had not long before had Jane. Faith found a way not to acknowledge this offer. Later he told her he thought she was a lesbian. Having her know that just must've seemed like a good idea. A class act is the Roger.

The long, wide, echoing dining hall has crisscrossed ceiling beams painted pink and light green and purple – something apparently appropriate to Bavaria. There are long green tables with pink plastic folding chairs meant to promote good times and family fun. Somewhere else in the inn, Faith is certain, there is a better place to eat, where you don't pay with coupons and nothing's pink or purple.

Faith is wearing a shiny black Lycra bodysuit, over which she has put on her loden knickers and Norway socks. She looks superb, she thinks. With anyone but Roger this would be fun, or at least a hoot.

Roger sits across the long table, too far away to talk easily. In a room that can conveniently hold five hundred souls, there are perhaps ten scattered diners. No one is eating family style. Only solos and twos. Youthful inn employees in paper caps wait dismally behind the long smorgasbord steam table. Metal heat lamps with orange lights are over-cooking the prime rib, of which Roger has taken a goodly portion. Faith has chosen only a few green lettuce leaves, a beet round, and two tiny ears of yellow corn. The sour smell makes eating unappealing.

'Do you know what I worry about?' Roger says, sawing around a triangle of glaucal gray roast-beef fat, using a comically small knife. His tone implies he and Faith lunch together daily and are picking up right where they've left off; as if they didn't hold each other in complete contempt.

'No,' Faith says, 'what?' Roger, she notices, has managed to hang on to his red smorgasbord coupon. The rule is you leave your coupon in the basket by the breadsticks. Clever Roger. Why, she wonders, is he tanned?

Roger smiles as though there's a lewd aspect to whatever it is that worries him. 'I worry that Daisy's going to get so fixed up in rehab that she'll forget everything that's happened and want to be married again. To me, I mean. You know?' Roger chews as he talks. He wishes to seem earnest, his smile a serious, imploring, vacuous smile. Roger levelling. Roger owning up.

'Probably that won't happen,' Faith says. 'I just have a feeling.' She no longer wishes to look at her salad. She does not have an eating disorder, she thinks, and could never have one.

376

'Maybe not.' Roger nods. 'I'd like to get out of guidance pretty soon, though. Start something new. Turn the page.'

In truth, Roger is not bad-looking, only oppressively regular: small chin, small nose, small hands, small straight teeth – nothing unusual except his brown eyes, which are slightly too narrow, as if he had Finnish blood. Daisy married him, she said, because of his alarmingly big dick. That or, more important, lack of that, in her view, was why other marriages failed. When all else gave way, that would be there. Vince's, she'd observed, was even bigger. Ergo. It was to this quest Daisy had dedicated her life. This, instead of college.

'What exactly would you like to do next?' Faith says. She is thinking how satisfying it would be if Daisy came out of rehab and had forgotten everything, and that returning to how things were when they still sort of worked can often be the best solution.

'Well, it probably sounds crazy,' Roger says, chewing, 'but there's a company down in Tennessee that takes apart jetliners. For scrap. And there's big money in it. I imagine it's how the movie business got started. Just some hare-brained scheme.' Roger pokes macaroni salad with his fork. A single Swedish meatball remains on his plate.

'It doesn't sound crazy,' Faith lies, then looks longingly at the smorgasbord table. Maybe she is hungry. Is the table full of food the smorgasbord, she wonders, or is eating it the smorgasbord? Roger has slipped his meal coupon back into a pocket. 'Do you think you're going to do that?' she asks with reference to the genius plan of dismantling jet airplanes.

'With the girls in school, it'd be hard,' Roger says, ignoring what would seem to be the obvious – that it is not a genius plan. Faith gazes around distractedly. She realizes no one else in the big room is dressed the way she is, which reminds her of who she is. She is not Snow Mountain Highlands. She is not even Sandusky. She is Hollywood. A fortress.

'I could take the girls for a while,' she suddenly says. 'I really wouldn't mind.' She thinks of sweet Marjorie and sweet but unhappy Jane sitting on the Danish modern couch in their sweet nighties, watching her trim the rubber-tree plant. Just as instantly she thinks of Roger and Daisy being killed in an automobile crash. You can't help what you think.

'Where would they go to school?' Roger says, alert to something unexpected. Something he likes.

'I'm sorry?' Faith says, and flashes Roger, big-dick Roger, a second movie star's smile. She has let herself be distracted by the thought of his timely death.

'I mean where would they go to school?' Roger blinks. He is that alert.

'I don't know. Hollywood High, I guess. They have schools in California. I guess I could find one.'

'I'd have to think about this,' Roger lies decisively.

'OK,' Faith says. Now that she has said this without any previous thought of ever saying anything like it, it immediately becomes part of everyday reality. She will soon become the girls' parent. Easy as that. 'When you get settled in Tennessee you could have them back,' she says without conviction.

'They probably wouldn't want to come back,' Roger says. 'Tennessee'd seem pretty dull after Hollywood.'

'Ohio's dull. They like that.'

'True,' Roger says.

No one, of course, has thought to mention Daisy in preparing this new arrangement. Daisy, the mother. Though Daisy is committed elsewhere for the next little patch. And Roger needs to put 'guidance' in the rearview mirror.

The Pageant of the Lights is just now under way – a ribbon of swaying torches swooshing down the expert course like an overflow of lava. All is preternaturally visible through the panoramic window. A large, bundled crowd has assembled at the hill's bottom, many members holding candles in scraps of paper like at a Grateful Dead concert. All other artificial light is extinguished, except for the big Christmas spruce at the top. The young smorgasbord attendants have gathered at the window to witness the pageant yet again. Some are snickering. Someone remembers to turn the lights off inside the Tyrol Room. Dinner is suspended.

'Do you downhill?' Roger asks, manning his empty plate in the half darkness. Things could really turn out great, Faith understands he's thinking. Eighty-six the girls. Dismantle plenty jets. Just be friendly.

'No, never,' Faith says, dreamily watching the torch-bearers schuss from side to side, a gradual sinuous dramaless tour down. 'It scares me.'

'You get used to it.' Roger suddenly reaches across the table where her hands rest on either side of her uneaten salad. He actually touches then pats one of these hands. Roger is her friend now. 'And by the way,' he says creepily, 'thanks.'

Back in the condo, all is serene. Esther is still at the skating rink. Roger has wandered back to the Warming Shed. He has a girlfriend in Port Clinton. A former high-school coun-sellee, now divorced. He will be calling her, telling her about the new plans, telling her he wishes she were with him at Snow Mountain Highlands and that his family could be in Rwanda. Bobbie, her name is.

A call to Jack is definitely in order. But first Faith decides to slide the newly trimmed plastic rubber-tree plant nearer the window, where there's an outlet. When she plugs in, most of the little white lights pop cheerily on. Only a few do not, and in the box are replacements. Later, tomorrow, they can fix the star on top – her father's favorite ritual. 'Now it's time for the star,' he'd say. 'The star of the wise men.' Her father had been a musician, a woodwind specialist. A man of talents, and a drunk. A specialist also in women who were not his wife. He had taught committedly at a junior college to make all their ends meet. He had wanted her to become a lawyer, so naturally she became one. Daisy he had no specific plans for, so she became a drunk, and, sometime later, an energetic nymphomaniac. Eventually he had died, at home. The paterfamilias. After that her mother began to shrink. 'I won't actually die, I intend just to evaporate' was how she put it when the subject arose. It made her laugh. She considered her decrease a natural consequence of loss.

Whether to call Jack in London or New York or Block Island is the question. Where is Jack? In London it was after midnight. In New York and Block Island it was the same as here. Half past eight. Though a message was still the problem. She could just say she was lonely; or had chest pains; or worrisome test results. (The last two of which would later need to clear up mysteriously.)

London, first. The flat in Sloane Terrace, a half block from the tube. They'd eaten breakfast at Oriel, then Jack had gone off to work in the City while she did the Tate, the Bacons her specialty. So far from Snow Mountain Highlands – this is the sensation of dialling – a call going a great distance.

Ring-jing, ring-jing, ring-jing, ring-jing, ring-jing. Nothing.

There was a second number, for messages only, but she'd forgotten it. Call again to allow for a misdial. *Ring-jing, ring-jing, ring-jing. . . .*

New York, then. East Forty-ninth. Far, far east. The nice,

small slice of river view. A bolt-hole he'd had since college. His freshman numerals framed on the wall. 1971. She'd gone to the trouble to have the bedroom redone. White everything. A smiling picture of her from the boat, framed in red leather. Another of them together at Cabo, on the beach. All similarly long distances from Snow Mountain Highlands.

Ring, ring, ring, ring. Then *click*, 'Hi, this is Jack' – she almost speaks to his voice – 'I'm not' etc., etc., etc., then a beep.

'Hi, Jack, it's me. Ummm, Faith. . . .' She's stuck, but not at all flustered. She could just as well tell everything. This happened today: the atomic-energy smokestacks, the rubber-tree plant, the Pageant of the Lights, the smorgasbord, the girls' planned move to California. All things Christmassy. 'Ummm, I just wanted to say that I'm . . . fine, and that I trust – make that hope – that I hope you are, too. I'll be back home – in Malibu, that is – after Christmas. I'd love – make that, enjoy – hearing from you. I'm at Snow Mountain Highlands. In Michigan.' She pauses, discussing with herself if there'd be further news to relate. There isn't. Then she realizes (too late) she's treating this message machine like her Dictaphone. And there's no revising. Too bad. Her mistake. 'Well, goodbye,' she says, realizing this sounds a bit stiff, but doesn't revise. There's Block Island still. Though it's all over anyway. Who cares? She called.

Out on the Nordic Trail, lights, soft yellow ones not unlike the Christmas-tree lights, have been strung to selected fir boughs – bright enough so you'd never get lost in the dark, dim enough not to spoil the spooky/romantic effect.

She does not really enjoy this kind of skiing either – height or no height – but wants to be a sport. Though there's the tiresome waxing, the stiff rented shoes, the long, inconvenient skis, the sweaty underneath, the chance that all this could eventuate in catching cold and missing work. The gym is better. Major heat, but then quick you're clean and back in the car. Back in the office. Back on the phone. She is a sport but not a sports nut. Still, this is not terrifying.

No one is with her on night-time Nordic Trail 1, the Pageant of the Lights having lured away other skiers. Two Japanese men were at the trailhead. Small beige men in bright chartreuse Lycras – little serious faces, giant thighs, blunt no-nonsense arms – commencing the rigorous course, 'the Beast', Nordic Trail 3. On their small, stocking-capped heads they'd worn lights like coal miners to shine their way. They have disappeared.

Here the snow virtually hums to the sound of her sliding strokes. A full moon rides behind filigree clouds as she strides forward in the near-darkness of crusted woods. There is wind she can hear high up in the tall pines and spruces, but at ground level there's no wind – just cold radiating off the metallic snow. Only her ears actually feel cold, they and the sweat line of her hair. Her heartbeat is hardly elevated. She is in shape.

For an instant then she hears distant music, a singing voice with orchestral accompaniment. She pauses in her tracks. The music's pulses travel through the trees. Strange. Possibly, she thinks between deep breaths, it's Roger – in the karaoke bar, Roger onstage, singing his greatest hits to other lonelies in the dark. 'Blue Bayou', 'Layla', 'Tommy', 'Try to Remember'. Roger at a safe distance. Her pale hair, she realizes, is shining in the pure moonlight. If she were being watched, she would look good.

And wouldn't it be romantic, she thinks, to peer down through the dark woods and spy some great, ornate, and festive lodge lying below, windows ablaze, some exotic casino from a movie. Graceful skaters on a lighted rink. A garlanded lift still in motion, a few, last alpinists taking their silken, torchless float before lights-out. Only there's nothing to see – dark trunks and deadfalls, swags of snow hung in the spruce boughs.

And she is stiffening. Just this quickly. New muscles visited. No reason to go much farther.

Daisy, her sister, comes to mind. Daisy, who will very soon exit the hospital with a whole new view of life. Inside, there's of course a twelve-step ritual to accompany the normal curriculum of deprivation and regret. And someone, somewhere, at some time possibly long ago, *someone* will definitely turn out to have touched Daisy in some way detrimental to her well-being, and at an all too tender age. Once, but perhaps many times, over a series of terrible, silent years. Possibly an older, suspicious neighborhood youth – a loner – or a far too avuncular school librarian. Even the paterfamilias will come under posthumous scrutiny (the historical perspective as always unprovable, yet undisprovable, and therefore indisputable).

And certain sacrifices of dignity will then be requested of everyone, due to this rich new news from the past; a world so much more lethal than anyone believed; nothing the way we thought it was; if they had only known, could've spoken out, had opened up the lines of communication, could've trusted, confided, blah, blah, blah. Their mother will, necessarily, have suspected nothing, but unquestionably should've. Perhaps Daisy herself will have suggested that Faith is a lesbian. The snowball effect. No one safe, no one innocent.

Up ahead in the shadows, Ski Shelter 1 sits to the right of Nordic Trail 1 – a darkened clump in a small clearing, a place to wait for the others to catch up (if there were others). And a perfect place to turn back.

Shelter 1 is open on one side like a lean-to, a murky school-bus enclosure hewn from logs. Out on the snow beside it lie crusts of dinner rolls, a wedge of pizza, some wadded tissue papers, three beer cans – treats for the forest creatures – each casting its tiny shadow upon the white surface.

Though seated in the gloomy inside on a plank bench are not schoolkids but Roger. The brother-in-law, in his powder-blue ski suit and hiking boots. He is not singing karaoke at all. She has noticed no boot tracks up the trail. Roger is more resourceful than first he seems.

'It's effing cold up here.' Roger speaks from inside the shadows of Shelter 1. He is not wearing his black-frame glasses now, and is hardly visible, although she senses he is smiling – his narrow eyes even narrower.

'What are you doing up here, Roger?'

'Oh,' Roger says from out of the gloom, 'I just thought I'd come up.' He crosses his arms, extends his hiking boots into the snow-light like a high-school toughie.

'What for?' Her knees feel knotty and weak from exertion. Her heart has begun thumping. Perspiration is cold on her lip, though. Temperatures are in the low twenties. In winter the most innocent places turn lethal. This is not good.

'Nothing ventured,' Roger says.

'I was just about to turn around,' Faith says.

'I see,' Roger says.

'Would you like to go back down the hill with me?' What she wishes for is more light. Much more light. A bulb in the shelter would be very good. Bad things happen in the dark which would prove unthinkable in the light.

'Life leads you to some pretty interesting places, doesn't it, Faith?'

She would like to smile. Not feel menaced by Roger, who should be with his daughters.

'I guess,' she says. She can smell alcohol in the dry air. He is drunk, and he is winging all of this. A bad mixture.

'You're very pretty. Very pretty. The big lawyer,' Roger says. 'Why don't you come in here.'

'Oh, no thank you,' Faith says. Roger is loathsome but he is also family. And she feels paralyzed by not knowing what to do. She wishes she could just leap upward, turn around, glide away.

'I always thought that in the right circumstances, we could have some big-time fun,' Roger goes on.

'Roger, this isn't a good thing to be doing,' whatever he's doing. She wants to glare at him, not smile, then realizes her knees are shaking. She feels very, very tall on her skis, unusually accessible.

'It *is* a good thing to be doing,' Roger says. 'It's what I came up here for. Some fun.'

'I don't want us to do anything up here, Roger,' Faith says. 'Is that all right?' This, she realizes, is what fear feels like – the way you'd feel in a late-night parking structure, or jogging alone in an isolated area, or entering your house in the wee hours, fumbling for a key. Accessible. And then suddenly there would be someone. A man with oppressively ordinary looks who lacks a plan.

'Nope. Nope. That's not all right,' Roger says. He stands up, but stays in the sheltered darkness. 'The lawyer,' Roger says again, still grinning.

'I'm just going to turn around,' Faith says, and very unsteadily begins to shift her long left ski up out of its track, and then, leaning on her poles, her right ski up out of its track. It is unexpectedly dizzying, and her calves ache, and it is complicated not to cross her ski tips. But it is essential to remain standing. To fall would mean surrender. Roger would see it that way. What is the skiing expression? Tele . . . Tele-something. She wishes she could Tele-something. Tele-something the hell away from here. Her thighs burn. In California, she thinks, she is an officer of the court. A public official, sworn to uphold the law, though regrettably not to enforce it. She is a force for good.

'You look stupid,' Roger says.

She intends to say nothing more. Talk is not cheap now. For a moment she thinks she hears music again, music far away. But it can't be.

'When you get all the way around,' Roger says, 'then I want to show you something.' He does not say what. In her mind – moving her skis inches each time, her ankles stiff and heavy – in her mind she says 'Then what?' but doesn't say that.

'I really hate your whole effing family,' Roger says. His boots go crunch on the snow. She glances over her shoulder, but to look at him is too much. He is approaching. She will fall and then dramatic, regrettable things will happen. In a gesture he himself possibly deems dramatic, Roger – though she cannot see it – unzips his blue ski suit front. He intends her to hear this noise. She is three-quarters turned. She could see him over her left shoulder if she chose to. Have a look at what the excitement is about. She is sweating. Underneath she is drenched.

'Yep. Life leads you to some pretty interesting situations.' There is another zipping noise. It is his best trick. Zip. This is big-time fun in Roger's world view.

'Yes,' she says, 'it does.' She has come fully around now.

She hears Roger laugh, a little chuckle, an unhumorous 'hunh'. Then he says, 'Almost.' She hears his boots squeeze. She feels his actual self close beside her.

386

Then there are voices – saving voices – behind her. She now cannot help looking over her left shoulder and up the trail toward where it climbs into the darker trees. There is a light, followed by another light, little stars coming down from a height. Voices, words, language she does not quite understand. Japanese. She does not look at Roger, the girls' father, but simply slides one ski, her left one, forward into its track, lets her right one follow and find its way, pushes on her poles. And in just that amount of time and with that amount of effort she is away. She thinks she hears Roger say something, another 'hunh', a kind of grunting sound, but can't be sure.

In the condo everyone is sleeping. The rubber-tree lights are twinkling. They reflect in the window that faces the ski hill, which is now dark. Someone, Faith notices (her mother), has devoted much time to replacing the spent bulbs so the tree can twinkle. The gold star, the star that led the wise men, lies on the coffee table like a starfish, waiting to be properly affixed.

Marjorie, the younger, sweeter sister, is asleep on the orange couch under the Brueghel scene. She has left her bed to sleep near the tree, brought her quilted pink coverlet with her.

Naturally Faith has locked Roger out. Roger can now die alone and cold in the snow. Or he can sleep in a doorway or by a steam vent somewhere in the Snow Mountain High-lands complex and explain his situation to the security staff. Roger will not sleep with his pretty daughters this night. She is taking a hand in things. These girls are hers. Though how strange not to know that her offer to take them would be translated by Roger into an invitation to fuck. She has been in California too long, has fallen out of touch with things middle-American. How strange that Roger would say 'effing'. He would also probably say 'X-mas'.

Outside on the ice rink two teams are playing hockey under high white lights. A red team opposes a black team. Net cages have been brought on, the larger rink walled off to regulation size and shape. A few spectators stand watching. Wives and girlfriends. Boyne City versus Petoskey; Cadillac versus Cheboygan or some such. The little girls' white skates lie piled by the door she has now safely locked with a dead bolt.

It would be good to put the star up, she thinks. Who knows what tomorrow will bring. The arrival of wise men couldn't hurt. So, with the flimsy star, which is made of slick aluminum paper and is large and gold and weightless and five-pointed, Faith stands on the Danish dining-table chair and fits the slotted fastener onto the topmost leaf of the rubber-tree plant. It is not an elegant fit by any means, there being no sprig at the pinnacle, so that the star doesn't stand as much as it leans off the top in a sad, comic, but also victorious way. (This use was never envisioned by tree-makers in Seoul.) Tomorrow they can all add to the tree together, invent ornaments from absurd and inspirational raw materials. Tomorrow Roger will be rehabilitated and become everyone's best friend. Except hers.

Marjorie's eyes have opened, though she has not stirred. For a moment, on the couch, she appears dead.

'I went to sleep,' she says softly and blinks her brown eyes.

'Oh, I saw you,' Faith smiles. 'I thought you were just another Christmas present. I thought Santa had been here early and left you for me.' She takes a careful seat on the spindly coffee table, close beside Marjorie – in case there would be some worry to express, a gloomy dream to relate. A fear. She smooths her hand through Marjorie's warm hair.

Marjorie takes a deep breath and lets air go smoothly through her nostrils. 'Jane's asleep,' she says.

'And how would you like to go back to bed?' Faith says in a whisper.

Possibly she hears a soft tap on the door. The door she will not open. The door beyond which the world and trouble wait. Marjorie's eyes wander toward the sound, then swim with sleep. She is safe.

'Leave the tree on,' Marjorie instructs, though asleep.

'Sure, sure,' Faith says. 'The tree stays on forever.'

She eases her hand under Marjorie, who by old habit reaches outward, caresses her neck. In an instant she has Marjorie in her arms, pink covers and all, carrying her altogether lightly to the darkened bedroom where her sister sleeps on one of the twin beds. Gently she lowers Marjorie onto the empty bed and re-covers her. Again she hears soft tapping, although it stops. She believes it will not come again this night.

Jane is sleeping with her face to the wall, her breathing deep and audible. Jane is the good sleeper, Marjorie the less reliable one. Faith stands in the middle of the dark, windowless room, between the twin beds, the blinking Christmas lights haunting the stillness that has come at such expense. The room smells musty and dank, as if it has been closed for months and opened just for this night, these children. If only briefly she is reminded of Christmases she might've once called her own. 'OK,' she whispers. 'OK, OK, OK.'

She undresses in the master suite, too tired to shower. Her mother sleeps on one side of their shared bed. She is an unexpectedly distinguishable presence there, visibly breathing beneath the covers. A glass of red wine half-drunk sits on the bed table beside her curved neck brace. The very same Brueghel print as in the living room hangs over their bed. She will wear pajamas, for her mother's sake. New ones. White, pure silk, smooth as water. Blue silk piping.

She half closes the bedroom door, the blinking Christmas lights shielded. And here is the unexpected sight of herself in the cheap, dark door mirror. All still good. Intact. Just the small scar where a cyst has been removed between two ribs. A meaningless scar no one would see. Thin, hard thighs. A small nice belly. Boy's hips. Two good breasts. The whole package, nothing to complain about.

Then the need of a glass of water. Always a glass of water at night, never a glass of red wine. When she passes the living-room window, her destination the kitchen, she sees that the hockey game is now over. It is after midnight. The players are shaking hands in a line on the ice, others skating in wide circles. On the ski slope above the rink, lights have been turned on again. Machines with headlights groom the snow at treacherous angles.

And she sees Roger. He is halfway between the ice rink and the condos, walking back in his powder-blue suit. He has watched the game, no doubt. He stops and looks up at her where she stands in the window in her white pjs, the Christmas lights blinking as a background. He stands and stares up. He has found his black-frame glasses. Possibly his mouth is moving, but he makes no gesture to her. There is no room in this inn for Roger.

In bed her mother seems larger. An impressive heat source, slightly damp when Faith touches her back. Her mother is wearing blue gingham, a nightdress not so different from the muumuu she wears in daylight. She smells unexpectedly good. Rich.

How long, she wonders, since she has slept with her

mother? A hundred years? Twenty? Odd that it would be so normal now. And good.

She has left the door open in case the girls should call, in case they wake and are afraid, in case they miss their father. She can hear snow slide off the roof, an automobile with chains jingling softly somewhere out of sight. The Christmas lights blink merrily. She had intended to check her messages but let it slip.

Marriage. Yes, naturally she would think of that now. Maybe marriage, though, is only a long plain of self-revelation at the end of which there's someone else who doesn't know you very well. That is the message she could've left for Jack. 'Dear Jack, I now know marriage is a long plain at the end of which there's' etc., etc., etc. You always think of these things too late. Somewhere, Faith hears faint music, 'Away in a Manger', played prettily on chimes. It is music to sleep to.

And how would they deal with tomorrow? Not the eternal tomorrow, but the promised, practical one. Her thighs feel stiff, though she is slowly relaxing. Her mother, beside her, is facing away. How, indeed? Roger will be rehabilitated, tomorrow, yes, yes. There will be board games. Songs. Changes of outfits. Phone calls placed. Possibly she will find the time to ask her mother if anyone had ever been abused, and find out, happily, not. Looks will be passed between and among everyone tomorrow. Certain names, words will be in short supply for the sake of all. The girls will learn to ski and enjoy it. Jokes will be told. They will feel better. A family again. Christmas, as always, takes care of its own.

ACKNOWLEDGMENTS

ELIZABETH BOWEN: 'Green Holly' from *The Collected Stories of Elizabeth Bowen* by Elizabeth Bowen, copyright © 1981 by Curtis Brown Limited, Literary Executors of the Estate of Elizabeth Bowen. Used by permission of Alfred A. Knopf, a division of Random House, Inc. 'Green Holly' from *The Collected Stories of Elizabeth Bowen* by Elizabeth Bowen, Jonathan Cape, 1980, copyright © 1980 by Curtis Brown Limited, Literary Executors of the Estate of Elizabeth Bowen. Used by permission of Curtis Brown (UK) Limited.

TRUMAN CAPOTE: 'A Christmas Memory' from *A Christmas Memory* by Truman Capote, copyright © 1956 by Truman Capote. Used by permission of Random House, Inc. 'A Christmas Memory' (4,809 words) from *The Complete Stories of Truman Capote* (Penguin Books, 2005). Copyright © Truman Capote, 1956. Reproduced by permission of Penguin Books Ltd.

JOHN CHEEVER: 'Christmas is a Sad Season for the Poor' from *The Stories of John Cheever* by John Cheever. © 1978, John Cheever. Used by permission of Alfred A. Knopf, a division of Random House, Inc., and The Wylie Agency (UK) Limited.

RICHARD FORD: 'Crèche' from *A Multitude of Sins* by Richard Ford. Used by permission of the author and Alfred A. Knopf, a division of Random House, Inc., and Rogers, Coleridge & White, London.

Everyman's Pocket Classics are
typeset in the classic typeface Garamond and
printed on acid-free, cream-wove paper
with a sewn, full-cloth binding.